THE LION'S WHELP

In his gratification, he admitted his hopes and intentions.

"I thank you! That is good, good! It means that I will have something to offer her, offer Agnes. A house. The means to keep her." He took the plunge. "Agnes Crichton."

His mother reined over, to smile at him, and his father grunted.

"We wondered when you would come out with it," the thane said. "You have been seeing a lot of that young woman, have spoken often of her. We guessed that this would be the way of it. But – Crichton! Have you considered what you would be taking on if you wed the man's daughter? It is scarcely a family I would have chosen for my son to marry into!"

"Agnes is not like her father. He is hard, a stern man. She is kindly, generous. And very fair."

"You love her?" his mother asked.

"I do. I do."

"And Crichton himself? Will he permit this?" Sir Patrick wondered.

"That I do not know," Alec conceded. "We may have to wait until Agnes is of full age. A year yet. That is, if she will have me! I have not asked her yet."

"But you think that she will?" Lady Lyon sounded sympathetic.

"Who knows? But she is . . . friendly."

"I hope that you are not stirring up trouble for yourself!" his father said.

They left it at that.

The Lion's Whelp

Nigel Tranter

CORONET BOOKS
Hodder and Stoughton

First published in Great Britain in 1997 by Hodder and Stoughton
A division of Hodder Headline PLC
First published in paperback in 1998 by Hodder and Stoughton
A Coronet Paperback

10 9 8 7 6 5 4 3 2 1

British Library Cataloguing in Publication Data

Tranter, Nigel, 1909–
The Lion's Whelp
1. English fiction – 20th century – Scottish author
2. Scottish fiction – 20th century
I. Title
823.9'12 [F]

ISBN 0 340 65999 8

Printed and bound in Great Britain by
Mackays of Chatham plc, Chatham, Kent

Hodder and Stoughton
A division of Hodder Headline PLC
338 Euston Road
London NW1 3BH

Principal Characters in order of appearance

Alexander Lyon: Son of Sir Patrick Lyon.

Sir Patrick Lyon: Thane of Glamis.

Queen Joanna Beaufort: Widow of murdered James the First, King of Scots.

Agnes Crichton: Daughter of Sir William Crichton of that Ilk.

William, Lord Borthwick: Scots noble.

Sir William Crichton: Keeper of Edinburgh Castle, Chancellor of the realm.

James Stewart, King of Scots: Second of that name.

Bishop James Kennedy of Dunkeld: Later Primate. Uncle of king.

William, 6th Earl of Douglas: Chief of the Black Douglases, Duke of Touraine.

James, 3rd Earl of Angus: Chief of the Red Douglases.

Princess Arabella: Youngest sister of the king.

Sir James Stewart, Black Knight of Lorne: Second husband of the queen.

Sir James Douglas of Dalkeith: Great Scots noble.

Alexander, Earl of Ross, Lord of the Isles: Great Highland chief.

Alexander, Earl of Huntly: Great noble. Later lieutenant-general.

Princess Margarer: Eldest sister of the king.

James, 7th Earl of Douglas: Known as James the Gross.

Princess Jean: Another sister of the king; later Countess of Angus.

William, 8th Earl of Douglas: Eldest son of James the Gross.

Alexander, Earl of Crawford: Great noble, known as the Tiger Earl.

Hugh Douglas: Brother of Earl William, created Earl of Ormond.

Archibald Douglas: Brother of Earl William, created Earl of Moray.

John Douglas: Brother of Earl William, created Lord Balveny.

Arnold, Duke of Gueldres: Low Countries prince.

Mary of Gueldres: Daughter of the above. Wife of James the Second.

Aeneas Silvius Piccolomini: Papal Nuncio. Later Pope Pius the Second.

William Turnbull, Bishop of Glasgow: Lord Privy Seal and founder of Glasgow University.

Sir Patrick Gray: Son of the Lord Gray and captain of the royal guard.

Lord Gray: Father of above, and notable soldier.

Kim Graham: Blacksmith of Mollance, near Kirkcudbright.

John, Lord of the Isles and Earl of Ross: Son of Alexander thereof.

James, Lord Hamilton: Powerful noble.

James Stewart, Duke of Rothesay: Infant son of the king.

Margaret of Anjou, Queen of England: Wife of Henry the Sixth.

Edward, Prince of Wales: Son of above.

PART ONE

1

Alexander Lyon stared at his father. "The king dead!" he gasped. "Dead?"

"Aye. Slain! Murdered by those dastards! Assassins! Sir Robert Stewart, grandson of Atholl, Sir Robert Graham, and another. At the Blackfriars Monastery in Perth three nights past. In the presence of Queen Joanna. James slain! The King of Scots! A deed unknown since MacBeth's murder. And at the behest of one of his own earls and kinsman, Walter Stewart of Atholl, his uncle."

"But . . . why? Why?"

"Spite! Hatred! Atholl seeking the throne, it may be. Revenge for the death of Murdoch of Albany, his nephew. Who knows for certain? But Scotland has lost her monarch. Trapped in some cellar of the friary where he was lodging. A strong, a fine king, gone. Now what?" Sir Patrick Lyon of Glamis strode to and fro in the withdrawing-room of the castle hall of Glamis, in Strathmore. "A six-year-old son left to reign over us. Here is disaster!"

Alexander shook his head. "To slay His Grace! Their sovereign-lord to whom they will have sworn fealty! It is scarce to be believed. It is not some canard, some coggery?"

"That wandering friar, Anselm, told me. He had come from Perth. He is honest, and said that it is truth. James was about to seek his bed, with his wife. Her lady-in-waiting, Catherine Douglas, with them. And a younger Douglas maid. That evil dastard, Stewart, his own kinsman, and Graham and others, broke into the monastery. They overcame the few guards. Monks shouted

3

the alarm, the friar said. The king heard it, and took refuge in some cellar beneath the bedchamber. With a trapdoor. The queen, when she heard them in the outer room, lay on it, the trapdoor, to hide it. They came up, the murderers. The Lady Catherine sought to hold the door, the room door. Used her arm as a drawbar – a stout-hearted woman! But they burst in, breaking her arm. They knew that the king was there – and no other door. They struck the queen, dragged her away. Found the trap. They went down to the cellar. He was a great fighter, was James. Always was. But he was for his naked bed. Had no arms. They had dirks and swords. They stabbed him to the death. James Stewart! Myself, I was hostage for him those years back, in England . . ."

"What . . . what is to be done?" Nineteen-year-old Alexander wagged his head, still hardly believing it.

"The good Lord knows! Vengeance on the assassins, aye. But – the rule of the land? Young Rothesay but a child. They, the murderers, will seek to get rid of him also, I would think. To make Walter Stewart, Atholl, the king."

"Atholl was uncle to the king?"

"Aye. Robert the Second was wed twice. By his first queen he had John, Earl of Carrick, whose name was changed to Robert, John being an unhappy name for any king. Then he had Robert, who became Duke of Albany, and this Walter of Atholl, David of Strathearn and the Lord Brechin. Carrick became Robert the Third and his son David, Duke of Rothesay, and this James. Albany murdered young Rothesay to gain the throne. And would have slain James also. But he escaped for France, but was captured by the English, and held there. Now Walter of Atholl has done what his brother Albany could not do! Scotland is set for strife and turmoil! Again!"

"What is to be done?" the young man repeated. "Can *we* do anything?"

"God knows! I will have to think. Consider well. I will go to see your grandsire, at Auchterhouse. Sir Alexander is sheriff of Angus. Has a good head on his shoulders still, old as he is. Something we *must* do. *I* am Thane of Glamis!"

"The prince. Rothesay? He will now be rightful king. But . . . six years! He was not with his father and mother?"

"No, heaven be praised! Or they would have killed him also, I swear. He will be at Stirling in the care of Livingston. If care that can be named! I do not trust Alexander Livingston!"

Alec nodded. He knew sufficiently of the dislike between his father and Sir Alexander Livingston, keeper of Stirling Castle, the royal fortress. "The queen? What of her, now? She is a strong woman, is she not? What happened with her? Do they hold her?"

"I know not. The friar did not say. They would not slay her, I think. Too close to the English throne. Her uncle, the Cardinal Beaufort, High Chancellor of England. They would not want war with England, as well, belike, as civil war in Scotland!" He stopped pacing. "See you, Alec, go tell your mother that I must visit her father and brother at Auchterhouse. She might wish to accompany me."

Alec found the Lady Isabel in the vaulted kitchen below, before the great arched fireplace and the stone ovens, instructing the cook on what she wanted for the midday meal. In front of the kitchen scullions he thought that he should not mention the dire news of the king's death, so merely told his mother that Sir Patrick was going to Auchterhouse, which was eight miles south-west in Strathmore, nearer to Dundee, on receipt of sudden news, and wondered whether she would wish to go with him. Surprised, Lady Isabel did not question her son, but went off to see her husband.

Alec went to tell his two younger brothers and his sister the terrible tidings.

That evening, when Sir Patrick and his wife got back from Auchterhouse of the Ogilvys, he was much exercised. His old father-in-law had not heard of the tragedy for Scotland, and was greatly concerned at the news. He also did not trust

Livingston of Calendar, who would now in effect become the governor of the young king. He had been favoured by King James, and had indeed been one of the jury which had tried and condemned to death the returned monarch's enemy, Murdoch, second Duke of Albany, on the king's return from his twenty-year captivity in England which had been contrived by Albany's father – so his reputation was sound enough. But he had failed Sir Patrick's own father at the foul Raid of Roxburgh in 1422, resulting in the older Lyon's capture and imprisonment in England, and this had never been forgotten. He was known to be friendly with Atholl, who, it was said, had gained him the appointment at Stirling. The queen should be warned, and either dismiss Livingstone or possibly meantime remove her son from his care. Whether she was still at Perth they did not know. But Sir Patrick would ride there on the morrow. He would take Alec with him. Perth was only some thirty miles distant.

That young man was nothing loth. He had been aiding his father in many activities these last two years, but mainly in the management of the large Glamis estates and lands, and in some measure in the affairs of Strathmore, that wide and fertile vale in the centre of the shire of Angus, north of Tay. But he had never been involved in any national causes or matters of state. That his sire deemed him fit to accompany him on this vital and possibly dangerous mission elated him more than a little.

Early next day then they set off westwards, accompanied by an escort of a dozen armed men, as befitted the Thane of Glamis. The Lyons were proud of that ancient title and style, little used now but once so important in Scotland, with the only other thanage, that of Arbuthnott, none so far off. The Lyons, admittedly, had no ancestral ties with the famous Thane of Glamis who had featured so prominently in the reign of King MacBeth four centuries before, having only gained the lands and lairdship when Sir Patrick's grandfather, who had been Chancellor of the realm, had married Jean, daughter of King Robert

6

the Second, and had been granted Glamis as her dowery. But at least this royal connection gave them prestige, and some authority in approaching the queen at this period of crisis. Alec was not averse to telling his friends that he was a great-great-grandson of that King Robert, and therefore a descendant of the hero-king, the Bruce.

They rode up Strathmore that breezy late February day of 1437 by Meigle and Coupar Angus and Balbeggie, passing near the site of MacBeth's castle of Dunsinane, north of the Sidlaw Hills, and so came to the Tay, near to Scone, coronation seat of the Kings of Scots, at the sacred point, in pre-Christian days, where the fresh water of the great river overcame the salt water of the tidal estuary, and fertility triumphed over the sea god's destructive power. From Scone it was a mere three miles down river to St John's Town of Perth.

They found the town still in a stir over the dire happenings there four days earlier, the citizens cowering away from the sight of one more group of armed horsemen. Sir Patrick knew the provost, and made for the Tolbooth, to ask if Queen Joanna was still in the town. A bailie there informed them that she had, the day before, departed for Stirling Castle.

This news presented a problem indeed. Should they go on to Stirling, where they could find Sir Alexander Livingston as well as the queen, when it was against the said Livingston that they wanted to warn Joanna, for her young son's sake? Sir Patrick should have thought of this. Yet not to do so would be failing in their duty to their new monarch. It was decided to press on, some risks as this might represent. It was always possible that the assassins might also have repaired to the royal fortress.

It was only noon, so they had ample time to reach Stirling, some thirty-five miles to the south, before even February dark. They rode over into Strathearn, and by Auchterarder into the Allan Water vale, and so reached Dunblane. There, on the higher ground, they could see down to the River Forth to where, southwards still, in

7

the sinking sunlight, they viewed the mighty castle on its towering rock above the levels where this other great river also reached the salt waters of the Firth of Forth, that vital first crossing-place of the seventy-mile-long barrier to travellers, which the fortress guarded. What sort of a reception would they have at that citadel?

Clattering through the narrow cobbled streets of the town, which climbed steeply towards the rock-top castle, impregnable there on its dizzy perch between Highlands and Lowlands, they reached the wide dry-ditch and gatehouse beyond. They found the drawbridge down, but well guarded by spearmen. Sir Patrick announced with every appearance of confidence that the Thane of Glamis had come to see the Queen's Grace, and craved audience.

Dismounting, they waited there at the gatehouse arch, wondering whether admittance would indeed be granted. Livingston, when he heard of the identity of the callers, might well refuse entry; after all, he could say that the queen, in her distress, was seeing no callers, lofty or otherwise. And if the king's murderers were indeed there . . . !

However, it was not Livingston but the captain of the royal guard who came down to the gate, one Sir Robert Menteith of Rusky, kin by marriage to the keeper, but with whom Sir Patrick had no quarrel. A good-looking youngish man, he greeted the Thane of Glamis respectfully, led the Lyons in, and said that he did not know whether the queen would see them, in her present state of loss, but he would inform Her Grace. He mentioned that the keeper, Sir Alexander, was absent meantime, the queen having sent him off on urgent errands connected with the shocking death of her royal husband.

That was some relief, at least, for the visitors.

They were conducted up to the wing of the fortress containing the royal apartments. There, in an anteroom, they were left, their escort remaining near the gatehouse.

When Menteith returned he had a companion, a man

with a bandaged hand, whom he introduced as Sir David
Dunbar, another member of the royal household. Her
Grace would see the Thane of Glamis.

This Dunbar, of middle years, leading them upstairs
without asking what was their business with the queen,
did indicate that Her Grace was in a state of much grief
and hurt but was maintaining the spirits of her young
family. He hinted that the visitors should not remain
with her for overlong, Sir Patrick agreeing. For his part,
he asked why Sir David had his hand so fully bandaged,
to be told, briefly, that he had had three fingers cut
off. At this unusual answer he could not but enquire
further, and learned that Dunbar had been at Perth those
four nights ago, and had sought to prevent Stewart and
Graham from intruding on the royal couple, and had had
his hand slashed with a dirk in consequence, by Graham,
to the loss of his fingers – although he had managed to kill
one of the wretches. What comment were the visitors to
make to that?

They heard children's voices, cries and laughter, before
ever they reached the royal chamber, girlish voices
predominating and scarcely sounding like a mourning
family. James and Joanna had had six offspring, five
daughters and one son; Margaret, the eldest, of eight
years; Jean, the youngest, but three. So no doubt the
queen was concerned that grieving for their father should
not too greatly upset them.

The callers were ushered into the royal presence, and
bowed low, only too well aware that their coming was in
the nature of an intrusion. The queen sat at a table, with
papers before her, while the six children played vigorously
around, the boy on hands and knees on the floor, with his
smallest sister sitting on his back, as though horse-riding,
a pleasing domestic scene. Alec wondered whether he
should bow again, to the new king.

Joanna Beaufort was a strikingly beautiful woman, and
despite all her child-bearing, had retained an excellent
figure, tall and fairly slender. She had notably fine eyes,

patrician features and a firm chin, her long chestnut-brown hair looped back with a fillet with no coif, a woman who had proved herself as one to be reckoned with, as well as admired for her looks. She would be in her thirty-fifth year.

"Ah, Sir Patrick, it is some time since we forgathered," she said, as he approached her, and offered her hand for him to kiss. "Greetings! Even in these sorry circumstances, I could not fail to receive the Thane of Glamis, remotely of my husband's kin." And she turned that handsome head to shush her children to make less noise.

"Highness, what am I to say?" Sir Patrick answered. "It is beyond all words, all acceptance, all belief! We come, offering you our sympathy, our compassion and understanding, our devotion. And our fealty and duty towards our new liege-lord – indeed our lives, if necessary." And he did bow towards the boy on the floor, Alec also now.

"You are good, kind, Sir Patrick. I, and he, shall need all the service you offer, I think! For there is much to be done. I am planning some of it now!" And she gestured to the papers. "I will see some justice done, God helping me!" She brought a fist down on the table in a strange gesture for a woman, but significant enough. Then, expression changing, she opened her hand towards Alec. "And this? A son, I think?"

"Yes, Your Grace, my eldest. Alexander. And eager to be at your aid and support."

"My service, or rather my son's, may be less than pleasing, I fear, my friends. There are deeds to be done which will demand . . . strong wills!"

"That is why we are here, Highness. We know it."

Behind them, Dunbar, of the Earl of March's line, spoke. "I have told Her Grace that there are many, many awaiting to do her royal bidding. To wreak vengeance on those foul miscreants!"

"Oh, yes, I will have vengeance, if I may!" That was said

in tones which were almost steely, despite her normally light and pleasing voice.

"Vengeance, yes," Sir Patrick agreed. "Dire vengeance! But first, I say, safeguards, precautions. For His young Grace, here."

Joanna eyed him keenly.

"See you, Highness, those dastards, had your son been with you at Perth, would have slain him also, I think, child as he is. They want the throne. For Atholl himself, or for his grandson Robert Stewart. If they could slay the father, they could slay the son, an only son. And then their way is open. With Murdoch of Albany executed, and his son, Atholl is next in line for the crown. I would say that they are not finished their evil tasks yet!"

She pursed her lips. "You think so, dear God!" She half rose, the mother in her superseding the queen. "But he is safe enough in this stronghold of Stirling."

"Is he, Your Grace? A stronghold is no stronger than its keeper!"

"What mean you by that?"

"I mean that Sir Alexander Livingston *may* be assured. Of good faith. Leal. But . . . he may not be. He betrayed my father once, out of spite and self-gain. And he is said to be friendly with both Stewart and Graham. If he thinks that he might do better under Atholl as king, or even Robert Stewart, and they come chapping at your gate here, I say that he might, *might* just, let them in!"

"No, no, Sir Patrick! Not that. I trust Livingston. He is loyal, I swear. My husband trusted him. Made him keeper here. He would not fail me. Or young Jamie."

"Perhaps not, Your Grace. Perhaps I wrong him. But conditions have changed. A child king can unsettle all in a kingdom, unsettle all who are, or would be, in power. You will find that so, I greatly fear."

"But I have sent Sir Alexander to apprehend the murderers! Or some of them. If he can . . ."

"M'mm. Yes. But I would advise caution, Your Grace, to ensure the young king's safety. In cases of possible trouble. See you, Edinburgh Castle is as strong as this one. In the care of Sir William Crichton, a good man, stoutly leal, trusted. Placed there by your royal husband. And no friend of Atholl and the others."

"Sir William is a Gentleman of the Bedchamber, yes. I know him well."

"I would suggest, Highness, that you send your son, His Grace, to Sir William's keeping meantime. Until the present unrest is past. All go to Edinburgh, if so you wish. There is bound to be upset for a time, while you seek your . . . redress. And this Stirling will be at the centre of it. The murderers will know that you will take vengeance, if you can. They may act further, therefore. And quickly. I say that this is no place for the young king. And for Your Highness's self, in this time. Even if you can trust Livingston."

"Y-e-e-es. Perhaps. You believe that they will strike again? And in force? Soon?"

"Having gone so far as to assassinate the king, they will not leave it at that, to be sure. And they can raise many men, Atholl in especial. I would advise that Your Grace does the same. Raises men, to deal with these traitors. Many, many men will rally to your cause. Aye, including the Lyons and the Ogilvys. Use Crichton to muster them all. And, I mind you, his daughter is wed to the Gordon chief, the Earl of Huntly. He has great numbers of his clan. And up there, near to Atholl's lands. Huntly could pose a dire threat to Atholl."

"You have me all but convinced, Sir Patrick . . ."

"I would agree with the thane, Your Grace. Edinburgh would be safer than here," Dunbar put in. "Crichton is a good man. My own kinsman, the Earl of March, none so far from there, in the Merse, could raise his thousands – Dunbars, Homes, Swintons and the like."

"We will think on this." Joanna had to raise her voice to counter the children's noise, these becoming impatient for attention. "We will talk of it over our repast. Once these noisy ones are abed. Sir David, find you a bedchamber for the thane and his son. And a servitor to attend them. We shall eat in an hour or so, Sir Patrick. And . . . Alexander, is it?"

Audience over meantime, they bowed themselves out, Sir Patrick reasonably satisfied that his advice would be taken.

In that he was proved right when, later, at table, the queen clearly had decided on a move to Edinburgh, Sir Robert Menteith now also agreeing that it would be wise, the talk really centring on how best to arrange it all, and how quickly.

Alec, not a little bemused to be part of this exalted company, presently was further exercised when he heard his father suggesting that he, Alec, should act messenger to Crichton at Edinburgh Castle, to have Sir William come and collect, and escort in strength, the royal party to his citadel, the three knights present all conceiving it their duty to remain with the queen and her family in the interim, while *he* could be spared. He would be given a letter . . .

Much flattered by this acceptance of his usefulness in such high affairs, his dwelling on it all was interrupted when he realised that the talk over the wine had switched to the subject of vengeance on the murderers, when and if they could be taken. And listening, he learned that women, however beautiful and fair-seeming, could be just as forceful and stern in their attitudes and judgments as could men, Joanna Beaufort making it entirely clear that she desired the harshest measures to be taken against her husband's killers and all connected with that foul deed. Menteith, as captain of the royal guard, was to ensure it, as opportunity arose.

Alec shared a bed with his father that night, for the first time, and took some time to sleep, unlike his progenitor, his sudden initiation into affairs of state scarcely restful on the mind, even though he had ridden over seventy miles that day and was bodily tired.

2

In the morning, then, it was more riding, although not so far, Stirling being but thirty-five miles from Edinburgh, going south-eastwards, as it were down Forth. Taking two of the Glamis escort, and with a letter in the queen's hand, he set off soon after first light, to go by the Tor Wood, Falkirk, Linlithgow and Niddry-Seton, whereafter they soon came in sight of the majestic, lion-like isolated hill of Arthur's Seat in the distance, with lesser ranges to the south nearby and the long barrier of the Pentland Hills beyond, the loftiest seen since leaving the Highland Line.

A dozen more miles and they were in the capital city with its walls, not clustering beneath its castle rock like Stirling but slanting up more gradually to a very similar precipice-sided fortress, from the Abbey of the Holy Rood, below that Arthur's Seat, a ridge-back mile to the tourney-ground before the citadel. The two castles themselves were remarkably alike, in buildings and fortifications as in site. Alec had been here only once before, when he had accompanied his father to a parliament.

He had more difficulty in gaining access than they had had at Stirling, he not being able to claim that he was the Thane of Glamis, only the son thereof, seeking Sir William Crichton, keeper. And when he did win admittance over the drawbridge and moat, it was to learn, to his concern, that the keeper was absent, having gone the day before to his own castle of Crichton in Middle Lothian. And it was not known just when he would be back.

What, then? Alec's mission was as urgent as it was

important. Nothing for it but to go on to this Crichton, unknown territory, apparently south-eastwards beyond Dalkeith and Cranstoun on the upper Lothian Tyne, some fifteen miles.

Beyond hilly enough Edinburgh, they rode on, to reach the Rivers Esk, North and South, and come to the Black Douglas castle and town of Dalkeith. The Douglases, Black and Red, were possibly the strongest family in all Lowland Scotland; and Alec wondered how they would react to the present critical situation. The Earl of Douglas was based on Lanarkshire and Galloway. His mother had been the daughter of Robert the Third, while his grandfather had married a daughter of Robert the Second, so the links with the royal house were close. Would he support the queen, or his kinsman Atholl? Again, the Lord of Dalkeith, the secondary branch, had also married a daughter of Robert the Third. What of him?

After Dalkeith they faced a long climb to the Cranstoun area, where they could see the long green summits and folds of the Lammermuir Hills on their left and the more rugged ranges of the Morthwaites on their right, the Pentlands now behind them. Alec had not realised how hilly were the Lothians, and in consequence, well supplied with rivers. After Cranstoun they had to dip down to another of these, the Tyne, flowing eastwards, which they had to ford at a place called Pathhead, and thereafter were instructed to turn right-handed and follow the river up for another three miles to Crichton.

They came into closer country now of grassy braes and narrow glens, and presently, at a bend in the river, found themselves in a hidden valley, quite deep but wider, oddly enough the mouth of it seeming to be guarded by a large church with parapeted tower rather than the castle, although this could be seen on a mound further up half a mile. This was Crichton, it seemed, and a secluded entity it was. Even the castleton hamlet was near the church, not the fortalice.

As Alec rode up towards the latter, he saw that it was

strongly sited above the water meadows of the river, on a steep bluff, but not large as such houses went, a simple square battlemented tower within a high curtain wall, with the usual landward ditch, or moat, and gatehouse. There was, however, an unusual feature, especially in view of that large church back there, of a chapel-like building not far beyond the castle itself. Were the Crichtons so holy a family?

The newcomers recognised that, holy or not, and secluded as was their seat, the Crichtons were nowise careless as to security, for, glancing behind them, they saw that they were being followed up from the castleton by fully a score of men on foot, the sunlight glinting on steel.

The drawbridge was down and the gatehouse portcullis up, a banner flying from a flagstaff at the tower head. A large bell hung from a gibbet at the bridge-end, and this Alec clanged, to the startled sidling of the horses.

Immediately there was response from the gatehouse parapet, indicating that their approach had not gone unnoticed. "Who comes to Crichton unbidden?" was demanded.

"Alexander Lyon comes, son to the Thane of Glamis," he called. "To see Sir William Crichton."

"Sir William is not here," came the brief reply.

Alec frowned. "We come from Edinburgh Castle seeking him. I bring important word for him. I was told that he was here."

"He was. But he is gone."

"Gone far? Will he be back?"

There was silence for moments. "We shall seek information. Wait you."

They sat their horses.

It was some time before there was further contact, with the score of men behind now forming a semicircle not far off, waiting also. It was a feminine voice that they heard presently. "Was I told aright?" came to them, high and clear. "Glamis, was it? Lyon of Glamis? You come from Glamis, seeking my father?"

"I do, lady. I am Alexander Lyon. With a message, a weighty message. From, from the queen." Somehow Alec felt foolish saying that.

"The queen!"

"Yes, lady, the Queen's Grace. A letter."

There was no reply to that. But presently a young woman appeared within the gatehouse arch, and waiting there, beckoned the trio forward.

They rode into the courtyard, and dismounted.

"I am Agnes Crichton," the young woman told them. "My father has gone to Borthwick, none so far off. You have come all the way from Glamis, sir? From beyond Tay?" She was probably about Alec's own age, a well-built and attractive female, dark of hair and eyes, with a wide mouth and dimples in her cheeks. She eyed Alec with frank interest.

"No, lady, only from Stirling, this day. We called at the castle of Edinburgh, where Sir William is keeper, but were told that he had come here. It was urgent, so I came on."

"From the queen, you said? She will be . . . in much distress. Is she?"

"You know of the grievous deed, then? The shameful slaughter of the king?"

"Yes. That is why my father is come here. And gone to Borthwick. And my brother over into Lauderdale. But – come you within." She was not clad for standing outside in February.

Leaving his men to see to the horses, Alec followed the young woman into the redstone keep of the castle, and on up a winding turnpike stairway into the first-floor hall, where a log fire burned brightly in a wide ingle-neuked fireplace. She rang a bell for a maid to bring refreshments, and told her to see that the escorts were served also.

Seated on the two stone ingle-seats on either side of the fire, Agnes Crichton told her visitor, as they sipped wine and ate oaten cakes, that her father had been shocked to hear of the king's murder, as had they all, shocked and dismayed and anxious. For he feared that this would not be the end of it, that there would be more grievous trouble and evil deeds. He believed that it was a bid to snatch the throne. And it had to be countered.

Alec said that that was his own father's reaction, and his Ogilvy grandsire's. They had gone to Stirling at once, to offer the queen and the new boy-king warning and aid. His father had predicted further infamy, and that it would almost certainly centre on Stirling. And Sir Alexander Livingston was keeper there. His father did not trust Livingston, although the queen and the late king had done so. He, backed by the captain of the guard, had proposed that the boy James should be taken to Edinburgh Castle meantime, in the care of her father, a secure haven, until all was safe for him to return to Stirling. That was why he, Alexander Lyon, was here, bringing a letter for Sir William from the queen. It was necessary that he delivered it soon.

"Borthwick Castle is but a mile or two," she told him, pointing south-westwards. "Were it not for that ridge between, you could see it from here. My father has gone to see the Lord Borthwick. Have him raise his men. He has many, and was a good friend of the king. And my brother James has gone to Lauderdale to raise our folk of Glengelt, Oxton and thereabouts. Also the Maitlands."

"So, Sir William wastes no time! A good friend of the crown. But this of getting the young king to Edinburgh demands haste also. More haste. My father fears that the assassins may strike again, and quickly. At Stirling . . ."

"Yes. I do not know when he will be back – my father. You had best go to Borthwick, friend. See you, I will take you. Less than two miles as the corbies fly, it is a deal further to reach, and the way a little difficult, round-about."

"I will find my way, lady."

"It is finding the two fords that is difficult. No, I will

take you. And, sir, do not name me lady! My name is Agnes."

"And mine Alexander. But Alec to most!"

"Very well, Alec. Give me a short time to change my garb for riding, and we will go." She rose. "If you look out of that window, and see between two standing stones on yonder ridge and an old bent hawthorn, you may glimpse the topmost tower of Borthwick Castle, but only just. It is hard to make out, a very fine new house, built but a few years ago by the proud new lord! His brother Nicholas is wed to my Aunt Elena. He built it very high, so that his watchmen could see warning beacons lit on our tower-top, this in case of invaders from England, or even Borders raiders. Wait you, then – I shall not keep you long."

Much taken with this practical young creature, Alec went to the window and peered out through the thick glass above the shutters. He had no difficulty in seeing the couple of tall standing stones on the skyline, less than a mile away, nor the bent, wind-blown tree; but gaze as he would he could not distinguish any tower beyond.

In commendably brief time Agnes Crichton was back, clad in heavy coat and long riding-boots, dark hair tied in a scarf. She declared that she had had her maid go tell a groom to have her horse saddled and ready.

They went downstairs to the vaulted kitchen where the two Glamis men were being entertained and out to the courtyard for the horses. Alec gallantly aided the girl up into her saddle, little necessary as this was.

The four of them riding out, he pointed to the chapel-like building nearby and asked what it represented, to be told that it was a strange combination, vaulted stables on the ground floor and a little chapel and lodging for the priest of the large church higher. Her grandfather had built it thus for some reason.

Agnes led the way down a steep zigzag track to the water meadows, their mounts having to tread warily. And once on the cattle-dotted levels, Alec soon saw why he had been provided with a guide, for they had to turn up the riverside for quite some distance, and not seemingly in the desired direction, before they came to a shallow enough stretch for fording, their horses splashing through. Thereafter, it was necessary to head back as they climbed the far side, less steep but much longer, thanks to that ridge, making for the standing stones.

Once up on the high ground they could see Borthwick Castle clearly enough, down there on another mound in another valley, that of the Gore Water. It was clearly a notably tall fortalice of unusual construction, E-shaped apparently and six storeys high. But although less than a mile away, reaching it was still less than simple, for this Gore Water, rushing off the nearby hills, had also to be forded, and this entailed another detour, a still larger one, downstream. When they reached this, it was to find it guarded by a smaller fortified house, which they were told was Catcune Castle, which had been the seat of the Borthwicks until they became too great for it and the present chief, another Sir William, the first *Lord* Borthwick, had erected his splendid lofty fortalice upstream, this on land bought from the Hay family and really called Lochquhariot, or Locherwarth. Agnes laughed as she recounted all this, for the name Borthwick itself was quite unsuitable, for the real Borthwick, on the Borthwick Water, where the family had come from, was far away down in the Middle March of the Borders near to Hawick; but the Borthwicks were not going to change their illustrious name to Catcune or Lochquhariot, so Borthwick Castle it was. And the girl added a twist to her story, declaring that a son of the Hay seller, who still owned the ground on the other side of the river, and close by, had deliberately built a water mill there, with a great and noisy wheel, so that the proud lord above would not be able to sleep of a night for the clacking of the Lochquhariot mill-wheel. So much for pride and dignity!

They came up to the castle, and Alec had to admit that he had never seen anything quite like it. Within its courtyard wall, it soared to fully one hundred and ten feet, to a lofty parapet walk, with stone-slabbed and gabled garret chambers higher, a massive main block with two great square towers projecting westwards, these with a gap between. Agnes, clearly a born raconteur, as they approached, pointed to that gap and said that it was some twelve feet across, and with its own significance. For the Lord Borthwick, as a feudal baron, like her father, had the power of pit and gallows, meaning that he could imprison or hang at his own decision without recourse to higher authority. No doubt Alec's father had the same? And Borthwick used this gap between the towers as an adjunct to his judicial system. He did not bother with gallows and hanging. If the verdict was death, he gave the sinner the opportunity to save himself. If he could leap across from one tower's parapet to the other, he could go free, and sin no more. If not, Borthwick provided a regiment of iron spikes down at ground level, one hundred feet below, for those to fall on who did not quite make it. And, to be sure, there was no space for the leapers to make a run for it, and with those parapets to get over, there were assuredly few who won their way to freedom.

Alec was duly impressed, and hoped never to fall foul of the Lord Borthwick.

Actually, when they met the said lord in his splendid hall with its minstrel-gallery and vast hooded fireplace, he did not appear so fearsome, a heavily built man of later middle years, and affable towards the visitors. Indeed Sir William Crichton seemed the sterner of the two, tall, hawk-faced and beginning to grey at the temples – not that his daughter seemed in any awe of him. His scrutiny of Alec was keen as he took the queen's letter.

Opening the seal, and reading, he nodded. "You know what is in this?" he asked.

"I know of the decisions which brought the queen to write it, sir," he answered. "My father urged it, the taking of the young king to Edinburgh Castle. Sir David Dunbar

21

and Sir James Menteith supported him. And the queen decided."

"Aye." Crichton turned to Borthwick. "The Thane of Glamis, whom we both know, and regard well, has advised Queen Joanna to come to Edinburgh for safety, believing the boy James to be in danger at Stirling. I would agree. How say you?"

"I say that is right, wise. Those scoundrels will stop at nothing. And you can hold the boy secure at your fortress."

"Yes." Crichton turned back to Alec. "What does Livingston say to this, young man?"

"He was not there, sir. The queen had sent him off to try to apprehend the killers."

"So! I think that he will not succeed in that! If he tries to!" The two older men exchanged glances.

"My father scarcely trusts Sir Alexander Livingston," Alec added.

"He is not alone in that! Unfortunately the king did. And no doubt the queen also." Crichton tapped the paper. "This commands me to repair to Stirling Castle at the earliest. In some force. Then to escort the queen and her family to Edinburgh." He shrugged, turning. "I must needs go forthwith, Will. You – you will gather the men? Your own and mine, and those my son brings from Lauderdale? Bring them to Edinburgh. We shall muster there. So soon as may be."

"Three days? Four? It will take time to bring mine up from the Borders. And yours from Sanquhar."

"That will serve, I judge. It will take me two days to get men to Stirling. Another to bring the royal family to Edinburgh . . ."

So it was agreed. There was no undue delay before father and daughter, with Alec, rode off back for Crichton, for soon it would be dark.

That evening, back in the ingle-neuk, Sir William and his guest discussed the situation into which Scotland had been plunged by this dire deed, sought to gauge

22

the consequences and to weigh up the strengths for and against the queen and her son. There was no doubt that the vast majority of the magnates, like the people themselves, would be loyal enough, for the king had been popular; but there was always the reluctance to have a child monarch, with all the problems of governance and regency which such involved inevitably, the struggles for power of ambitious lords, the uncertainties and manoeuvrings. Some might opt for Atholl or his grandson on the throne, even while deploring the means by which they had won it.

Agnes meanwhile intermittently plucked the strings of her harpsichord, and sang them ballads in a lightly melodious voice.

It had been a long day for Alec. Soon he was yawning, and the girl, nodding at him, escorted him to his room up on the third floor of the keep. Her mother long dead and her older sister married and away, she obviously ran the establishment, and firmly, despite her lack of years. She now assured herself that all was in order in his chamber, the fire well-doing, the hot water steaming in its tub, the warming-pan in the bed, before wishing Alec a goodnight and pleasant dreams. Much taken with his hostess, he was bold enough to reply that he might well dream of *her*, and, he hoped, warmly on this cold night; at which she flicked a reproving hand at him but smiled as she did so, those dimples deepening.

In the morning their setting off for the capital was delayed while Sir William collected as many men as could be raised and horsed locally for the required escort, although he would be able to add to these from the guard at Edinburgh Castle. Alec was surprised but nowise displeased to find that Agnes was coming with them. It seemed that her father thought that with the Lady Catherine Douglas's arm broken and much of the royal household presumably left at Stirling, the queen might well be in need of an extra lady-in-waiting at Edinburgh.

The weather had changed, with flurries of snow, as the party of some forty rode northwards. Passing Dalkeith in due course, Sir William wondered about the Douglases. Was their powerful support assured? The present Sir James Douglas had married as his second wife Janet, daughter of Lord Borthwick; and his first wife had been Elizabeth, third daughter of King Robert the Third and sister of the late king. But that made her also a niece of Atholl, to be sure! And the Douglases were apt to be a law unto themselves.

At Edinburgh Castle, Crichton assembled more of the guard, while his daughter set about preparing quarters for the queen's family. This citadel, although a royal one, was very much a military establishment, a fortress rather than any sort of palace. There was a royal wing, yes, but it was seldom occupied, kings and queens when visiting the capital much preferring the more comfortable quarters in the abbot's house of Holyrood, looked upon as all but their own. Queen Joanna had never dwelt in the castle. Agnes was very busy.

By early afternoon they were ready for the thirty-five-mile ride to Stirling. Somewhat reluctantly, Alec took his leave of the young woman, but said that he might well be back with the royal company on the morrow or the next day. He did not know what his father's plans were.

They reached Stirling just before dark, in time to see the distant lofty peaks of the Highland Line snow-covered and gleaming. They found all in order at the castle, if that was the right term, for the keeper, Sir Alexander Livingston, was back, and apparently disapproving of the projected move to Edinburgh, declaring that the royal household was better, safer, with him in this stronghold, whatever Lyon, Menteith and Dunbar said.

The meeting between the two fortress governors was significant, although there was no overt clash, however much their mutual dislike was evident. When Crichton asked how successful the other had been in apprehending the murderers, Livingston said briefly that the guilty ones had straight way fled into the Highlands. He had managed to capture only one of their retainers, Chambers by name, and had him in custody.

Livingston was a handsome man, tall, somewhat younger than Crichton. Looking from one to the other, Alec saw them as likely to be key figures in the land in the days to come. The Livingston territory, from which he took his name, was in Western Lothian, whereas Crichton's was in Middle, none so far apart, some twenty-five miles. It looked as though there would be a tug-of-war across those miles.

But meantime it was all preparations for the royal move to Edinburgh the next day, despite Livingston's disapproval. Sir Patrick, Menteith and Dunbar all said that they would accompany the queen's party, to see them all safely installed, and to consult with Borthwick and the others who would be assembling with their forces at the capital, to see what was to be done for the realm's security. A parliament obviously should be called, and speedily. Normally forty days' notice had to be given for such, but in these exceptional circumstances probably a lesser interval could elapse. Crichton said that he would get in touch with Bishop Cameron of Glasgow, the Chancellor of the realm, whose duty it was to call a parliament in the king's name and preside thereat. He would urge him to convene it as soon as possible. Admittedly that might mean that some entitled to attend would not be present, if they were based far away in the north, the Highlands or the Hebrides; but most should make it in a deal less than forty days.

That night Alec again shared a bed with his father and, with the castle crowded indeed, one of Crichton's lairdlings had to sleep on the floor of the same room. Alec preferred his bed-going at Crichton Castle.

With the women and children to be readied and horsed, it was mid-forenoon before the large company set off for Edinburgh. If Livingston's assertion that the conspirators had fled into the Highlands was accurate, there was little likelihood of any enemy attack on the way, so the numerous escort was not really necessary. Inevitably they made a slow journey of it, the little girls being scarcely practised horsewomen, although young James rode well for a six-year-old. He was a lively, confident boy and scornful of his sisters' feebleness in the saddle.

It was almost dark before they reached the capital and climbed the round-about route from the West Port gateway in the walls, through the Grassmarket and up the West Bow to the Lawnmarket, to reach the castle. There Alec had nothing to do with the settling-in process, so he did not see Agnes Crichton, who would be much involved – that is, until late in the evening, when she it was came seeking him in his humble quarters below Queen Margaret's Chapel. She was full of tales of the royal children and the queen's calm and assured authority. She said that it seemed to be taken for granted that she was to be an extra lady-in-waiting meantime; so Crichton Castle would have to manage without her for a while, although it looked as though her father and brother were likely to be otherwhere anyway, with an army being assembled.

Alec was again sharing quarters with others, so the young woman's company was shared likewise, and appreciatively; but he did presently contrive to escort her back to the royal block of buildings further down the rock-top – and that rock-top being naked stone, uneven and wet with rain, he found it expedient for her safety to hold her arm tightly, even her waist now and again, she patting his hand in mock gratitude.

They paused outside her doorway, inclement as was the night, that entrance unfortunately guarded by sentries – there were altogether too many people in this Edinburgh Castle – and turned to face out over the darkened city.

"Will you enjoy waiting on the queen?" Alec asked. "I do not think, somehow, that you are one for fetching and carrying at anyone's behest, even a queen's!"

"No? You judge me proud, haughty, do you, Alec Lyon? I wonder why? Have I treated you so ill?"

"No, no. It is but that, that you seem very much assured of yourself. Very much your own mistress."

"I am certainly no one else's mistress!"

"That I believe! Although you are fair enough to have many seeking it!"

"You say so? Flatterer! Do not think that that will win you much! No, I judge that I shall quite enjoy waiting on Queen Joanna. She seems to be a strong woman, but not haughty nor harsh. And the Lady Catherine Douglas, her chief attendant, is kindly, friendly, however much she is pained by her broken arm. A brave soul!"

"Yes. They went through a terrible night, both of them. Those murderous wretches! Nothing, no fate, would be too dire for them. If they can be defeated and caught."

"They will be, if the queen has aught to do with it! I heard her tell the Lady Catherine that she will know no mercy, especially on Graham. He is uncle and tutor to the young Earl of Strathearn. My father has sent up to Strathbogie, in the north, to Huntly, who is wed to my sister Elizabeth, to rally his Gordons, and he has his thousands, and to lead them down into the Atholl country to seek to grasp that earl. He is behind it all."

"Think you that there will be battle, then? Armies fighting?"

"It may be so. But my father thinks that, if they can capture Graham and Robert Stewart first, quickly, and assail old Atholl in his own lands, then there will be no rebel rising. It is to be hoped so. Then you will not have to seek to prove yourself a hero, Alec Lyon!"

"So! What other could I do to impress you?"

"You have impressed me sufficiently – with your forwardness towards womankind!"

"Not *all* womankind!"

"There you go, see you! Now, I escape, before you practise your arts further! But – a goodnight to you." And she touched his arm before turning and flitting indoors between those two sentries.

3

Edinburgh was a busy city in the days which followed, not to say uproarious, with the loyal magnates assembling their forces on the Burgh Muir, the common grazing land on the skirts of the Braid and Blackford Hills, and these spilling inevitably into the town's streets, not always to the citizens' delight. The castle became still fuller, with their leaders, and sleeping accommodation therein more packed. Sir Patrick was considering going back to Strathmore and raising a force of his own men and Ogilvys.

He delayed doing this however, and for two reasons. There was the forthcoming parliament, which Bishop Cameron had agreed to call for only ten days hence, and which the thane must attend; also because the word reaching the capital – and Crichton proved to be very well informed – was that there was no armed uprising developing meantime, the conspirators appearing to be lying low in their various upland territories. The queen was urgent that these should be taken, without delay; and Crichton, who was more or less automatically taking the lead, sent out strong parties to the Graham and Stewart lands of Dundaff and Strathearn.

Alec meantime hung about the fortress, seeking to see as much as possible of Agnes Crichton and, because of her new position, was able to see also quite a lot of the royal children, to which she was all but acting as governess, this suiting him very well. Naturally he found the boy king easiest to cope with, and they got on very well together. James, advanced for his years, lively, indeed headstrong, was ever ready for activity, exciting if possible. He was very disappointed that Edinburgh Castle provided no hurlyhackit slopes, as did Stirling, for grass-sledging down on an ox skull, a favoured sport. He would also have liked to go hawking round the braes and lochans of Arthur's Seat, but this was forbidden in case of kidnap or other attempts, and any large guard with him would have driven off any game for the hawks to stoop on. So he had to be content, if that was the word, with archery practice on the tourney-ground in front of the gatehouse, javelin-throwing, fencing with sticks instead of swords, and bowls. Alec being the youngest man apt to be haunting the royal quarters, he became all but a kind of squire to the king, the official Gentleman of the Bedchamber well enough pleased to leave the monarch's entertainment to the Thane of Glamis's son. Thus he saw the more of Agnes, she putting up with him in head-shaking amusement.

The vital parliament was held in the greater hall of the castle in due course. Alec was able to attend, for the first time, only as a spectator to be sure up in the minstrel gallery, but then, was not that the position of Queen Joanna herself and the Lady Catherine, Agnes having to be left in charge of the young princesses? It was King James's first parliament also, the monarch, youthful as he might be, having to be present, otherwise it was not a true parliament, only a convention, and limited in what it could debate and decide upon. When all others had taken their seats, officers of state, earls, lords, bishops, mitred abbots and representatives of the shires and of the royal burghs, the Three Estates, the boy was ushered in, to trumpet flourish, by the Lord Lyon King of Arms, to take his seat on the throne, Keith the Earl Marischal and Hay of Erroll the High Constable standing behind him. The young monarch was not in the least abashed by it all, gazing around him with excited interest, and even waving to his mother up in the gallery, and again when he spotted Alec there also.

The Bishop of Glasgow now took charge, as Chancellor, standing behind his table near the throne. Bowing to the king, he announced that with His Grace's permission he would declare this parliament now in session. He called for Bishop James Kennedy to open the proceedings with prayer, the Primate, Henry Wardlaw, Bishop of St Andrews, being unfortunately too infirm to attend.

A very able cleric, young to be a bishop, and an appointee of the late king's own, Kennedy came forward and skilfully incorporated into his appeal to the Almighty for aid in their deliberations and decisions, some indication to all of the nation's great loss in the dire murder of His Grace's royal father, the dangers of the present situation, the need for unity behind the new monarch, who would be crowned immediately hereafter, and a call for divine vengeance on the forces of evil which had brought about this crisis in the nation's affairs.

Thus suitably prepared, the assembly got down to its tasks.

Bishop Cameron, who undoubtedly had been given his instructions beforehand, commenced by announcing that he felt that he had occupied the chancellorship for sufficiently long, and that this emergency in the realm's governance was the occasion for a man of more experience in military matters, and the disposition of armed forces, to take and hold the position of chief minister. He hoped that parliament would agree, and so appoint.

The response to this was immediate. Borthwick arose in the lords' benches and, declaring that the bishop's most valuable services to the realm were appreciated by all, and would no doubt be used in other ways, he agreed that he was right in assuming that a Chancellor used to the handling of armed men was vital at this stage. He felt that none could fill the position better than Sir William Crichton, keeper of this castle and Master of the Household, and so proposed. The Thane of Glamis stood to second that.

There were cries of agreement, but one or two contrary shouts. These last had the powerful Earl of Douglas rising to move a counter-motion: that Sir Alexander Livingston of Calendar, keeper of Stirling Castle and Gentleman of the Bedchamber, be appointed Chancellor, this promptly seconded by Sir James Douglas, Lord of Dalkeith, whose aunt was Livingston's mother.

Thus early were the lines drawn between these two, and the favour of the Douglases indicated. That was, the Black Dougles. The Red line, to which Lady Catherine belonged, might think differently.

There was much noise and argument in that hall, so that the bishop had to beat the table with his gavel for quiet. When he obtained it, he asked if there were any other nominations. There was none, and no one suggested that he himself should stay on as chief minister.

So the matter was put to the vote. By a fairly large majority, Crichton was elected.

Alec felt like cheering, as probably did many there, but he noticed that Queen Joanna looked doubtful.

Sir William lost no time. Coming forward, he bowed to the throne, and going to the table before it, shook hands with Bishop Cameron, and picked up the Chancellor's gavel, turning to face the assembly. As his predecessor made his way down to the clerics' benches, after more bows to the king, Crichton banged on the table-top strongly, and went on banging, undoubtedly some indication of the sort of role that he intended to play.

Without preamble or any remarks on his appointment, he plunged into the first duty of the parliament: to ensure the security of the realm and their support of its lawful monarch, King James the Second, this against all would-be rebels and enemies, within and without; and the apprehension and due punishment of their late sovereign-lord's assassins. There was also the question of England's reactions to be considered. Invasion might develop, the auld enemy thinking to use this period of crisis and uncertainty to further their age-old aims of conquering Scotland. All this involved the mustering of the nation's forces forthwith, and their allocation to the various parts of the country where threat was most likely, especially

31

along the borderline with England. Already there were a substantial number assembled on the Burgh Muir here, but these must be added to very considerably. The Earl of Huntly, his own good-son, was rallying in the north to assail Atholl, who was behind this evil situation; but other great lords should enlist their strengths. He hoped that this would include the great houses of Douglas; and suggested that it would be most suitable if they took on the defence of the Borderland.

There was something of a hush as Crichton paused there, on account of this overture towards the Douglases. There was no actual response from that earl nor from Dalkeith, but nor was there any disclaimer. And the Earl of Angus, a noted soldier, chief of the Red line, rose to announce support for the proposal.

There was relief in most parts of the hall, for the Douglas power was always a matter to be reckoned with in Scotland, their wealth almost certainly greater than the monarch's, their large lands in France contributing – the Earl of Douglas was also Duke of Touraine in that country. Crichton carefully went on to try to consolidate his advantages by declaring that all this military preparedness would require a Council of Regency to be appointed by parliament, on which, he suggested, the Earls of Douglas and Angus should sit. None sought to contest that. The Earl Marischal, from behind the throne, moved that such council be appointed, but not by the entire parliament, its membership a matter of much weight and requiring much consultation; it should be decided hereafter by a committee of the Lords of the Articles. This was promptly seconded by his companion, Hay of Erroll, High Constable.

None contesting this, the new Chancellor went on to remind all that extra moneys would be required for the necessary preparations, the equipping, maintaining and provisioning of these hosts, the strengthening of the border defences, and the sending of envoys to foreign courts, especially their Auld Alliance partners of France, and, needless to say, King Henry the Sixth of England, assuring him of the goodwill of the new regime in Scotland while also informing him of its readiness to defend its frontiers and coasts. The council would have to decide on the raising of such necessary moneys, but it was to be hoped that Holy Church would contribute generously.

This last aroused cheers throughout the hall. Alec wondered how Queen Joanna felt about the references to England. After all, she herself was related to the English royal house, and her uncle was High Chancellor of England.

Thereafter followed decisions on the day-to-day governance of the realm, appointments to various offices, sheriffdoms and the like, as well as the state of the revenue. This was got over with the minimum of talk and delay, save for certain manoeuvrings as to influential positions – for most there were concerned that the coronation ceremony which was to follow was not unduly held up.

When Crichton was able crisply to bring matters to a close, and sign to the Lord Lyon to bring forward his trumpeters, there were not a few sighs of relief that all had gone reasonably well, save for the ambitions of the Livingston faction. All stood for the king's exit, and James, who had latterly been fidgeting and twisting about in his chair, jumped up and all but ran for the dais door, leaving the Marischal and the Constable to hurry after him, dignity a casualty.

Thereafter there was much bustle in the castle as the great ones readied themselves, and formed up for a procession down through the city to the Abbey of the Holy Rood, womenfolk now included. The queen and princesses and some others would ride, but the men would walk, including the monarch, so that the citizenry could see him, and hopefully cheer, the boy now in a fine flowing purple velvet cloak and bonnet. Alec found himself being beckoned by the monarch to his side, to the frowns of the Marischal, the Constable and various earls, and he had to shake his head, effectively refusing a royal command, punishable offence as that was. Agnes, making faces at

33

him from the saddle beside the princesses, did not help. To the beat of drummers, after much argument as to precedence in position by the magnates, the procession eventually moved off, being joined at the High Kirk of St Giles by a choir of singing boys, the drummers and the singers somewhat competing.

The crowded streets duly rang with cheers.

Holyrood, founded by King David the First three centuries before, was a magnificent establishment, its church all but a cathedral, its monastic buildings extensive, its abbot's house palatial, Holy Church at its most splendid. This would be its first coronation, however, for Scone, up near to Perth, was the traditional crowning-site for the Kings of Scots, former resting-place of the Stone of Destiny. But Scone was behind the Highland Line, and considered to be too dangerous an area to take young James to, in present circumstances, close to the Graham and Strathearn lands; and anyway, the precious Stone was now none knew where, save for the MacDonalds of the Isles. Holyrood would serve.

The great church was already packed when the royal party arrived, and ringing to the praises of choir and instrumentalists and the chatter of hundreds, vastly more than could ever have got into the comparatively small church of Scone Abbey. James and his mother and sisters, and their attendants, with the officers of state, were able to enter by the abbot's door to the vestry area, but Alec had to squeeze into the overcrowded nave, where all had to stand, benches removed. Making himself unpopular, he eventually managed to find his way to his father's side near enough to the chancel steps to be able to see all that went on. The queen mother, princesses and their ladies were taken to occupy the choirstalls.

Owing to the absence of the aged Primate Wardlaw of St Andrews, John Cameron of Glasgow, the next senior bishop, was to officiate, assisted by Kennedy of Dunkeld. There was an added cleric to take part, in the person of Antony, Bishop of Urbino, the Papal Legate, who had arrived on a visit to Scotland on the very day of the king's murder, and who was able to add the Vatican's fulminations against the assassins.

There was a problem, in that the hereditary coronership for the crownings of the monarchy had been vested in the family of the MacDuff Earls of Fife; but this line had died out, and the office had fallen to the royal house of Stewart itself; and as it happened, the present Coroner was actually Walter Stewart, Earl of Atholl. This sorry circumstance was overcome by the appointing of the Earl of Douglas and Duke of Touraine to fulfil the task, the most powerful subject in the realm, and whose mother had been the Princess Margaret, daughter of Robert the Third, and sister of the slain monarch.

The service and ceremony were comparatively brief, however important, Bishop Kennedy again opening with prayer, then the Bishop of Urbino addressing all in Latin, and conveying the Pope's blessing on the boy king, who was then led over to a throne-like chair by the officers of state. The Lyon King of Arms, acting as the successor to the ancient Celtic Sennachies, then read out the lengthy list of the monarch's predecessors, from prehistoric times down through the Pictish and Albannach periods, score upon score, some indubitably imaginary, and so to more modern days, naming Duncan and MacBeth and Malcolm Canmore, down to Bruce, David the Second, Robert the Second, Robert the Third and James the First. Then, bowing low towards the throne, he ended up with James the Second, by the Grace of God.

Bishop Cameron of Glasgow then consecrated the sacred oil and went to anoint James therewith, to the youngster's grins. Then the Earl of Douglas stepped forward, not exactly to place the crown on the six-year-old's head, much too small to support it, but to touch the head with it and then hold it over the boy for a few moments, while the Lord Lyon King of Arms shouted, "God save the King's Grace!" and the cry was taken up throughout the church.

The precious and ancient symbol of monarchy was then placed on James's bent knees, where he held it more or less straight, this by Douglas who was the first to kneel in front of the boy to take the oath of fealty. This involved holding the monarch's right hand between the oath-taker's two palms, and declaring due and lifelong loyal duty, to the death if need be, the process requiring the youngster to remove that hand from its holding of the crown of heavy gold, with the result that it all but fell to the floor and had to be grabbed by Bishop Cameron and saved. Advisedly the proud relic was then placed on the chair's seat alongside the small occupant, where it would be secure, for the fealty-making by all the other earls, lords, barons, knights and magnates present would take a considerable time as they all came forward in due precedence, guided by the Lord Lyon's heralds, to kneel and hold the royal hand, a process which took longer than all the rest of the ceremony.

Long before the last of the oath-swearers had finished their fealty, King James was showing signs of restlessness and of having had more than enough of such formalities for one day, frowning and looking over towards his mother for help, she making down-calming gestures with her hand, to the boy's scowls.

But at length it was over, and Bishop Kennedy closed the service with another mercifully brief prayer and the Bishop of Urbino pronounced the papal benediction on all. Trumpets blared, and James, jumping up, made for the door without waiting for mother and sisters, to go darting about outside while the church slowly emptied, the procession reformed, the choir boys began to chant and the drums to drown them out. Somewhat raggedly the return was made up to the castle.

Scotland had a crowned and anointed monarch again, undoubtedly, proclaimed and sworn allegiance to. So much for the reigning. But what of the ruling?

* * *

The very next day, something of the quality and style of that rule was demonstrated. Word came from Perth that Sir Robert Graham had been run to earth and captured. Queen Joanna was in no doubt as to what to do about that. She wrote specific instructions to Sir Alexander Livingston at Stirling that Graham was to be brought to Edinburgh, put on a cart, naked, and led through the streets, his right hand nailed to a post, red-hot hooks, knives and irons, from a brazier in another cart, constantly thrust into him, and thereafter his son, who had taken part in the conspiracy, disembowelled before his eyes. If he himself was not dead by evening, he was to be executed by the common hangman at the Mercat Cross the next day.

Alec and Agnes, discussing this, were distinctly shocked. Was this how they dealt with treason and murder in the queen's England? Edward the First, Hammer of the Scots, had similarly treated William Wallace. But at a woman's command? The queen mother had a husband to avenge, yes. But, this! The Thane of Glamis told his son never to underestimate the spite and venom of women where their loved ones had been violated and wronged.

Joanna's hatred and vengeance was accepted apparently by most as just and suitable. She did not however go to see the actual sentence carried out on the man whose dagger had slain the king, the parade through the streets, the despatching of his son, or his hanging the next day; presumably while her mind could conceive of the grim details, her female stomach would turn at the sight of it all. Crowds of others, nevertheless turned out to watch the spectacle, women and children by no means excepted.

It was four days later that the Earl of Atholl and his grandson, Sir Robert Stewart, with the man Chambers, were brought in chains to Edinburgh. Their punishment was only a little less fearsome. Stewart and Chambers were lacerated with sharp instruments and then hanged, drawn and quartered, heads sent to adorn the gates of Perth. Walter of Atholl, being an earl and a king's son, could not be dealt with in quite that fashion. But he was executed by the axe, and an iron crown clamped on his decapitated head and this put on a spike above Edinburgh's Tolbooth.

So perished the king's enemies, went out the warning.

Sir Patrick Lyon reckoned that it was high time that he got back to his duties in Strathmore, and took Alec with him, although the younger man would have lingered. But he did win a kiss from Agnes Crichton on parting, with the instructions to haste him back.

4

In the event, Alec Lyon was back in Edinburgh sooner than expected, to his surprised satisfaction. A messenger came to Strathmore, from the queen no less, announcing that her son had taken a fancy to Lyon, Younger of Glamis and sought his attendance, at his early convenience. Alec would have been off that same day if his parents had not restrained him.

However, his arrival at Edinburgh Castle produced a certain disappointment. The queen was not there, and in consequence neither was Agnes Crichton. Young James Stewart was, and greeted Alec warmly, even though Sir William Crichton eyed him less so, distinctly cool.

The king told him that his mother was now lodging down at Holyrood. He wished that he could go there also, but was not allowed to. He was glad to see his friend, for he was, it seemed, bored and indeed lonely. There was nothing but old men about this castle, he claimed.

Wondering at all this, and aware of an atmosphere almost of tension about the place, Alec asked why this situation had come about. He knew that the abbot's house was much more comfortable than the royal quarters in this fortress, and could see that the queen mother might prefer to stay there; but why not take her son with her? The boy did not know, but said that he thought that his mother did not like Sir William.

Yet the queen had sent for him, Alec, to be with the youngster. This was all rather strange.

Crichton had always been of a stern nature, not easy to win close to, and his attitude to Alec did not encourage questioning. Needless to say, the younger man would have gone off down to Holyrood without delay, to see Agnes and discover the reason for this state of affairs, but James was so glad to see him, and eager for some activity, that he felt that he could not leave him too quickly. So it was archery practice and fencing, and when rain halted that, indoor games. It seemed strange to be feeling sorry for the King of Scots, but that was Alec's reaction.

Next day he approached Sir William, to tell him that since Queen Joanna had sent for him it was incumbent upon him to go and report to her that he had obeyed her call. He suggested that he should take the king with him to see his mother.

Curtly Crichton told him that this was not possible. The young monarch's safety was at stake, there being many who would seek to seize him for their own ends; and his own instructions from parliament were that he was to hold the boy secure in this castle.

So, to the youngster's disappointment and glowers, Alec set off alone for Holyrood.

On arrival at the abbot's house at least the looked-forward-to meeting with Agnes was no disappointment, that young woman greeting him with a hug and frank affection. And she was eminently huggable, as he told her – to a cautionary tweak of his ear. They had been apart only for two weeks, but he asserted that it had felt like two months.

She responded, more soberly, that it had been a difficult two weeks, with trouble between the queen and her father. She judged that Joanna had never really liked him, preferring his more genial enemy Livingston, and it seemed that they had had a serious quarrel about something, resulting in the queen declaring that she was going to take her son back to Stirling. Her father had said that this was forbidden by the council appointed by parliament, which had ordered that the boy be kept secure in Edinburgh Castle in *his* care. The mother had contested this, but he had been adamant; and it had ended by her asserting that she could no longer dwell in the same establishment with him. She would go down to Holyrood Abbey and take her son with her. This also had been prohibited, as far as the king was concerned. And now this ridiculous situation had developed, mother and daughters here, and the son a mile away, and no coming and going between them, the boy not allowed to leave the castle and the queen too proud to go up there and seek permission to see her own son.

Agnes blamed them both, her father over his harsh stubbornness and holding to the council's command too literally, and the queen's pride and suspicions. It put herself in a difficult position, but Joanna seemed to assume that she was on her side, as in a way she was. She had sought to change her father's attitude, but had failed quite. This was mainly why the queen had sent for him, Alec, to act as a go-between.

Much concerned by all this, he was taken to see the queen mother in her palatial suite of rooms.

Joanna welcomed his appearance, and straightway launched into a very similar account of affairs to that which he had just heard. She wanted him to act as a link with her son, take him messages and gifts, and bring accounts of his communications to her. Crichton would realise, of course, that this was going on, but he could scarcely stop it.

Alec agreed so to act, as courier, if hardly intermediary, and it would allow him to see Agnes frequently. But it was an extraordinary situation, and he doubted if it could go on for long.

Back at the castle he explained the position to James, the boy seeming not so much upset about not seeing his mother and sisters as over the constrictions on his own freedom and being shut up in this rock-top citadel. He wanted to go riding and hawking and hunting, and with that Arthur's Seat so close. But it was not allowed. He hated the man Crichton, a monster!

The said monster sent for Alec to give an account of his visit to Holyrood.

"What did the queen say to you, Lyon?" he was asked. "How is it with her? Has she gathered others around her? Visiting her there? There could be danger in that."

"Not that I saw nor heard of, sir."

"Some could see it as opportunity to advance their own fortunes. When Livingston hears of it, as hear he will, he could seek to use it."

Alec shrugged.

"And . . . my daughter? How does Agnes see this? Is she intent on staying with the queen?"

"I think so, yes. She did not say otherwise."

"Does she understand the position? Perceive the dangers? See that there could be grievous trouble, even war in the land, in endeavours to hold the king. I have to keep him secure, safe, here. The woman Joanna leans towards Livingston. And those who will use him to gain fullest power in the realm. I do not trust the Douglases!"

"That I know naught of, Sir William. Nothing was said of the like."

"When next you go, then, seek to learn the queen's intentions. My daughter may know of them, in some measure, and will perhaps tell you. It is important."

Wagging his head, Alec saw himself as being used by both sides in this tangle, as some sort of an agent, a spy almost, and did not like it.

"Sir, would not much be improved for all if the queen could see her son? Frequently. And he, who is much exercised over being confined here all but alone, almost a prisoner, feel more free? So there would be less of displeasure. And therefore of any danger such as you mention. You have many guards here. If I could take the king riding and hawking round yonder hills. Under strong guard. None could capture him. And he could call and see his mother and sisters on occasion."

"Did she, the queen, tell you to say that? Or my daughter?"

"No, sir. It is my own suggestion. I say that it would help."

"It is not to be considered, man! Do you not see the danger? No guard such as I have here could ensure the boy's safety. The Douglases, and others, could raise thousands! In a day or two. If they heard that the king was going riding abroad, they could descend on him, overwhelm any guard. Dalkeith, a Black Douglas seat, is but five or six miles away. It is not possible. Livingston's own lands of Calendar none so far off. Young James must bide herein. My daughter knows that, if Joanna Beaufort does not!"

The younger man shrugged again, and went back to his small liege-lord.

So commenced a period of very uneasy living for Alec Lyon, he seeking to keep James Stewart not content but occupied and diverted from his feelings of confinement, acting as all but his tutor although scarcely book-learned himself; and making quite frequent visits down to Holyrood and being questioned there, and again when he returned to the castle. He much disliked this double-sided role, and told Agnes so, admitting that he was much more in favour of the queen's attitude than Sir William's but could not reject her father's questioning, or almost certainly he would be expelled from attendance on young James, for whom he had much understanding and liking. Agnes sympathised and told him to be patient. This could not go on for very long, she felt sure.

At least it did mean that he could see quite a lot of the young woman, unfortunately seldom alone, save momentarily, for she always had the five princesses with her, save when these were abed, and that was not the time for Alec's visits, with the fortress closed up securely at nightfall, drawbridge up and portcullis down. He did achieve some improvement in this matter of association with Agnes, he suggesting to the queen that the princesses, all but Annabella, the youngest, would be the better of being taken horseback-riding round Arthur's Seat's foothills, Agnes accompanying them of course. This being agreed, they did quite a lot of riding, as the winter passed into spring and the weather improved, even though the young girls were less than expert in the saddle, and it was possible for talk to be exchanged between their elders when riding side by side, with their charges trotting ahead. And sometimes they could dismount and sit together, as at the shores of Dunsappie and Duddingston Lochs, with the youngsters playing at the waterside, Alec making the most of such opportunities and the young woman not actually discouraging him. These were no ideal courting conditions, but a deal better than nothing, and perhaps good for a man whose enthusiasm might have outstripped his moderation; for Alec had decided that he was in love with this female Crichton, whatever he felt about her father.

Once or twice they had company on these rides, as the weeks passed: the queen herself. This was accounted for by the arrival on the scene of a new character in the drama, one Sir James Stewart, known as the Black Knight of Lorne, a son of the Lord of Lorne, a darkly handsome character, distantly linked with the royal house and also with the Black Douglases. Based in Argyll, he had come to Dalkeith on a visit to Douglas kin, and while there had called to see his late royal kinsman's widow to express his condolences and outrage. And he had come back, and more than once, evidently being sufficiently well received, and now served as a riding companion for the queen. Alec found Sir James easy to deal with.

Whether it was at the Black Knight's suggestion or otherwise, Agnes's prediction that the present situation could not go on indefinitely was fulfilled. In early March, on one of Alec's visits, she intimated that the queen desired a word with him, and led him into the presence, to find Sir James Stewart with her.

"My friend," she said to him, "we have come to a decision. And a means of carrying it out. And we seek your help. An important decision, to serve your sovereign-lord King James. In an unlikely, indeed somewhat desperate method of effecting it, your aid will be required. We aim to rescue James from confinement in Edinburgh Castle. Will you assist us?"

What could he say but yes? But he glanced at Agnes, since this must be contrary to her father's interests. She nodded.

"It must be secret, wholly secret," Joanna went on. "You swear not to reveal it, Alexander Lyon?"

He swallowed. "If it is for the king's true weal, I do, Your Grace."

"Oh, it is, it is." That was Sir James. "Have no fear of that. Even if it may . . . lack dignity!" And he actually laughed.

"Dignity?"

"Yes," the queen said. "It may seem lacking in majesty for a crowned monarch, even a small one. But we believe that it will be effective. It demands the aid of Agnes and yourself."

Wonderingly Alec looked at them all.

"Here is the way of it. I left not a little of my clothing and belongings up at the castle. I am entitled to have them. Some in a large wardrobe-chest in my bedchamber. I can send Agnes to claim it and have it brought to me here. That will not be forbidden, surely. The plan is for some of the gear to be taken out of the chest, and my son put in! It is large enough to hold him. Then it to be brought down to me, with him inside. It is a heavy oaken box, carved and deep. James does not weigh so heavily. It should not be evident that there is not only my gear inside. A rope tied around, to keep the lid closed. A cart required, for it is much too heavy for any horse. Get some of the guard to carry it down to the cart. Then here with it."

Alec all but gasped. "The king! In a wooden chest!"

"He will be well enough. He will likely see it as a notable ploy! We will be waiting here, with the horses. Sir James will have a boat hired to be waiting at Leith haven to take us all up to Stirling. What think you of that?"

"It is all but beyond belief!"

"But so simple," Stewart said, "and like to be successful, I judge. How often does Crichton come to see the king? Will he be apt to miss him, if he is gone? Quickly? We shall have to be ready to ride at once. In case . . ."

"He sees him but little. Many days not at all."

"Then it should be little trouble," the queen said. "Agnes here will go up to the castle with the cart. You will be ready for her, James prepared. She will tell Sir William of my need of my clothing and gear. Then get men to carry the chest down to the cart."

Alec looked at Agnes. How was she taking this extraordinary move against her own father?

His questioning gaze obvious to her, she shook her dark head. "It has to be," she said. "The king has to be with his mother and sisters. It is for the best."

"Yes. And when is this to be?"

"The sooner the better," Joanna said. "The morrow. In the morning."

"I will have the vessel ready at Leith before noon," the Black Knight agreed. "We should be at Stirling in three hours or so, once we sail."

"You will prepare James. Warn him not to talk of it. A secret! He likes secrets. You will do this, my friend? With Agnes's help."

Alec nodded. "As Your Grace wishes. I, I will have to come with you, with the king, to Stirling?"

"You are the king's attendant, yes. Your place is with him."

He bowed, and with Agnes, went to rejoin the princesses.

"This is a wonder!" he said, when they were out of the room. "It is Sir James's notion? Your father . . . ?"

"He will much condemn me, yes. But I cannot refuse the queen. And it is best for young James – that I am sure. Keeping the boy from his mother, at seven years, is not right."

"But it was the mother who left *him*! At the castle."

"She knows her own mind. And has her daughters to think of also. Are you against it all, Alec?"

"No-o-o. The boy is not happy, shut up there, alone. A captive, or next to it. He should be with his family, yes. It is just that I mislike seeming to betray Sir William."

"How think you that *I* feel – my own father! But I see him as in the wrong in this. Holding the king so close."

"He will, I think, see it all as of Livingston's contriving."

"It is not. Sir James Stewart does not know Livingston. I heard him tell the queen that he had never met him. All this is of his proposing."

"At least we will be together again!" Alec said.

"And you conceive that as of importance?"

"I do, yes. Do you doubt it?" And he squeezed her arm.

"So! I will *need* a friend after this, I think!"

He was about to say that he aspired to more than just friendship, but recognised that this was probably not the time to say it.

When Alec left the abbey in due course, it was with the arrangement that he would see the girl, with a horse and cart, next forenoon, up at the castle gatehouse. He would be on the watch, and have James ready.

Later, at supper with the boy, alone, he told him of the project – and had to press him down when he would have jumped up from the table in his excitement, having to keep repeating the word secret, secret. They could not have had more enthusiastic co-operation, at any rate. Gulping down the rest of his meal in haste, nothing would do but that they should go through to his mother's former bedchamber to inspect that wardrobe-chest, Alec a little anxious lest servitors should see them, and wonder. But with the queen and princesses gone, this wing of the establishment was all but deserted, and they went unobserved.

The vital piece of furniture was very evident in the bedroom, a massive dark bog-oak chest, almost five feet in length by half that in width and depth, used for storing clothing, indeed having dried lavender perfume

47

in amongst the dresses, skirts, petticoats and the like when they opened the lid. James had much of these out on the floor right away, then climbed in and lay down, knees to chin, although there was ample room for him. He bade Alec lower the heavy lid, whereupon there were gurgles of laughter from within. Other chests and hanging-presses were about the large room, but this was clearly the one meant.

Getting the boy out, Alec said that they would need a rope or cord to tie round the chest in due course, lest the lid got lifted and the contents seen. James, grubbing about in a garderobe, produced the girdle of a bathrobe, which would serve. They went back to their own quarters, the would-be escapee all but dancing.

The King of Scots was difficult in getting to sleep that night, to a lesser extent his gentleman-in-waiting also.

Alec was down at the tourney-ground with his young charge, at the archery, fairly early next morning, considering this the best means of keeping the boy in hand until Agnes should arrive, afraid that his excitement would somehow communicate itself to servants and guards. He had not seen Sir William since his return from Holyrood, nor wished to.

They had some time to wait, and Alec was wondering whether something had gone amiss with their plans, when at length a heavily plodding horse with its cart made its appearance from the Lawnmarket, a burly carter driving and Agnes sedately walking behind. James, dropping bow and arrows, ran to meet them. Alec, not knowing whether to feel relieved or the reverse, still foresaw that so much could yet go wrong with this venture.

The young woman however appeared calm and unruffled. She explained that there had been some delay, as the carter had been delivering herrings from Newhaven to the Fishmarket stalls; certainly there was a strong smell of fish about the vehicle.

Agnes was, of course, well known to the gatehouse

guards as the keeper's daughter, and had no difficulty in gaining access for herself and conveyance. She went off ahead for her father's quarters, and John and the monarch led the carter and cart up the rocky slope to the entrance to the royal wing.

There was further delay, and again Alec grew anxious. Would Sir William be suspicious and come to investigate? Or merely forbid the removal of chest and clothing? James, impatient by nature, was in a state of agitation, waiting at the door.

When at length the girl appeared again, Alec drew a quick breath when he saw that she was not alone. Then sighed with relief when he recognised that her father was not one of the four men with her. When she came up, she announced that these were members of the guard who would help to carry the heavy chest down to the cart. She raised significant eyebrows at him as she said this, and addressing the carter, suggested that he should turn his dray round for its downward progress. Taking the hint, Alec grasped James's arm and hastened him inside and upstairs before Agnes and the guards could follow.

So it was straight into the box with the boy, some of his extra clothing already in before him. Alec hurriedly tied the robe-girdle round, to keep the lid from being opened. He was uttering warnings to his liege-lord not to stir nor make any sounds until safely in the cart when the young woman and the four men came up into the bedchamber.

Alec nodded to her, and she pointed at the chest, which the men considered assessingly and went to test the weight. Apparently satisfied that they could carry it, two in front and two behind, they bent to hoist it up, and adjusting their positions, indicated readiness to move.

Agnes, preceding them, warned that descending the winding turnpike stair would demand care. It certainly did, the bearers all having to to go one step at a time, and cautiously, the forward ones inevitably bearing the greater weight. Alec wondered whether he could assist, but decided that this would be impracticable in that narrow twisting space.

Slowly they got that awkward burden round and down, and then out through the door, Agnes maintaining her air of cool unconcern. There followed the business of getting the chest up on to the floor of the cart, but at least Alec and the carter could help in this, and the transfer was accomplished. Agnes thanked the four bearers, the carter climbed to his seat, slapped the old horse's rump, and moved off down the bumpy slope, Alec and the young woman walking seemingly casually behind, however much they wondered how the royal passenger fared inside.

Out beneath the gatehouse arch cart and walkers passed, to the interested gaze of the guards there, and on down over the tourney-ground towards the cobbles of the Lawnmarket.

It had all been almost absurdly easy and straightforward, save for the getting down that twisting stair.

Sighing with relief, Alec asked how Agnes had got on with her father.

"There was no difficulty," she told him. "Save that I felt ashamed of my deceiving him. He suspected nothing, and agreed that the queen should have her clothing, riding-boots and the like. How he will consider me when he finds James gone, I do not like to think!"

Her companion was in no position to reassure her on that, his own part in it on his mind. He was a little concerned that the king might not be getting sufficient air in that chest, but had tied the cord not so tightly that the lid could not be raised a little way, if necessary.

They walked on down to the abbey.

There all was ready for them, the horses saddled and waiting, Stewart with them, luggage packed. The Black Knight went indoors to collect the queen, princesses and the Lady Catherine Douglas, or Barlass as she was now being admiringly nicknamed, while Alec climbed into the cart and untied the girdle to let the gleeful escaper out, he seemingly none the worse for his incarceration. He jumped down and danced a jig there beside the cart, Agnes shaking her head over him.

Quickly the royal family emerged, and there was a joyful reunion, the children vociferous. But Stewart was anxious to see them on their way, lest any hitch should occur, any pursuit develop from the castle – not that this seemed likely.

The abbot came to see them off, and produced two mounted monks to escort them, and to bring back all the mounts, including two laden pack-horses, from Leith haven.

So it was off with them, a party of fourteen riders, on the two-mile road to salt water. Stewart had already been down to the harbour on the firth that morning, ensuring that all was ready and in order. So the boat, a fishing vessel, was prepared for them and the crew waiting. They boarded over the gangplank, James skipping, to his mother's alarm, the baggage was transferred; and they said goodbye to the monks. To cries of mutual satisfaction the craft was pushed off, the sweeps put out and the sail half hoisted.

With only the firth's waters between them and Stirling now, monarch, family and attendants turned their faces westwards thankfully. Edinburgh Castle on its rock was still visible but no longer threatening.

5

Sir Alexander Livingston, trustworthy or otherwise, needless to say received the royal party with much satisfaction and effusive enthusiasm, a very different man from Crichton, hearty instead of stern, voluble instead of gruff, seemingly eager to please, at least towards this company. Yet Alec did not take to him, for one, perhaps unreasonably; his own father had not trusted him, he reminded himself.

Few at Stirling thereafter had any doubts that Sir William Crichton would not tamely accept this change in circumstances, Livingston himself in especial. He soon got word that his enemy had approached the Earl of Douglas for support, and although the rumour was that that most powerful individual, the lieutenant-general of the realm, had not committed himself, precautions had to be taken. Livingston, in the king's name, sent a messenger to Bishop Cameron of Glasgow declaring that his resignation of the chancellorship at the Edinburgh parliament, and Crichton's succession thereto, was now deemed to be irregular, and that he, the bishop, was still in fact Chancellor, Crichton disgraced and reduced. A new parliament was necessary to establish the king's rule and governance, and the bishop must accept the authority to call it, and swiftly.

What Cameron thought of this was not known. But he evidently was a realist, and recognised actualities when he saw them. At any rate, he sent word back that he was prepared to accept the decision, since it came in the king's name, and the call to parliament could go out as from himself. Livingston did not delay, and again ignoring the forty days' notice, sent out the summons, to carefully selected addresses, for an assembly at Stirling in ten days' time, two of the especial recipients being the Earl of Douglas and the Lord of Dalkeith, whom he hoped to wean to his cause in the present situation, stressing Sir James Stewart of Lorne's links with the house of Douglas.

Alec wondered at the ethics and legitimacy of all this, but was not in any position to affect matters; and the queen and Stewart appeared to approve. One of the summons went out to his father at Glamis.

It was in fact a very questionable convention which met in Stirling Castle in due course, more notable for who was *not* present than for who was; and amongst the absentees were the Douglases, likewise Sir William Crichton and the Lord Borthwick. Alec had word with his father before the assembly, and found Sir Patrick highly doubtful about the entire proceedings, his mistrust of Livingston nowise diminished. But he had felt that he had to attend, to see what transpired and to choose his course accordingly.

Alec and Agnes, with the queen's party, watched all from a gallery at the rear. James had been given his instructions as to behaviour.

Bishop Cameron, anything but confident and assured, presided. The main business, as arranged by Livingston, was to achieve the downfall of Crichton and the restoration of the fortress of Edinburgh to royal control. To effect this, a new council was appointed, none of the Crichton faction upon it, although the Douglases were in theory co-opted. This was necessary if a large armed force was to be raised to assail the capital and citadel, the Earl of Douglas being lieutenant-general of the nation's armed might; but a deputy was appointed, in case of non-co-operation, in the person of Sir Alan Stewart of Darnley, who had held the lofty position of Constable of the Scots Corps in France, a kinsman of Sir James. The assembling of the desired army was ordered, the lords and chiefs present, or some of them, indicating their contributions in men.

Alec noted that his father did not; in fact he made no contribution of any sort to the deliberations. It looked as though Scotland was divided into three factions: those pro-Livingston, those pro-Crichton, and those who held aloof from both. Nevertheless it was decided that wherever rebels and offenders against the throne had taken refuge in their castles or fortalices, it was the duty of the lieutenant-general to raise the loyal lieges to besiege such holds and to arrest the miscreants – pointing a fairly obvious finger at Crichton.

The notably brief session broke up, with the decision that parliament should in future meet twice every year.

It did not take long for Livingston to put into action the will of that so-called parliament, that very same afternoon indeed, having Stewart of Darnley, as the lieutenant's deputy, immediately summon all available forces to meet at Stirling in three days' time, to march on Edinburgh.

Sir Patrick Lyon was much disturbed over this, and told his son that it was tantamount to a declaration of civil war. It would result in dire bloodshed, would gravely offend the Douglas power thus being superseded, and worse, present opportunity for an invasion by the English, ever on the lookout for such, to bring Scotland under subjection, that age-old endeavour. No Glamis contingent would contribute to this army's strength, nor any other where he had influence.

That evening, when King James was abed, and the young princesses likewise, Alec sought out Agnes, and proposed a walk, to discuss with her the day's doings. In the half-dark they went up to the high north-eastern summit of the castle rock, where the steep grassy slope dropped to the peculiar terrace of narrow meadowland named Ballengeich, pasture for the fortress's half-dozen milk-cows, an extraordinary feature, with a sheer drop below to the plain of Forth, these upper slopes the site for the sledging sport of hurlyhackit so much appreciated by James, a favourite spot in that rock-bound citadel – and the better this mild evening for the king being safely asleep.

Halfway down to that Ballengeich terrace, the couple found a stone outcrop to sit on, and to gaze out towards the unseen Highland Line which closed off the north.

"How think the queen and Sir James Stewart over this of the parliament?" Alec asked. "This of marching on Edinburgh, and, and . . ." He refrained from adding on her father. "My father is much against it."

"They are not happy," she told him. "Any more than I am. The queen, in that Livingston intends to take James, the king, with him, with this army. To give the royal authority. She says that it is not right, not suitable, for a seven-year-old. And the Black Knight is against this of probable offence to the Earl of Douglas, appointing a deputy and using him to muster some of the nation's armed men. He says that it will in fact rouse the Douglases to fury, the most powerful line in the land. That there will be grievous trouble. Folly. He says that there is no need for this, with the king safe here. My father can be left in Edinburgh Castle. *He* will not come marching against Stirling."

"No. Livingston is consumed with hatred for Sir William. It is that which drives him on, my father thinks, rather than concern for James and the realm. The queen, he believes, is foolish to trust him."

"She always has done. Her husband did."

"If the king is taken on this armed venture, then I will have to go also, I think. As his close attendant."

"Alec, will you? I had not thought of that." She turned, and grasped his arm. "Need you, indeed? There could be much danger in it all. War. Fighting."

"Not for the king himself, surely. And therefore for myself. I would hold near James. I do not want to go, but I see little danger in it, for me." Nevertheless, her obvious concern for him was a useful by-product of these fears, and he took the opportunity to put his arm round her, on that stone, and held her close.

"I could plead with the queen not to let her son go," she said.

"Do that, yes. Would she heed you?"

"Perhaps not. But if I spoke through the Lady Catherine? She is good. We get on well. Or, better still, through Sir James Stewart. He might convince her. The queen has become very fond of the Black Knight, I think. I should not wonder if they became . . . closer! She needs a man to cherish her."

"Do not all fair women!" That was another opportunity too good to miss. He leaned over, to kiss her, first on her hair, then her brow, and when she did not turn away, on her lips. Not finding himself rejected he repeated the salutation, and this time he distinctly felt her lips stir beneath his own and even open a little.

"My dear!" he got out. "I, I have been longing for this! Hoping. For long . . ."

A gurgle of small laughter issued from between those lips. "Long, Alec? Then . . . you have taken your time!"

"You say that! Agnes, you say it?" He all but shook her. "You mean that . . . ?"

"Think you that only men can feel an affection on occasion, stupid?"

"I . . . I . . . could not be sure. I could only hope and pray that, that . . ." He gave up such foolish waste of breath and time, and concentrated on action rather than halting words. Both arms round her now, he cupped her breasts, and if she would have voiced any protest at this advance in intimacy, he ensured that she did not say it, lips clamped firmly on hers.

Agnes eased herself more comfortably within his arms.

So they sat there in the gathering darkness. They did not notice the hardness of their seat, the kingdom's problems and woes for the moment forgotten – and those moments multiplied, themselves unheeding, time standing still.

When eventually they stirred, in more than their embracings, it was to rise and hand-in-hand climb the slopes to make for the royal quarters. They did not speak, thought sufficient, Alec assured that the world had changed for him. Whatever happened hereafter, and their future was uncertain to say the least, he had gained something which he would never lose, a woman's love and trust.

The knowledge and the joy of it, presently, did not prevent him from knowing also a grievous sense of frustration when he had to say goodnight to his companion at her bedroom-door, however prolonged the leave-taking.

6

Three days later the host assembled down on the King's Knot tourney-ground to the south-west of the castle rock, a large horsed company of some four thousand. Undoubtedly Sir Alexander Livingston had hoped for more, but at least he had the king's presence, having persuaded Queen Joanna to let him go, on the promise that the boy would be kept well out of harm's way, and on the understanding that the royal presence might well ensure that Crichton would surrender Edinburgh Castle at the king's command, without fighting and bloodshed. It also should help to keep the Douglases from interfering, whatever the Black Knight thought.

In fact, to ride at the head of a large armed force was very much to young James's taste, and he would have been very upset if his mother had not allowed him to go. She did order Alec Lyon to go with him, and to see that the boy got into no danger.

The royal family, with Agnes and Stewart, came down to the Knot to see them off, Alec getting more instructions from Agnes as to safety. In front of all the others there could be no affectionate farewells, looks and murmurings having to serve. None could guess just when the company would be back.

In front of the host of Grahams, Erskines, Buchanans, Oliphants and the rest, banners flying, plumes tossing, steel glinting, they made a gallant sight for James to lead, his cries of delight resounding. In theory Sir Alan Stewart of Darnley was in command, but all knew that Livingston was in charge.

The Tor Wood, which they had to traverse, much

intrigued the king, Alec having to restrain him from dashing off through the glades and shaws, hoping to see deer or even wild boars. For his age, he was a good horseman.

At Falkirk they were into Livingston territory. Sir Alexander was laird of Calendar and that property lay just east of the town. Here they picked up reinforcements from the Haining of Almond, from Slamannan and from Livingston itself, and more at Linlithgow, the western Lothian shire very much under that family's influence.

It was late in the day when they approached Edinburgh, and it was decided to halt and camp in the Corstorphine area, the walled city being no place for an army at night. But Holyrood Abbey lying outside the walls to the east, the leadership group, with the king, rode on thither, to partake of its comforts. It was strange for Alec to be back in the abbot's house in very different company from heretofore.

In the morning they rejoined the host and entered the capital. No doubt by then Sir William Crichton was well aware of their presence.

There was no way that the bulk of the host could get anywhere near the castle on its rock-top, as Livingston well knew; so he deployed most of the men on the fairly level ground beyond the Nor' Loch at one side and in the Grassmarket area on the other, both entirely visible from the fortress, where Crichton could see the size of the force come against him. Then, with the king, Stewart of Darnley and most of the leaders, with a couple of hundred supporters, he rode up to the open tournament-ground, banners flying. As expected, the gatehouse was closed up, the portcullis lowered and the drawbridge raised.

Under a different sort of banner, a white flag, Livingston, with James and Stewart and a few others, went forward, Alec tagging on behind. Before the gatehouse they reined up. It was Stewart who raised voice.

"In the name of the King's Grace, here present, I, lieutenant-general-depute of this realm, require the attendance of Sir William Crichton, keeper of this royal citadel," he shouted.

Promptly came a reply from the parapet, their arrival obviously awaited "You have it, sirrah, although I know not your authority. I am Crichton. What would you with me?"

"I am Sir Alan Stewart of Darnley. We would have you to deliver up this castle to the King's Grace, forthwith."

"*You* would? I jalouse that you mean that Sir Alexander Livingston would! Let him speak for himself."

"Whoever speaks, it is for the king here. His is this castle."

"Has Livingston lost his tongue, as well as his wits! Sitting there at your side."

"The King's Grace is also sitting at his side, Crichton." That was Livingston. "You, as his keeper here, are required to yield up this hold."

"Required by whom? By you, I swear! With that child in your power. I yield nothing."

"You disobey the royal command? That is treason!"

"I do not accept that it is a royal command. Coming from you, or this new lickspittle of yours! In proof of which I give you all my own command. Be off! If you do not depart from this place without delay, I will send you on your way with cannon-balls!"

"You would not dare, Crichton! With the king here before you."

"Would I not? I see no king, only some captive child, who may be anyone's brat whom you have taken. Be off! I have my cannon loaded and primed."

"You shall suffer for this!" Livingston shouted, and reined his mount round, as did the others, Alec reaching over to tug at James's bridle.

They had not gone thirty yards back towards the waiting supporters when the horses all reared and sidled, and men and boy clapped hands to ears, as cannon-fire thundered out behind them amidst clouds of smoke. Whether in fact an iron ball crashed out with it, or it was only exploding powder, they did not know; but the message was clear enough. Controlling their steeds, they spurred for the safety of the town buildings, the waiting party already turning to do the same.

After the first shock of the noise, young James was in a fever of excitement, yelling his stimulation, almost ecstasy. Real war, battle! He waved his arms at Alec.

In the Lawnmarket, there being no more gunfire, Livingston drew rein to confer with his leaders, not exactly shaken but angered. Clearly Crichton was not going to yield, and this use of cannon changed the picture. They had no artillery to counter him; and the walls of that fortress were thick. Siege was their only resort, although they could send to Stirling for some cannon of their own. But that would take time, days, to get the heavy, slow-moving, oxen-drawn pieces over the thirty-five miles; and it was doubtful whether the Stirling bombards would be as powerful as were these Edinburgh ones. Besieged, how long would Crichton be able to hold out? There were wells up there on the rock, an essential for any fortified site. It would be food, starvation, which would bring about surrender. How much provision would be stored there? With quite a large garrison, as Alec reported, much essential provender would be needed. Day and night watch would have to be kept, that none was smuggled in. Always an armed presence must be maintained and evident. Their thousands of men were of little use in this situation.

There was always the danger, also, that Crichton's friends, Borthwick, Maitland, Seton and some of the Border chiefs, might come to his aid. And Douglas, that ever-present question mark? Not that the Douglases were in any way allies of Crichton; but their earl might well resent this armed usurpation of his over-all generalship, and act to quell it. So, for how long could a siege go on?

It was decided to station their host in three encampments, to east, south and west of the city: there at the foot of Arthur's Seat, up on the Burgh Muir, and back towards the Corstorphine area, to guard against any hostile forces' approach. And to send to Stirling for cannon, which could at least make some challenge against Crichton's artillery. Meanwhile, the leadership would make use of the ecclesiastical comfort of Holyrood.

James Stewart said that it was all very feeble, not his idea of campaigning at all.

They settled in at the abbot's house.

The days passed with little activity. No hostile forces came to aid Crichton; nor did any supplies reach him to feed the garrison. The Stirling bombards were slow in arriving, and when they did come, were insufficiently supplied with the equally heavy and slow-of-delivery cannon-balls. A gesture was made, to James's approval, of firing two pieces from the Lawnmarket-head at the castle walls and gatehouse; but although the bangs and clouds of smoke were highly satisfactory to the monarch, the range was on the long side for these moderate-calibre weapons, and the spurts of dust and flying chips off the stonewalling resultant was disappointing – especially when return balls came crashing back at them and a hasty retreat was called for.

So the king had to content himself with riding and hawking around Arthur's Seat, and more than once climbing, with Alec, to the top of the great hill, to admire the vast prospects of land and water spread out all around, and the city crouching below to the west, with even the impregnable castle dwarfed.

Thus ten days passed, with no sign of surrender from the fortress, and the encamped troops, and their leaders also, becoming restless and out of hand. Siegery was very dull work, it seemed, and not only for seven-year-olds.

With no evident progress being made, whatever the state of the castle's larders, it was Sir Alan Stewart's suggestion that perhaps an approach should be made to the Earl of Douglas. He was probably offended over this military activity without his authority, but might be persuaded to join forces with them, and consequently take over a greater say in the affairs of the realm, if it was made in the king's name, possibly take over the chancellorship. At the various Douglas castles there was known to be cannon, and his adherence to their cause could well bring about Crichton's downfall. At first Livingston was very doubtful about this, but as the days went by without progress, he came to think better of it. *He* would not go cap in hand to the earl himself, being scarcely on friendly terms with him; but Stewart could go as lieutenant-depute, and take young James with him, to offer the royal authority.

Douglas was thought presently to be at his kinsman's house of Dalkeith none so far off. So next morning Stewart took the boy, Alec in attendance, with quite a large escort, for appearances as well as safety, southwards for Dalkeith. But when they reached Dalkeith Castle it was to learn that the earl had gone to one of his lesser establishments, Restalrig, between Edinburgh and Leith, Sir James Douglas with him, it seemed. So it was on northwards, thither, another six miles.

They found the two Douglases at a small fortalice above a little loch, a miniature Edinburgh citadel on its modest rock-top. And the earl was unwell. He was a man of middle years, fine-looking but now features drawn. In his bed, had it not been for the young king's presence, his kinsman, a brooding man of similar age, probably would not have allowed the callers to see his chief, his attitude to Sir Alan scornful, Alec ignored.

The earl, sitting up, inclined his greying head towards the monarch. "Your Grace, you honour this poor house," he said. "I regret that I must greet you thus. I suffer some fever. But I wonder what brings you here, Sire?" And he looked at Stewart. "Are you he who calls himself my deputy?"

"I am, my lord, appointed so by parliament."

"You call that a parliament? An assembly of pretenders, I would say!" Although his voice was not strong, his words were sufficiently so. "Friends of the man Livingston, I

63

judge. When I require a deputy, I shall appoint him myself."

"His Grace here was present, my lord. The queen mother also. So the parliament was lawful. And its appointments likewise."

"The king, in Livingston's keeping, would be taken to it, as to any other gathering where his royal presence would be useful! And Joanna Beaufort has no authority now." He sank back on his pillow. "What is the purpose of this visit by His Grace?"

"With Sir Alexander Livingston and other lords and knights, who have called upon Sir William Crichton, keeper of Edinburgh Castle, to yield that royal fortress to the King's Grace, I have acted. Crichton has refused to so yield, and has used cannon to defy the royal orders."

"Think you that I do not know that, man! I may be sick, but I am not lacking in knowledge and my wits! You need not have come, and brought His Grace, to tell me that."

"No, my lord earl. We have come to seek your guidance. And to urge that you, the lieutenant-general, join us in the regaining of the royal citadel to the king's keeping. Or, since your lordship is presently unwell, your Douglas power."

"Why should I, sir? What advantage to have Livingston keeping Edinburgh Castle as well as Stirling?" And the earl looked at Sir James of Dalkeith, who had been listening to all this, grim of face.

"Two rogues!" that man declared. "One no better than the other."

"The parliament ordered it, my lords."

A wave of the hand dismissed that parliament. "The man Crichton has also sent word to me," the earl went on, his voice failing. "Seeking my aid against you, sirrah. Or against your master, Livingston. I ignored his pleas, as I shall ignore yours. A plague on both your houses, I say!" As he got that out, the earl was convulsed by a fit of coughing, before sinking back, eyes closed.

Young James, who during this exchange had been gazing

round the room, bored, at this fit of coughing and the invalid lying back, eyes shut, was suddenly interested. "Is he going to die?" he asked.

Alec cleared his throat. "His lordship is weary, Sire," he said. "He has been less than well. We . . . intrude."

"Whoever you are, you speak truth!" Dalkeith declared. "I suggest that you leave his lordship. And now."

"Yes," James agreed, turning away.

The earl had opened his eyes again. "Who is this young man?" he asked weakly.

"I am Alexander Lyon, son to the Thane of Glamis, my lord."

"Ah! How come you into this company? I know Sir Patrick, your father. A good man."

"I but attend on His Grace."

"But not sufficiently well to keep him out of ill company!" That was Dalkeith.

"My lords, you misjudge, I say," Stewart put in. "We but seek the weal of the king's realm."

"Weal, you say! These two, Livingston and Crichton, scoundrels both, seek only their own weal, not the realm's. Even though they do not agree. I would that . . . they should destroy . . . each other! For the *king's* weal!" That said, with an effort, the Earl of Douglas closed his eyes again.

Dalkeith tapped Alec's shoulder. "Come," he ordered. "Leave him now."

"I think that he *is* going to die!" James said, interestedly.

Alec took the royal arm, and steered him to follow the other Douglas out of the bedchamber, Sir Alan nowise reluctant to go also.

Offered no hospitality by Dalkeith, they rode off back to Edinburgh, the boy doing most of the talking, much concerned over the details of dying.

Livingston was concerned over Stewart's account of the Douglas visit, not so much that he was over-disappointed about the non-co-operation, as to which he had never been so hopeful as was Stewart, but on account of the proclaimed Douglas hostility towards himself, and the dangers this implied. If they translated that hostility into action, then there would be cause for anxiety indeed. The Douglases could field ten thousand and more without any difficulty. He was interested, too, in that Crichton had also approached the earl, and likewise had been rebuffed. This gave him occasion for much thought.

That thought, after a few more days of unavailing siegery – and with the possibility of swift Douglas action tending to haunt him – culminated in action, and very surprising action at that. Astonished, his supporters heard his decision. It was to be another white-flag occasion.

Surprised or not, none actually protested, even Sir Alan Stewart. All were wearying of the situation, and the Douglas shadow lay over all.

On the morning of 1st May the same party as before rode up, under a banner of truce, to the castle gatehouse, and word was requested with Sir William Crichton. This time they had to wait for a response.

When at length Crichton's voice sounded from the parapet, it was as stern as ever, and certainly gave no hint of possible surrender.

"What have you to say now, Livingston, that may be worth my coming to hear?" he demanded.

"Quite a deal, Sir William," he was answered. "I suggest a conference between us. For, I think, our mutual benefit."

"Mutual? You, man! I judge where you are concerned, benefits are like to be less than mutual!"

"I say that you misjudge. In especial today, when we both are threatened by Douglas."

There was silence then, for long moments.

"You approached Douglas," Livingston went on. "And were rejected. That one is too powerful for us, either of us. I say that we would be foolish not to confer."

"Confer on what, sir?"

"On our own interests. And on His Grace's weal. And the realm's."

Another silence. Then, "This is no device? No trickery to win you my person?"

"No, Sir William. Rest assured. Confer here, if so you will. At your own gatehouse. Each with no large company."

"So-o-o! I will have to consider this. Come you back, Sir Alexander."

"When? Soon, I say. Douglas could strike."

"This day. Later. After noon."

"Very well. I will be back. Consider well." Waving his party round, Livingston's people, or more properly the king's, trotted back for Holyrood. No cannon-fire followed them this time.

In the afternoon James and Alec were not asked to accompany Livingston, Stewart and the small group which rode back to the castle, the boy thankful, but Alec intrigued to know the outcome. They went hawking around Arthur's Seat instead, after the wildfowl which haunted the various lochs.

When they got back to the abbot's house, Alec at least was astonished to find Sir William Crichton there, and clearly no sort of captive. Never an affable man, he was not evidently ill at ease nor showing hostility to those around him, although he did give Alec a less than friendly glance before bowing to the king.

From Stewart, Alec learned the results of their conference. An accord had been reached between the two enemies, more than just a truce in their conflict. They were going to share power, control of the sovereign and his realm, and unite against the Douglas threat. Livingston would continue to hold the king at Stirling but Crichton would retain his keepership of Edinburgh, and become chief minister and Chancellor, Bishop Cameron being got rid of, co-operation the policy. He, Stewart, would remain lieutenant-depute, nominally in command of the joint supporting forces. There was, in fact, to be a celebratory supper up at the castle that evening, the king to be present, as it were to seal the compact. And on the morrow, it would be a return to Stirling.

Alec was almost past being surprised, extraordinary as was this development. But it was good news, of course, excellent news – although how long this amity would survive was another question. Now, so much depended on the Douglases. Perhaps, in the circumstances, it was as well that the earl was ill.

That evening, at the castle, all went well, however warily lesser men on either side eyed each other. Crichton and Livingston sat on either side of the king, and behaved amicably enough without being actively friendly, James showing no interest in either of them, and occasionally waving to Alec, placed far down the table. It was not a particularly hearty nor plenteous meal, the castle's stores no doubt all but empty, but banqueting was not the object of the exercise.

James Stewart was late in getting to his bed that night, down at Holyrood. And in the morning, thankfully, it was back to Stirling, leaving Crichton to hold his fort. Alec wondered whether this new situation, as regards her father, would help to further his relationship with Agnes. It seemed grievously long since he had seen her.

The satisfaction at Stirling Castle, not only that of Alec Lyon and Agnes Crichton and those close to the queen and the royal family, was, sadly, of short duration, even though the news of the death of the Earl of Douglas a week or two later enhanced the prospects of peace, for he left only two young sons, the elder but seventeen years; and in these circumstances the Douglas power was unlikely to flex its muscles. Troubles quickly developed elsewhere, however, not so much between the two principal actors on the scene as between their respective adherents. It was caused, in the main, by the handing out of offices and appointments to the said supporters, and jealousy rearing its head almost inevitably, Crichton's friends tending to feel that they came off second-best. This animosity was exemplified all too grievously by the waylaying and slaying of Sir Alan Stewart of Darnley, who was laying claim to the earldom of Lennox through his mother, killed near Falkirk by Sir Thomas Boyd of Kilmarnock, a Crichton follower. This was swiftly avenged by the Lennox Stewarts, his brother, Sir Alexander "Bucktooth" and his sons ambushing Boyd and murdering him, feud between the two lines following.

Sir Robert Erskine, claiming the earldom of Mar, which had fallen to the crown, surprised and took over the royal castle of Dumbarton, and could not be dislodged from that difficult fortress on the Clyde, this to bring pressure to bear to aid his claim. Another earldom was claimed, that of Ross, this by none other than that great Highland chief, Alexander, Lord of the Isles, who saw opportunity in this duality of power, and threatened Crichton with setting all the Highlands in turmoil if it was not granted. Innumerable other demands by lesser magnates added to the disarray. Scotland was used to upheavals by unruly lords, but seldom indeed had there been such chaos as this. Double rule clearly was proving unworkable.

Agnes told Alec that the queen was greatly concerned, and had come to the conclusion that she must try to do something about it. She had little or no actual power in the land, to be sure, but as the monarch's mother felt a responsibility. She was greatly influenced by the Black Knight these days, and he persuaded her that the answer to the situation lay with the house of Douglas, so closely linked to the royal family, yet lying quiescent since the death of its earl. He advocated an approach to the Lord of Dalkeith, to have him urge the new seventeen-year-old earl to act, to muster the full strength of the line, assume the vacant lieutenant-generalship and impose order on the realm. He, James Stewart, could go to see Dalkeith, with the queen mother's blessing.

Alec recognised the need for some such move, but wondered whether a seventeen-year-old could assume such status, and be able to wield the power wisely. Would not a parliament have to grant him the lieutenant-generalship in the first place? And how would such an inevitably divided parliament act?

His doubts were scarcely lessened by the news Agnes brought him the very next evening. The queen and the Black Knight had gone riding that day, attended by herself and the latter's brother, Sir William Stewart, supposedly hawking. But in fact they had gone to nearby Cambuskenneth Abbey, and there had been secretly wed by the abbot. How much this was a demonstration of affection, if not love, and how much to give Sir James authority, as now the king's stepfather, was a matter for conjecture.

Whichever it was, the word of it was not long in reaching the ears of Sir Alexander Livingston; no doubt he had his spies amongst the royal household. He acted drastically and without delay. Armed guards arrested both Stewart brothers, and they were cast into the fearsome pit of Stirling Castle, a hole carved out of the solid rock, with no access save by a trapdoor in its ceiling. And the Queen and Lady Catherine Douglas were locked into two secure rooms outwith the palace block, strictly guarded and no leaving permitted nor any visitors.

Appalled, Alec, with the king, and Agnes with the princesses, were faced with an unheard-of situation. Livingston appeared to have gone power-mad.

When the princesses called at their mother's new quarters to see her, they were refused permission. Alec took young James to make a like attempt, but even though the boy was instructed to say that it was a royal command and admission could not be refused, the guards declared that they had to take their orders from the castle's governor, and allowed no access.

Alec and Agnes cudgelled their wits as to what they could do. Would the young woman's father, Crichton, be able to prevail on Livingston? Or be willing to do so? Alec deemed not, Agnes herself doubtful. But they felt that they had to try to do something. In the end they decided that, as the Black Knight had advised, the Douglas power was the only answer likely to be effective. Alec should go to Dalkeith Castle and seek Douglas help, in place of the queen's new husband.

How was this to be effected? Livingston might well be keeping a keen eye on him, in these circumstances. But, if he and the king, with Agnes and the six princesses, all were to go riding? They would not be allowed to do so without an armed escort of course; but in the Tor Wood it might be possible for Alec to dash off into some thickets and escape, mounted on his better horse than the guards' mounts. And then ride on for Lothian and Dalkeith? It was agreed to attempt this the next day.

The king's security, as ever, being vital, on obtaining permission for the ride to the Tor Wood, Alec and Agnes found themselves saddled with no fewer than a score of guards, no doubt with their strict instructions about ever letting the young monarch out of their sight. The boy did not normally ride abroad with his sisters, being scornful of their abilities in the saddle; but on this occasion, being let into the secret and much elated thereby, he promised to cooperate, and was given his instructions. Agnes did not confide so fully in the girls, however, in case they chattered.

It was not very far to the first outliers of the great wood, across the higher ground above the links of Forth, where the great battle of Bannockburn had been fought, the party of nearly thirty trotting much more sedately than was usual in the boy's ride-outs, Alec thankful to note the all but holiday mood of the troopers.

Once into the wood itself, Alec had to restrain James, who would have started to play his part almost at once, excitement mounting. Presently he was allowed to dash off down lanes and glades amongst the trees, pointing and shouting, and the guards, or some of them, hurriedly spurring after him, the excuse being that he was spotting deer or other creatures lurking in the bushes. Always he allowed himself to be conducted back to the main party after these preliminary forays. Alec went with him on the second, but thereafter remained with Agnes and the princesses.

That man thought that he knew the Tor Wood well enough by this time to select a likely spot for his endeavour. Perhaps a couple of miles in, he remembered a large and dense thicket area of scrub, elder, thorn and birch, which he hoped would serve. Sure enough, it was as he recollected it. And just before they all reached it, he gave the eager James his signal.

Almost too promptly the boy yelled, gesticulated and spurred off down a shaw on the left, fully half of the escort resignedly riding after him. Then Agnes played her part, suddenly calling to the younger girls and reining off, again to the left, in amongst the trees. Somewhat doubtfully the princesses pulled round to follow, some more of the escort after them. Alec rode on easily, regardless, now with only five of the guard behind him.

Keenly he was keeping that thicket on the right under observation. When, after a couple of hundred yards or so, he saw a gap, he cried out as though he too had spotted some animal, and kicked his mount into a canter. In to the narrow gap he drove.

He had anticipated at least some of the troopers to come after him, but presumably they suspected nothing by this time, thought that narrow entry into the bushes uninviting and probably unprofitable anyway, or were just weary of all this folly of chasing shadows. None of them followed on – at least not by the time that Alec was well out of their sight amongst the clutching and enclosing foliage. Crashing through it, his horse clearly not enjoying the process, he came to a more open space, and drew rein, to pat his beast's neck and listen. No noise of pursuit sounded behind him.

Scarcely crediting that his escape had been so easy, he headed on westwards through deep woodland, until he felt that he could safely turn to face the midday sun and head due southwards.

He wondered what was going on now far behind him.

After that it was all just straightforward riding – or at least as straightforward as the dense forest would allow. So long as he rode into the sun he could not go far wrong; and for many a mile he saw no human being, but plenty of roe-deer and a woodland stag or two, until he came on a group of wood-cutters, who told him, a seemingly lost horseman, that their village of Auchenbowie was just a short distance ahead. Alec trotted on. He was only some seven miles north of Falkirk.

By that town and Linlithgow he journeyed on to Edinburgh. Avoiding the city, to the south, by early evening he approached Dalkeith. The castle was north of the town, in a strong site on the bank of the River North Esk.

When Alec announced to the guards that he came to see their lord, in the name of Stewart of Lorne, he had no difficulty in gaining access, and was ushered into the presence of Sir James Douglas, and his youngest son at their evening meal, at which he was invited to join them. Gratefully he sat, and explained the circumstances and the reason for his mission.

His hearers were greatly disturbed, Elizabeth Stewart outraged, that Joanna Beaufort should be imprisoned, and her husband much concerned for his friend the Black Knight, although surprised to hear of his marriage. They agreed that the realm was in a dire state, and that something would have to be done about it.

"What the queen and her new husband urge is that the Douglas power be assembled, to help to put matters to rights," Alec told them. "They believe that the new Earl of Douglas should claim his father's office of lieutenant-general. That would, they say, require parliamentary authority. So, a parliament called, backed by Douglas strength. Sir William Crichton is Chancellor. They judge that he would probably be prepared to call it, for he cannot be happy with what is being done by Livingston, even though they are now in seeming alliance."

"Alliance against Douglas!" Dalkeith interjected.

"That was the position yes, sir," Alec admitted. "But the situation has changed. There is this great trouble in the kingdom. This of the two working together has not succeeded. All in disorder. And Livingston imprisoning the queen and her husband. This makes the king hate him. It will make it very difficult for him to gain the boy's response with royal authority. I think that Sir William Crichton will not fail to see that, and seek to change matters. To his own advantage, yes – but also to the realm's."

"It may well be so. And the queen and Sir James look for Douglas aid to win their freedom?."

"And also to keep Crichton under some control, in *his* place! They see Douglas as the key to the kingdom's fair order in this coil of affairs."

"I see it so also," the Princess Elizabeth said. "You must so tell Archibald, James. He is young, but with your guidance will do well enough as lieutenant."

"M'mm. Perhaps. It is time, yes, that Douglas took a hand, I think. When would this assembling be required?"

"So soon as you can effect it, sir, to be sure. The captives freed, the Lady Catherine Douglas one of them."

"Aye, Barlass deserves better than Livingston's keeping!"

"How long to muster your Douglas strength, sir? If it was there, assembled, it would make Crichton and the parliament, if he will consent to call one, the more . . . heedful!"

"To be sure. There will be no forty days' notice, I think, in this broil. Give me, or leastwise the Earl of Douglas, ten days. Much of our strength is far off, in Galloway and the Dumfries dales. But – Crichton? He may not play his part. How is he to be brought to it?"

"He may well see the need. And when he knows that Douglas is taking to arms, he will I think agree. I have a letter for him from his daughter, who attends on the young princesses."

"So! You are going to Crichton?"

"I must." Alec was certainly not looking forward to that part of his mission; but he had agreed that it was necessary. "I go from here to Edinburgh Castle."

"You are, I think, a brave young man!" That was Princess Elizabeth.

"I am not, lady. But someone has to go. And I have this letter."

"Then you will bide the night here. And go well sustained in the morning."

"Aye. And speak for Douglas!" her husband added.

So that was that. Half his task achieved.

At Edinburgh Castle, announcing that he had come to see the keeper at the behest of his daughter Agnes Crichton, Alec gained the information that Sir William was gone to

Crichton Castle meantime; so that meant another dozen miles riding southwards, to the Tyne valley. At least the man would be more accessible there.

At Crichton, in due course, Alec found Borthwick with the laird. He was greeted less than warmly, but that was only to be expected.

"So here is the young man who stole the King's Grace from my keeping! By an artifice," he was challenged. "I wonder that you dare to approach me, Lyon!"

"I come at your daughter's bidding, Sir William. And that of the king, I did at the queen's command. Not to be refused by such as myself. His Grace is eager to see his mother."

Raising his eyebrows, the other looked at Lord Borthwick.

"At least he is bold enough to come and seek you in your own house," that man said.

"I come, because it is of great moment," Alec declared. "From not only your daughter, sir, but from the Lord of Dalkeith."

"Ha! Dalkeith! What does the Douglas want of me?"

"He urges you, as Chancellor, to call a parliament, sir. So does Agnes."

"A parliament? Here's a jest! What does the Douglas want with a parliament? And judge that I should heed him? And what has it to do with Agnes, that fool girl!"

"It concerns all who are loyal to the King's Grace, Sir William. You know of the queen's fate?"

"I know that she is in Livingston's pocket, yes."

"In more than his pocket! In his prison."

"Prison?"

"You have not heard, then?" Alex went on to relate the situation at Stirling Castle, the queen locked into two rooms, not permitted to see her son and daughters, and Stewart of Lorne and his brother thrown into the underground pit. This because they believed that only the Douglas power could bring order to the nation's affairs in this pass, with the new earl succeeding his father as lieutenant-general. So he, Alexander Lyon, had gone to Dalkeith, as the Black Knight had meant to do. And the Douglas had agreed that a parliament would be necessary to appoint the young earl; meanwhile he would muster the Douglas strength.

Crichton and Borthwick eyed each other.

"Imprisoning the queen!" the latter said. "Is Livingston run mad?"

"I knew naught of all this." Crichton frowned. "He, Livingston, was to keep me informed of all of consequence. Here is folly, and worse!"

"So say we all," Alec agreed.

"You could do worse than heed the Douglas," Borthwick said. "If they are assembling their men."

"If the parliament appoints the young earl as lieutenant-general, with Dalkeith aiding and advising him, Livingston could be curbed indeed," Alec added. "Forced to free the queen and Lorne. And yield up the king."

Crichton nodded, but said nothing.

"Lyon speaks sense," Borthwick went on. "Livingston has overshot his mark! He must be brought down. And Douglas, with a parliament, could do it."

"We shall consider it."

That was as far as Alec could push the matter. But he thought that Crichton was probably persuaded, Borthwick certainly so. He took his leave, not being invited to linger.

It was midday and, with the late August daylight, he thought that he might just make it home to Glamis, a lengthy ride indeed. But his horse was a fine one. For, of course, much as he would have liked to return to Stirling, and Agnes, that was not to be considered. Livingston would almost certainly imprison him, with the Stewart brothers, possibly that the least of it. His liege-lord would have to do without his attendant meantime.

Avoiding Stirling, then, as well as Edinburgh, Alec made for Queen Margaret's Ferry, where a scow took him and his mount across Forth, and on through Fife, all the miles to Ferryport-on-Tay, to pass over that second wide estuary to Dundee, and so north to Strathmore and Glamis, a daunting journey by Perth avoided. Even so it was some eighty-five miles, and dark before he rode his weary horse up to Glamis Castle, thankful indeed to reach his home. It had been long since he had seen his family.

8

It was on his fourth day at Glamis that Alec learned that his efforts had not been in vain, when a messenger arrived to inform the thane that a parliament was to be held on the ninth day of September and, surprisingly, at Stirling, at Cambuskenneth Abbey, not at the fortress, this in the name of Chancellor Crichton. Well satisfied, Alec wondered why Stirling was chosen as the venue. Presumably Crichton considered that greater pressure would be brought to bear on Livingston by the assembly being held there under his very nose, as it were. Or perhaps it was a Douglas decision?

Sir Patrick would attend, and Alec accompany him. How soon would parliament's orders and the Douglas threat suffice to bring Livingston to heel, free the captives – and allow him to see Agnes again?

On this of Agnes, Alec had been doing a lot of thinking. He wanted that young woman, desired and needed her, was determined to have her if it was humanly possible – and reckoned it just conceivable that she might give herself to him. And, since he would be of full age the very next month, he could wed without his father's permission, although he had gained no hint of parental disapproval despite the girl being daughter to Crichton, whom his sire by no means admired. But Crichton himself? Unfortunately, Agnes was a year younger, and so in law still in her father's keeping; and he could prohibit her marriage to anyone contrary to his choice. And could that man be expected to approve of a son-in-law who had tricked him as Alec had had to do? He would probably forbid the match. So they might have to wait for at least another year, until Agnes too came of full age, and could, if so she chose, defy her father. But in that case, Sir William might think to marry her off to someone of his own choosing, and she powerless to refuse – dreadful thought as that was. What was his best course? To say nothing meantime so as not to arouse Crichton to active opposition? A year to wait! All but eternity! He need not wait till then to put his proposal to her, of course . . .

His own father it was who, without actually touching on the subject of marriage, did allow Alec to marshal his thoughts somewhat. One morning, while they rode, with Lady Lyon, to her Ogilvy former home, Sir Patrick did refer to his son's forthcoming majority, and declared that they had decided to mark the event by settling on him Balharry and Cardeun in Strathmore, and Pitteadie in Fife, the latter with a small castle, presently unoccupied. What thought he of that?

Alec was much elated. He would be his own laird and have a home to offer Agnes. He had only once been to Pitteadie, years before when an uncle held it, with whom his father did not get on, and who was now dead. But he remembered it as a pleasantly situated place near to Kinghorn, which was another possession of his father's. In his gratification, he admitted his hopes and intentions.

"I thank you! That is good, good! It means that I will have something to offer her, offer Agnes. A house. The means to keep her." He took the plunge. "Agnes Crichton."

His mother reined over, to smile at him, and his father grunted.

"We wondered when you would come out with it," the thane said. "You have been seeing a lot of that young woman, have spoken often of her. We guessed that this would be the way of it. But – Crichton! Have you considered what you would be taking on if you wed that man's daughter? It is scarcely a family I would have chosen for my son to marry into!"

"Agnes is not like her father. He is hard, a stern man. She is kindly, generous. And very fair."

"You love her?" his mother asked.

"I do. I do."

"And Crichton himself? Will he permit this?" Sir Patrick wondered.

"That I do not know," Alec conceded. "He has no reason to love me. I aided him, perhaps, in this of the parliament and the Douglases. But before that . . . !" He shrugged. "We may have to wait until Agnes is of full age. A year yet. That is, if she will have me! I have not asked her yet."

"But you think that she will?" Lady Lyon sounded sympathetic.

"Who knows? But she is . . . friendly."

"I hope that you are not stirring up trouble for yourself!" his father said.

They left it at that.

When they rode for the parliament, with Ogilvy of Inverquharity and Rattray of that Ilk, it was a company wondering what they were going to be involved in, what direction Scotland was going to be steered into now. How grievously uncertain was the fate of a nation when its monarch was in childhood. None there esteemed Crichton much more highly than they did Livingston; it was the Douglas involvement which interested them especially. If that great house could and would take the lead in the affairs of state, there might be a steadying influence, a period of comparative quiet, for the Douglases were sufficiently strong to make most of the unruly magnates think twice before disturbing the peace in any major way. If they could support, and act for, the king until he reached man's estate, the realm might become a land worth living in again.

At Cambuskenneth Abbey, set in the levels amongst the meanderings of the Forth just before it widened to the salt waters of the estuary, the newcomers were scarcely enheartened by finding scores of Highlandmen roaming around, armed to the teeth, in their kilts and tartans, and being eyed askance, but heedfully, not provoked by the trains of the Lowland lords, something fairly new for a parliament. These proved to be the clansmen of the Lord of the Isles himself, that great Hebridean potentate having deigned to attend a parliament in person, highly unusual, despite having had such short notice. What did this portend?

The abbot – he who had married Queen Joanna and the Black Knight – and his monks were proving excellent hosts to the large numbers attending, for, of course, in the troubled state of the kingdom, no magnate travelled the land without an adequate train of men-at-arms; so even the wealth of Holy Church was taxed to provide adequately for all. But the unpopularity of Livingston, up at the castle, ensured that the abbot did his utmost, especially for the great ones.

That evening, well fed and in comfort, Alec wondered how Agnes was faring only a mile or so away on the rock-top, and whether Livingston had sought to punish her in any way when she had returned from the Tor Wood ride without him – although that man would not know of Alec's reason for flight, even though he might have his suspicions now. He did not forget the queen and Lady Catherine either, nor the Stewart brothers in their pit. It was to be hoped that the parliament could somehow better their state, free them if possible.

Next forenoon, it was not really a parliament at all, only a convention, for the king had to be present for the former and he was not this day, although the Chancellor had sent the Lord Lyon King of Arms up to the castle to command Livingston to allow His Grace to attend – with predictable results.

Everybody present, including those watching, like Alec, from the clerestorey of the abbey-church, was highly interested to see who had come and who had stayed away. There was, needless to say, a good attendance of Douglas barons and lairds, under the good-looking young earl and his brother, the Lord David, and James of Dalkeith. The Earls of Huntly, Angus, and Marischal, the Lords Seton, Haliburton of Dirleton and Boyd, Murray of Tullibardine and others, with the Bishops of Glasgow, Moray, Ross and Dunblane, and notably the resplendent Lord of the Isles and some of the other Highland chiefs. But there were notable absentees, and not only amongst the known Livingston supporters, many no doubt waiting to see which way the wind would blow.

The displaced Chancellor, the Bishop Cameron of Glasgow, opened the proceedings with prayer, beseeching God's blessing on the King's Grace, and His mercy upon the captive queen mother and her shamefully imprisoned husband and good-brother, not exactly calling down divine vengeance on the perpetrator but leaving no doubt that was intended. Thereafter he sought heaven's guidance and benison on the assembly's deliberations and decisions. Then he handed over to his successor, Crichton.

That man, as ever, wasted no time, coming straight to the point, his harsh voice contrasting notably with the sonorous tones of the other. He declared that the realm was in chaos, disorder rife, and that mainly the fault of the keeper of Stirling Castle, so nearby, Livingston of Calendar, who held the king in his grip, had imprisoned the queen and her husband, and encouraged violence and disharmony throughout the land. The situation must be amended, and forthwith. It would require strong measures. The nation's loyal forces must be marshalled, and ably led. To that end none was better able to take the lead than the House of Douglas in all its branches, and it allied to the throne. It was now his suggestion that the present Earl of Douglas should be appointed lieutenant-general of the realm in succession to his late father, with Sir James, Lord of Dalkeith as deputy, the former deputy having been slain. Were these nominations the will of the commissioners here present?

The Earl of Huntly jumped up so to propose, and the Lord Borthwick seconded.

Was there any contrary motion?

Only one voice spoke, that of Alexander, Lord of the Isles, a musical lilting Highland voice somewhat at odds with its owner's reputation. "Sir Alexander Livingston has promised me that he will advise King James to grant me the earldom of Ross, which should rightfully be mine, whatever. I would be after expecting a like promise here, if I am to support the present motion."

There was silence for long moments in that church.

Crichton cleared his throat at this most evident example of pressure and exaction. He glanced over at the earls sitting at the front, near the chancel step. "I cannot speak for others, my lord," he said at length. "But, for myself, I would so avow, accepting your right."

The young Earl of Douglas stood. "I agree."

"As do I," Dalkeith added.

There was murmuring in the company, but none of it in actual protest.

"I then am after voicing no contrary motion," the Islesman declared.

After that there was no opposition expressed. The entire Weight of the Western Highlands was now involved.

Sir Robert Erskine seized his opportunity. "I claim the earldom of Mar," he called. "I am undoubted heir, through Elyne, only child of Gratney, the eleventh earl."

Before the Chancellor could speak, Sir Alexander "Bucktooth" Stewart, the late Sir Alan of Darnley's brother, cried out, "You have taken and hold the castle of Dumbarton, in Lennox. And I claim the earldom of Lennox, my brother dead, murdered. The Earls of Lennox are hereditary keepers of that royal hold."

"Give me Kildrummy Castle up in Mar, and you can have Dumbarton back!" Erskine returned.

Crichton, frowning, thumped fist on table for silence and order.

"This is a convention of parliament," he declared. "It

is not a market-place! I move, I suggest, that a council of earls be set up to decide on these matters and hear these claims. Part of a wider council of state, to carry out the convention's will in other matters, free the King's Grace, his royal mother and the other prisoners, and order the realm's affairs."

"I so move." That was Dalkeith.

"Seconded," Huntly said.

"Any contrary motion?"

There was none, but Sir Patrick Lyon rose to say that the appointments to the proposed council of state were of vital import, not to be left to any small group, but the business of this convention.

There were shouts of agreement from all around.

"Nominations, then?" Crichton jerked. "But first, is it agreed that the Earl of Douglas be appointed lieutenant-general? And Sir James of Dalkeith his deputy?"

With an army of Douglases camped nearby, where the Bannock Burn entered Forth, none contested that.

"Then I say that the first duty of the lieutenant-general is to send up to Stirling Castle to demand that the keeper release the queen mother and the other captives, and to yield up the King's Grace to this convention." That at least to cheers.

"Now, nominations for the council – but not over-many," the Chancellor moved.

There followed the lengthiest and most argued-over part of the proceedings, as parties sought their own ends and preferences, the Chancellor's thumping fist much in use to maintain some sort of order. There was no lack of Douglas claimants, with even Dalkeith having to tone them down. Alec, watching all from aloft, was pleased to see his father appointed. All three would-be earls were included. How effective a council it would make remained to be seen; but at least it would be united against Livingston, the principal object of the exercise.

At length the convention broke up, and practically the entire company, save for the Lord of the Isles, decided to accompany the new lieutenant-general up through the town of Stirling to the fortress to inform Livingston that his ascendancy was over.

Up there before the gatehouse, Alec, thinking that he was now only some hundreds of yards from Agnes, for one was surprised to hear that it was not all threat to Livingston, but an offering also, presumably concocted between Crichton and Dalkeith beforehand. It took some time before Livingston consented to come to the gatehouse parapet and be addressed; admittedly he could have refused all contact, for his citadel was impregnable. But when he did come, and was confronted by the very evident strength of the opposition, and their power in the land, he bowed to the inevitable, however sourly – especially when he was told that if he yielded up his prisoners forthwith, he would be permitted to retain the keepership of this Stirling Castle, and even given an annual grant of four thousand merks, allegedly for its due maintenance. Alec wondered how this sum was arrived at, the reason behind it, and whence it was to come? The Douglas army would be clearly visible from the fortress, so there was little likelihood of its keeper attempting any armed resistance, however large his castle garrison; nevertheless it was thought fit that the formal surrender and handing over of the prisoners should take place the next day, and not here at Stirling but at Perth to the north, this for reasons which eluded Alec and others also.

The ultimatum delivered and received, Crichton rather than the lieutenant-general doing most of the talking – or shouting, rather, since the two parties to the dialogue were separated by a moat, ditch and raised drawbridge – the victorious company turned and went back to the abbey. It had been a peculiar performance. The Thane of Glamis, now a councillor of state, confessed to his son that he was mystified by this of going to Perth on the morrow, mystified and slightly suspicious.

Alec, needless to say, was more concerned over what Agnes was thinking of it all up there on the rock-top.

The thirty-mile ride to Perth next morning was made without the Douglas host, which was left at its encampment as signal to the castle that the threat remained, to inhibit any possible efforts at defiance. There was no sign of any Livingston party as they left.

At St John's Town of Perth, Alec thought that perhaps he could see a reason for this journey northwards. A large Highland force was gathered there. The Lord of the Isles had presumably come prepared to enforce his claim, if necessary, to the Ross earldom; and knowing of this, Crichton had thought to use the evidence of this powerful support to impress Livingston. The two greatest houses of Highland and Lowland Scotland were now ranged against him. Let him see it, and heed.

But when, presently, Livingston's company arrived at Perth, he proved that he could also use his wits to effect, for although he brought with him Queen Joanna, her husband and his brother, and the princesses, he did not bring King James, to Crichton's and the others' concern. When this was voiced, he announced that His Grace was safe and secure.

The queen and the other captives appeared none the worse for their incarceration, although the Stewart brothers had a somewhat haggard look to their features. Their joy at release was very evident, especially the womenfolk, however darkly they all eyed Livingston and, somewhat suspiciously, Crichton also, reserving their gratitude for the Douglases.

Agnes was with them. Alec, for his part, could not restrain his joy at seeing her again, and apparently well and her spirited self. He ran to fling his arms around her, there before all, discretion abandoned. He was not repulsed.

The arranged meeting-place was the open parkland known as the Inch, just to the north of the town, an odd designation since it was no island, as the name implied, close to the Tay river as it was. There the Highland array was encamped. What Joanna Beaufort thought of this return to the scene of her former husband's murder was not to be known; but she found time to come to thank Alec for the part he had played in gaining her release. She did add that she was worried that her son remained shut up in Stirling Castle, however. Others were equally so, undoubtedly.

Clearly this was Livingston's bargaining card. So long as he held the king, he was in a position to ensure his own safety and some furtherance of his interests.

A strange situation it was, with the Lord of the Isles all but acting host, his clansmen and those of the other Highland chiefs being there temporarily settled and able to offer food and drink in plenty to the travellers; how this had been obtained was not specified, the citizens of Perth not in evidence to explain. But no prolonged lingering was desired by anyone. What now then?

Dalkeith proposed that the queen mother and the princesses should be taken to her dower-house of Linlithgow meantime, since none but Livingston himself was for returning to Stirling Castle, save in the by-going, to gain the person of the young monarch. The Lord of the Isles, his purpose achieved, was for returning to his Highland fastnesses, assured that he would be created Earl of Ross hereafter. The others prepared to ride back whence they had so recently come, all a most curious arrangement, with Livingston with them as though innocent of any offence, however carefully the queen's group avoided his company.

It was only as they were preparing to ride off that most there realised that Crichton was no longer with them. Alec's father, who had no further call to remain with the queen's party, and was for home to Strathmore, discovered and told his son that in fact Crichton had departed quietly almost as soon as he learned that the King was not with Livingston, with just what in view was not clear, save that he had told the Earl of Douglas that he was off to arrange the payment of those four thousand merks allowance for Livingston, where from not specified.

Thereafter Alec, riding side by side now with Agnes, although mystified by these strange proceedings, was not greatly concerned. He was reunited with his love, that was what mattered mainly to him.

The queen-mother and the princesses were now in the care of the Douglases, Livingstone riding with his own small group well to the rear. When they reached the Stirling vicinity, it was their encamped army at the Bannock Burn which concerned the young earl and Dalkeith. They gave orders for the host to come on southwards the next day, and Livingston's return to his fortress went all but unnoticed. But at the camp they all learned that Crichton had not been so much interested in raising the four thousand merks allowance as in gaining custody of James, King of Scots. He had gone up to the castle, declaring that he had come in the keeper's name to take His Grace to his mother and sisters, under the new arrangement, and had been permitted to collect the boy. He had ridden off with him, presumably for Linlithgow.

This news much concerned all, the fact that Crichton had said nothing of this intention to anyone beforehand looking suspicious indeed. It might be fair enough, of course, and the king be awaiting them at Linlithgow. But there were fears otherwise. Whosoever held the monarch . . . !

So the Douglas chiefs took the queen and her daughters, with their attendants, on the further fifteen miles to Linlithgow Palace, reaching there at the darkening. No sign nor word of Crichton nor the king awaited them there.

Not only the Douglases were much troubled. Fairly obviously this meant that Crichton was seeking to play his own game again. No doubt by now he had young James safely held in his castle of Edinburgh once more, and so in a position largely to call his tune in Scotland, his association with the Douglases, brief as it had been, ignored or much reduced. He might still intend to work together with them and the others when it suited him, but this secretive and deceptive way of going about it was scarcely encouraging.

Agnes was, as so often before, distressed over her father's actions. But what could she say? He was obsessed with the wielding of power. That was what mattered to him; how the power was obtained of little concern.

They all spent the night at the palace above the loch, decisions being made. The Douglases would care for the royal family, less the monarch, meantime at Dalkeith Castle, the earl's Lanarkshire and Galloway seats being less conveniently placed. Agnes would continue to attend on the girls, whatever her father's behaviour. As for Alec, there was question. His place was with the king. But would Sir William Crichton agree to accept him at Edinburgh Castle, when he had previously contrived the boy's escape therefrom? It seemed highly unlikely. Meanwhile Alec had to choose. He could go home to Glamis. Or he could temporarily attach himself to the queen's company, and so remain close to Agnes. Not surprisingly, he chose the latter.

So it was a general parting of the ways on the morrow, with a certain stiffness developing between the pro-Crichton lords such as Borthwick, Seton and Dirleton, these heading for their own territories, and the Douglases, all wondering what the sequel would be, Alec Lyon not the least of them, his wondering not only over national affairs.

9

Dalkeith Castle was large enough, in its enclosed Esk valley, for the queen's group to occupy a small wing and tower of their own, the Princess Elizabeth proving a sympathetic and attentive hostess. Alec shared a room with the Black Knight's brother Sir William Stewart, a man only a couple of years older than himself, and with whom he got on well. No one seemed to question his attachment to the queen-mother's party, and in the circumstances he found himself acting as a sort of esquire to the young princesses, which suited him very well. The eldest of them, Margaret, was now in her tenth year, and looked as though she would develop into an attractive young woman. All six were easy to get on with, their eventful upbringing and lifestyle helping them to associate easily with all. So life went pleasingly enough for Alec Lyon in the month which followed.

Nevertheless there was frustration in it also, to see so much of his love yet seldom being able to be alone with her for more than a few moments at a time, the tower of the castle being hardly spacious enough for over a dozen people to gain privacy, and the royal youngsters packed off to bed early. Agnes was kind and sympathetic, and when they were out riding with the girls up the Esk valley and over the rolling Lothian landscape as far as the skirts of the Pentland and Morthwaite Hills, there were occasions when they did manage to gain short spells of near-privacy, but these were all too few and brief, at least for the man.

No word came from Edinburgh Castle as to Sir William Crichton's intentions nor the king's state. In the circumstances, probably, no news was good news. Livingston also appeared to be lying low meantime, with that autumn blessedly uneventful.

Alec, very much aware that his services at Dalkeith were hardly essential, thought to seek short leave of absence to go and inspect the coming-of-age property which his father had allotted him in Fife, this a bare twenty miles away from Dalkeith as the crows flew but with the wide estuary of the Firth of Forth in between. But before going, he decided to, as it were, test the water with Agnes, this as to the place's future, as far as he was concerned. Somehow he had to contrive an occasion when he could have her to himself, those six princesses ever present, she even sharing a bedchamber with two of them.

Eventually he devised a plan, when the girls were heading bedwards one evening, their attendant with them. When he had said goodnight, with a squeeze for Agnes's arm, he allowed them only a very few minutes before excusing himself to William Stewart, and went upstairs, hoping that that man would not follow him immediately; and instead of proceeding further up to their own bedroom at the top of the tower, he paused at the third-floor doorway below, and knocked, trusting that the undressing and washing process would not yet be far advanced within. As hoped for, it was Agnes who came to the door, fully clad as yet.

"The queen requires your attendance, Agnes," he told her. "Some privy matter. I hoped that you were not yet abed."

"Now? That is strange," she said. Then, "Very well. I shall go to her." She turned back to call to her companions that she would be gone for a little, to their mother, and came out to join Alec on the landing.

But instead of conducting her down the twisting turnpike stairway to make for the queen's private apartments in the adjoining wing, he took her arm and directed her upstairs.

"I lied to you, lass," he confessed. "The queen does

not need you. I had to see you, see you alone. It is so difficult. Never alone. I could think of no other way."

"Poor Alec!" she commiserated. "I know that you are ever seeking opportunity! But this . . ." She did not however hold back from mounting those steps with him.

"It is important. To me," he declared. "Possibly to you also. That is my prayer! I have to put it to the test." He led her past his own bedchamber doorway, and on the few more steps to another door confronting them, this opening out on to a little parapet walk which encircled the tower-top. Out into the September night he took her, looking out over the river, and without delay he enfolded her in his arms.

"You must be . . . desperate . . . this night!" she got out, when she could free her lips to speak.

"I am, yes. But not only for, for this. Lass, you know of my house in Fife. Pitteadie, near to Kinghorn, that I have told you of. That I want to visit. I have never seen it. And, and it is my hope that one day . . ." He took a deep breath. "That one day you will visit it also, do more than visit, will, will share it with me!" There, it was out. "One day . . ."

She searched his features in the half-dark. "Alec, are you saying . . . are you saying . . . ? Is this a wooing, a suit? Is it . . . a proposal of marriage?"

"It is yes, lass – yes! Could you, would you, think of it? Consider it? To wed me. It is my greatest wish and hope, my dream! Is it possible? Can you think of it?"

"My dear!" That came out on a small laugh, a little tremulous. "Think of it? I have thought of it. Often. Think you that I would have allowed our small . . . affections had I not thought of you as, as one day perhaps, my, my . . ."

She got no further before her lips were closed again, closed and then parted, and her person all but shaken, this against the crenellated parapet, actions much more eloquent than words. She did not attempt to complete her admission.

When he could bring himself to speak again, he was less

lucid, his joy and thankfulness tumbling out in incoherent spate, hands busy about her.

The young woman had much better control of herself, stroking his hair when she could get an arm free to do it, and chiding him.

"You did not think that I would refuse you, Alec Lyon, when I had granted you . . . lesser favours?" she asked. "I am not of that sort, although no saint! I had wondered when you would come to say the word!"

"We are so seldom alone! Those princesses!"

"Poor Alec! Waiting, waiting! And still you will have to wait. For some time, I fear. For your, *our* fullest coming together. Our felicity. For my father will scarcely see you as a favoured son-in-law, I think!"

"I know it. After I deceived him over James. What are we to do? He still will have your marriage in his right."

"Yes. It will be almost a year yet before I reach full age and I can choose for myself. We could, I suppose, abscond and wed secretly. But he could have the Church annul it. And you proscribed. He has power. And he is sufficiently displeased with me already, for continuing to wait on the queen and princesses."

"No, that would serve nothing. It seems that we must wait, a grievous trial. For me, at least. But we know now that we have each other. In our hearts, lass!"

"True, my dear. But we must not show it openly, to all. Or my father may hear of it and marry me off to someone more of his choice meantime."

"God forbid! No, we must seek to be patient, little as I am good at that! It will be hard, hard. But a year will pass, I suppose. And meanwhile what do I have to do? I cannot remain, unbidden, with the princesses overlong. It will be too plain that it is you I seek to be with. I cannot go back to the king – your father will not have me, I judge."

"Perhaps we will think of something . . ."

They left it at that, this opportunity too precious to waste on mere words. And Alec had no reason to complain of rejection on Agnes's part, at least, there on the parapet walk.

When at length she felt that they could hardly prolong her absence from her charges further, they had to return downstairs. Even so, the parting at that bedroom door was a trial, and took a little time. However, when he was eventually bedded down in his own chamber, and said goodnight to Stewart, Alec Lyon knew a great joy, if not content. Somehow, it would all come right in the end, he prayed.

On the morrow he approached the queen for leave of absence in order to visit his inheritance in Fife, this being granted with a somewhat quizzical look, she, nowise lacking in wits and perception, no doubt having her own notions as to reasons and hopes. She forbore to ask whether he intended to try to wait on her son again, but said that he would be welcome back in her company at any time, and that her daughters thought highly of him.

So he was off to Fife, back to Queen Margaret's Ferry, fifteen miles, then across Forth and eastwards along the other coast, by the ancient burgh of Inverkeithing, by Dalgety Bay and Aberdour, a Douglas place, to Burntisland of the Wemyss family and so to Kinghorn, where Alexander the Third had ridden over a cliff to his death, leaving no male heir, in 1286, thus precipitating the Competition for the Crown and the subsequent Wars of Independence, with William Wallace giving the lead and Robert Bruce completing the mighty and challenging task.

It was all new territory to Alec, and at Kinghorn he had to ask where Pitteadie was situated. He learned that it lay two miles or so inland, on the south-facing slopes of the modest hills which separated the coast from the Tool valley of central Fife, flanked by the lands of the Wemyss family and those of Kirkcaldy of Grange.

He found his inheritance, a pleasingly placed property of south-facing, grassy slopes and open woodland, with fine views over the estuary; and in the centre, in no particularly strong position, a square stone keep of five storeys, modest in size compared with Glamis or Crichton, set within a high courtyard wall, a small farmery nearby. Within the enclosure, its gate not barred, he found further access not possible, for the doorway, with its round-headed arch, was up at first-floor level. A stone mounting-block, with steps, did arise some ten feet away, but there was a gap between, requiring some gangplank to be run out from the said door to gain admittance. No such gangway was in evidence that day.

The tower had only narrow arrow-slit windows at ground level, although larger above. Up at parapet level the angles had open rounds corbelled out to give defence of the walling. Over that unreachable, and only, arched doorway, at parapet level, was a projecting machicolation for the dropping of unpleasantness upon unwelcome visitors who might penetrate that far. The little castle had an air of emptiness about it. Alec's uncle, the previous tenant, had died some years before.

The new laird, seeing no way of getting inside, had to ride to the farm and seek help.

He found the farmer, Durie by name, and three sons stacking oats, and introducing himself, asked how access was to be gained to his property. He was told that planking was hidden in bushes, outwith the courtyard, at the lower end of the orchard – one of the sons would show him where – and after climbing the stone steps to the platform, these could be run over to corbels projecting below the doorway, to base them on, and so the door reached. It was held shut by a drawbar and slot, but this was greased and would slide open readily enough. There was an iron-grated yett behind, but this was not locked. The gangway for normal use was kept available within the thickness of the walling inside, so that occupants could push it out and draw it in, as required.

Clearly Pitteadie Castle was not to be readily entered by enemies.

Accompanied by a Durie son, glad enough to escape the back-taxing labour of picking up and erecting corn-stacks, Alec was taken and shown the process of entry to the unoccupied premises, crossing the gap gingerly on narrow planks which shook somewhat and which he feared might come adrift from their far-side corbel supports and deposit the crossers on to the stone-cobbled yard below. But they both made it safely, and duly slid back the drawbar into its greased slot, opened the massive bog-oak door, iron-studded, and the heavy yett behind it, and so in through the ten-feet-thick walling, with the true gangway lying there ready in the passage.

Much aware of the musty smell of disuse, Alec passed into the first-floor floor hall, the main living-room of the house, his home-to-be, a fine apartment, with a circular stair in the eastern angle, up and down, a stone-slabbed floor strewn with worn deer-skin mats, a lengthy oak table and benches therefor, four windows each with stone seats in the ingoings, and a handsome hooded fireplace at the west end, this provided with an ingle-neuk stone seat also. Birch logs were stacked in the wide fireplace.

Accompanied by young Durie, Alec descended to the dark vaulted basement, wherein were stored items of furniture, blankets and plaids, old clothing and the like; and in the centre of the stone floor a wooden lid, which, raised, revealed a deep well shaft beneath. So the water supply was conveniently available, vital in any sort of siege.

Climbing back up to the second floor, they found the withdrawing room, above the hall, where the laird and family could withdraw for privacy when desired, this with a small bedroom off provided with a garderobe in the thickness of the walling, for sanitary purposes. The two main floors above, and then the attic storey within the parapet walk, each contained two more bedchambers and storage space.

All admittedly had a neglected air about it, for the previous laird had been a widower and had lived alone and sparsely; but there was nothing decayed nor ruinous about the house, and Alec reckoned that it could all be made comfortable enough, with extra furniture and plenishings, the chill air dispersed with fires lit. A woman's touch would see to that – and he believed that he would have a woman available.

There was nothing that he could do therein meantime, and after going through the locking-up and descending process, and the hiding of the gangplanks, Alec bade farewell to the Duries, and went for a ride around the property. It was not very large, some eight hundred acres, but was all worthy land, with three small farms with their cultivation riggs, good pasture and scattered woodland, and three small burns running down, all with those notable views out southwards over the islanded firth to the Lothian coast, and far further to the Norse Sea itself. He could live here well content, he decided – provided he had the right company, and the nation's affairs allowed it.

It was still only early afternoon, and he decided that he should probably go and see his parents and the family at Glamis while he was thus far on the way. He ought to be able to reach Ferryport-on-Tay by nightfall, spend the night at the monks' hospice there, and cross in their ferry-scow in the morning. Holy Church did provide these useful services for travellers, and garnered considerable wealth therefrom.

That he did, and was home in Strathmore by noontide next day.

10

Alec found his father, while thankful for the present comparative peace and breathing-space in the realm's affairs, concerned that it was not going to last, the word he had from various sources indicating that all too clearly. Livingston was sending out messengers far and wide through central Scotland, and as far up as this Angus and Aberdeenshire, to his supporters to be ready for action, just what unspecified. It was unlikely indeed that, in the circumstances, Crichton had not been doing the same further south. The Lord of the Isles, now styling himself Earl of Ross, was seeking to bring all the Western Highlands under his control, and far enough south as to be near Glasgow, having perpetrated a massacre of the Clan Colquhoun on Loch Lomondside. There was plague in Edinburgh, and such visitations always had the effect of raising unrest as well as sad casualties, with folk flocking out of the cities and towns to escape the infection and causing trouble in the process, and the conditions for lawlessness. The Douglases had so far not seemed to exert their authority to any marked extent, and the lieutenant-general, away in Galloway, was hardly in touch with current affairs. Sir Patrick feared that dire happenings would again convulse the nation, and soon. This precarious balance could not last.

His son thought that the thane's forebodings were unduly gloomy. What could Livingston do without the king's authority? He was now only keeper of the royal castle of Stirling again. The Lord of the Isles was more dangerous, but he was unlikely to trouble more than the Highlands. And Dalkeith would advise the Earl of Douglas as to effective action. Father told son not to underestimate Livingston, nor Crichton either, two men avid for power, and both short as to consciences.

Alec did not remain long at Glamis, drawn back to Dalkeith by an attraction stronger than the filial. And when he arrived back there, it was to learn extraordinary news. The two power-seekers had joined forces again. Livingston had come to Edinburgh, with the Bishops of Aberdeen and Moray as go-betweens, and had prevailed on Crichton to meet him at St Giles Church there to confer, in theory how best to use the power of Douglas for the weal of the realm. It seemed that the young earl, being also Duke of Touraine in France, had apparently sent to that country for an armed force of his French tenantry to come over to Scotland to support his role of lieutenant-general – this, Dalkeith admitting, not on his advice, and probably unwise. At any rate, the two castle-keepers had come to terms, with Crichton actually yielding up the king to Livingston's care again, and in return given what amounted to control of all offices and appointments in the nation and its government, with access to the monarch at all times, and a pension of seven hundred merks per year until the king's coming of age. This, and mutual co-operation of their joint supporters to keep the Douglases in their place.

Needless to say, Dalkeith was direly angered by all this, and was not long in departing for Threave Castle in Galloway, the earl's favourite seat, to see that young man, advise and admonish and counsel. Queen Joanna was also much concerned, foreseeing all but civil war breaking out again in her adopted country, her son as ever to be a pawn in the game. If French troops did land, the English, always on the watch for French aggression under the Auld Alliance with Scotland, might well take a hand and move an army north, as she, an Englishwoman of royal birth, knew well. Then there would be worse than civil war, disaster indeed.

Agnes Crichton was likewise perturbed by all this, and

confided in Alec that her father would not have come to terms with Livingston without very good reason, letting the king out of his keeping when he need not have done so. She too feared very positive developments.

The couple's love-makings were nowise forwarded in consequence.

Surprises were by no means over, either. Shortly after Dalkeith's departure for Galloway, a messenger arrived at his castle, and from none other than Crichton himself – but for Alec Lyon, not its lord. The Chancellor requested, indeed ordered, that young man to repair forthwith to Stirling Castle to resume his attendance on King James, and to act as intermediary between himself and the monarch.

Alec was more than astonished to receive this demand, and in two minds whether to ignore it or to obey. It was not, after all, a royal command. On the other hand, his place presumably was with the king, and he had come to be fond of the boy, unfortunate as he was. Agnes said that he ought to go; it was his duty, she felt. Also there was the point that to do as her father said might bring him to look on Alec more favorably as a son-in-law! But she was going to miss his company meantime – not that he could have gone on thus at Dalkeith indefinitely.

In a couple of days then, it was farewell and off to Stirling. He went with some misgivings. What would his reception there be?

His greeting by the young monarch was sufficiently enthusiastic, at least, almost heart-warming, James Stewart seldom doing anything by halves. Clearly his company had been much missed, the boy lonely, the attendants and his two tutors provided by Livingston not his choice. Sir Alexander's own reception was not as Alec anticipated, being not exactly friendly but not uncivil either, nor suspicious. Evidently he was expected, the arrangement being made between the two keepers. No reason for it was offered, but Alec guessed that it was part of a mutual co-operation against the Earl of Douglas, whose position

101

and power, and his French connection, offered a threat to both.

So commenced a new sort of life for Alec Lyon, different from his previous spells of duty at Stirling, for James was growing fast and very active, demanding much of his companion, and Livingston obviously thankful to be spared the task of dealing with him, and having to try to tie him down. Daily hurlyhackit sledging, archery, quarterstaff bouts, fencing, and above all riding abroad, hawking and hunting, became the norm; and in the last, little as they were desired, an escort of a score of men was always provided for the royal safety, no doubt with strict orders never to let the monarch out of their sight, as had their predecessors. In wet weather, and it was now early winter, indoor pastimes tended to be active, even boisterous, rather than leisurely, and certainly not studious, James not being that way inclined, his tutors despairing of him, not of his intelligence but of his unconcern with learning.

Co-operation between Livingston and Crichton, however much they misliked each other, was emphasised by two errands for Alec to go to Edinburgh, one before Yuletide and one after, with letters and documents with the king's signature and seal for the Chancellor to endorse. On the first, Crichton received the messenger with stiff formality and no confidences, requiring him to remain only an hour or so at the citadel, and to depart with return documents – which had its advantages since it allowed Alec time to make his way back to Stirling by a round-about route, by Dalkeith in fact, this providing a most welcome if all too short reunion with Agnes, made the most of, needless to say. The queen and the princesses were glad to see him also, and he was pressed to stay for a second night. There was no particular news for him at the castle, save that Dalkeith had persuaded the Earl of Douglas to countermand his order for French troops to come to Scotland in the interests of peace and avoidance of any English threat.

But on the second Edinburgh visit, in January, Crichton was slightly more forthcoming, possibly because he had his friend Borthwick with him, a more amiable character, and went so far as to ask whether Alec had seen his errant daughter recently – so he was none so ill-informed.

In fact, however, on his devious return to Stirling again, by Dalkeith, it was to find the queen and her daughters gone therefrom, and Agnes with them. Apparently the Douglas had sent them on to Dunbar Castle, a score of miles southwards – just why was not explained. This was a blow to Alec. That extra twenty miles seemed to put his love far away from him.

The winter passed fairly uneventfully on the national scene, with no major upheavals, although word from the Highlands told of the Earl of Ross ever increasing his sway, his evident ambitions beginning to alarm Livingston. Alec's relations with the latter were peculiar, to say the least. When they met – which was seldom, considering that they dwelt in the same castle; but Stirling was a large fortress and the royal bloc separate from the keeper's – the older man was civil, with even a surface affability at times, but the smile never reached his eyes which were warily cold; for his part, Alec could not pretend to like nor respect the other.

Trouble loomed in April. It was reported that the Earl of Douglas, in his nineteenth year, was claiming that he should be on the throne, not James Stewart; that Robert the Third's son, the late monarch, like his brother David of Rothesay, was born before their father's marriage to Elizabeth More, and was therefore illegitimate; so the succession should have come to the son of Robert the Second's younger son the Earl of Strathearn, by his second marriage to Euphemia Ross, and whose only child was the Douglas's mother. Therefore he should now be the king. And as well as this claim, he had sent Sir Malcolm Fleming, one of his senior vassals, and Alan Lauder of the Bass, to France, conveying his oath of allegiance to King Charles the Seventh thereof, a significant move in the circumstances, and not necessary to offer as titular Duke of Touraine. Alarm rose. It might all be youthful folly but could indicate desire for French pressure to help make a bid for the crown. That this was the lieutenant-general of the realm, the nation's armed forces commander, making the gestures, added to their seriousness.

Alec was sent to the Chancellor to urge the calling of a council of state, and possibly a parliament later, which the earl should attend.

At Edinburgh, Alec was sufficiently bold, once he had delivered his message, as to suggest to Crichton that the queen-mother, who had links with Douglas through the Black Knight, ought to be informed of all this, and her good offices used if possible to bring pressure to bear on the young earl to withdraw his claims against her son, and to renounce allegiance to France. Crichton, eyeing him one eyebrow raised, said that he doubted whether Joanna Beaufort would have any influence on the young fool; but there was no harm in making trial of it, especially as she might be useful in reassuring the English monarchy that this French folly had no general support in Scotland. So the opportunity for a visit to Dunbar was contrived.

Alec had never had occasion to travel down the east coast of Lothian and the Merse coast of Berwickshire, where the Lammermuir Hills came down to the sea, Haddington being as far as he had reached hitherto. He found it a pleasing and fertile land, divided by the vales of Tyne and Peffer, Hepburn country, their castle of Hailes impressive, set on the Tyne below Traprain Law, where once King Loth had reigned, who gave name to Lothian and whose daughter had produced St Mungo, who founded Glasgow. On through the vividly red-soiled countryside, past the mouth of Tyne and the village of Beilhaven, he came to Dunbar. If Hailes had been impressive, Dunbar Castle was more so, a stronghold unique in being built on a series of individual stacks of rock rising out of the sea, a tower on each rock-top all linked by narrow bridges with covered passages. The third of these was over a wide enough gap to allow access below for vessels to the quite large harbour of the adjoining town – which access could be blocked by simply lowering a sort of outsized portcullis, this enabling the lord of the castle to demand a tithe of all fish caught by the many fishing craft which used the harbour, an extraordinary sort of baronial toll. Not that the present Earl of Dunbar and March profited by it, for he was an exile in England, forfeited for treason to the late king, and his castle put in the care of the Red Douglas, Earl of Angus, in nearby Tantallon, with Hepburn of Hailes its constable, hence this secure choice of haven for the queen-mother and the princesses.

The gatehouse tower of this peculiar fortalice was the only part actually based on the mainland, and the first of the bridges spanning the gap beyond was a drawbridge, which could be raised, thus cutting off the remaining towers from approach by land. Once Alec got past the guard there, he felt almost as though aboard ship.

He was well received by Queen Joanna and her daughters, and embraced quite frankly before all by Agnes, their relationship now apparently accepted, this in the second of the islanded towers, which was the main keep of the castle, the constable's lodging being in the first.

Alec's errand regarding the Earl of Douglas's claims produced the expected reaction of dismay and concern; that and an assertion from the Black Knight of Lorne that he would personally go to Threave Castle in far Galloway to reason with and try to persuade his distant kinsman of the foolishness and dangers of his assertions and ambitions. Young King James and his troubled realm had sufficient problems to cope with without that. The queen-mother said that the earl's claims were mistaken anyway, for although David, Duke of Rothesay, starved to death by his uncle, Albany, at Falkland Palace, *had* been born before his father's marriage, Robert the Third's second son, her own late husband, had been born in true wedlock, and therefore had been rightful king, and her son likewise so.

Alec was able to tell them all about James and the conditions at Stirling, of the boy's rapid growth into youth, his lively spirits and enthusiasms. They passed a pleasant evening, with the princesses and Agnes entertaining all with music and dance, there above the surging waves.

When it came to bedtime, the visitor discovered that the girls, and Agnes with them, were occupying the outermost tower, the one across the harbour entrance, the bridge, he was informed, being no less than sixty-nine feet long, giving the stack-top building a great sense of isolation. Apparently he himself was to bed down in the attic chamber of this. So when goodnights were said, he elected to go with the other young people – after all, he had had a long day's riding – and was nowise restrained.

With an entire tower of four storeys to themselves, there was ample room for all, and Agnes had her own chamber, this on the third floor, Alec's attic directly above. In due course, after seeing the girls to their rooms, when he escorted her up to this, she did not pause at her door but went on up with him, to ensure that the chambermaid had prepared all adequately for his comfort; hot water, a little fire burning and a bed-warmer between his sheets.

And there, testing the last, Agnes found herself turned round, sat down on the bed, and enfolded in urgent arms.

"My dear, my dear!" he said, kissing her, and kissing again. "At last! Oh, lass, how I have waited and longed for this!"

"For . . . just what . . . Alec Lyon?" she wondered, a little breathlessly, inevitably. "See you, you have set me down on the warming-pan! Scarcely . . . to my comfort!"

Bodily he moved her over, and pressed her back at the same time, so that she part lay. "Comfort!" he exclaimed. "Comfort *me*, girl! Who have waited and ached for it for so

106

long. Ached and desired and hoped. And now, and now
. . . !" His busy hands caressed her person while his lips
explored.

"And now – what?" she gasped. "You judge . . . that
you have me . . . at your mercy!"

"The mercy should be yours, woman! Mine, the need!
You, with all that I desire, all that I have been missing
for so long, *missing* I tell you!"

"Not only you can miss. I have missed you also.
But . . ."

"You have? You have, girl? Oh, lassie! To hold you
thus. Here is heaven! Or, or . . . all but heaven!"

"All but, yes, my dear. All but! See you, do not tear my
fine bodice with those hands of yours! I am scarce rich in
clothing here." And she patted those busy fingers at her
bosom.

"But Agnes lass, you are so lovely, so fair, so warm! I
want you."

"Then you shall have . . . just a little of me, demanding
one! Only a little . . . for now! Since you are so deprived . . .
so needful!" And drawing aside his hand, she unbuttoned
that clinging bodice.

Alec Lyon had two hands, however, and the second
one was not slow in slipping into the opening, to cup
one of those firmly rounded breasts, so warmly enticing,
its delicious neighbour swiftly dealt with by the other
hand, while lips met and complemented the fingerwork,
hers opening.

So they lay, words become superfluous meantime.

But before long, the female lips had to content themselves with kissing the man's hair, for his head was down
to transfer his attentions to the challenge of those breasts,
finding much to kiss there, her nipples proud, the heaving
of that bosom only adding to his provocation.

She murmured small endearments, stroking his head
now, but his lips were too busy to respond, like his
hands. But presently, inevitably, the male hands began
to slide downwards over lower parts, the belly and

then the thighs, and, sighing a little, Agnes reluctantly called a halt.

"Enough, my dear, enough for the present," she said into his hair. She reached for those hands. "We must have patience, no? Our time will come, I promise you. But not . . . thus. Wait you, Alec my dear . . . until we can, can . . ." She left the rest unsaid.

He almost protested, but managed to control himself. Unspeaking, he gave a lingering salute to her bosom, came up to her lips, and then lifted himself off her and off the bed.

"Thy will . . . be done!" he got out.

"Thine also, Alec my heart?" she asked, all but pleaded, and when he nodded, reached up to stroke his cheek. "Better this way, until, until . . ."

"Yes. No doubt." He did not sound fully convinced. "When do you come of age?"

"In seven more months."

"I shall count the days! Then, your father could not have our marriage annulled?"

"I think not. But, who knows, he might come to approve of you earlier. Now that you are working with him, in some measure."

"Scarcely working with him. Nor with Livingston, in truth. Only for the king. And the peace of the realm. If peace there will ever be! James needs the help of even such as myself. And now I do not know whether I can even trust the Douglases!"

"It is only the young earl, the power he has inherited going to his head, it seems. Perhaps our Black Knight will make him see reason." She had risen, and was adjusting her clothing. "Now, I shall leave you to seek peace in sleep, Alec my heart. Will you dream?"

"I wonder? Perhaps I shall win fulfilment then? But, lass, forgive my, my concern with my man's body! I should be rejoicing. I do, yes – I rejoice. In what I have been given this night. Your kindness, your caring, your loveliness. I thank you, indeed." And he took her in his arms again.

Laughing a little, she pushed him from her. "Dear Alec, do not start it again! A goodnight to you, then. And to myself." And she turned for the door.

He went down with her, however, to her own room, where he let her go reluctantly.

In the morning, it was the sixty miles back to Stirling.

11

The council meeting was duly held, but without the Earl of Douglas, neither Dalkeith's nor the Black Knight's efforts at persuasion apparently effective. Indeed the meeting was not well attended at all, doubts over the future of the kingdom and personal loyalties and priorities apparently inhibiting counselling rather than encouraging it as might have been expected. But decisions were made, to the fair satisfaction of Crichton and Livingston, those unlikely allies, and a parliament was called for August. The Thane of Glamis did attend, so Alec saw his father.

He saw nothing of Agnes, however, that summer. He was sent on no missions to Edinburgh, and spent all his time with young James, being active, save for one brief visit to Strathmore with sundry papers for his father to scan and sign. He presumed that the queen was still at Dunbar.

His relationship with the king burgeoned into real friendship. James, at ten years, could scarcely be called a youth, but he was very advanced in person and spirit for his years, if not in learning and always in judgment. He made lively and challenging company, and although there were others who waited on him, apart from his despairing tutors, Alec was his principal and favoured companion, on most days the only one, apart from the inescapable escort to go with him outwith the fortress – and most of those summer months were spent largely in the saddle. Being Gentleman of the Bedchamber to James the Second was no mere formal appointment.

The king's hatred of his captors, Livingston and Crichton, was inevitably great, and grew by the month.

Alec often wondered how these two visualised their fates when their royal charge finally reached man's estate and took over the rule of his realm. They were hardly storing up a favoured future for themselves, he judged.

The parliament assembled at Stirling in due course, this occasion much better attended, and all agog to see whether the Earl of Douglas would present himself. He did not, although the Earl of Angus, the lord of Dalkeith and sundry others of the name did. It seemed that the great house was divided. Whether that was for the good of the kingdom or otherwise was a matter for debate.

Not that this parliament could directly debate it, with so many of the name present – and not only of the name itself, but of its associate lords. Douglas sons and daughters had for generations been marrying not only into the royal house but into some of the most distinguished families in the land.

The Chancellor started out discreetly, for him, by seeking to ensure that the bishops and senior clergy were firmly on his side; advisable after his displacing of Bishop Cameron in the chancellorship. He urged that Holy Church should be maintained by all in freedom and respect, and that the persons and property of all ministers of religion be protected, this on account of sundry recent and shameful assaults by unworthy lieges. Livingston promptly rose to turn that into a motion, which was duly seconded by the said Bishop of Glasgow, and passed unanimously, that prelate then declaring piously that Almighty God would reward all who so supported his heavenly kingdom here on earth, as well as His Grace's kingdom of Scotland. Still to create the required atmosphere in the assembly, Crichton next declared the council's concern that justice was not being upheld and administered adequately throughout the realm, to His Grace's officers' concern. He sought a motion to be put forward that all justiciars, sheriffs, lords of regality and provosts should sit in judgment in their various courts at least twice in a year, so that the common folk could be assured of their rights and safety being upheld. The Lord Borthwick so proposed and the Bishop of Aberdeen seconded. There was no contrary motion, despite the presence of not a few lords of regality and justiciars who had not held their courts with any regularity.

Livingston then rose to propose that, in order to reassure the people of the kingdom on this matter of justice being ensured for all, the king himself – and His Grace had agreed – should ride in person to the scene of any rebellion and misrule, there to see that the sheriff of the county, or other relevant officer of the law, did his duty suitably and promptly. Alec, from the gallery, wondered just what this move signified. It was the first that he had heard of it, James certainly not having mentioned it. But since Livingston had the monarch in his keeping, it would mean that man would be in a position to act in the royal name whenever he saw fit.

The Red Douglas, Earl of Angus, rose to ask why this should be necessary, and was informed that it was to emphasise the crown's desire that the ordinary folk should recognise that their sovereign-lord, although young, was concerned and exercised for their welfare. Somewhat doubtfully the motion was passed.

There were two or three other issues raised and dealt with before the real reason for this parliament came up – and even so it was raised heedfully and in sufficiently general terms, so as not to rouse the Douglases and their allies to outright opposition. It was that the peace of the realm was endangered by talk of English fears that the King of France might have interest in sending forces to Scotland, under the age-old terms of the Auld Alliance; and that parliament should make it clear that no such move was desired or acceptable in present circumstances, and the King of England so informed. Put that way, with the Earl of Douglas's name not mentioned, it was difficult to object to. Dalkeith rose to ask why the English should suspect any such French move, and was told by the

Chancellor that they had it from no less a source than the Papal Legate, recently come from Versailles. His Holiness in Rome was concerned that peace should prevail amongst the nations of Christendom.

This subtle answer precluded any overt Douglas opposition, and the assertion of the Scots non-requirement of French intervention, and the expression of goodwill towards England, was passed; and with it, if unexpressed, the assumption that those in power in the realm would be authorised to take all necessary steps to ensure that parliament's will was enforced.

Sundry appointments to office wound up the proceedings, including one or two, tactfully, for Douglases, the Earl of Angus being made justiciar of Lothian. The assembly broke up, James, bored with it all, glad to escape from his throne.

Sir Patrick Lyon told his son that he had a shrewd notion that what had been unsaid at this parliament of 1440 was more important than what had been said, Alec prepared to believe it.

It was not long thereafter before there were developments, however little they appeared, on the surface, to relate to parliamentary decisions. James was asked to sign an invitation to certain persons, not worded as a royal command but in fact practically that, including William, Earl of Douglas and David his brother, to attend a celebratory dinner at Edinburgh Castle in two weeks' time, to mark the monarch's tenth birthday – although that date was some way past – with the flattering assertion, in this instance, that the occasion would not be complete without the presence of his kinsmen, the Douglas brothers, heads of the most illustrious house in the land, the earl the esteemed commander of the armed forces of the crown. The king, who had never had such a festivity before, was delighted to sign. Alec wondered, in fact, since the dinner was to be held in Edinburgh Castle, not Stirling's, that the reason might be to get the boy into Crichton's keeping again; although in that case why would Livingston be thus supporting it?

It took ten days for a reply to come from Galloway. The Douglas brothers would attend His Grace's dinner, and bring suitable presents.

So it was for Edinburgh two days later, Livingston escorting the king in person, with a fine train, a highly unusual circumstance, Alec still wondering.

They found the capital, seemingly recovered from its visitation of the plague, all prepared for the occasion, the streets decorated with bunting and pine branches, crowds cheering, and Crichton there to greet them at the West Port and to conduct them through the Grassmarket and up the West Bow to the castle. The Douglases were not expected until the next day.

So James and Alec were back in their old quarters in the citadel, and there left to their own devices, all the display meantime over. The boy was looking forward to the morrow. After all, he was to be the principal character, was he not, a new experience for the King of Scots. His friend was not so sure, but did not say so.

The Douglas brothers made their arrival in style, with a large train, including Sir Malcolm Fleming of Cumbernauld and Biggar, their chamberlain, and Douglas of Cavers, their seneschal. They came to Crichton Castle, where the Chancellor met them, and led them to Edinburgh, where, there being no room for the numbers of their followers, these were left in the royal park below Arthur's Seat and Holyrood. As promised, the brothers brought gifts for the monarch, two magnificent Barbary mares, with saddlery and heraldic trappings, a gold and jewelled casket, and a battle-axe reputed to have belonged to Bruce's friend, the Good Sir James Douglas. Much was made of the presentation ceremony.

Earl William was notably youthful-looking to have gained the reputation he had, however splendidly attired and bearing himself determinedly proudly. His brother, at seventeen a year younger, was nervous-seeming and fidgety. They gave no impression of being a menace to the throne and cause of national apprehension. James got on well with them from the first meeting. He was delighted with the horses, and insisted on riding them in turn round the castle tourney-ground.

Alec noted that the distinguished company invited to the birthday dinner included no other Douglases.

When the time came to commence the feasting, all the lesser guests, including Alec, were required to take their places at the lengthy table in the banqueting-hall, and to remain standing. Then heralds led in the principals, the Douglas brothers, followed by Crichton and Livingston, and finally the Lord Lyon King of Arms ushering in the king, to a trumpet flourish, James grinning broadly. He was led to a throne-like chair between those of Crichton and Livingston, with the Douglases across the table, directly opposite. All could now sit.

The repast which followed was superb, quite the most ambitious Alec, or James himself, had ever sat at, course succeeding course, all to music from instrumentalists up in the minstrel gallery. There were soups, sea-fish, salmon and eels, swans' breasts, peacocks with tails spread, duck, venison, wild-boar ribs and oysters, sweetmeats already on the table. Throughout James talked animatedly with Earl William across the board, although Crichton sought to discourage this.

When the courses were at last finished and only the sweets and fruit remained before them, at a sign from a herald the musicians up in the gallery halted their tuneful accompaniment, and instead commenced a solemn rhythmic beat with a drum, very different. This went on for some time, and then, in at the hall door came a small procession, led by another herald, with two cooks bearing a huge platter on which sat a great black bull's head, steam rising from the mouth and nostrils and up between the horns. At the sight, all who recognised the significance of this development held their breaths.

Not so James Stewart. Staring, he clapped his hands,

exclaiming at the sight, while still the drum sounded its steady, solemn pulse as the heavy dish was placed on the table between the monarch and the young earl.

The drumming ceased, and apart from James's boyish applause there was silence in that hall. Then Crichton spoke.

"Your especial provender is before you, my lord! You have earned it!"

Clearly the Black Douglas knew what the bull's head purported, even if the king and his brother did not. It was for doom. He started up, pushing back his chair, eyes wide.

Livingston added his voice. "Treason!" he declared. "Highest treason! The throne menaced. His Grace's crown besought."

"No, no!" the earl got out. "Not . . . that!" He shook his head. "Never that."

His brother had now risen also, looking bewildered. "What? Will, what is this?" he wondered.

No one informed him.

"Lyon! Remove these two traitors hence, to await their trial and sentence." Alec looked startled at this command by Crichton, then realised that it was directed not at himself but at the Lord Lyon King of Arms. And as that dignitary moved forward, a guard of armed men came into the hall, to assist him. All had been most carefully timed and planned, evidently.

Most were on their feet now, as the two Douglases were roughly grasped and marched off, to James's cries of protest, the boy in a state of agitation, tugging at Crichton's arm and being shaken off.

Alec hurried round to the monarch's side.

Livingston sought to quieten his charge, declaring that this was all for the best, that treason had to be dealt with or the throne would fall, that these Douglases might well have had him slain in their bid for the crown.

Crichton glancing meaningfully at certain of the other guests at this birthday dinner, signed for Livingston to follow him out and to bring the king with him. Uninvited, Alec, seeing it as his duty, went with them.

There was no delay now. Straight into a nearby lesser hall Crichton led them, James reaching for Alec's hand and declaring that this was bad, bad. The Douglas brothers were therein, strictly guarded. A small number of the guests came in behind them, including the Lords Borthwick and Haliburton, these all selected members of the council of state. Crichton, very much in charge, waved the others into a semicircle facing the prisoners, the king still clinging to Alec.

"These, William and David Douglas, stand before us charged with sedition and highest treason," he asserted, without preamble. "They have declared that His Grace, here present, is not truly King of Scots, and that the elder, William, should be on the throne, the other his heir. They have sought foreign aid to support their shameful claims, and thereby endangered the realm, not least by raising the threat of English invasion. I say that they are guilty of misprision and perfidy in the highest degree, and represent a threat and menace to the nation as well as to His Grace. Does any here deny it?"

"I do! It is false, false!" the Earl William cried. "Lies! I only have stated that the crown *could* be mine. That in blood I am in direct succession. As none can contest. Here is no treason."

Crichton ignored him. "As Chancellor of the realm, I declare these here present of the council to be sufficient to see justice done, to serve as the required court. I so name it. Does any council member speak in favour of the accused?"

Only Livingston spoke. "None who is loyal to the King's Grace and this nation could so speak," he asserted.

Alec wished that his father, who was a councillor, had been present, for he himself could nowise speak up, having no status other than as Gentleman of the Bedchamber. The guests here had been carefully chosen.

None raised voice.

"I declare, then, that William Douglas, and David his brother, here before you, are guilty of treason in the highest degree." He pointed a finger at them both. "They must pay the due price! The penalty for treason is execution by the axe. In the name of the council, I so order. That they shall be taken from this place and so executed. And forthwith. This as required by the laws of the land."

"No! No!" That was James. The sequence of words spoken may not have meant much to him, but this of execution by the axe he did understand. "Not that. Do not kill them! No!"

Crichton flapped a hand at his sovereign-lord, and Livingston gripped the boy's shoulder.

"The sentence stands. See to it." That was to the Lord Lyon King of Arms.

"No!" James yelled. "Alec, stop them! Stop them!"

That man tried his best. "It is a royal command!" he exclaimed. "The king has said it. No execution."

"The king, while a minor, is represented by his council," Crichton said flatly. "In matters of state. As is this. Let sentence be carried out."

As the guards took the Douglases' arms to lead them out, James ran forward to clasp the earl's free arm. "It must not be!" he cried. "They must not do it." Tears in his eyes, he clung to the other, to the concern and confusion of the guards.

"Lyon, restrain him!" This time Crichton did speak to Alec. "Have him back, man!"

"I cannot . . . lay hands on the King's Grace!" That was desperate. "That also could be treason!"

James himself spared his friend that offence. He turned to fling himself upon the Chancellor, beating his fists on the man's chest. "No! No! No!" he cried.

The guards took the opportunity, and hurried the Douglases from the chamber.

Livingston turned to Alec, pointed at the king, and then at the other door peremptorily.

Alec saw nothing that he could usefully do better than

118

to obey. He went to the boy and took his arm, there in front of Crichton, and urged him away. Was this likewise *lese-majesté*? The boy, gulping back his sobs, allowed himself to be led out.

They went back to the royal apartments unhappily.

"Perhaps they will not kill them," James said. "Only to frighten them."

"I fear that they would not have contrived all that, and in front of so many, had they not intended to slay them. Freed, Douglas could raise ten thousand and more, to wipe out his fright."

"It is so wrong! Wicked. He was not against me, as they said. If they kill Douglas I will hate them, hate them both, for ever!"

"They have the power, meantime, Crichton and Livingston. And would keep it. That is why they are killing these two. No others in the land could bring so many against them. Save perhaps the Lord of the Isles, but he concerns himself only with the Highlands."

They heard later, from a servitor, that the Earl of Douglas and his brother had indeed been beheaded, there and then, in a back-court of the castle, the perpetrators watching. It had been no fright for those two youths – but it was for the nation.

What would happen now?

12

Crichton and Livingston had calculated shrewdly, however grimly. The great earldom of Douglas would pass to another, and its power none the less fearsome to them for the loss of those two brothers. Their heir would now wield it. But the heir was James the Gross, Earl of Avondale; and the two fortress-keepers knew it, and knew their man. James Douglas, great-uncle of the young victims, was their nearest in blood, and therefore the new Earl of Douglas, chief of the name. He had four sons in their early teens, but himself was a man in his sixties, if a man he could still be called. Reputedly weighing some thirty stone, he had been a handsome, indeed dashing character once, wed to a sister of the proud "High" St Clair, Earl of Orkney; but as he grew towards middle age, so had he grown and grown in size and girth and bulk until he had become a mountain of quivering lethargic flesh, why none knew. Now he existed, rather than lived, a corpulent, immobile hermit in Abercorn Castle, in Lothian, near to Queen Margaret's Ferry, his sons and daughters reared elsewhere. Such was now the head of the Douglas power. James the Gross would not avenge his grand-nephews – and *his* heir, and the other three sons, too young to lead the clan. The executioners had done their calculations.

Scotland resounded, of course, with the news of the appalling deed, the Black Dinner set to become a black mark indeed in the nation's history. But the fact remained. For the first time in centuries the house of Black Douglas was leaderless, and like to remain so for some time.

So, although there were rumblings and threatenings throughout the land, and calls for bloody vengeance, for a great rising and a coalition against the murderers, the Red Douglas, the Earl of Angus, with Dalkeith, the loudest of voice, nothing such eventuated immediately thereafter.

In fact, however desperate and uncertain the situation, it did have one redeeming factor for Alec Lyon, in that it provided him with an opportunity to see his Agnes. Crichton and Livingston, very aware of the dangers they had conjured up, took steps to amend it for their advantage. The latter sent for Alec one morning.

"Lyon, I have a mission for you to undertake," he said. "You have proved none so ill at acting the envoy. This is on behalf of the realm, from the Chancellor and myself. You are to go to the Earl of Angus at Tantallon Castle. Also to the king's mother at Dunbar. Queen Joanna first. I will give you letters to them both. Aye, the queen first. It is of importance. She will receive you, her son's attendant. This is to assure peace with England, a continuation of the truce between the two realms. She is well known to the King of England, kin indeed. He will heed her. She should write him, in her son's name, assuring him that Scotland is now secure from any ambitions of the Douglases, and any threat of French coming. You have it? She will do this, we believe. She is concerned, as are we, for peace between the kingdoms."

Alec inclined his head.

"There is talk," the other went on, "that she is seeking to arrange the marriages of some of her six daughters – or, leastways, their betrothals. This for suitable and worthy matches for the princesses, ever important. This could also work for the weal of Scotland. We desire that, in despite of the fall of the Douglases, no ill-will is offered to France. We want no French efforts to succour their Douglas friends, and using this as excuse to aid themselves against the English; ever they seek such. So, tell the queen-mother that we, the council, will aid her in any moves for the marriages of her daughters. To French husbands, even to the Dauphin himself, as has been spoken of. And to the son of the Duke of Bretagne. I will write it, but you to understand, if she questions you."

Alec drew a deep breath. "This is all too much! Too great a matter for such as myself."

"You are the king's closest companion. You are the son of the Thane of Glamis, whom the queen favours. And you are in, shall we say, friendship with the Chancellor's daughter, attendant on the princesses. You will serve."

What was he to say to that?

"There is more – this of Angus, the young Red Douglas. He is important in avoiding any Douglas uprising. Even though less in power than the Black. He is to be assured of the council's favour. If this was shown by having him marry into the royal house, one of the king's sisters, that would please him well, we judge. So I will suggest this also to Queen Joanna Beaufort. A match for another daughter – and she has plenty! She would agree that, I think. If she does, tell you Angus so."

"Why myself? The Earl of Angus does not know me."

"He knows your father, man. And you are of an age with him. And come from the king. Make not so many excuses! On the morrow, then, you will ride for Dunbar."

Alec went back to James with all this, his head in a whirl.

The king was not greatly interested, save to wish that he could go to Dunbar with his friend; only they both realised that this would never be permitted.

It was now mid-December, coming up for Yuletide, and the days at their shortest. There was frost on the ground for that long ride, but fortunately no snow, although the Highland mountains gleamed white. Alec made a start before sunrise. He had to follow the Forth estuary down all the way for some sixty miles, cold miles.

Arriving at Dunbar Castle with the sunset, having passed Tantallon on the way, he had to cross over the bridges and through the main keep before he could reach the further princesses' tower, so that he saw the

122

queen mother before he could reach Agnes. As always she received him kindly, a beautiful, calm and poised woman. She declared that it seemed long since they had last met, and with so much having happened in the land in the interim, dire doings indeed. Not that aught of it made great impact here at Dunbar, greatly concerned as she and her husband were; this castle was like some calm backwater in a turbulent river, where they only heard the rush of the waters, experiencing nothing of it all. She took Livingston's letter, but her interest was in hearing how her son was faring in all these troubled times; how she wished that she could see him. But they were as good, or ill, as prisoners here, under the man Hepburn of Hailes, governor here for Angus.

Leaving her to read her lengthy letter, without declaring that he himself knew of the contents, he went on in search of Agnes.

As usual, they fell into each other's arms, but only briefly. Getting her alone was difficult, and the greetings had to be of lower key than the man would have wished, until, on pretext of having a Christmas gift for him up in her room, Agnes managed their escape from the princesses.

Aloft, their embraces were more comprehensive and prolonged, Alec delighted to perceive that his love seemed to be almost as requiring of demonstration as was his own need. For a while expressions of their mutual ardour were physical rather than vocal.

Then a great spate of less than coherent chatter followed, with so much to be said to each other, not all of it by any means of realm-wide concern, or over the reasons for his present long-delayed visit. The man did get out the question as to how long now? How many months? She chided him that she had told him before; she would be twenty-one years in April. Had he forgotten? He had not, but the asking was in the nature of a reassurance.

They almost forgot the present-giving. It proved to be a pair of sheepskin wool-lined riding-gloves, which Agnes had fashioned and sewn, and had managed to enhance with a needlework design of the Lyon family motto, *In te Domine Speravi*, In Thee Lord I Put My Trust. Bearing these proudly, he reluctantly returned with her downstairs.

Alec considered the six princesses with rather different eyes now, with their future as brides for sundry great ones in mind. But he could scarcely refer to this subject in front of them; and he did not see Agnes alone again before he felt bound to return to the main keep for his interview.

The queen had her husband with her now, a man much frustrated, his marriage having made all but a prisoner of him, exiled from his great estates in Lorne of Argyll. As well that he and Joanna Beaufort were so evidently fond of each other.

"You know something of what Sir Alexander Livingston has written to me?" she asked Alec. "He says that you are going to visit the Earl of Angus hereafter."

"Yes, Your Grace. He has told me something of it. But I am only the messenger."

"Angus holds this castle meantime, of the crown," Sir James Stewart said. "Hepburn only its keeper, for him. But when he comes, he is sufficiently . . . friendly. An odd situation for him, we think, to be as good as our gaoler!"

"I judge that he is embarrassed," the queen said. "He is young, and mislikes the part he has to play."

"Does he require to play it, Your Grace?" Alec wondered. "He is the Red Douglas. I would have thought that he was powerful enough to refuse to act thus for Livingston and Crichton. To do their bidding."

"He did not agree with the late Earl of Douglas, nor yet with his father. Any more than with this new one, Avondale. The Red and Black Douglases do not always see eye to eye, however powerful. Like other families!" Such was Stewart, to whose own family that applied notably.

"I think that he is a little unsure of himself," the queen

went on. "He appears so, when he comes here. But the girls approve of him!"

That was the lead which Alec sought.

"Yes." Angus was not the only one unsure of himself and able to feel embarrassed. "This of a marriage, as is, I understand, suggested? Would Your Grace be prepared to consider such for one of your daughters?"

"Sir Alexander now urges it, yes. He says, for the good of the realm! Just why, I am unsure. But, yes – I would consider it." She half smiled. "Marriage, for princesses, is ever required, I fear. The trouble there, perchance, is which one! My daughters all appear to think highly of the Earl James. They see so few young men, to be sure. There might be some jealousy!" She shrugged. "And he might well make a better husband than some unknown French princelings!"

"Then I can so tell him, Your Grace?"

"Do so. Perhaps he will have his own other preference. Or, it may be, choose elsewhere."

"I think not, Highness. To marry into the royal house. And with such attractive a choice!"

"Ha, there speaks the courtier! But it may be that you are right. When here, he ever spends more time with my daughters than with myself! I wonder which he would select?"

"Jean, I would judge," Stewart said. "Leastways, she speaks of him most often."

"But she is the simplest, yet most outspoken."

"Does the earl have the choice of *six*?" Alec wondered.

"Ah, no. Margaret, the eldest, is suggested for the Dauphin of France. And Isabella to the son of the Duke of Bretagne. But the others . . ."

"The French, yes. This of keeping the French from offence, over the Douglas murders. And the English, therefore, also. This concerns the council, I am told. And Your Grace with influence in this difficult matter. Maintaining the balance, as it were. For Scotland's safety . . ."

"That is also in Sir Alexander's letter, yes. I shall do what I can. This of the marriages, or betrothals at least, should help with France. As for England, King Henry may heed me. He is less warlike than some of his advisers. I am left in no doubts, by your friends, that no daughter of mine should marry into the English royal house. They fear the age-old desire of England to take over the Scottish crown, and with some reason. And my son James has no closer heir than one of his sisters. How much this fear is justified at this time. I know not. But it is there, ever in your friends' minds."

"Highness, they are not my friends! I would have you to know it, if I may. I am but their messenger in this. Useful to them on occasion. I am the king's friend, if I may dare so to call myself, but not these others'."

"And yet you are the friend of the daughter of one of them, no?"

"That does not make me to love her father!" Alec wagged his head. "She mislikes much that her father does also, I know."

"Yes. It is difficult for her. We owe much to Agnes, an excellent young woman. We wish you and her well. But – this of England. Sir James and I have often spoken of it. And now, with this letter. See you, he has been shut up in this strange castle for months – no life for any man. I cannot go to London to see Henry, leaving my daughters. But he could go, see the king, and tell him of the situation and that England has nothing to fear now from your Auld Alliance. That is, if Sir Alexander Livingston and Agnes's father would permit it. That would be best. I cannot send him myself; this Hepburn would never let him go. He keeps us fast here. But if my lord of Angus was to urge and sanction it . . ."

"I would be gone but two weeks," Stewart put in.

"I can speak of that to the earl," Alec agreed. "He would, I think, require permission from the Chancellor."

"Yes. But if he recommends it, through yourself."

"Gaining one of the princesses in marriage, surely he would do that."

With the arrival of the girls and Agnes for the evening repast, it was all left at that.

Thereafter, another pleasant interlude was spent, with music and singing and dance after the meal, with Alec, when bedtime came, not pretending that he did not want to go off with the other young people, his concern with Agnes now apparently recognised by all. Indeed there were knowing glances and giggles coming from the royal sisters when goodnights were said at their respective doors.

Agnes shook her head over them, as she and Alec mounted the further stair. "I fear that they think of me now as, if not a fallen woman, one on the brink!" she said.

"Would that you were! Or perhaps . . . ?"

"Impatient one! Would you spoil the great day for us, with only four months to wait now?"

"Those months could be an eternity! *Will* be! Unless . . ."

"Unless what, Alec Lyon?"

"Unless you allow me some further foretaste of my bliss then! To savour, to cherish, as I wait!"

"You already have had something such, have you not? Last time . . ."

"Only enough to make me the more demanding, the more needful. You do not realise, lass, how enticing you are, how you draw me to your person, set me afire!"

"It is but my person, then? My woman's body only? Not me, myself, the being I am, the inner creature that is Agnes Crichton!"

They had paused outside her bedchamber door.

"No, no! Not that. You it is that I love, girl. But being near you rouses me. And it is always wait, wait . . ."

"Poor Alec! I scarcely see myself as so dire a creature!"

But this time she did not precede him up the stairs to his attic, but opened her own door, and entered without any goodnight gesture. He followed her within.

She went over to the fire which blazed welcomingly in every bedroom, beside the steaming water-tub. "Do not think that I am uncaring over the delay we must endure," she said, looking down into the flames. "Women have their needs also. I would but save our fulfilment for the day, or the night, when we have won the fullest right to it."

"No doubt you are right. But . . ."

"But, indeed, Alec my love. I shall be most fully yours, then. But I am yours now, yes. And so would prove." She took his hand. "A foretaste, you said? Then take it, lad, take it. So far as, as . . ." She did not finish that.

"I will also try to prove that I am not . . . beyond control! And that I believe that you are right in this. If you will help me." And he took her in his arms.

Even as they kissed his hands were busy, fondling, caressing, searching. But quickly his fingers concentrated on those buttons of her bodice, freeing them. Open, he bent to kiss what became available there, the division between the swelling of her bosom. But even so the hands were not idle, turning the bodice material back over her shoulders, she not hindering, indeed twisting one shoulder to aid in the process, and withdrawing one arm, then the other. The garment fell to the floor.

His lips returned to hers, but he was not finished lower. The slip that she wore was scanty at this level, and was readily made to slip indeed. It slid to her middle, where it was held by the skirt-waist, to hang. With a cry of sheer delight he held her away from him at arm's length, to gaze at her loveliness, there in the firelight, all above that waist now his to view, Agnes by no means shrinking nor using arms or hands to cover her full and shapely breasts, these stirring with her deep breathing.

As his eyes devoured her, words failing him, hers did not.

"I do not . . . disappoint?" she asked, voice as stirred as the rest of her.

As answer to that, he dropped down on his knees there before her, in a kind of worship, to kiss and kiss, tongue more active and eloquent than any words, she stroking his head the while. Then she too sank to her knees, to enclose him in her own arms, crooning and rocking him gently, pressing his face to her smooth swelling warmth.

So they settled there on the deerskin rug and fallen bodice before the fire, he alean against the heavy water-tub, she against him. Alec, schooling himself and his urgent desires, was able to relish the comfort and sheer bliss of it, as distinct from his more passionate responses, even though a hand did now and again stray down to stroke thigh and hip, covered as these remained.

For how long they continued thus, they knew not nor cared, there in the fire-glow with the waves crashing far below them. They spoke little, content – or almost so. It was that fire sinking to smouldering embers which brought them to recognise the passage of time, and eventually the young woman stirred in other than just affectionate reaction.

"Is it enough, Alec?" she wondered. "So good. So much of . . . promise! And joy to come." She gave a little laugh. "The washing water will be grown cold. Perhaps to our advantage!"

He did not let her go quite yet, even so. But presently they rose, and hand-in-hand she led him over to the door, still naked to the waist, her clothing trailing unheeded.

"My dear," she said. "The rest awaits you. But the love you have now, and for always. You may sleep with that, at least!"

He kissed her, unspeaking, and took the further stair.

In the morning, however brief his sleeping and inadequate his farewells, Alec was off northwards for Tantallon, ten miles with the great bay of Tynemouth to get round. That castle, although somewhat less extraordinary than Dunbar's was also highly unusual, crowning a lofty headland above the waves, in fact consisting principally of a single long and high battlemented wall cutting off the cliff-point, this incorporating storeys of chambers on its inner side, all but within the thickness of the walling, and with a great drum-tower keep in the middle and lesser towers at either end. A series of deep ditches and moats protected the approach; and within the walled-off area, spacious before the sheer drop to the sea, were lean-to buildings, chapel, laundry, barracks, stabling, storerooms and the like, and a deep well. Red Heart Douglas banners flew from all three towers.

Alec found James, third Earl of Angus, at a favourite pastime, fishing for rock-cod from an open window. This could be done only in calm weather or in a fairly gentle westerly breeze, for, facing due east, the long lines would be blown against the rock-face or otherwise made unmanageable, spray from the breakers far below blinding the fisherman. Alec was interested in this unusual procedure, which could be pursued at Dunbar Castle also and was glad to sit beside the earl, watching, while he disclosed his mission.

The other of a similar age to his own, was a slim but wide-shouldered young man of open countenance.

The visitor, who had debated with himself how best to put to the Red Douglas what he had to say, found that, with this of the fishing preoccupying the other, it was all easier than he had anticipated. Declaring that he would recommend this sport to the princesses at Dunbar Castle, where conditions were somewhat similar, it was a simple matter to go on to speak of their possible marriages, these for the realm's weal, and therefore the concern of the Chancellor and Livingston. Thus to the point: a bride for the Red Douglas.

The earl's reaction was sufficiently positive for him to pull up his line a little way and gaze at Alec. "Marriage? Mine? To one of the princesses? Myself?" he demanded. "Is it spoken of? Possible?"

"Queen Joanna says that it is. If you would so wish, my lord."

"This, this is a notable matter! A surprise. Aye, a surprise!"

"But a fair one, I would hope?"

"Which one?" That came out a little breathlessly.

"Not the Princess Margaret. Nor yet Isabella, my lord. These, I understand are all but promised otherwhere. To France. But . . ."

"Jean!" Angus said, without hesitation.

Alec heaved a sigh of relief. "That would be possible, I think. They all think well of you, I am told. But . . ."

"Jean is the best. I have been bidden by my kin to consider marriage. But have not done so, not yet. But Jean Stewart – yes! I would well consider that. She is pleasing. My father's mother was a princess – Mary, daughter of Robert the Third . . ." The earl was gabbling somewhat, clearly stirred, but of a sudden this was interrupted by a tugging at the line which he held over one hand and forearm. He had evidently let it sink again into the water. A catch! A catch! Less urgent matters were promptly thrust into abeyance.

Jerking his line strongly, to ensure that the baited hook became firmly fixed in the mouth of whatever tugged it, Angus had quite a task ahead of him. Rock-cod can be quite large fish, and by the strength of the pull this was no feeble specimen, in energy at least, probably in size, for it twisted and swung and wriggled vigorously as it was being hoisted, the line swaying this way and that, and now having to be held in both hands to control as well as to raise, for with all the lively movement it could get caught on projections of the cliff face. It took minutes to bring the heavy, flapping creature up to the open window for the earl proudly to display to his companion.

"Eight pounds if an ounce!" he announced. "That mallet," and he pointed to the tool for killing the catch.

Alec, handing it over, was duly impressed. He had never gone in for sea-fishing. Perhaps, once he had settled into Pitteadie, near the opposite coast, he could try his hand at it.

The hook extracted and rebaited, and the line let down again, they could resume their discussion. And now Alec

131

found it easy, the atmosphere having become propitious. He had no difficulty in gaining Angus's agreement that Sir James of Lorne should be sent to King Henry of England to assure that Scotland was posing no threat to that kingdom, with French help or otherwise. For his own part, he assured the earl that Livingston and the Chancellor would approve of the Red Douglas's help in furthering the realm's weal. And he took the opportunity to suggest that Angus had a word with Hepburn of Hailes that he should be less stern towards the hostages at Dunbar Castle, this being conceded readily enough.

There was one disappointment, however, a private one. Alec had hoped that he might make the information that the earl was happy to have one of the princesses as his betrothed as an excuse to return to Dunbar for further dalliance with Agnes. But Angus declared that he would now halt his fishing and go thither himself, to announce his satisfaction at the marriage suggestion, and indeed make the proposal forthwith to Jean Stewart and, of course, her mother. Alec, in the circumstances, felt that he could hardly propose to accompany the other on this personal errand. There was nothing for it but to head back for Stirling, mission accomplished, especially with Angus declaring that he would put his own ferry-boat, at the North Berwick harbour, at his visitor's disposal, to sail him and his mount up-Forth to Airth, near to Stirling, which would save him not a few hours of riding.

So the two young men rode out of Tantallon Castle to a friendly parting, the earl to head southwards his ten miles, Alec the mile or so to North Berwick, with the castle's steward, who would arrange the boat journey.

He hoped that the Chancellor would consider his mission a success and be the more kindly disposed as to his association with the daughter. Livingston he was less eager to please, despite the closer links, enforced as they were.

13

Alec would have sought leave to go home to Glamis for Yule, but King James pleaded with him not to go and leave him alone with those tutors of his, to spend a dull Christmastide. He could not refuse the boy, but he did seek to improve the situation by suggesting, not very hopefully, to Livingston that the young monarch should be allowed to visit his mother and sisters at Dunbar for the festive occasion – and was flatly refused, however large an escort might be ordered to go with him. So a less than merry Christmas was spent in the fortress, in no atmosphere of love and peace, at least for the two all-but prisoners.

The year 1441 started with upheavals, not amongst the nobility and landed folk, for once, but in Holy Church. The aged Bishop Wardlaw, of St Andrews, the Primate, incapacitated for years, had died; and Pope Eugenius appointed in his place, not the most senior cleric, Bishop Cameron of Glasgow, former Chancellor, but the youngest of the prelates, Bishop James Kennedy of Dunkeld – this to some heart-searching amongst his fellow clerics. Kennedy had royal blood, to be sure, and was related to some of the highest in the land, the Earl of Angus amongst them. His mother had been the Princess Mary, daughter of Robert the Third and former Countess of Angus, who, on her husband's death had married Kennedy of Dunure. This was her second son, so he was a cousin both of the king and of the Earl of Angus. He had been appointed Bishop of Dunkeld, at James the First's recommendation on taking holy orders, at the age of thirty-two; and now a few years later, he was primate – nepotism indeed. Yet apart from jealous prelates, all spoke well of him, an able and conscientious cleric, strong-minded but concerned for the wellbeing of the nation and its people. For years the primacy, the leadership of the Church, had been all but dormant, allowing quarrels and dispute amongst the bishops and abbots, of which Cameron had taken advantage. Now undoubtedly there would be changes. Alec wondered how this would affect Livingston and Crichton. After all, the captive monarch was Kennedy's nephew.

It did not take long for the new primate to make his weight felt. On his advice his friend the Pope – Kennedy had lived for some time in Florence, where he had become friendly with Eugenius – dismissed from their sees sundry troublesome and greedy prelates and appointed in their places the Primate's nominees, much worthier characters. Various failings and malpractices were amended, and neglected services, institutions and teachings revived – not without opposition and resentment. But Kennedy was a match for all clerical opponents, and his sway prevailed. Holy Church, so long enfeebled and corrupt, was set to become a power in the land, and, it seemed, a power for good. With the papal authority behind him, the Primate could make a major impact on state as well as religious affairs. The Vatican, on his soliciting, could pronounce excommunication on any individual, however lofty, and no excommunicate could take the oaths of office; even a monarch could not be crowned.

Sir Alexander Livingston, for one, was quickly made aware of the changing situation. Bishop Kennedy presenting himself at Stirling Castle to see his nephew, could not be forbidden, and soon had the young king approving of him; Alec Lyon also. James spilled his complaints to his uncle, whom he had never met before, as to the conditions under which he was held, and his hatred of both Livingston and Crichton. He was told that he must not hate; that was against the God of love's commands. But wrongs must be put right, and their perpetrators redirected. He would have a word with Sir Alexander.

That word was effective, for there followed notable improvements in conditions for James, and therefore for Alec also, in their quarters, the king's clothing, the servants who waited on him, and his freedom of action, even though armed escorts were still insisted upon outwith the fortress's perimeter. This freedom was demonstrated notably within a month of the Primate's calling, when an invitation arrived for James to visit his uncle at St Andrews in a week's time, and Livingston proclaiming no opposition. Here was improvement indeed.

James was greatly excited over the prospect of his first excursion, save ferrying as a captive between Edinburgh and Stirling, since his father's death. They would go well guarded, of course.

The great day arrived, and they set out for Fife, with an escort of two score, larger than usual, this probably Livingston's way of indicating to the bishop that he still held power over the monarch. Alec was keen to visit Pitteadie on their way, and although this was not on the shortest route to St Andrews from Stirling, the escort, seeing it all as something of a holiday, made no objections.

They rode by the Mar castle and township of Alloa, past the Bruce stronghold of Clackmannan, where Alec was able to point out the large standing stone erected in pre-Christian Pictish days in the worship of Mannan, the sea god, just why here, some way back from salt water, not known. Then on down Forth to Culross, where St Serf had reared the child of Thanea, who had become Kentigern or St Mungo, Glasgow's founder. They were into the western division of Fife here, known as Fothrif, young James agog at all that he saw, and expecting Alec to be able to tell him the significance of every feature and landmark, savouring this freedom to roam and gaze and question. His guide failed him frequently.

But not at Dunfermline, the capital of Fothrif, with its great abbey, one of the richest in the land, and the adjoining palace which James was told had been King

Malcolm Canmore's seat, and to which he had brought the renowned Margaret, queen and saint, and where were born three of James's predecessors on the throne, Edgar, Alexander the First and David the First, the palace presumably now the boy's own property. Alec had difficulty in getting his charge away from Dunfermline, after a meal provided by the abbot.

On by the port of Inverkeithing on its bay, the main trading centre, a prosperous place providing much of the wealth of Dunfermline Abbey, and beyond, by Dalgety and Donibristle and Aberdour and Burntisland, the last fishing havens, to Kinghorn, where the monarch was shown the cliff over which another of his predecessors, Alexander the Third, had ridden over on a dark night to his death, leaving no male heir and thus precipitating the Wars of Independence, with William Wallace and Robert the Bruce having to fight so long and bloodily for Scotland's freedom from Edward Longshanks's bid for English domination.

Pitteadie, only that mile inland, had to be only briefly inspected, for time was running out and there were still many miles to go to St Andrews. But Alec was proud to display his own little lordship to his liege-lord, and his hope that it was here he would bring Agnes Crichton as his wife before long, which had James questioning as to what was to become of *him* if his friend was dwelling here, and not at Stirling? To which he got no very definite answer.

The Durie family at the home farm, busy at the spring ploughing, were quite overawed to be presented to the King of Scots.

Thereafter it was all haste to get over the low hills, by Leslie and Falkland, another royal palace, into the Howe of Fife, its great central strath, and on eastwards by Letham and Cupar and Dairsie and so down to the coast again, the Norse Sea coast now, not the Forth, and into the religious metropolis of Scotland, a walled town above its large harbour, with its splendid cathedral,

136

bishop's castle-palace and more monastic institutions of the various orders and abbatial establishments and hospices than anywhere else in the kingdom, undoubtedly the realm's wealthiest location.

The master of it all, Bishop Kennedy, received his nephew kindly, although he frowned at the size of the escort, and wondered at the time it had taken for the journey from Stirling. The visitors were installed in the most handsome quarters it had ever been their lot to occupy, and an excellent feast of eatables likely to appeal to a boy provided, with acrobats, musicians and even a dancing bear to entertain him. James was quite overwhelmed with gratitude, admiration and esteem for his uncle. He was hard to get to sleep that night.

The next day Kennedy devoted entirely to the part entertainment, part education of his nephew, taking him round to see some proportion of what St Andrews had to offer, starting at the mighty St Regulus Cathedral. There he told the story of its founding far back in the ninth century by Angus mac Fergus, High King of Alba, as a shrine for the relic-bone of Saint Andrew himself, Simon Peter's brother and first-called of Christ's apostles, whom that monarch believed had saved his Albannach and Scots army from defeat by the Saxons, with his saltire cross of white cloud in the blue sky indicating divine intervention, Andrew thereafter being adopted as patron saint of the two kingdoms and his cross the national flag. James was even allowed to touch the fragment of finger-bone in its jewelled casket.

They went on to inspect the building work on the new college of St Salvator which Kennedy was founding as a seat of learning, the first such in the land, not only for clergy but for the nation, the boy more interested here in the construction craft than in the reasons for it, book-learning and the like never having been his preferred interest.

Next they were taken down to the harbour area, to inspect the warehouses of the largely Flemish merchants, to admire their imports of cloths and clothing and robes, their wines and cheeses and other eatables, their metal work and the rest; then the Scots exports of wool, salted meats and fish, salt itself by the sack, candles, hides, deerskins and suchlike, all contributing to the Church's wealth, the bishop pointing out how important this all was for the nation, with the nobility and gentry too foolishly proud to engage in trade. Alec duly took note.

They went aboard two of the vessels moored at the quays, to the boy's delight; indeed it was difficult to stop him exploring below and above decks, the latter even extending to a desire to climb the tarred ratlines and rigging of the masts, from which he had to be dissuaded.

Altogether they passed a busy and rewarding day, all quite new to James's experience, and giving him a valuable insight into much that a good monarch should know as to his people's lives, other than that of palaces and courts.

Another evening's entertainment and excellent eating followed.

At bedtime, Kennedy revealed to Alec that he had to go north over Tay the next day, to instal a new prior in an appendage of the great abbey of Arbroath. He would be gone for two days; but if his visitors desired to wait until he returned, they were very welcome.

Alec had been wondering how he might contrive a venture which had not failed to form itself in his mind. Livingston had announced no actual day for their return to Stirling, not to himself at least, although he might have done so to the leader of their escort. But now the chance presented itself. They were probably not expected back for two or three days yet. And Bishop Kennedy was sympathetic and understanding.

"Would it not, my lord Bishop, be a good opportunity for His Grace to go to visit his royal mother and sisters at Dunbar?" he asked. "He has not seen them for many months. Livingston would never allow it, I fear. But if we went from here, with your lordship's blessing, that would be different. May we do so?"

"Why, that would be an excellent move, my friend," he was told. "James should certainly see his family, quite wrong that he has been kept from them for so long. And his mother entitled to see her son frequently. Do that. When are you expected to return to Stirling?"

"Nothing was said as to that to me. Nor to the king. But the man Carruthers, who leads our guards, may have been given his orders."

"I will have a word with him. Go you tomorrow. It is unfortunate that you have so large a party with you. I could have sent you by sea, in a scow, to North Berwick or Dunbar havens, saving long riding. But I have not vessels which could carry forty horses. I myself will be using a scow to take me to Arbroath. A pity. It will take you two days to ride to Dunbar, using the Queen Margaret's Ferry across Forth. Bide you over the night at Dunfermline Abbey; I will send one of my people with you to inform the abbot, and he will see to your crossing of Forth. And, look you, as you pass Tantallon Castle, as you will do, call you in there to see my other nephew James, Earl of Angus. I understand that he is to wed the Princess Jean. Give him my congratulations. I have not seen him of late. Tell him, if he will bring his bride here to St Andrews, when the day comes, I will marry them, and gladly. It will not be without benefits if he now sees his kinsman and sovereign-lord James Stewart, in the by-going. Probably they have not met since the late king was slain. With the Douglas power now in the limp hands of Black James the Gross, it is time for the Red Douglas to take some grip of it, to the nation's good, I judge. Tell him so. Tell him to come and visit me."

Alec was much impressed by Scotland's new Primate. Next morning he and James were on their way south.

At Tantallon, the afternoon following, they had to wait for some time for Angus to return from visiting some of his sheep-runs in the Lammermuir Hills. When he arrived, it was to his astonishment to find his monarch being shown by Alec Lyon where the cliff-top fishing was pursued, with the younger James eager to try his hand at the sport. The two got on well from the start, and very quickly lines were out for a demonstration, this while Alec passed on Bishop James's messages and advice. There seemed to be a lot of Jameses on the scene – Stewart, Douglas and Kennedy.

They caught no fish in the short time available, to the king's disappointment, although Angus did get one bite, but despite his tug the hook was evidently insufficiently imbedded in the victim's mouth, for it fell back into the sea before it could be hoisted up.

With still ten miles to go to Dunbar, Alec thought that they should not delay longer, or they would not be in time for the evening meal there. The earl announced that he would come with them, as was only suitable, to see his bride-to-be over this of a St Andrews wedding by the Primate. Not to be outshone by Livingston's forty guards, the Red Douglas summoned his own escort of horsemen to accompany them. So it was quite a large contingent which bore down on Dunbar Castle that evening; and owing to the peculiar siting of that stronghold, with no accommodation for large numbers of horses, all these troopers had to be left down in the township to fare as best they might in the inns and taverns there, with only doubtful welcome. But the earl was master of all, so the situation had to be accepted.

The arrival of James Stewart at the castle was the occasion for much surprised rejoicing, quite overshadowing that of his two companions, even though they too received individual welcomes. Queen Joanna actually shed tears of affection over her son, and the princesses exclaimed over how he had grown – to the boy's embarrassment. In fact, much as he was glad to see them all, his attention was to some extent distracted by the extraordinary situation of the fortalice on its rock stacks, he hurrying from tower to tower exclaiming.

In the circumstances, Alec was unable to be alone with Agnes, although in all the excitements and chatter they did manage to stand aside together not infrequently, hold hands at their backs and murmur their own felicitations, she congratulating him on having achieved this forgathering.

At the repast, sitting beside her, he was able to inform her of the situation with Bishop Kennedy, and the distinctly more hopeful conditions they might look forward to. But of course the main thought in his mind, and he prayed in hers, was that it was now only a month until her coming of age, and what that signified. Four weeks . . . !

Angus, sitting beside Jean, was likewise preoccupied; and James, between his mother and eldest sister, was the one who did greatest justice to the meal. They were told that Sir James of Lorne had indeed gone to England to see King Henry, and was still away.

With the king having to share Alec's attic room for the night, there was still no opportunity for physical exchanges; but as they said goodnight at the young woman's door, Alec did mention Sir William Crichton. Agnes said that it would be good if he could somehow see her father soon, before mid-April. If he would give permission for the match, it would be so much better than any hurried secret marriage. Alec wondered whether seeing Sir William would be of any use, any advantage, with that man having but little cause to love him.

But in the morning, the girl managed to have a word with him as they awaited Angus at his saying his farewells and praises to the princess.

"The earl, Alec," she said urgently. "If you could have Angus to go with you to my father. Show him that you are friendly with him. And with his uncle, the bishop. My father and Livingston will wish for Red Douglas support. Indicate that you are seeking to aid in this. He would think well of that. And might look more favourably on you, I think."

"Would Angus go with me? And James? That Carruthers, of the escort, would never allow me to take the king to Edinburgh Castle in case your father held him there, gained control of him again. I cannot think that Livingston and he trust each other."

"No. But if you sent James on back to Stirling with his guards, you to follow later. They could not force you to stay with them. You are a free man, even if the king is not."

"It might serve. Worth the trying. If the earl will do it."

"He owes you something, does he not? And you are close to the king, whose sister he is to wed. He should feel for you, in *your* quest for a wife!"

"Perhaps . . ."

Goodbyes said, with Angus promising to come back and teach the princesses the art of cliff-top fishing, it was down to the town to collect the two escorts. On their way, Alec was not long in putting the proposal to the earl of coming with him to Edinburgh Castle, emphasising that his links with the new Primate could greatly aid King James, and the Douglas power help stabilise conditions in the realm. The other made no objections, indeed saying that he would be as well to meet Crichton, whom he had never spoken to, although he had seen him acting Chancellor. So it was agreed.

Angus kept his Douglas guards with him as they rode past Tantallon and proceeded on westwards towards Edinburgh. Passing in due course south of the city, by the Burgh Muir, it was the earl who spoke to the man Carruthers, telling him authoritatively that he and his friend were going to call on Sir William Crichton at the castle, and that the Stirling escort should take the king directly back to Sir Alexander Livingston, Alec meanwhile explaining to the somewhat alarmed monarch that all was well and that he would be rejoining him in the evening.

The boy had no wish to see Crichton, so he accepted his companion's assurance. The Stirling party did not contest the issue.

It was all as easy as that. How the interview with the Chancellor would go was another matter. Alec hoped that he was not away at Crichton Castle, or elsewhere.

At the citadel gatehouse the Earl of Angus announced that he required speech with the Chancellor of the realm, as was his right, and they were not long in gaining admittance. Brought to Crichton, he eyed them with his usual calculating gaze, both of them, but allowed his visitors to explain their presence. It was Alec who led off.

"Sir William, my lord Earl of Angus, who is to wed the king's sister, the Princess Jean, recognises that the nation requires an end to struggle and faction. Also that the new Earl of Douglas is a sick man. He, the Red Douglas, feels that he can aid in this, as representing the power of that great house. And his uncle, the new Bishop of St Andrews, so urges. As Chancellor, you, being chiefest minister of the crown, must be concerned for this likewise. My lord Earl wishes to assure you of his support in the necessary efforts towards uniting the realm for peace under its young monarch, peace here and peace also with England and France." Alec had been preparing that speech in his mind all the way from Dunbar.

"That is so," Angus added briefly.

"So-o-o! What is it that you require of me, my lord?" Crichton asked, although it was at Alec that he looked.

"Your understanding of my position, sir. My concern for the King's Grace. And my suggestion that you, the Chancellor, should call a parliament as soon as may be, this to seek to bring about the unity and peace required. It is the Primate's wish also, the Pope Eugenius likewise concerned." That last meaningful addition the two young men had decided upon as they rode.

Crichton did not fail to perceive the significance of that, all but threat, nor his awareness that they now had

143

a new force to be reckoned with on the Scottish scene, Bishop Kennedy, of royal lineage, strong views and with the might of the Vatican behind him.

"A parliament is perhaps advisable, my lord," he acceded cautiously.

"I accompanied His Grace to see his uncle, Bishop Kennedy," Alec added. "He is much exercised over the state of his royal nephew's realm, and would see . . . improvement."

"As would we all," Crichton jerked. "I heard that the king had gone to St Andrews." He looked from one to the other. "This visit, then, is to have me call a parliament? At the Primate's bidding."

"His and others, sir, including mine," Angus said.

"And Sir Alexander Livingston's?"

"He, no doubt, also had the nation's need in mind." That was the best that Alec could do.

"Very well. Douglas, I gather, will be well represented thereat! Unlike on some occasions!"

"If wed to the king's sister, I see my duty to seek to aid in the welfare and peace of His Grace's kingdom." That was in the nature of an assertion.

"To be sure. And when, my lord, is the wedding to be?"

"Shortly, sir. A parliament takes forty days to call. It will be before that, I deem. My uncle will marry us."

"Ah, yes. A notable occasion, no doubt."

Alec took his opportunity. "Sir William, on this of weddings. It is my wish, my very strong wish, to wed your daughter Agnes. Her wish also, that we wed. She sees little of you, in this coil. But . . . she would have your blessing on the marriage. As, sir, would I!" There it was, out.

Crichton considered him assessingly. "I wondered when it would come to this!" he said. "I have known of your concern with my daughter for long. Whether you, Lyon, would have been my choice for a goodson is not now so important for her, is it? For she is about to come of full age, I have not failed to note! Nor have you, I judge!"

Alec swallowed, but said nothing.

"So she wishes my agreement. But . . . !"

"We both do, sir."

"And if I said no, young man?"

"Then we . . . your Agnes would have to consider, sir. And, and decide."

"Decide, aye! That one was always headstrong! As you will discover! But . . . so . . . so be it. I will not contest her choice. But shall expect that my goodson does not work against me hereafter!"

"Then you consent to her marriage?"

"If I cannot stop her, what worth my not consenting? Yes, I agree the match. But treat you her well, sirrah. She is still my daughter."

"I will! I will! I shall greatly love and cherish her. I thank you!"

"Your thanks are scarcely to the point, young man. But I wish her well in it all."

After that, there was little more to be said, for any of them. Crichton was not a man for light and easy conversation. The two young men were not long in taking their departure.

When they in turn parted thereafter, down in the town, Angus eastwards, Alec to ride north, the former promised to go to Dunbar shortly and tell Agnes Crichton of the outcome, the latter saying to tell her that he would come and see her just so soon as he could contrive it; she would understand the difficulties.

Elated, Alec Lyon headed for Stirling, however much he would have preferred to be going in the other direction.

14

Livingston, well aware of the change in circumstances and the wisdom of tacking with the new wind, was prepared to allow another visit of the king to his mother after a comparatively brief interval, on the pretext of James having to give the royal approval of the marriage of his sister with Angus, together with the signing of sundry charters of royal lands to the earl as the Princess Jean's dowery.

So a mere ten days later, no more, it was back to Dunbar, with the king gleeful over this change in his fortunes, and his party of guards becoming quite happy with their duties and all but friendly. They called at Tantallon in the passing, and found Angus more than ready to accompany them onwards; he had been going to visit Dunbar the next day anyway, to make the vital marriage arrangements, for he was going to take his bride and her family to St Andrews the following week for the wedding. When Alec heard this, he did not fail to perceive opportunity.

"The family?" he demanded. "All of them? The queen and princesses?"

"To be sure. It will be a great occasion. Jean's mother and sisters must be there," the earl declared.

"And this will be allowed? They are as good as prisoners at Dunbar . . ."

"Allowed? I will allow it! None will stop me taking them, I promise you! They are in my charge, given by the council. Certainly neither Crichton nor Livingston will stop me."

"Then Agnes will go also? With her princesses."

"If so it is desired, yes. You will be there, with the King?" He turned to James, at their side. "You, Sire, will attend your royal sister's wedding?"

"Yes – oh, yes. That will be so good. I have never been at a wedding. What do we do?"

"Your Grace will give your sister to the bridegroom – myself. If you will be so kind, since she lacks a father. Before the bishop, in the church."

"How do I do that?"

"Just a gesture. A wave of the hand will serve. A token of assent."

Alec was seeing the possibilities. "Then, then *we* could be wed also! Agnes and myself. Not at the same time. Or by the Primate. But there at St Andrews. While we are both there anyway. Could that be? A wonderful opportunity! Two weddings!"

"Why not? Yes, that would be the way for it. My uncle – our uncle, for he is Your Grace's also – would, I think, wed you, Alec." They were on first-name terms by now. "You are the king's attendant. His Gentleman of the Bedchamber."

"Not us at a royal wedding, no. Not at the same time. That would not do. But thereabouts. Some other priest would do it. If Agnes will agree to this. And I think that she will."

"I would come to your wedding also!" James declared. "I would like that."

In high spirits the trio rode on, no Douglas escort being called for this time.

At Dunbar, similar satisfaction prevailed over the proposed arrangements. Agnes had no hesitation in agreeing to a quiet wedding at St Andrews, quite reconciled to none of her family being present. She had an elder sister who was married to the Earl of Huntly, up in Aberdeenshire, whom she had not seen in years. She would wed perfectly satisfactorily on her own! She did not require anyone to give her away, did she? For her father would not be there, that was certain.

"I can give you, can I not?" James, listening, said. "If I can do it for Jean. Could I do that?"

"You are the king, and can do anything for any of your people. You are the father of the nation!" Angus asserted.

Their sovereign-lord clapped his hands.

So it was settled. St Andrews in six days' time, the Eve of St Mark. It would be the first time that the queen and her daughters had been out of Dunbar Castle, for any distance, for months. The Black Knight of Lorne had returned from England, his embassage seemingly successful, and he would accompany them and act groomsman for Angus.

That night, the fact that there was no chance for loving gestures could be put up with; having waited this long, they could wait six days more.

On the Eve of St Mark, 24th April, Alec took the king to Fife, to find that the Dunbar party had already arrived at the castle-palace of St Andrews, and all dispositions being made. Bishop Kennedy would gladly marry Agnes and Alec the next day, just prior to the royal wedding, so that the pair could attend the second ceremony as husband and wife. The king could practise his giving-away role at the first, in the forenoon, and then the greater affair would take place in the afternoon.

In accordance with age-old custom, the brides' and grooms' parties did not occupy the same premises for the previous night. So Angus and Alec were allocated rooms in the house of one of the Primate's officials nearby, while the royal family, with Agnes, stayed in the bishop's castle. A splendid feast was provided for all before they parted, however, Kennedy proving an excellent host. Very significant goodnights were said thereafter between the couples, Alec given instructions to be at the northern side chapel of the Cathedral of St Regulas by eleven of the clock, Angus assuring that he would accompany him.

In the morning, clad in his best, such as it was, he and the earl presented themselves in good time at the great church, much impressed by its splendour. One of the bishop's chaplains was awaiting them, to conduct them to a robing-room off one of the aisles where, to goblets of wine, they were advised as to the order of procedure, and assured that he, the chaplain, would be on hand to guide them throughout. They were left to wait.

Presently they heard the singing of a choir, and soon some commotion nearby, and what was clearly the king's voice upraised and excited.

It took some time for the chaplain to return, now in alb and chasuble over his black cassock, to lead them out into the side chapel. There they found the queen and princesses and Stewart of Lorne sitting, Alec much gratified that all the royal family had come to attend this lesser nuptials, a token of their esteem for Agnes. They all smiled to the pair as the chaplain led them forward to the step up to the little chancel. This aisle-side chapel was not large enough for any choir, and the choristers were singing in the main cathedral nave beyond the pillars, instrumentalists accompanying them. This was to be no hole-in-corner wedding, despite comparison with the next one.

At a sign from the chaplain the choir changed its singing to a more rhythmic chant, and out across the cathedral paced the Primate, mitred and in full canonicals, attended by a couple of acolytes. He came to bow before the altar, and turned to face the little congregation, raising both hands in a sort of blessing.

The chaplain signed for all to rise, and then went off, to return with the king and Agnes, she holding the boy's arm rather than he hers. He clearly considered that their guide was walking too slowly, and the young woman restrained him. They were brought up to stand beside the groom and groomsman, James grinning at Alec.

That man had eyes only for Agnes. She was looking very lovely, flushed but nowise appearing nervous, clad in white silk trimmed with gold braid, having a long tight bodice and sleeves with a trailing edge, the skirt full, and wearing a lace coif over her dark hair. With eyebrows raised at Alec, she guided James to stand between them.

The watchers sat and the Primate commenced the service.

It was commendably brief, prolonged wedding rites being but little to most participants' taste, they usually scarcely in full awareness of what was being said and done, Alec certainly not on this occasion, his thoughts less than concentrated or coherent, his glances at the bride, over the royal head, being as frequent as at the celebrant. That is, until the time came for action, and Bishop Kennedy asked who gave this woman to be wife to this man.

James, jogged by Agnes, burst out with, "I do!" and turned to push her bodily at her chosen one, laughing, and looking back down the chapel to see the impact on his family.

Then it was Angus's turn, to produce the ring, and also to draw the king over to stand at his far side, the boy obviously doubtful as to what to do now.

Alec managed the ring exchange and fitting without the dreaded dropping of it, Agnes squeezing his hand in the process. The ring, in fact, had been furnished by the earl, Alec not being supplied with the like. It was on the large side for the young woman's slender finger, but she held it secure. Then the great moment, as the celebrant declared them man and wife, and Alec's heart leapt within him. She was his now, his until death did them part, and thereafter beyond.

That recognition got him through the brief remainder of the service, and the benediction – there was no nuptial mass, that to be shared with the second couple in the afternoon – and Alec found himself leading Agnes, arm-in-arm now, James at his other side, down to the congratulations of the company, the monarch demanding to know if he had played his part well. The choir resumed its singing, in triumphant fashion now, competing with the chatter of six princesses. Alec, longing only to get his bride to himself, sought to behave suitably, but was distracted by the dimples in her cheeks, which seemed deeper and more provocative than ever.

But there was to be no privacy yet. Clearly the bridal pair were expected to return to the castle with the others, in preparation for the royal wedding, no doubt also some sort of meal first, Agnes apparently still with her duties towards the sisters. The new husband and the bridegroom-to-be found themselves at something of a loose end – not what might have been looked for in the circumstances.

For want of better employment they went for a walk together down to the harbour, to fill in the time, a sense of anticlimax upon Alec Lyon.

However, back at table, with Kennedy in his avuncular role now, and complimenting Agnes, changed now out of her bridal wear, on her looks, behaviour and even her choice of husband, he felt better, especially when she found opportunity to run light fingers over his thigh as they sat together. He whispered to her, amidst all the talk, as to how soon they could decently get away after the next ceremony? He was determined to take her to his own house of Pitteadie for that night, if at all possible, a thirty-five-mile ride. She murmured that there was bound to be a bridal feast after the wedding, and they could not go before that. But soon thereafter, and they would be on their own at last. It would be worth the waiting for, she assured.

Alec seemed to have had to do a deal of waiting, one way or another.

So presently they all trooped back to the cathedral, the Princess Jean now the centre of attraction, Angus and Alec together again, and feeling all but superfluous. Were bridegrooms always thus at marriages, the males a mere required appendage at a female occasion?

This time the service was held in the main nave and chancel of the vast church, the choir reinforced and quite a congregation assembled, mainly clerics, to see the king's sister wed. The groom and Alec went back into the same robing-room as before, roles reversed, with the same chaplain acting as guide and adviser. They waited, shaking heads over it all.

When at length they were conducted out into the nave, it was to find all more or less as before, save in scale, more people, louder and more varied music, longer waiting and, when the Primate appeared, it was with a train of richly robed ecclesiastics. Agnes, Alec noted, was now sitting alone towards the rear. But in essence it all developed into a rerun of the earlier ceremony. Alec, prejudiced to be sure, decided that Jean Stewart, quite bonny and more splendidly gowned, did not compare with Agnes Crichton as a bride; but her groom looked as though he found no fault. King James was displaying entire confidence. He strolled up with his sister, eyeing all around as though this was all of his own devising, even though the vivid red flush of his cheeks, which on occasion caused some to call him Fiery Face when he was excited, was more in evidence.

The service proceeded, this somewhat longer because of intervals of singing and chants and extra prayers, but basically the same, the monarch giving the bride away with an exaggerated flourish, and she giggling a little. When it came to Alec producing another ring from the Tantallon jewellery chest, the earl fumbled a little with it, to another giggle, but got it safely in place, as Bishop Kennedy blessed the circlet and she who now wore it. Then Angus uttered the required promises of taking and holding, of honouring, and of sharing worldly goods.

The announcement that those whom God had joined together let no man put asunder was greeted with relief, Alec however wondering how this did not seem to apply to the Pope in Rome, since he appeared to be able to pronounce marriages invalid. Not that he was likely to do so in this case.

There followed a triumphal singing, and then the brief nuptial mass for the principal participants, which included Agnes and Alec, and the general benediction. Then it was all congratulations.

It was all over. There was but the wedding feast, and then . . .

They had a word with the queen and their host beforehand, Alec explaining his desire to spend their first night together in his own new house, but that this meant over three hours' riding to get to Pitteadie. It was accepted understandingly, and agreed that they should slip away quietly after they had partaken sufficiently of the provision, Agnes assuring that she would return to her duties with the princesses, at Dunbar, in a few days' time. It was not so easy informing James, who wanted Alec back at the earliest. His uncle promised to keep the boy, and therefore his escort, for, say, four days, whereupon Alec should come for him to take him back to Stirling; longer would be difficult for the Primate, for he had to pay an official visit to his old diocese of Dunkeld to instal a deputy there for his successor – which all meant that Alec would have only two days with Agnes at Pitteadie before taking her to Dunbar. Having royal appointments had disadvantages as well as privileges. However, what must be, must – and meantime, bliss! Or so they anticipated . . .

With the banquet only half over, and Alec worried over the time, during a musical interval they rose from the table, and bowing and curtsying towards the king, his mother and Bishop Kennedy, they made their escape. It was late afternoon, all but evening, but there ought to be four hours of daylight yet. Alec hoped that the Durie wife and daughter had carried out his instructions adequately, and made the little unused castle comfortable, at least the hall, kitchen and principal bedchamber, especially the last, with good blankets, linen and warming-pan. Agnes told him not to fret; she was perfectly capable of domestic functions, as he would discover.

They rode westwards into the sinking sun, man and wife.

*　　*　　*

153

That sun had set, but it was scarcely dusk when they reached Pitteadie, Alec relieved to see smoke rising from three of the chimneys. They found Mary Durie and her daughter Peg in the kitchen, with one of the sons, awaiting them, with a meal prepared, the young man to look after the horses. After the day's eating at St Andrews the bridal couple had little appetite for more food, but they had to make some acknowledgment of the kindly provision, the wine giving them most appreciation. When the Duries took their farewell, belatedly as far as Alec was concerned, they were barely out of the door when he arose and took Agnes into his arms.

"At last! At last! Mine! Mine, my beloved! Aye, and I yours!"

"We have been that for long, have we not, foolish one?" she reminded. "In our hearts, if not in, in . . ."

"I have wanted more than just that," he declared. "Blessed as it was. Is that so ill a need? You are so desirable, so, so alluring, so provoking, woman! In this tempting person of yours!" And he ran urgent hands over her. "Do you blame me?"

"No," she said. "I would have it so." That was the simplest invitation.

He did not fail to take it as such, and pulled her towards the hall's door and the stairway.

Halfway up, however, he paused. "Forgive me," he got out. "You would be alone? Have some privacy? For a little. Before, before . . . ?" That took not a little effort to suggest.

"Perhaps it would be best, yes," she acceded, smiling, and patting his cheek. "Not long. I will call down," she promised.

Shaking his head, in something of turmoil, he turned and went back. Anyway, he had forgotten to blow out the hall candles.

Urgent as he was, Alec had no cause for complaint. Agnes was as good as her word. His pacing of the hall was soon ended by a melodious summons from above. He all but ran up those twisting steps.

154

The bedroom door stood open, and he burst in – to halt abruptly. There in the warm glow of the firelight and candles, she stood awaiting him, completely naked, a sight to take any man's breath away, loveliness itself, in sheerest beckoning form. And even as he stared, she held out her arms.

His emotions choking him, he went to her. And arms still out, she came to meet him.

Coming together, they clung to each other. And now her hands and lips were as busy as his own, stroking, pressing, exploring, her shapely rounded person moving enticingly against his own, kissing ardently, murmuring as she did so.

Alec was so overcome with joy, desire and wonder as to render him for the moment scarcely so assertive as might have been, his wits like his feelings in riot, the sheer delight of her warm, curvaceous and mobile body in his grasp, the urgency of her lips, the scent of her even, and above all the realisation that she was eager, evidently as eager as he was, affecting him tellingly.

But his lack of assertion did not last for long. Schooling his wayward hands, he picked her up bodily and strode with her to the large four-poster bed; holding her thus his face was buried between those softly heaving breasts, she running her fingers through his hair the while. Setting her down on the blankets, he sank to his knees, to start kissing where he had not reached previously, downwards, over her belly and the dark triangle at her groin, to the long firm thighs and smooth calves and wriggling toes. Having got that far, he commenced the return journey, lips by no means wearying.

Nor was Agnes inactive, leaning over to unbutton his doublet, and slipping a hand within the neck of his shirt and feeling down to the hairs of his chest.

All this soon had him rising to his feet, to commence to tear off his clothing, she assisting in this also, getting up off the bed to do so more effectively, and laughing mirthfully as their haste got him entangled with his breeches fallen about his ankles and all but falling upon her as he tried to step out of them, this pushing her back on to the bed. As naked as she was, he stood before her.

Alec had not said a word throughout, however eloquent his actions had been, unlike his more declamatory wife.

Her acclaim was nowise inactive however. She reached out to him and in a single involved but purposeful movement pulled him over on top of her as she sank back on the blankets, on top of them not under them, long legs wide, he panting now, his need as urgent clearly as was hers.

They became one indeed, then, she taking him into her, with thereafter a gasp compounded both of brief pain and blessed consummation, he groaning his response in possessive satisfaction.

After that it was all fulfilment, and swiftly so for both, a minimum of vehement activity required. After all, they had both waited long for this. Even as the man came to final triumphant, masculine achievement, he was aware of another kind of joy, that his woman was equally liberated while yet enthralled. Who and what was he to deserve this?

They lay, holding each other in a kind of rapture rather than contentment, speaking but little. It had been worth the waiting for, to be sure.

It was not long, however, before the man's hands began to stray again, with all that delight so close, so available at last, so demanding indeed. Nor was he rejected, Agnes quite frankly responding in kind, to his own further gratification. And those responses of hers were effective, sufficiently so, for in remarkably short time he was all but ready for further developments of their joint appreciation, and she, perceiving it, considerably aided the process by rolling herself over on top of him in loving ardour and invitation.

His reaction was all that could have been hoped for. Moaning her joy, ecstasy, she received him to her again, active in her contribution to their mutual fusion into togetherness.

This time they were the less hurried and the more rewarded still by the depth and worth of their passion, discovering each other with an intimacy neither could have anticipated or even imagined before.

For how long they maintained their coalition of zestful felicity they did not know, for time did not apply in this experience. But when at length the woman uttered a cry of sheerest gratification, and convulsed her body in his arms, Alec knew and reached the height of masculine attainment, and allowed himself to join her in the abandonment of climax and accomplishment.

When presently she rolled herself off him limply, she summoned up just enough energy to kiss his cheek in a more chaste salute.

"My love!" she murmured. "My own and dear love! We are . . . truly one, now! One!"

His hand did all the answering necessary.

He was almost asleep some indefinite time later when he was roused by Agnes's pressure again – on this occasion for ablutionary rather than amatory exercise.

"Let us be clean, at least," she said, almost guiltily. "To wash! The water will scarcely be warm now. But I must wash, see you." And she drew aside the blanketing and rose, to go and light a candle from what remained of the fire.

Alec was less immaculately inclined perhaps, but at least he enjoyed watching the washing process, even if he yawned. He decided that the least that he could do now, was to offer to dry his wife's back, and other parts while he was at it. So he forced himself upright, to provide his services, his first experience of aiding in feminine ablutions. He suffered a fairly cursory wash himself before returning to bed.

Some minor and sleepy love-play followed, but slumber won the night fairly soon.

St Mark's Day had been their day also.

*　　*　　*

They were late in rising in the morning, with Agnes proving her assertion that she was competent in matters domestic by rising first and disappearing downstairs, in only a bedrobe, to revive the kitchen fire's glowing embers, get water heating and a breakfast of sorts prepared. Alec was duly appreciative of this, as of all else.

That day, well pleased with each other, they explored the Pitteadie property and the area surrounding, something Alec had not done in any detail previously, but he avoided any contacts with their lairdly neighbours, having no desire to share these halcyon days with others. They did not have to call the Duries, however, for the women of the family presented themselves early at the castle, to provide services required, the man arriving later to offer any help suitable.

In their roaming around, the couple decided that Fife was a pleasing county to live in, although how much of their time they would be able to pass at Pitteadie remained to be seen, both very much aware that theirs could not be the normal married life of consorting, at least for the foreseeable future, with their duties to monarch and princesses precluding that. Alec wondered whether there could be any possibility of James and his mother and sisters resuming family living, at Stirling or elsewhere, and so allowing themselves to serve together; but Agnes said that the queen's hatred of Livingston almost certainly precluded any return to his custody; and that man would never release his grip on young James unless he was forced to. Their only hope was that Bishop Kennedy might attain sufficient power and authority to improve the royal situation further, indeed get the king out of Livingston's grasp, yet not into Crichton's. Until then their time together would inevitably be less than they would wish, they feared, erratic and patchy. James, it was evident, would never allow his friend and attendant to leave his service, his royal command meaning something between them at least; and Agnes believed that the same would apply to her duties with the royal girls.

The possibility of the pair of them settling down as laird and lady of Pitteadie seemed remote. But they had known that all along. They would contrive as many contacts as they possibly could, that went without saying.

This awareness made their so brief stay at their new home the more precious and to be savoured to the full, and this they achieved, for the next day they would have to be off to Dunbar, if Alec was to collect the king the day following at St Andrews, as the Primate had instructed. That night was a delight and excitement of new discoveries and appreciations of each other's persons and potentialities, the sleeping being fairly intermittent. Alec had not realised that women could be so deliciously challenging.

So in the morning it was farewell to the Duries and riding for Queen Margaret's Ferry, to win across Forth into Lothian, and east again for Dunbar. They would call in at Tantallon, to see if their fellow newly weds had returned there. Agnes still felt some responsibility for the new countess-princess.

They did find the Anguses at home, and happy with each other; happy also, it transpired, to accompany them onwards to Dunbar, for Jean to see mother and sisters. As they went, they did not exactly exchange notes as to married bliss, but did not fail to indicate mutual satisfaction.

Their reception at the stacks-top castle was as lively as it was welcoming, the five unwed sisters agog to hear details from Jean, and not uninterested in Agnes's experiences also. The young men were eyed assessingly, especially by Queen Joanna and the Black Knight. Even Hepburn of Hailes came to pay his respects, a man not usually forthcoming.

That third night together continued the Lyon couple's education and voyage of discovery, whatever it did to the Anguses'. They were all too well aware that it might well be some time before the process could be recommenced

The parting in the morning was dire inevitably, and made only slightly the more bearable by Angus's offer of his sea-going scow to take Alec by water all the way from North Berwick to St Andrews, this allowing him to delay his departure for an hour or two.

Back to duty, then.

PART TWO

15

Thanks to Bishop Kennedy, as they had hoped, the situation improved for members of the royal family, and therefore for Alec and Agnes Lyon. Oddly enough, troubles at the Vatican itself aided in this, especially increasing the Primate's power and influence. A schism developed in the papacy, a faction amongst the cardinals rebelling against Eugenius and setting up, at Basle, Amadeus, Duke of Savoy, as Pope Felix the Fifth. A majority at Rome itself supported Eugenius, but a number of important states favoured Felix, for political reasons. So there was now the scandal of two Popes. This had its impact on Scotland, and Kennedy, for Eugenius, seeking to strengthen his position, sent special nuncios to various lands, one not unexpectedly to his friend in Scotland. This was one Bishop William Croyser, a Scot himself from Rome, and with him two aides named Turnbull and Lithgow. These were to remain with Kennedy more or less permanently, not just on any visit, but to counter efforts by Felix from Basle. They took up residence at St Andrews, and greatly enhanced Kennedy's position. To have a papal nuncio as his constant support was as highly advantageous as it was unusual.

So the Church in what Eugenius was calling his loyalest northern kingdom was very much in the ascendant, and its Primate in a position to exert major weight and sway. His nephew King James was a primary beneficiary. He was to have much greater freedom at his castle of Stirling, Livingston being left in no doubt. And with Queen Joanna and the princesses in the care of his other nephew Angus, at Dunbar, with Hepburn dismissed, conditions there were likewise bettered. Now James was allowed to visit his family frequently, which of course meant joy for Alex and Agnes.

Indeed just three weeks after their marriage, one such opportunity occurred. This was the arrival of envoys from France to interview and more or less inspect the Princess Isabella as bride for Francis de Montfort, heir to the Duke of Bretagne, this match mooted for some time. It was considered important that the King of Scots should meet these envoys, so it was back to Dunbar for Alec, and for a three-day visit.

Perhaps such intervals between their cohabitation actually had the effect of making their comings together the more exciting and stimulating? The pair certainly made the most of them.

The Frenchmen brought satisfactory assurances and conditions, also gifts, and themselves went away satisfied. Isabella was the quietest of the family, but very pretty. She would go to Brittany in the autumn. The envoys would also report back to the King of France regarding the other daughters of Joanna as to an alternative wife for his heir the dauphin.

Bishop Kennedy came to see James twice that summer, leaving Livingston suitably aware as to what was expected of him. Surprisingly little was heard of Crichton, at Edinburgh. He certainly did not come to see his son-in-law, nor indeed visited his daughter either. The nation was undergoing an interval of blessed peace.

Young James celebrated his eleventh birthday with a visit to Dunbar.

Then there was a development which, although not in itself sensational, had its possible significance for the realm. James the Gross, Earl of Douglas, died. Few, if any, would miss him probably, even his widow; but it meant that there was now a new head to the house of Douglas, his eighteen year-old son William, known to be of a lively and vehement character. Under the Red Douglas, Angus, that great and potent line had been lying more or less quiescent; but now he would be superseded, who knew with what results?

Not a few anticipated trouble. After all, the new earl could claim to be heir to King James through lines of descent, the Douglases having made a habit in the past of marrying into the royal house of Stewart.

Bishop Kennedy, himself kin to the Black Douglas as well as to the Red, saw the possibilities not only of trouble but also of opportunity for good. He had King James summon the new Earl William to Stirling Castle, and went there himself to meet him. Angus was invited also.

Alec Lyon was much impressed by William Douglas, not least in that he came without any great train of his men, indeed with two of his brothers and a very small group. He was good-looking, personable, and obviously a young man to be reckoned with, Black Douglas or none. In fact, Alec liked him, as did James Stewart, who got on well with him from the start; indeed Alec thought that he saw a certain similarity of character and outlook between these two cousins, much more so than between the monarch and the less assertive Angus. With Kennedy himself, they made a fascinating group of kinsmen.

What the Primate and the new Earl of Douglas discussed in private was not disclosed, but the visit certainly gave the impression of being amicable and successful, however sour Livingston's attitude. That man undoubtedly saw his own power and status on the wane. It looked as though Kennedy was preparing to promote the Douglas cause, which could mark the end of his own and Crichton's dominance of the kingdom's affairs.

Thereafter, Earl William was quite a constant visitor to Stirling Castle. He took the king hunting in the Tor Wood, the Flanders Moss and the Ochil Hills, Alec in attendance; also, to be sure, Livingston's armed escort. And once James took him to see his mother and sisters, to Alec's satisfaction.

The Princess Isabella departed for France, her mother

and elder sister Margaret, with the Black Knight also, Angus and Agnes left in charge of the remaining unwed four.

Later in that year of 1443 a parliament was held, a strange and rather special parliament, this not called by the Chancellor, Crichton, but by the king himself, on the advice of the Primate; this because Crichton was no longer in a position to call it. For Kennedy had convinced a majority of the council to proclaim that man as unfit to be Chancellor, for having in the past abducted the monarch and held him prisoner in Edinburgh Castle, and for having presided over that grievous Black Dinner there and, with others, engineered the unlawful and shameful execution of the sixth Earl of Douglas and his brother. The summons to that parliament was as good as a writing on the wall.

Crichton did not appear.

Alec, up in the minstrel gallery, watched it all, a well-attended gathering, with a notable number of Douglases present, James on the throne, flanked by the hereditary officers of state, the High Constable, the Earl Marischal and Lyon King of Arms. Livingston occupied a comparatively lowly position in the hall.

The Primate opened the assembly with prayer, and then, with no one presiding at the Chancellor's table, called on Lindsay, Bishop of Aberdeen, to chair the further proceedings. That rubicund prelate went to the table, took up the gavel, banged it, and declared that, His Grace the King permitting, he would declare this parliament in session.

James shouted yes, and all could sit.

Bishop Lindsay was not long in coming to the point. With Sir William Crichton demoted from the position of Chancellor and chief minister, it was necessary for parliament to appoint a new incumbent to the office. The Privy Council had agreed that the most suitable candidate should be the Primate himself, the Lord Bishop of St Andrews. He so proposed to the assembly.

From the earls' benches, William Douglas jumped up to second that, Angus beside him adding his support.

Was there any contrary motion, or alternative nominee? the other bishop asked.

In the circumstances, it would have been a brave man who so moved. None did so.

Bishop Lindsay declared Kennedy Chancellor of the realm, bowed to him and handed over that symbol of office, the handsome gavel, and returned to the bishops' benches.

His replacement at the table turned to bow to the king, who clapped his hands.

James Kennedy faced the company as the most powerful man in the land, head of Holy Church and chief minister of the crown. Seldom indeed had the two appointments coincided. None there could be in any doubt as to the significance of the situation.

The new Chancellor tapped the gavel, and thanked the king and the assembly for the confidence they all had placed in his hands, of questionable worthiness for the responsibility, and assured them that he would endeavour with all that was in him to fill the notable and demanding office to the best of his abilities and to the accord of his conscience, before God and man. And he asked for the support of all leal and honest men in the kingdom.

Removing a paper from a pocket in his robe, he resumed. "The first business of this parliament, I conceive, is to require the former Chancellor, Sir William Crichton, to yield up to the king forthwith the castle of Edinburgh, of which he has been keeper, as he is unworthy to hold that royal fortress. Is this agreed?"

"I so propose." To Alec's surprise, that was Sir Patrick Lyon's voice. He had not noticed his father being present below the gallery. It was long since he had seen him.

Douglas of Dalkeith seconded.

No amendments were forthcoming. That was simple enough, but carrying the resolution into effect might well be less so.

Kennedy nodded. "Next, it seems right and wise to propose that the office of lieutenant-general of the realm, vacant since the slaying of the sixth Earl of Douglas, should be filled. It seems also wise, prudent, that William, eighth Earl of Douglas, be appointed to this important position of commander of the armed forces of the crown, he having the greatest manpower in the land at his disposal, as well as being all but hereditary in his family. Also he being in kinship to His Grace. Does any so move?"

"I do." Alec was the further interested to hear his father's voice again upraised. This was notable. Was he now thinking to take some greater part in the rule of the realm than in the past? Did he see opportunity for the furtherance of wellbeing now, support for Kennedy? Had the Primate and he been in touch? The Thane of Glamis had lain fairly low on the national scene, other than that of Strathmore and the province of Angus, since the murder of the late king, for whom he had acted hostage in England for three years.

Bishop Tulloch of Ross seconded.

"Any contrary motion?"

Once again, opposition would have demanded courage and strong convictions. None was forthcoming.

Earl William rose, bowed to the throne, to the Chancellor, and turned around, nodded to the assembly, and sat down. Douglas and Kennedy were now most evidently the power in the land, at least in theory.

Alec wondered whether Livingston was sitting down there, tense, thinking that he might well be next to be singled out, and scarcely favourably. Was he to be dismissed from the keepership of Stirling? Or would that have the effect of reviving his association with his rival Crichton, creating a very formidable and dangerous alliance at this stage?

Such was not proposed then, at any rate. A succession of appointments was put forward, some from the Chancellor, others from the benches, most accepted without debate, including a number of Douglas nominations, and, Alec was intrigued to hear, Sir Patrick Lyon, Thane of Glamis, as Justiciar of the Regalities of Kincardine and the Mearns. It looked as though his sire and Kennedy had come to an understanding.

When the more humdrum but necessary parliamentary business had been dealt with, and the session prorogued, Alec had to go to attend on the king; but he soon sought leave to go in search of his father, and discovered that he was closeted with the Primate and the Earls of Douglas and Angus, this confirming his conjecture that there had been some sort of pact arranged between them. He could not, of course, intrude on such deliberations, but was able to greet his parent when presently he emerged.

"I was going to look for you, Alec," Sir Patrick greeted him. "I have been hearing much of you, at a remove. But last night, from my lord of Angus, and the good bishop, who wed you both. They appear to approve of you!" He patted his son's shoulder. "How goes your married life, lad?"

"Well – well, indeed! Notably. Save in that we do not see each other sufficiently. Agnes is tied to the princesses, and I to the king. But . . ."

"You must have known that before you wed. But it will not concern you for overlong, I think, with the princesses getting married off. And your service with young James will stand you in good stead one day."

"I enjoy my attendance on him, Father. And he needs someone who is not in Livingston's pocket. He hates that man!"

"Aye, no doubt. But I fear that he will have to put up with him for some little time yet. Bishop Kennedy cannot afford to make an enemy of both Crichton and Livingston at the same time, see you. But give us time, and we shall spare His Grace Livingston's company, I think!"

"You are now working closely with the bishop? What moved you to that, Father?"

"I admire him greatly. I have known him long. And conceived it my duty to the king. I was his father's friend, and owe his son my caring as well as my due loyalty. And I conceive of him requiring it, of us all."

"Yes. He is in need, and deserving, a strange boy, all but a youth now, growing fast. He has been reared without a friend almost, since his father died. He needs friendship. Headstrong, suspecting all, which is not to be wondered at. But with warmth in him, also. And he sees me as a friend. I must hold to him, not fail him."

"Do that, lad. I stood captive three long years for his father, when you were a child. Hostage. You spare a year or two more for the son."

"Yes. This of you being made justiciar? Is this to your wish?"

"It is something that I can do, yes. Something of worth in the realm."

They left it at that, parting with good wishes for Alec's mother, brothers and sister; the last, he was interested to learn, had become betrothed to a Highland chieftain, Robertson of Struan. He promised to bring his Agnes to see them all at Glamis just so soon as it was possible.

It was back to duty – but a duty with its satisfactions. And the future looked brighter undoubtedly for them all – all, that is, who sought the peace and goodwill of the land.

16

That peace was not long in being upset, whatever the wellbeing at large. Sir William Crichton saw to that. A year later he ignored parliament's demand that he should resign the keepership of Edinburgh Castle, and refused to yield up that fortress. This could not be accepted, of course, and the new lieutenant-general was responsible for seeing that it was not. The Black Douglas did not temporise in this, the first call upon his services – he was not that way inclined. He mustered a sizeable force and marched on Edinburgh, to require the submission of the citadel; and when this was ignored, laid siege to it.

Such action was correct and approved, and in normal circumstances would no doubt have sufficed. But the circumstances here were scarcely normal. Edinburgh Castle was all but impregnable, save against very heavy artillery, and itself boasted the heaviest and most powerful cannon in the land. And Crichton had not failed to lay in a large stock of provisioning for the garrison, the citadel having its own deep well. Siegery was less than effective.

Douglas, to be sure, sent for such cannon as he could lay hands on, all the way from his castle of Threave in Galloway, and from elsewhere. But once these arrived, it was quickly made evident that they were less than adequate. Their first salvos were answered by the resounding crash of much larger and deadlier pieces, which shook the city and caused a hasty withdrawal of the Douglas guns out of range, one of these being smashed and its team decimated. The fortress's lofty rock-top site meant that effective bombardment was only feasible from due east, by the approach from the city, and here the longer range of Crichton's artillery made it impossible. Cannon could not be fired from amongst tall, close-set housing; and Crichton was not the man to worry if his own shot damaged the said buildings. It was stalemate.

The Douglas did not just give up, needless to say. He established a more or less permanent encircling force to sit and wait, much to the resentment of the citizenry. Time must tell in the end, he reckoned.

Meanwhile, although the nation waited on the outcome tensely, elsewhere a kind of peace prevailed, Kennedy's firm hand telling at the helm – save in the remoter Highlands and Hebrides where the Earl of Ross, Lord of the Isles, was intent on extending his sway.

Queen Joanna came back from France, and minus both daughters, for as well as seeing Isabella wed in Brittany, she had concluded the betrothal of the other, Margaret, and the dauphin. It had been decided to bring forward the actual marriage to take place while the mother was there in France. So Margaret Stewart was to be the next Queen of France.

That left three unwed daughters. King James was permitted now to visit them frequently, so Alec saw quite a lot of his wife.

St Andrews also became a quite frequent destination for the monarch and attendant, for the Primate was anxious to see much of his nephew, and as Chancellor often required the royal signature and seal on edicts, charters and the like; and with all his ecclesiastical duties to see to also, it was much more sensible and convenient for young James to visit his uncle than for Kennedy to come to Stirling – and much preferred by the king. In fact, now the boy was no longer Livingston's prisoner, the latter retaining the style of keeper of Stirling Castle, the principal seat of the monarchy, but no longer keeper of the sovereign's person.

James revelled in his comparative freedom, even though the Primate also insisted that he should always ride abroad with an armed escort.

So 1444 passed into 1445, and still Crichton held out in his citadel. Douglas took his revenge by destroying Barnton Castle, west of Edinburgh, the seat of Crichton's cousin, Sir George, Sheriff of Linlithgow; and when that did not produce the desired result, sent Forrester of Corstorphine to demolish Crichton Castle itself, Agnes's old home. Nor did this solve the Edinburgh problem. The situation was a major drawback and impediment for the new regime, so evident to all that parliament and government were powerless in this matter.

Young James demanded to know why they could not manufacture more powerful cannon of their own which could outdo those in Edinburgh Castle. It had to be explained to him that no one in Scotland had the knowledge, expertise and facilities to construct such great pieces. Flanders and the Netherlands were where the wrought iron necessary for the like was available. The boy did not accept that. When *he* was in command of his kingdom . . . !

There came sad news from Dunbar. Queen Joanna was sick. Whether or not she had contracted some sort of infection in France, as was suggested, she had become very unwell, and seemed to be making no betterment. This did have the effect of letting Alec see more of Agnes, for James visited his mother oftener, but that was scant cause for satisfaction, especially as each time they saw the queen she was looking thinner and more wan, even haggard. The physicians shook their heads over her.

Agnes said that Joanna accepted that she was going to die, and did not dread to do so. What she was concerned over was her three unmarried daughters. She would wish to see their futures assured before she went. Marriage for princesses was something that could not be left to chance or personal choice, for linkage with the royal house had to be carefully considered always. Bishop Kennedy was the queen's adviser in this, he too becoming a frequent visitor at Dunbar.

Some of Joanna's concern for her daughters was partly

eased by the arrival of a Flemish ship at Dunbar harbour, bearing the Lord of Campvere. He was the heir of the Duke of Burgundy, whom the queen had met in France, and who was interested, or his father was, in a suitable royal marriage. At Stirling, the first they heard of this was when the young man turned up there in person, to seek the king's permission to wed his sister – Mary, it seemed, being his choice. He spoke little or no English, so converse had to be in French, at which James was less than expert and Alec only a little more fluent. So the little-used tutors had to be called in. He seemed to be an agreeable character, and the king found no fault, whatever his sister thought. At Alec's suggestion, he urged the suitor to go on to St Andrews to gain the Primate's confirmation. Kennedy would be a good French speaker, and a good judge also.

So, all being well, that left only Eleanor and Annabella unmatched.

The Earl of Angus thought that his far-out kinsman, the young Douglas of Dalkeith, could be doing with a wife. He liked him, and would sound him out.

Queen Joanna died in June, and was buried beside her first husband at the Charterhouse of Perth. There was a notable funeral, at which, with the royal family and the Primate, who conducted the service, Alec met Agnes once more; and with Kennedy taking the king and his three sisters to St Andrews for a brief spell, Alec seized the opportunity to ask if he might take his wife to Glamis, to visit his family and old home. This was readily granted, the Primate offering to let him use his own vessel, known as the Bishop's Barge, to sail them across Tay to Dundee and so save many miles of riding.

So it was Strathmore for the Lyons, and a very happy occasion for all, his people much taken with Agnes. Two nights of bliss, and then it was back to duty for them both. Sir Patrick revealed that Kennedy, as Chancellor, was to advise the king to create him a lord of parliament. So he would become Lord Glamis, and Alec, his heir, the Master thereof. Agnes wondered whether that would make her the Mistress of Glamis, despite being married to him!

The following month there took place a most extraordinary development on the national scene. The siege of Edinburgh Castle still went on and had, in fact, become something of a farce. The young Earl of Douglas was humiliated, his first task as lieutenant-general made to look feeble indeed, and himself ridiculous. Yet the situation remained dangerous. It was believed that food was being hoisted up the precipitous castle rock-face by night, using ropes; and although the besiegers, who had become all but settlers in the city, sent out patrols around the rock's perimeter, nothing of the sort was seen or intercepted; after all, the circuit of the said rock extended to well over a mile, the Nor' Loch intervening and providing possible supplying by boat or raft.

Douglas did not waste his time conducting this prolonged siege in person. But the embarrassment and chagrin of his ineffectual efforts were ever with him, and did his reputation, and that of the Chancellor's administration, no good. The royal fortress remained in Crichton's hands.

In the end, it was decided that this could not go on, enough harm done. And yet the besiegers could not just pack up and steal away. Some climbdown was inevitable – but not that. It was Bishop Kennedy, on a visit to Stirling who told James what had most reluctantly been decided, and the king had to be informed, since it involved his royal signature. Edinburgh Castle must be restored to royal keeping. And to achieve that, Crichton had to be bought out, as it were, chastening and expedient as this must be. Crichton was to be offered a full pardon, if he surrendered the fortress, and not only that, further inducement by being allotted an honour. He would be made a lord of parliament if he would yield.

Alec, for one, was astonished. And James declared that he would never sign such appointment; he hated the man, just as he hated Livingston. But patiently Kennedy explained that, such as it was, the rule and governance of the kingdom on occasion demanded such sacrifices and manoeuvres, the lesser evil accepted in order to avoid the greater. Edinburgh was the greatest city of the realm, and its castle dominated it. The present situation could not be allowed to continue. The ennobling of Sir William Crichton was a price worth paying for its surrender.

James, with bad grace, signed the paper. He signed another one for Sir Patrick Lyon at the same time, with more satisfaction.

The Earl of Douglas would by no means treat with Crichton over this humbling transaction, so Kennedy asked the Earl of Angus to do the negotiating, a somewhat less proud Douglas. And Crichton agreed without over-much debate. No doubt he himself was not a little weary of being shut up in the citadel, on scanty provision, for so long. At any rate, he and his garrison marched out that July of 1445, and Edinburgh Castle was freed from his grip after many a long year.

The new Lord Crichton was faced with the task of rebuilding his own castle of Crichton, which Douglas had wrecked. Meanwhile he went to reside at his kinsman's house of Sanquhar in faraway Dumfries-shire. Not that anyone thought that he would bury himself there for long.

William Douglas licked the wounds to his esteem.

17

The two new lords, Crichton and Glamis, had opportunity to attend as such at a parliament at Stirling that autumn, sitting nearby on the lords' benches behind the earls, where Douglas and Angus carefully avoided any acknowledgement of the presence of the first, while warmly greeting the second.

Crichton, however, was not long in asserting himself and his new authority when, after Kennedy as Chancellor had announced the proposed sequence of business for the session, he rose to introduce the first motion, and to reveal, if that was necessary, that he had a long memory, and that old sores might be covered up for a time but did not always heal.

"Sire, and my lord Chancellor," he began, in that gravelly voice of his. "I have recently been aquitted and absolved of an offence against Your Grace, on holding you secure in Edinburgh Castle, when in fact I was saving your royal person from those who would use you for their own ends and advantage, first amongst these Sir Alexander Livingston, keeper of this castle of Stirling." And he turned and gestured scornfully towards that man, his ancient rival and enemy, who sat behind amongst the commissioners of the shires. "I was charged with unlawful holding of His Grace's person, dismissed from the chancellorship, and finally beleaguered in the said Edinburgh Castle. Livingston, however did gain the charge and custody of you, Sire, in this hold, and still does so. I claim before this parliament that this is not only contrary to all justice but is an offence against the monarch and his parliament. I therefore move that Sir

Alexander Livingston be pronounced rebel, dismissed from the keepership of this castle, and tried for treason." He sat down.

There was a profound silence in that hall, as men stared at each other, until the Lord Borthwick, beside Crichton, rose to second the motion.

Then exclamation, talk and debate broke out, James half rising from his throne in excitement, and continued for some time until Kennedy, clearly as surprised as most others, banged his gavel for quiet.

"I have the Lord Crichton's motion, duly seconded," he declared, even-voiced. "Is there any contrary motion?"

"I move to the contrary." The Earl of Crawford, known as the Tiger Earl, or Beardie, a fierce character who had frequently co-operated with Livingston, announced. "This Crichton is a rogue and a perjured turncoat. He should not be sitting in this parliament. I move that he be dismissed from this session."

"That is a new motion, however unsuitable, my lord," the Chancellor ruled. "I sought any contrary motion to that of Lord Crichton's."

"I so move," the Lord Hamilton said. "Crichton's accusation is false. And Sir Alexander has been the king's protector these many years. The motion is calumny and envy."

"I second." That was Hepburn of Hailes, a friend of Livingston.

Up in the gallery the new Master of Glamis, almost as aroused as was his liege-lord, sought to assess the situation. When put to the vote, how would it go? Both Crichton and Livingston had their allies and enemies. But how would the majority present see it, the many lords temporal and spiritual, officers of state, commissioners of the shires and provosts of royal burghs, who had no axes to grind for either?

Alec's wondering was all but brought to an end, and by none other than William, Earl of Douglas. He rose to announce to the assembly that he conceived the Lord

Crichton's motion to be fair, wise and for the good of His Grace and the realm. He sat down.

Angus voiced his agreement.

Again the hall resounded with outcry and comment. The great house of Douglas had chosen its course, despite its humiliation over the Edinburgh siege – or perhaps because of it? Did this signify a realignment of interests, a making of the best of ill circumstances, an accord with an enemy who had won a contest? It looked rather like it. At any rate, it was likely to clinch the issue, settle Livingston's fate. Few there would wish openly to counter the Douglases.

The Chancellor, seeking to seem suitably neutral, called the vote.

There was little need for actual counting. Clearly there was a large majority against Livingston. Amidst shouting and clamour the thing was done. The Lord High Constable was instructed to remove Sir Alexander Livingston from the hall and keep him secure in suitable accommodation until parliament's further decisions were duly implemented.

So fell one of the king's objects of hatred.

Suddenly, then, all was changed, for the king, his sisters and for Alec and Agnes, indeed in some measure for the realm itself. Stirling Castle was no longer to be a prison, any more than was Edinburgh. Robert Erskine, Earl of Mar, married to a sister of the Black Knight, was appointed keeper, but by no means keeper of the king. James was free to live there, or elsewhere, as he would. His unwed sisters could do the same, and promptly left Dunbar to return to their old quarters at Stirling, and of course Agnes with them. So now the Master of Glamis and his wife could live together as a married couple should. And all because of her father's bargaining.

Livingston was duly tried by a court of the council, presided over by the Chancellor, and although condemned to death for treason against the royal person, on Kennedy's recommendation the sentence was commuted to banishment to his own house and area, permanently, removal from all national affairs, and a forfeiture of the vast wealth he had amassed through the control of the royal lands and revenues – to the great benefit of the kingdom's treasury. Thankful to escape execution, he retired to private life, unlike Crichton, who made no secret of the fact that he intended to continue to play his part on the nation's stage.

Kennedy and Douglas were now in full and firm control of Scotland, the former as good as regent for his nephew, although he did not call himself that, Primate and Chancellor being quite sufficient for him. Apart from the rampaging of the Earl of Ross in the Western Highlands and Isles, there was peace in the land in general, although some inveterate trouble-makers did cause minor upsets, but on their local scenes, such as the Tiger Earl of Crawford, who constituted something of a headache for his area's justiciar, the Lord Glamis.

Alec found the quality of life now so improved as to be scarcely believable, not only because of Agnes's constant presence – and she proving herself a wife to cherish indeed – but James also the better company. He was growing fast, and taking full advantage of his new freedom, eager to roam the countryside and show himself to his people, as well as indulging in his pastimes of hunting, hawking, fishing and archery. So his Gentleman of the Bedchamber greatly benefited also; his sisters likewise, even though the youth was apt to be scornful of their abilities in some of his activities.

An especial source of gratification was James's interest in the royal hunting-seat of Falkland, in Fife, long neglected, and which Bishop Kennedy permitted him to have repaired and refurbished, indeed sometimes visiting there himself, for it was none so far from St. Andrews. And even nearer to Pitteadie, to Alec's further satisfaction. So all the refurbishment was not confined to Falkland, and the Lyons' little castle began to take on the atmosphere of a home. In fact, Agnes and the princesses on occasion lodged there while the menfolk were at their hunting at Falkland.

The king was also seeing much of the Earl of Douglas, who was cutting an ever-widening swathe on the national scene, indeed so much as to begin to worry Bishop Kennedy. For he got James to create his brother Hugh Earl of Ormond, a completely new title, Ormond being no more than a hill on the Black Isle of Ross. Also to agree to another brother, Archibald, who had married the younger daughter of the late Earl of Moray, becoming the new earl thereof, although she had an elder sister married to Agnes's brother James Crichton. And a third brother made Lord Balvenie. So now the Douglases had four earldoms, if Angus was included, as well as two new lordships to add to others, Dalkeith and Balvenie, giving them a notably powerful voice in any parliament. Moreover, Earl William himself had just married the heiress of the earl murdered at the Black Dinner, the Fair Maid of Galloway, a noted beauty, which brought him an enormous increase in wealth and manpower, practically all of Wigtownshire and Kirkcudbrightshire and much of Dumfries-shire, which he had not held already. Small wonder that the Primate feared that the lieutenant-general was becoming so powerful as to be able, if so he wished, all but to impose his will on the nation. And his mother's brother, the Earl of Orkney, had great influence in the north.

The king's sixteenth birthday, celebrated at St Andrews, was a very splendid occasion, organised by the Primate, the Douglases there in force, the new Lord of Dalkeith paying particular attention to the Princess Annabella. Kennedy confided in his other nephew, Angus, that he was a little concerned over all this concentration of might and sway in the Black Douglas's hands. A word in the Earl William's ear might be advisable.

As it happened, however, that power and sway was the cause of praise and congratulation in the realm shortly thereafter, rather than fears. For the Auld Enemy, England, long quiescent, suddenly stirred and bared her teeth towards Scotland. The reasons for this were strange, but the effect grievous, ominous. The English monarch, Henry the Sixth, was young, sickly and on occasion none so far from imbecility. As a consequence his ducal kinsmen of the houses of York, Lancaster and Gloucester were rivalling each other in their manoeuvrings as to who should exert control of, and possibly take over, the throne. And Richard, Duke of York conceived the strategy of using Scotland to further his cause and to embarrass Lancaster, who was for negotiating a peace with France, this by a token invasion of the northern kingdom, which would automatically bring the Auld Alliance arrangement into play, with France and Scotland aiding each other against English aggressiveness – a complicated machination. At any rate, the Earls of Northumberland and Salisbury, English Wardens of the East and West Marches of the Border, simultaneously, at York's behest, invaded Scotland, Northumberland winning as far north as Dunbar, which he burned – not the castle on its stacks but the town and harbour, and sundry shipping therein – and Salisbury ravaging the town of Dumfries, in the west.

Douglas, the lieutenant-general, acted, and swiftly; after all, Dumfries was in his own bailiwick, as it were, and Dunbar the Red Douglas's. He mustered his great strength, and on both flanks drove the invaders back over the border, and had them followed some considerable way thereafter, as far as Alnwick and Warkworth, where two quite major battles were fought, the Scots winning both.

The land rang with praise for Douglas – even though this scarcely soothed Kennedy's unease.

The King was delighted, and declared to all that he wished that he had been there, at the fighting.

The King of France reacted suitably, breaking off negotiations with the Duke of Lancaster, and assuring the Scots that he was prepared to help with arms and ships if further assaults took place. He also suggested that the Auld Alliance would be usefully strengthened, and the

English warned, if a French match for King James was to be arranged. In his seventeenth year, was it not time that he was considering marriage?

The King of Scots was duly appreciative, his interest in womankind having become evident of late.

The Primate's reaction to all this took the nation by surprise, the king and Alec Lyon no less than others. He decided that, whether he himself liked it or not, there was only one man in the kingdom who was of sufficient experience, determination and ability to help limit the overweening power of Douglas, and who had reason to wish to do so; and that was William, Lord Crichton, elderly as he was now. To the astonishment of all, Kennedy announced his resignation of the chancellorship, and recommended that Crichton should be chief minister in his place.

James, for the first time, was furious with his uncle, his dislike of his former gaoler still intense. But, although his marriage was now being considered, he was not yet of age, and he could not forbid the appointment. Why not his friend, the Earl of Douglas? he demanded. Kennedy asserted that Douglas was already much too powerful for the good of the kingdom, where a balance had to be kept amongst the greater nobility. Douglas's might and riches were now much more impressive than were the crown's – and he was a descendant of Robert the Second!

Sullenly James signed the edict appointing the Lord Crichton to be Chancellor of the realm once more.

Alec wondered whether in this the wise Bishop Kennedy had acted wisely. Many wondered the same.

What would Douglas do now?

18

Strangely, William Douglas did nothing, at least not immediately, although his inactivity went so far as to fail to attend the parliament called to instal the Lord Crichton as Chancellor and deal with the English-French situation, this a year later. No single Douglas lord was present, save for Angus, so it was a deliberate abstaining and snub, and, since the parliament was called in the king's name, a slight to James Stewart.

Out of that ill-attended parliament there came an unexpected development. If the Duke of York succeeded to the English throne, or displaced the young Henry, as seemed more than possible, his animosity towards Scotland might well result in all-out war. Therefore the French connection was recognised as the more important, the strengthening of the Auld Alliance the more necessary. This must be put into effect, not only in general understanding but in detailed arrangements, requiring a shrewd and authoritative embassage to go to the French king. And it could be suitably signalised by arranging the betrothal of the King of Scots to a worthy French bride. Sadly the Princess Margaret, young wife of the dauphin, had died suddenly, the cause unexplained, so that link had snapped. A courier was to be sent to Versailles to inform King Charles there that the Chancellor himself would come to deal with these important matters, so soon as it was convenient for that monarch.

James was not happy with this choice of envoy, Crichton almost the last person he would wish to select a wife for him. But Kennedy pointed out that it had to be a very highly placed emissary who went, and as well as being

Chancellor, Crichton was the most experienced and able functionary in the land. Douglas, James's choice, was much too young and unskilled in negotiations to be the ambassador, however high-born.

In due course the courier returned from France. King Charles would welcome an embassage from Scotland to discuss matters military. As for a bride for the King of Scots, he would suggest Mary, daughter of the Duke of Gueldres, a near relative of his own.

So – Mary of Gueldres! James had never so much as heard of her, nor of her ducal father. Where was Gueldres?

His uncle explained that Gueldres, often called Gelderland, was a province of the Low Countries, in Flanders rather than in France itself, but with ties to France, placed near the borders of Bavaria and Zeeland, a prosperous and quite important dukedom, and near to Burgundy where James's sister Isabella now lived. Chancellor Crichton would visit there on his way to Versailles and see the young woman.

The king scowled.

Later James spoke to Alec on the vexed subject. He was not going to accept a wife on the word of the man Crichton! He might have him married off to any shrew, strumpet or ugly hoyden, even a witch! Would Alec go with the party and see this creature Mary himself? Bring back a true description of her for him? Tell him whether she would make him an acceptable wife? She would become the Queen of Scotland – she must be befitting. Would he go?

Alec was perfectly prepared to do this for his friend and sovereign. But would Bishop Kennedy agree? And Crichton?

James said that he would order it. A royal command. They could not refuse that, could they?

Actually, when it was put to the Primate, he was quite agreeable, indeed in favour of it, seeing it as quite valuable to have another opinion than Crichton's on Gueldres as an ally and link with the Low Countries. Alec need not go on with the others to Versailles, where his presence would be of little value, but could return alone in one of the wool ships from Veere with his information. There was much traffic in shipping between the ports of Dunbar, Eyemouth and Berwick-on-Tweed and the staple-town of Veere, where all the Lammermuir wool was sent for the Flanders and Netherlands cloth manufacture.

Alec found himself as quite looking forward to this excursion, although it did mean that he would be away from Agnes for a period. But it seemed that it need not be for very long. Angus told him that it was about six hundred miles to Veere; he actually owned two of the ships which sailed with his hill farms' wool from Dunbar harbour. It was normally only a three-day voyage unless weather conditions were very bad. He could provide the vessel to take the embassage there. How far it was from Veere to this Gueldres he did not know, but some of the Flemish wool merchants at Dunbar would tell them.

So it was settled. What Crichton thought of having his son-in-law as travelling companion was not declared; but with the king and Primate ordering it, he could not object.

Agnes was going to miss her husband, but she agreed that they would have had longer partings in the early years of their marriage.

In the event, the king, Agnes and the Princesses Eleanor and Annabella all accompanied the envoys' party to Dunbar to see them off, taking the opportunity to visit Angus's wife, Jean, at Tantallon. Crichton and his daughter had not seen each other for long, and made no great demonstrations of affection. And with the king there, the Chancellor could display no objection to Alec's presence, even though his greeting was less than hearty. He had with him as assistants the Bishop of Dunkeld, appointed by Kennedy, and the Official of Lothian, one Nicholas de Otterburn, a fluent French speaker, each with a servitor.

From Tantallon Angus escorted them to Dunbar, where the quite large sea-going vessel, the *Beil Belle* was loading with great bales of Lammermuir wool, one of Scotland's principal exports. The town was being rebuilt after its sacking by the English, which gave added point to the need for this embassage. James was predictably angry at what he saw.

All went abroad the ship to inspect the quarters, less than luxurious, but hastily improved and furnished for the exalted voyagers, the oily smell of wool throat-catching. Alec was to share a small cabin with Bishop James Bruce, an amiable character.

The parting thereafter was, in the circumstances, fairly formal, with the king glaring at Crichton and whispering instructions to Alec, the latter more concerned with farewells to Agnes, the shipmaster, Ayton by name, and his crew, much preoccupied with the monarch's presence.

At length they cast off, to sail beneath one of those bridge-connections of the castle, Alec on his first major voyage by sea.

It all took a little adjusting for folk unused to shipboard life, with little or nothing for them to do, once they had got used to watching the shipmen's handling of the vessel and its sails and gear. They sought to identify the landmarks which they passed – for that first day they were never out of sight of land, on their southerly course. Crichton kept very much to himself, using the captain's cabin, but Bishop Bruce and Nicholas Otterburn were more sociable. Their servitors were equally at a loose end, and it was amusing for Alec to observe how these behaved more loftily towards the crewmen than did their masters. Fortunately the early spring weather was kind, and although the *Beil Belle* did roll in the south-west swell, none found occasion to complain of sea-sickness. Indeed until they became used to the oily smell of the fleeces, they found that more of a burden on their stomachs than the vessel's motions.

Off what they were informed was the North Yorkshire coast, the bishop held a brief vespers service, Crichton absenting himself, and the passengers retired to their bunks.

It was midday following before they eventually passed out of sight of the land to the west. They appeared to have the Norse Sea to themselves.

Alec sought to make some use of the idle hours by urging Otterburn to help him improve his French, of which he stood in some need. This did pass the time to some advantage, for in this Gueldres to which they were heading he would almost certainly require some command of the language, if hardly fluency.

The second evening the shipmaster, Ayton, told them that he was pleased with progress. If this westerly breeze continued, he would hope to have them entering the Veerse Meer by nightfall on the morrow.

Next day, in the afternoon, the passengers had to be informed that they were in fact approaching land, for they had not realised it. They had to have the darker band on the horizon ahead pointed out as the Netherlands coast, so low was it, unlike anything the travellers, used to a hilly country, had seen before. Ayton told them that indeed much of the land was actually below sea-level, the tides having to be restrained by great man-made banks called dykes – the Low Countries deserving that name. The Netherlanders and Flemings had reclaimed much from the sea, but it was a constant battle, with storms and northerly gales frequently undoing much that had been gained. Water seeping in all the time under the sands had to be pumped out into canals, this by windmills, to keep flooding at bay.

They were able to verify all this that evening as the *Beil Belle* drew in through a sort of gateway of high banks, to sail down what was more like an enormous canal than any seaway, with the land on either side so level as to be scarcely believable, and stretching seemingly to infinity, treeless, the endless plain of it dotted with isolated, slender upthrusting spike-like projections, which they were told were the steeples of village churches, these and windmills.

Of the villages themselves they could discern nothing. Actually, it seemed, the stretches on both sides were islands of a sort, Beveland on the east, Walcheron on the west. They were sailing down the Veerse Meer, and would be reaching Veere town and port within the hour.

After the empty-seeming Norse Sea, this Veerse Meer was a veritable hive of activity, with barges of every size, large scows and lighters everywhere, demanding of Ayton's helmsman no little heed, care and expertise. Clearly trade was all-important here, and equally evident that goods were largely transported by boat, presumably because roads were difficult to lay down across all this watery, flooded land. The Scots all were aware of the great trading reputation of the Low Countries, and their consequent wealth, but had not realised fully the conditions under which all this commerce was carried out.

The port of Veere, when at length they drew into it, manoeuvring amongst a pack of barges, was unlike their own harbours in Scotland in that it consisted not of a cluster of out-thrusting quays and piers but of a lengthy bank, solidly brick-built – apparently there was little or no stone available in this watery and sandy terrain, and brick was a necessary substitute – almost a mile of this, against which ships and barges were tied up, all backed by warehouses, and stores with houses sandwiched between, again all in brick, red brick with designs in black on the walling. Ayton had quite some difficulty in finding a gap into which to insert and berth his ship, his crewmen shouting and pointing at other vessels moored there which they recognised as Scottish. This was the main woollen centre of northern Europe, and the Scots contributed quite a large proportion of that commodity.

It seemed that the burgomaster of Veere, the chief magistrate or provost, always a great wool-merchant, was in the extraordinary position of deciding each year on the ruling prices for the various categories of wool, this known as the Staple at Veere, and having a major effect on the prosperity or otherwise of the Scots sheep farmers and lairds, as Angus knew only too well, whose wealth was largely from Lammermuir wool.

When the passengers landed, Ayton came with them to lead them to a tall many-gabled building amongst all the warehouses, above which they were surprised to see a large blue and white banner flapping in the breeze, the saltire, the St Andrew's cross, the national flag of Scotland. This was the Scots House, they were told, the base and centre for all Scottish trade in these Netherlands. Here they would find a welcome, and almost certainly accommodation for the night, and help for their onward journeying.

Their shipmaster was proved right in this, for they discovered at the richly furnished Scots House a big, burly man named Henderson, from Duns in Berwickshire, who it appeared was actually deputy burgomaster of Veere, he sitting with his large family at their evening meal, and who promptly insisted that the newcomers should join them; this even before he discovered that his visitors included the Chancellor of the realm, the Bishop of Dunkeld, the Official of Lothian and the Master of Glamis. His Dutch wife did not appear to be at all flustered by this invasion, and quickly had servants bringing in extra food and drink, this clearly a very prosperous establishment.

Over the meal, at which Ayton joined them, they learned that there were many Scots merchants and traders at Veere and its surroundings, just as there were numerous Flemings at Dunbar, Berwick and Leith, the links long-standing and strong. In the passing they were surprised to learn that the game of golf, more or less adopted as their own by the Scots, had in fact originated in these parts, where the Dutch called it *kolf*, although their version differed from that at home and could even be played on ice, on frozen polders, like a kind of curling.

They learned also as to how to get to Gueldres. They had assumed that they would have to hire or purchase horses; but no – barges were the answer. All the way they would go by water. Down the Veerse Meer again, across into the Ooster Schelde and so by the Mastgat into the great River Waal. Thereafter they would continue up that, one of the main waterways of the Netherlands, all the way to its junction with the Rhine, near Nijmegen, then north up a lesser stream to Arnhem, the capital of Gueldres, some one hundred and sixty miles in all. They need not change from the hired barge throughout.

Astonished at this, they were further told that their host would find them a suitable barge and crew, to leave in the morning. Their journey ought to take them no more than three days.

Well pleased, they sought their beds, these in a deal better conditions and comfort than on the *Beil Belle*.

True to his word, Pate Henderson led them in the morning to a berthingplace on a side inlet, where they were presented to the master of a medium-sized barge, named Molenaar, with a crew of six oarsmen. He would take them to Arnold, Duke of Gueldres's palace at Arnhem, for a fee in guilders, which Crichton agreed. There they said goodbye to Ayton, Alec enquiring for how long the *Beil Belle* would be remaining at Veere, and being told for possibly ten days or more, depending on how long it took to produce and load their return cargo of cloth, clothing, wines, cheeses and metalwork. So, Alec said, the ship might still be there when he got back to Veere, for his return to Scotland – but not to wait for him.

So they took leave of their helpful fellow countrymen, and seated themselves under a sort of awning at the stern of the barge, the long sweeps were pushed out, the master, Molenaar, took his place at the helm, and they pulled out into the Veerse Meer. It seemed as though it would be three days of sitting there. They learned that there were plenty of inns to serve them overnight.

In these circumstances, Crichton could nowise distance himself from his fellows, and although he by no means made an affable companion, he proved not too difficult to get on with. Alec in fact found him less of an ogre than he had expected. They would never be close, save in their present proximity, but he was able to feel somewhat more kindly towards his father-in-law. Actually the older man slept for much of the time, seeming to have a great capacity for drowsing. The bishop and Otterburn made fair associates, although both considerably older than Alec.

Their so idle journeying was less than exciting or dramatic, there being so comparatively little to see. So often these waterways were lined by high banks, to prevent flooding, for they were still on salt water, this penetrating deep into the heart of the land, these banks shutting out such views as there might be. Even when they did see for distances, there were few features to catch the eye other than the windmills and church spires. Such villages as they passed near seemed to have very low-set houses, with walls of whitewashed clay and reed-thatched roofs, Brickwork presumably reserved for the towns, save for those churches. The large numbers of these, dotted far and wide, impressed Bishop Bruce, who decided that the Dutch must be a very godly people. Would that the Scots were likewise!

The oarsmen appeared to be tireless at their task, very long slow rowing with their heavy sweeps, often chanting as they pulled, in monotonous rhythm. No doubt this assisted the Chancellor's sleeping ability also.

The first night they pulled in, with the dusk, to a town called Willemstad, on the edge of the wide Holland Diep, a fair-sized place with a busy dock area similar to Veere, red brick again in evidence and more step-gabled houses. They were led to a many-storeyed inn, where noisy but friendly company drank beer in huge tankards, and buxom maids served and slapped and giggled.

With all the inaction, it was long before Alec slept, especially with the noise continuing below.

The next day, passing near the city of Dordrecht, they reached the River Waal by midday. Now conditions were different. The land was a little less flat, there was more to see, even a tree or two. And the oarsmen had to work still harder, pulling against the wide river's current, so progress was slower. Alec wondered why these barges did not have masts and sails to help the rowers, for there was plenty of wind, as all those whirling windmills testified; but although they passed innumerable similar craft, none was so equipped.

By Gorinchem and Heerewaarden they entered Gelderland, indeed the town of Geldemalsen was pointed out to them some way inland to the north. They passed the second night at Tiel, smaller than Willemstad and with less noisy accommodation.

Soon the following forenoon they began to see a major change in the countryside, trees, indeed woodland, being frequent, slight slopes in the land, scarcely hills, relieving the monotony of the landscape, large houses, castles of a sort, in evidence. It was nothing like Scotland, but less strange to the travellers. They began to see roads, carts and horsemen.

Still on the Waal, they passed the city of Nijmegen, clearly a busy place, with much barge traffic to be steered through, evidently the commercial heart of Gelderland, and so to a tributary of the great river heading northwards, through now much wooded country. This brought them in the afternoon to Arnhem, the capital, their destination, less large than Nijmegen and less of a trading centre but with fine buildings, a cathedral or dom-kerke, squares and a market-place. Here they landed, and paid off their bargemen, and were directed towards a spacious park where rose the palace of the Duke of Gueldres, called Veluwe apparently. Why Gueldres rather than Gelderland? Alec wondered.

The travellers braced themselves for a change in conditions and behaviour, one week out of Scotland.

Their reception at the ducal house, more of a palace than a castle, was interesting and informative even though not what they had looked for, this because Duke Arnold and his friends were away at one of their sporting-lodges, apparently hunting wild boar. However, the visitors were very well received by two large and cheerful women, one very much the junior version of the other, who proved to be the Duchess Henrietta and her daughter Mary, plump, laughing, easy-going females, nothing like what Alec had anticipated as wife and daughter of a ruling prince. These Dutch did not seemingly stand on ceremony, rich and effective as they might be.

The Princess Mary admittedly was not beautiful, fair of hair but as rounded of features as she was of person, although sufficiently and pleasingly feminine, with an infectious, gurgling chuckle and roguish blue eyes. Alec liked her and her mother from the start, whatever the other envoys thought. He, being younger than his companions, Mary, of about twenty years, seemed to take on his entertainment as her responsibility, and an excellent and friendly, even warm, hostess she made, nudging him on occasion and patting his arm, in lieu of conversation, the language problems presenting difficulties, although she did whisper in his ear, just what he was uncertain, this at table. How was James Stewart going to like this one? Notably well, if Alec's advice was accepted, although his monarchial qualities might be called for at times to keep her in order. But he judged that there was no ill in her, however attractively roguish. Queenly she might not be, but she would make a lively and stimulating wife, in his opinion. Alec just wished that his French was better, to appreciate her sallies more fully – he had no Dutch at all, of course.

They were late in bedding that night, with all the good cheer and entertainment, Otterburn and he sharing a room again. They concluded that the princess had no objections to coming to Scotland to be a bride, and that what the former had told her of James seemed to please her reasonably well. Fairly obviously she would not have greatly appreciated a dull and solemn husband. She was older than he was by a couple of years, but most evidently young in heart, as was her mother still, who had flirted most frankly with Otterburn,

Crichton less than responsive and the bishop forbidden territory.

In the morning, Crichton decided that they should go on forthwith to Julich where apparently Duke Arnold was hunting, and from where he was not expected to return for some time, the duchess providing horses and guides. The Chancellor saw no need for Alec to go there with him, he having nothing to contribute to negotiations, and moreover, it seemed that they could proceed on to France from this Julich reasonably conveniently, better than by coming back here. This suited his son-in-law very well. He would stay at Arnhem for another day, enjoying the company, and then get back to Veere hopefully in time to catch the *Beil Belle* before it salled.

When the others were gone, the princess took Alec round the town, to see the handsome St. Walburger's Cathedral, the city hall, and the noisy shoutings at the fish market, which the young woman seemed to enjoy. And in the afternoon they went riding through extensive woodlands in what was apparently called the Hoge Veluwe, the high parkland, although its height was a matter of opinion. The evening was most pleasant, Alec the only guest, and gaining the duchess's attentions as well as her daughter's, he indeed dancing with them both, substantial armfuls. He decided that he liked the Dutch, if these were typical.

He was quite sorry to leave in the morning, and would have been welcome to stay on. But the risk that he might miss the *Beil Belle* if he delayed, and have to fill in time for who knew how long at Veere, awaiting another ship for Scotland, decided him. He was given the use of a fine ducal barge, and warmly kissed by mother and daughter, and sent on his way, assured that they would meet again. His task was accomplished, and most satisfactorily.

The journey back to Veere was speedier than the outward one, this for two reasons. The current of the Waal was now with them; and this ducal barge was provided with a sleeping cabin, handsomely appointed, at the stern, so they did not have to land and find overnight accommodation, the crew having their own bunks forward. They made it to Veere then in excellent time – to find the *Beil Belle* not yet fully laden. So Alec had two days more to fill in at the Schotse Huizen, with the Henderson family, before they sailed, which he used to visit the spinning-mills and cloth-making workshops, to see how the Lammermuir wool was processed. Also a tile-making factory, where so many of the red tiles on Scots house roofs came from.

Then it was to sea again, home and Agnes beckoning. He would have been away a mere eighteen days.

19

Agnes's welcome home was such as to make the parting almost worthwhile in itself.

The king was well pleased with Alec's report on Mary of Gueldres, declaring that she sounded as though she would make a wife that he might well like. Ever the impatient enthusiast, he was for having the marriage at the earliest. How soon could it be done, the princess brought from this Gelderland and the ceremony held? He would have a great festivity, masques, feasting, a tournament, races, a hunt . . .

His uncle pointed out that parliament first had to give official consent to the match. There was little doubt that it would do so, but the matter had to be put to it. Thereafter they would seek the Duke of Gueldres's convenience.

Forty days' notice, James exclaimed. And for a mere formality. Folly! What had a parliament to do with his wedding? His own concern only, was it not?

Until he was of full age, the Primate reminded, he had to be guided by parliament. He was only in his twentieth year.

Alec learned that there had been an alarming development while he was away; another invasion by the English, this time in the west only. What these comparatively small-scale raids signified was difficult to fathom. It was clearly not all-out war, or the Auld Enemy would put scores of thousands of men into it, large armies. Kennedy thought that it probably represented some manoeuvring of policies on the part of the English houses of York and Lancaster, York behind this one, in an effort to implicate the rival Duke of Gloucester and reduce his sway over the feeble King Henry. At any rate, there had been a battle, on the River Sark, in Dumfries-shire, after the Earl of Northumberland's son, young Percy, invaded from Carlisle, over the Solway, and ravaged some of lower Annandale. It was Douglas country, and that earl's brother, Hugh, Earl of Ormond, had gone to deal with it. He had won a notable victory, Percy markedly incompetent as a commander. There had been fifteen hundred English slain, and another five hundred drowned in the Solway when fleeing, for the loss of only twenty-six Scots, an expensive gesture, if it was indeed York's doing. Percy and his senior lieutenants had been captured, and their ransoms would further increase the Douglas wealth. Unfortunately Wallace of Craigie, a noted soldier, had died of his wounds, received while leading the Scots left wing. So the Douglases had this added advancement in prestige and power, which was worrying. There was talk of them heading a major invasion of England in retaliation, and that could lead to all-out war. The Primate was urging the king to ask parliament to sent an embassage to London to protest, and to seek to establish a lasting truce, this to forestall any such Douglas folly. Keeping the peace, and not only at home, must be the national priority.

Impatiently James Stewart waited for the forty days to pass.

The parliament, when it eventually met, was very much dominated by the Douglases. The ostensible reason for its calling, the approval of the royal marriage, was passed without debate, almost without comment. Crichton, who had recently arrived back from France, was congratulated on his efforts at Versailles, and the consolidation of the Auld Alliance. The Earl of Douglas then declared that the King of France should forthwith be urged to stage a vehement gesture against the English, mass a large army in Normandy, while the Scots drove down deep into England, to make clear once and for all that English aggression must cease. There was a fair amount of support for this, although Kennedy argued otherwise, that a peace mission should be given a chance to establish a lasting truce and concord, without bloodshed; he had a papal directive to that effect. That last carried much weight, but Douglas was not satisfied, and parliament divided. A decision was left with the Privy Council, in distinctly feeble fashion.

There was no such division and uncertainty, however, over the next business, the Douglases, like most others, united in decision. This was over the upsurging of the Livingstons. The old lord, admittedly, was still lying low; but his offspring and kinsmen were not. He had, while in power, had many of them appointed to positions and offices of power in the land, from which they were difficult to eject. For instance Robyn, one of his sons, was keeper of the royal castle of Dumbarton; another son, John, keeper of Doune, a third, Robert, of Linlithgow; and the eldest son and heir, Sir James, was claiming the keepership of Stirling as his hereditary right, even though he knew well that he would not be given it. But, much worse than that, this James was looking as though he would seek to rebuild the family's dominance in national affairs in some measure. He had formed an alliance with the new Lord of the Isles and Earl of Ross, the old earl having died. His successor was young and apparently aggressively minded, in more than just Highland affairs. An association between him and the Livingstons could spell serious trouble. Parliament decided that the lieutenant-general of the realm and his Douglases would be better employed in nipping any such confederation in the bud than in invading England.

That earl almost scornfully accepted this challenge, and said that he would deal with it forthwith.

He kept his word, and much more speedily than any there had anticipated. A bare ten days after the parliament, the news reached Stirling that he had led a force of some four thousand Douglases to a place called Inchbelly, near Kirkintilloch north of Glasgow where, on the Glazert Water, Sir James Livingston had his base, reasonably near the all but impregnable Dumbarton Castle, and was there awaiting the Lord of the Isles to concert plans. Caught unready, the Livingstons had been surprised and not so much defeated as overwhelmed, and all the senior members of the family and allies captured. The brothers Robert and Alexander were hanged there and then, Sir James, the leader, and in fact still High Chamberlain of the realm, was imprisoned, and their uncle Dundas of Dundas fled, to shut himself up in his own castle. Old Sir Alexander, the king's late gaoler, retired to his house of Calendar, was arrested likewise and imprisoned by the lieutenant-general. Douglas appeared to treat all this in an almost offhand manner, almost as a flourish and demonstration – to the further alarm of Kennedy, and even now of the king, who was beginning to see the earl as something of a possible menace to his own position, despite his former admiration.

However, James meantime was fully preoccupied with the arrangements for his forthcoming marriage. Alec got the impression that it was not so much the actual joining of male and female which was his main concern – not to be wondered at, perhaps, since he had never seen the bride – but the associations and festivities connected therewith, the receptions, the events and diversions which must accompany the event, and who would be there to witness it all. He was all for haste, couriers sent off to the Low Countries and France to speed matters up.

Kennedy shook his head over this nephew of his. Haste, in this as in so much else, should not be the criterion. With so many to be invited – for it was to be something of a family reunion as well as a state event, with his sisters and their husbands to come from far and near – careful planning was of the essence, not haste.

The weeks had to pass. Agnes had only the one princess now to attend, Annabella, and she was tentatively betrothed to the Duke of Savoy, whom she was to see at the wedding.

*　　*　　*

The excitement mounted as the agreed date drew near, James with almost no heed nor time for anything save the devising of the events of the great occasion, his first real hosting of a major royal undertaking. Although he would not be of full age for another two years, it was more or less accepted that, with his marriage, he would assume full kingly status and powers, and he was determined to celebrate this in appropriate style, he who for so many of his years had been little better than a prisoner.

The wedding itself was to be held at Edinburgh, the capital city, in the Abbey of the Holy Rood, and much of the relevant activities also, with the tourney-ground before the castle there suitable, and all the hunting-park of Arthur's Seat available, with its lochs for hawking, the Braid, Blackford and Pentland Hills offering further opportunities. Then a move would be made to Stirling, to sample its facilities, with the Tor Wood, the Flanders Moss, and the Highland hill-skirts to provide different varieties of sport. They might even go to Falkland . . .

The Primate sought to have his nephew dwell more on the solemnities, responsibilities and, yes, the joys, of holy matrimony. And he was much concerned over the ever-growing prominence and power of Douglas, of which he kept reminding the young monarch. Fortunately there were no more English raids, and Chancellor Crichton, sent to London on a peace-making mission, came back reasonably satisfied that York's aggressive attitudes would be curbed. Agnes and Alec were intrigued at how her father, from being seen as a menace and miscreant, was now being accepted as a useful intermediary. How long would this last? they wondered.

At last a ship-borne courier arrived from Veere to announce that Mary of Gueldres was on her way to Scotland, with a great company, so great indeed that it required thirteen ships to transport it, sailing from Amsterdam where this fleet had assembled. In much ado, James was for going out in a vessel to meet this armada and welcome it to Scottish waters; but Kennedy convinced him that this was hardly appropriate for the King of Scots, who would be better to greet his bride and her company on her landing on his soil. So James decreed that Alec should go instead, in his name, since he already knew the princess; and Kennedy agreed to lend the Bishop's Barge for the occasion. Agnes asked if she might go with him, on this errand, as suitable, for some of her former charges, the royal sisters, were to be of the company. There was no objection to this.

Alec and Agnes, then, went off to St. Andrews to join the Bishop's Barge, while the king and his uncle and a great train of nobles, knights and clerics set off for Edinburgh in fine style.

At St Andrews there was no undue delay in putting to sea, although they did not know just how near their destination the bridal fleet might be, making for the Firth of Forth. The barge's shipmaster suggested that their best course was to sail out to the Isle of May, situated fairly centrally in the mouth of the firth, and wait in the shelter of that quite large island, where they should be able to see and join the visiting squadron; presumably it would not enter the firth in darkness, if it arrived by night, but would lie off until daylight. This was agreed, and they set sail.

Agnes found all this much to her taste, a pleasing change from the distinctly enclosed duties as a lady-in-waiting. She was looking forward now to freedom from her long-standing appointment and her fuller enjoyment of wifehood at Pitteadie, the more so as the king's marriage would almost certainly mean less royal need of Alec's services. So they could hope to take up more or less permanent residence at their Fife house.

Neither of them had ever visited the Isle of May, however prominent it was as seen from both sides of the Firth of Forth. It lay nearer to the north than the south shore, about five miles from the eastern point of Fife, a fair-sized island, fully a mile long although comparatively narrow, cliffgirt, a great haunt of sea-fowl and seals, and with quite a notable history.

Sailing round Fife Ness from St. Andrews, they saw the May almost straight ahead, with lofty columnar greenstone cliffs stained white with bird droppings. Their shipmaster was quite knowledgeable about its story, coming from nearby Pittenweem, all seafarers being much concerned with it, this because, placed at the mouth of an important seaway notorious for storms, the isle had been a menace to shipping from the earliest times, and had indeed become the most suitable site for the first-known lighthouse in what was to become Scotland, this as far back as the sixth century. One of St. Columba's disciples, he who brought Christianity to the Picts, Ethernan by name, had chosen the May as his diseart, or quiet refuge, where he could retire from his missionary work to refresh himself spiritually and commune with his Maker, as was the custom of these Celtic saints. And on the island he had witnessed sufficient of its dangers to seafarers, in wrecks and strandings in the darkness, to realise that what was needed was a beacon lit by night to warn shipping of its position. Unfortunately, however, no trees grew on the isle, so the energetic Ethernan had set himself the task of fetching timber from the woodlands of Fife, to be ferried out constantly, and appointing custodians to see that the fires were lit each night, a major undertaking of very practical Christianity, for which seamen had been thanking him ever since, for the beacon, now elevated on a stone tower, still functioned although with improved fuelling arrangements. Sadly, Ethernan himself was no longer given the credit, for Queen Margaret, the later canonised saint, Malcolm Canmore's wife, in the great efforts to put down the ancient Celtic Church in favour of the Roman Catholic one, five centuries later, had changed the name of the founder to that of Adrian, who happened to be the Pope at the time; so now travellers blessed St Adrian instead of St Ethernan. Bishop Kennedy was quite concerned over this, but could hardly alter it now.

With no sign of any fleet of ships in the offing, Alec suggested that they might go ashore and explore the island while they waited. At the south-east end the cliffs sank away to low ground and reefs, and here was the landing-place, scarcely a haven but a sheltered inlet. Two boats they found moored therein, the property of the fishermen-custodians of the lighthouse, whose cottages were tucked into a neuk of the cliffs nearby.

These little hermit-like families were surprised but pleased to see the visitors, for they received few callers in this isolated spot, although on occasion they said monastic parties did come, in summertime, to pay respects to the remains of St Ethernan-Adrian, who had been slain, shamefully, by Norse sea-raiders. Their offer to take Alec and Agnes and their shipmaster to see the grave, up near a little lochan on the levels of the higher ground, with a ruined chapel nearby – this apparently built by King David the First, he who founded all the abbeys, that Queen Margaret's youngest son – was gladly accepted.

They traversed the isle thereafter, surrounded by hordes of screaming fowl, gulls, fulmars, kittiwakes, puffins and the like, reminiscent of the Bass Rock a dozen miles or so to the south, off Tantallon Castle, and having to dodge the droppings therefrom. They were much impressed by the dizzy heights of the cliffs, Agnes not venturing too near the edges, even to view the seals on the rocks far below. With evening's dusk beginning to fall, they returned to their vessel, no sign of the bridal squadron yet.

Although less sumptuous than the Duke of Gueldres's barge, this St Andrews one was comfortably appointed as to cabins, and the Lyons were able to bed down happily together, rocked as it were in the tides' cradle. Before sleeping, it occurred to Alec to wonder whether ever before there had been love-making on the Bishop's Barge?

In the morning they went ashore again for further exploration; and it was while up on the eastern clifftops that they saw the sails of many ships far to the south. The chances of such a fleet being anything but the Netherlands one being remote, they hurried back to the haven, to inform their skipper.

With the usual south-west breeze it was judged that the squadron would not be long in reaching the firth mouth; so sail was hoisted and they cast off, to head for a fairly central position to await a meeting. Out there, lying stationary, the rolling of the vessel emphasised the talk of the sea's turbulence hereabouts, and Agnes for one began to feel a little queasy. Their shipmaster helped her by raising a little sail and tacking to and fro into the tides, which much reduced the wallowing.

They had not long to wait, for soon the approaching ships drew near, nearer in fact than expected, for they seemed to be heading less into the west than was the obvious entrance to the firth, indeed as though making for the Isle of May itself. Surprised, the Bishop's Barge was moved to intercept.

They counted fourteen ships, not thirteen, being led by a large three-masted galleon, hung about with banners and heraldic painted sails, fairly obviously the ducal flagship. As the lone Scots craft drew closer, most evidently meaning to make contact, this leading vessel dowsed most of its sails and swung round to heave to. Behind it the array of followers did likewise.

Coming near, their shipmaster blew a horn, and cupping hands to mouth, shouted his loudest.

"Ahoy! Is that the Duke o' Gueldres's ships? Here is the Maister o' Glamis, sent by the King o' Scots to greet you and the Princess Mary. To welcome you to this land. Hail, I say – hail!"

Someone there must have had a fair command of the approximately English tongue, for after a brief pause the answer came back. "It is well. It is good. Yes. His Majesty of Scotland is good." That was pronounced goot. "Do you come? You wish speaking? You come?"

"Yes. The Maister o' Glamis will come aboard you, sir. Wi' His Grace's welcome."

So the barge was manoeuvred forward and alongside the larger vessel, and a rope ladder was dropped down. Agnes looked somewhat askance at this, but her husband declared that, despite its swaying, it would not be difficult to climb, so long as a good grip was maintained. In manly style, he proceeded to prove his assertion.

In fact, because of the sidelong lurching of the ship and the consequent swing of the ladder, it was less easy than he had said, and hard on the knuckles when knocking against the craft's timbers. But he made it without mishap, and at the top, as he clambered over the rail, hands were outstretched to aid him, one of those hands female, none other than Mary of Gueldres's own, she laughing and greeting him as Meister Glam-is, Meister Glam-is! When he was safely aboard, he was enveloped in warm arms, by the young woman first and then by her mother, loud in their greetings, a row of grinning dignitaries behind, one of whom came forward to push wife and daughter aside and introduce himself as Arnold, Duke of Gueldres, a great bear of a man, but all smiles.

Alec was so busy with these greetings that it was not until more feminine cries from behind turned him round that he discovered that Agnes had contrived the difficult ascent, skirts hitched high and offering the barge crew below much long white leg to admire, to be helped over the rail in turn amidst loud acclaim and hilarity. Breathlessly she smiled and gestured.

There followed a great to-do of introductions in mixed Dutch and French, much of it incomprehensible to the Lyons, although Alec did gather that the group seemed to be composed largely of dukes; Burgundy, Brittany, Saxony and even a grand-duke of Austria, this while Agnes was being embraced by her former charges, Mary, Isabella and Eleanor.

The Bishop's Barge drew off a little way, duty performed.

All the ships hoved to thus, and rolling inevitably, the two boarders were led aft to fine quarters and plied with refreshments. It was while so engaged that Alec was asked, in French, by Mary of Gueldres just what this strange island was. She had never seen anything quite like it, with its green and white cliffs and tall tower and all the large wheeling birds. Her sisters-in-law to be apparently did not know it, although they must have seen it often enough from Dunbar. Using Isabella, Duchess of Brittany as interpreter, Alec told something of the May's story – and then nothing would do but that the future Queen of Scotland had to set foot on this extraordinary fragment of that realm, especially to view the seals which Alec had mentioned, animals such as she had never seen. When the Grand Duke of Austria heard that there was a ruined chapel founded by the son of Margaret of Hungary, a distant forebear of his own, he declared that they should visit it to give thanks to their Creator for a safe voyage to this strange land.

Agreeing to this, Alec suggested that, in the meantime, one of their ships, the fastest one, should be sent onward to Leith to inform the king and his advisers that the flotilla had got this far and would be reaching them in a comparatively short time.

So the barge was hailed back again, to transport such of the visitors as wished to make a landing, for the little inlet would by no means harbour any large vessel. More rope ladders were lowered over the side, and amidst much merriment about a dozen of the company, including the Gueldres mother and daughter, climbed down, with varying degrees of expertise and agility, to shrieks of laughter, Agnes now leading the way. The bishop's crew had never seen the like, and would no doubt regale their cronies with accounts of it for many a day to come. These Netherlanders, Flemings, Burgundians and the others were clearly a lively lot, despite their reputation for hard-headed wealth-accumulation.

Landing them all from the barge was a less demanding performance, and with much exclamation the party pointed to the cottages and their astonished occupants, for never indubitably in its long history had the May seen anything like this magnificently garbed throng. The first sighting of seals drew cries of delight, as the party moved up to the chapel. There the Abbot of Arnhem, spiritual guardian of the expedition, conducted a short service of praise and thanksgiving, unintelligible to the Scots; and then the younger and more energetic members of the party proceeded to explore, while the others went back to the barge, the bride-to-be foremost in activity. Some splendid clothing was splattered with both mud and bird droppings in the process.

In due course the return was made to the waiting fleet, and climbing aboard activities were accomplished, Alec and Agnes staying with the ducal group, the Bishop's Barge drawing off to head back to St Andrews while the squadron set sail up Forth, amidst much pointing and exclamation at the flanking hills and precipitous shores and such outstanding features as the Bass Rock, the conical North Berwick Law and the fishing havens on the Fife side.

Alec wondered whether the ship sent ahead would have arrived in time to bring the king and welcoming party down to Leith, to be there to greet the visitors on arrival; and surely they would have had watchers posted on high lookout positions, such as Arthur's Seat, to give due warning of the fleet's approach.

Tacking into the wind now, it took almost two hours to reach Edinburgh's port at the mouth of the Water of Leith, with the sight of the lion-like hill of the said Arthur's Seat drawing astonished comment from these Low Countries folk, the Austrian grand-duke likening it to the Alps, surely an exaggeration. As they approached the riverside harbour, with its quays on both sides, small rowing-boats came out to greet them, with cheering occupants, although the cheers were soon drowned out by the distant boom of cannon-fire from Edinburgh's castle, this last heard at the Earl of Douglas's ineffectual siege.

Fourteen vessels could not, of course, all dock at once beside the one sent ahead as herald, so the flagship, guided by the harbour-master in one of the rowing-boats, edged its way in first to a clearing at the quayside. And there, under a painted canvas awning erected for the occasion, with a host of banners flapping above it, and scores of horses tethered behind, filling all the limited space between warehouses and water, was the royal party, with trumpeters, musicians and a choir of welcome, all competing with those far-off cannon.

Alec found himself having to act as introducer of Duke Arnold and his wife and daughter, first down the gangway, to James who was all but dancing with excitement, dressed in his best but still humbly compared with most of his guests, Bishop Kennedy at his back, much bowing and curtsying going on amidst a great gabble of languages. Quickly, however, the king's sisters were there to embrace their brother, and to introduce further and translate, and thankfully Alec could retire to Agnes's side. Presenting all the dukes and their ladies was a lengthy process in itself; and then the greater Scots nobles, the Earl of Douglas and his brothers foremost, extended their reception, with all the time more visitors coming ashore from the other vessels as they were able to dock. It developed into something like chaos there at the quayside, with servitors seeking to dispense refreshments, the lack of space, the new arrivals and the noise. The Lyon King of Arms and his heralds did their best to maintain some sort of order, but were faced with a major task. Alec came to the conclusion that it would have been better for James to have met his bride out at the Isle of May.

It was Douglas who eventually took charge and managed to impose his will on the disorder, however high-handedly, to royal frowns, clearing a way by main force for the principals to reach the horses. Isabella, Duchess of Brittany informed Agnes that the various dukes had brought no fewer than three hundred of their nobles, knights and gentry, as well as men-at-arms, to witness this royal marriage, so it was small wonder that there was some confusion.

There was an insufficiency of horses for all this company, numbers sorely underrated, so most of the Scots present had to yield up their mounts to the visitors. Even so the majority were left standing, and messengers were hastily sent up to the city to fetch more beasts, for it was well over a mile up to Holyrood Abbey, their destination. Cheerfully the ladies mounted behind their menfolk to ride pillion, which helped, James preparing to take his laughing bride-to-be, but Kennedy advising that this would not look suitable for the monarch on the official entry into his capital, Mary instead mounting behind the Lord of Campvere, her mother with her husband. Alec and Agnes, like many another, found themselves without steeds, and set off to walk up to the city – not that they saw this as any major trial. The Netherlanders undoubtedly would be assessing their method of transport, by water and barge, as much to be preferred.

Relays of horses did keep appearing, however, and most of the new arrivals eventually obtained mounts, even though many proud Scots nobles had to pace all the way to the abbey.

There even the extensive and rich establishment was taxed to provide accommodation for the foremost guests, the less distinguished having to be found quarters in the Blackfriars and Greyfriars monasteries in the city, and even up in the fortress-castle itself. James was much put about, none of his advisers ever having conceived of such a numerous invasion.

The monkish cooks and kitcheners had to exert themselves indeed to cope with the situation, but Holy Church did not fail the monarch. The visitors' servants also had to be catered for.

The banquet that evening at least was a success, provision ample and varied, from venison and boar to wild goose and duck, and even peacock and swan, the guests being particularly pleased with the salmon and trout, which apparently they knew little of. James sat at the high table, flanked by the Duke and Duchess of Gueldres, their daughter, at this stage, being placed less prominently amongst the princesses. Her time would come. From well down the hall Alec and Agnes sat and eyed all with interest and some amusement, the king clearly revelling in his first experience of hosting a major international event, and getting on well with the Netherlanders, despite language difficulties. Bishop Kennedy, with Aeneas Silvius Piccolomini, the Papal Nuncio, sat at a side table for the clergy, and kept a watchful eye on all.

The entertainment, after the feasting, was as varied as the provision, with dancers, acrobats, jesters, a performing bear, and dogs jumping through hoops, the monarch having to be prevented, by frowns and headshakes from the clerics' table, from joining in himself. It all made for late bed-going. The Lyons had to find sleeping quarters in one of the Canongate inns that night.

The next few days were more than fully occupied, with sightseeing, hunting and hawking, sports, a tournament up at the castle, displays of prowess, and of course more feasting and revelry – for the wedding itself was delayed for a week, this in order that an especial papal blessing and gift should come from the Vatican. A visit was paid to Stirling, for alternative sporting venues and activities; and here a highlight was a *combat-d'outrance*, that is, a battle to extremity, with three Burgundian champions challenging three Scots knights to a fight, on horseback, with lances, battle-axes, swords and daggers, to the death if need be. The Scots volunteers chosen were James Douglas, next brother to the earl, Douglas of Lochleven, and Sir John Ross of Halket, a noted warrior; and all were especially knighted for the occasion by James, even though they were all already knights. A fierce and exciting affray ensued amidst the clash of steel on armour and the shouts of the onlookers, until Lochleven crashed to the ground from the saddle, half stunned, and one of the Burgundians had lost shield and helmet. At this the king threw down his gauntlet, to bring the contest to an end before it became fatal, to the congratulations of all. Most Scots had never seen the like, and some doubts were expressed as to

211

its suitability, however dramatic and thrilling. Agnes declared it barbarous and to be deplored.

The hunting in the Tor Wood and the Ochil Hills was much to be preferred. They did not however get to Falkland. It was time to return to Edinburgh for the wedding, the Pope's handsome gift and blessing arrived.

Alec had been but little in the king's close company during all this crowded activity, but in preparation for the actual ceremony, as Gentleman of the Bedchamber, he had his duties, and was able to have private talk with his liege-lord. He found James much in a ferment, needless to say, but somewhat uncertain, unusual for him, over what was expected of him after the nuptials. He had had no experience of close association with femininity, apart from an occasional frolic with a serving-wench, and he was less than confident that he would perform as was expected of him, and as this Mary would wish. He liked the young woman, he said, and did not want either to disappoint or offend. Alec sought to reassure, and said that he felt that probably the bride would be fairly well versed in what the situation required, going by what he had seen of her, perhaps not more experienced than her groom but more knowledgeable, these Netherlanders being very down to earth. She would probably help in the bedding process quite effectively. He himself gave James some small practical advice in the matter.

The abbey-church was large, founded by the same King David who had had the little chapel built on the Isle of May, and was much admired by the visitors, especially the grand-duke. It was packed for this occasion, even the clerestorey galleries being crowded, Alec and Agnes up there and obtaining an excellent view of the proceedings. Kennedy, assisted by the nuncio Piccolomini and the Arnhem abbot, conducted the service, and guided the couple throughout. James looked nervous at first, but his bride's calm confidence no doubt helped him. She was looking very attractive, in a plumply generous way, fair and lively as though she was enjoying the occasion. Alec confided in his wife that he thought that she would make a very satisfactory bedfellow – to a dig in the ribs from Agnes.

The actual marriage over and the pair declared man and wife, the nuncio performed the brief nuptial mass, and then the new queen was ceremonially crowned there in the church. Thereafter it was all outside for congratulations, more revelry and feasting. Later the ritual of dowery and portion-giving was gone through, to much applause by the witnesses, Mary being given the dower-house of Linlithgow Palace, with royal lands in Strathearn, Methven and faraway Argyll, while the Dukes of Gueldres and Burgundy committed themselves to the bride's portion of no less than sixty thousand gold crowns, an enormous sum, to be delivered over the space of two years.

In mid-afternoon the newly weds rose from the table to take leave of their guests, to much acclaim and well-wishing. They were heading, it seemed, for Falkland, James's favoured retreat. Going, the king sought for and caught Alec's eye, well down the hall, and nodded, which that man took to mean that either he would remember advice given, or that his own attendance in Fife, in due course, would be expected – possibly both.

It was not long thereafter that the Lyons also made their escape, and thankfully, for Pitteadie. The Princess Annabella, the last of Agnes's charge unwed, had just been betrothed to the Duke of Savoy, and she would return with her sisters to the Low Countries, there to await her wedding. So now the Mistress of Glamis was a free woman, at last, to her husband's joy. Fife for them also, then.

20

Alec Lyon's own hopes of being largely freed from close
attendance on his sovereign were scarcely fulfilled. Not
that he was not fond of James, but he hankered after
the quieter life of a laird on his own land, especially a
happily married one, and courts and palaces he had had
enough of. But he was soon sent for. Fortunately James's
fondness for Falkland enabled Alec to be at Pitteadie, only
some twenty miles off, frequently. Fortunately also, Queen
Mary greatly enhanced the royal attendance duties. She
was a happy creature and with clearly some affection for
the Meister of Glam-is. She also came to look on Agnes as
a sort of extra lady-in-waiting, so, although still with their
courtly tasks, the Lyons were able to be together much of
the time. Agnes declared to her husband that this was just
as well, so that she could keep an eye on him and that so
demonstrably affectionate Mary of Gueldres!

James was eager to display their kingdom to his wife,
who was so admiring of its scenic features, so different
from her own land, and himself to explore it further, on
account of his so restricted childhood and youth having
seen so little of it. And he had an urge to get to know his
subjects, not just the nobility and gentry but the common
people, this on the advice of Bishop Kennedy. So there
followed much touring of the countryside, with Alec and
Agnes frequently in attendance, going to the many areas
unknown to that pair, as well as the monarch, seeing the
sights, viewing the towns and villages, the castles and
abbeys and monasteries, and showing themselves to the
folk. They traversed the Merse and the Borders, especially
intrigued by the Ettrick Forest; they visted the Ayrshire

and Galloway coasts, the cities of Glasgow, Dundee and Aberdeen, even going as far north as Inverness. They did not penetrate very far into the Highlands, especially the west and the Isles, for these were apt to be in turmoil and clan warfare, with the new Earl of Ross and Lord of the Isles by no means seeking to pacify them. But they did reach southern Argyll and Cowal, to view Mary's jointure lands there, where she much relished the splendid scenery of mountains and lochs and islands.

So that late summer and autumn took on something of a holiday atmosphere for the two couples, and they learned much, not only about the land but about each other. James had clearly come to love his Mary, and her influence on him was good, her happy, laughing and affectionate, yet strong, nature helping to counter his hot-headedness and over-reactions.

National affairs were not to be ignored, of course, and brought their worries, in especial the ever-growing dominance of the Douglases. That earl had made some sort of alliance with the Tiger Earl of Crawford and the new Earl of Ross, and between them they could all but control two-thirds of the country, this quite apart from Douglas's lieutenant-generalship. The dangers in this were obvious, greatly worrying Bishop Kennedy; but there was little that he and James could do about it.

They did call a parliament in January, at the Tolbooth of Edinburgh, Crichton still Chancellor, at which certain measures were put forward to try to ensure the rule of law and administration of justice, the king now no longer acting the figurehead but taking an active part in the debates, ruling as well as reigning monarch. His interventions and assertions were not always such as to enhance peace efforts, to his uncle's head-shakings, but at least he was acting the sovereign-lord, even though the Earl of Douglas might smile and shrug. The queen, with Alec and Agnes, watched proceedings from a gallery.

Instigated by the Primate, James proposed that all

justiciars, sheriffs and law officers should make perambulations of their jurisdictions at least twice every year, to show themselves to the people and ensure that the laws were being enforced. In his own recent journeyings, he had learned that the ordinary folk tended to be all but unaware that they had rights, and the protection from ill-doers and aggressors, with little or no faith in justice being maintained. This was passed. He also declared that lords and lairds must not, at will, eject tenants from land held on lease, this to aid farmers towards better and more sustained cultivation of the soil, to the increase of national wealth – this a less than popular proposal but grudgingly accepted by a majority present. On that subject of wealth, national and personal, an awkward matter was brought up by Kennedy. He pointed out that Queen Mary, whom God bless and protect, had as her dowery been promised not only lands and Linlithgow Palace but the sum of five thousand pounds per year to maintain them. That sum was not presently available in the royal treasury, owing to the non-payment of dues by many magnates and even clerics, some here present. This was to the dishonour of the nation and had to be rectified, he asserted.

The Earl of Douglas rose to ask if it was not the case that the queen's father and uncle had, those months earlier, promised the sum of sixty thousand gold crowns as the bridal portion? Was this vast treasure not sufficient to solve His Grace's treasury problem?

Kennedy pointed out that this amount was only promised to be paid within two years, and so far was not forthcoming. And it did not relieve the king from providing the Scots dowery moneys.

There was a brief silence, and then Douglas rose again, and with something of a flourish announced that he personally would donate the sum of one hundred pounds to aid in His Grace's dilemma.

That produced something of a sensation, James frowning from the throne, and comments coming from all over the hall. Bishop Kennedy himself, looking less than happy at this development, declared that personal donations were not being sought, but the prompt payment of dues, taxes and feudal fees. However, since the Earl of Douglas had been so loyally generous, he himself would give two hundred pounds, as a gesture, not from Church funds but from his own purse.

Out of the hush that followed, Chancellor Crichton rapped his gavel, and observed that since the realm's honour appeared to be at stake, he would add five hundred pounds to the total.

Agnes, at Alec's side, caught her breath, her father clearly seeking to buy his way back into royal favour – and her husband wondering just where all those pounds had come from.

After that, of course, there was something of a competition amongst the lords and prelates to display their loyal benevolence, although none reached the aforementioned figures, Douglas looking annoyed, James himself clearly not happy about it. He announced that he would look upon these offerings as loans not donations.

In the gallery, Queen Mary seemed much amused.

The monarch sought to improve his impoverished image by introducing the final item on the agenda namely the dire subject of treason. Now that he was bearing the rule of the realm, it was necessary that provision be made for due protection of his and his queen's persons and authority from ill-wishers, place-seekers and traitors, as in the past had occurred. The crime of high treason must be fully defined and its penalties enforced, immediate execution the retribution. To this end he proposed the setting up of a committee of parliament, consisting of four lords, four prelates and four commissioners of the shires, to apply the law before all, great and small. Was this agreed?

No one there was in a position to controvert or question the monarch. The matter was put, seconded and passed, and the committee appointed.

The session was adjourned, with Queen Mary much fascinated by her first parliament. Her husband, however, was less pleased. That gesture of Douglas's, offering him the one hundred pounds, rankled. He saw it as mockery, no less.

The earl was not invited to the royal table that night, although Angus was.

The Primate's growing concern, and now the king's also, was over what they saw as an increasing Douglas threat. It caused them to take steps to try to contain it, if not lessen it. Kennedy conceived of a plan, quite an involved one, which might be effective, at least getting the earl out of the country for a period, and hopefully taking his mind off advancing his dominance in Scotland, even though it might gain him prestige elsewhere. It was in connection with the French duchy of Touraine. This had been held by the Black Douglases since 1422, when the fourth earl had greatly served Charles the Seventh of France; but on the execution of the sixth earl and his brother it had fallen into abeyance, and was retained by the present King of France. So if Earl William was to go to France to claim the duchy and its lands, including the county of Longueville, he might well regain it, and thereafter seek to make his mark on the Continent, as his predecessor had done before him, and allow Scotland some breathing-space. It also occurred to Kennedy that this all might be advanced if it had the papal blessing. It so happened that the new Pope, Nicholas the Fifth, had declared this year of 1450 to be the Jubilee Year, to celebrate the end of the schism and to further his efforts to unite the warring factions of Christendom; and there were to be great observances and functions in Rome, in October. The Primate himself was going to be there, to take part. But if Douglas was to attend there also, possibly as representing the Scots nobility, all this might well help to redirect his ambitions, at the same time aiding his claims to Touraine. Not that they would go together, but at the same time. Pope Nicholas could be persuaded to be helpful, the nuncio Piccolomini suggested. Holy Church might well serve Scotland well in this.

But first there was a use for the Douglas nearer at home, and which would probably please that ambitious young man. The English affairs of state were under even more threat than were the Scots, with York and Lancaster in open warfare for control of the ineffective King Henry. Chancellor Crichton, on his visit to London, had learned that York was still using the alleged enmity of Scotland, in alliance with France, to advance his cause, thus endangering the recent truce. If that truce could be converted into a firm and enduring peace pact, the situation would be much improved as far as the northern kingdom was concerned. The continual raids over the border were the ongoing threat to peace, deliberately stirred up; and if these could be halted, the way would be cleared for such pact. So if the lieutenant-general, with his especial Galloway and Dumfries-shire interests in the West March, could come to terms with the English Wardens of the Marches, it would be to great advantage.

James was at first unwilling to seek Douglas aid, as he saw it, in this matter or in any other. But his uncle persuaded him that it was for the realm's weal, and should not in any way advance the Douglas cause vis-à-vis the crown. The king eventually agreed, so long as the Red Douglas, his brother-in-law, whom he trusted, went with the Black, to see that there were no underhand dealings. Kennedy said that he would add a couple of bishops to the delegation, for the same purpose.

Douglas was summoned to Stirling then, in June, and given his instructions, making no objections. And the Primate took the opportunity to speak of the Touraine project and the visit to Rome. That certainly was well received.

Kennedy judged that he had probably achieved some advantage in the power struggle, perhaps only temporarily but an amelioration at least.

Douglas duly arranged his visit to the borderline, with Angus, Crawford and the Bishops of Dunkeld and Brechin, and, on the West March at Gretna, met the English wardens under Northumberland. Despite a difficult start, with the English earl asserting that any peace pact must not seem to invalidate King Henry's hereditary claim to overlordship of Scotland, angrily denied, some sort of agreement was arrived at, and the Duke of York's activities and ambitions condemned.

Then it was all preparations for the Continental and Rome visits. So much interest was aroused in this Papal Jubilee that James himself got caught up in the fever, and told his uncle to inform His Holiness that he was prepared personally to lead a crusade of the united nations of Christendom against the infidel Ottoman Empire which was occupying the Holy Land, Kennedy seeking to play down this royal enthusiasm.

Douglas departed for Flanders, on the way to Paris and Rome, in August, taking with him his brothers the Earls of Moray and Ormond – James Douglas being already in France – accompanied by a semi-royal retinue of six knights, fourteen lairds and eighty men-at-arms as escort, this requiring three ships to sail from Leith. He left his younger brother Balveny to look after his interests in their absence. Kennedy, much more modestly, and heading directly for Rome, followed in a wool-ship from Dunbar two weeks later, Turnbull, Bishop of Glasgow, a rising prelate, left to aid Chancellor Crichton in minding affairs for the king.

Scotland settled down for a period of peace and quiet.

The king and Mary departed for Falkland, and Alec and Agnes for Pitteadie. It was the prime hunting season, and sport and domestic bliss were to be the order of the day, and of the night.

21

Alas, it was not to be. It was not long before word reached
Fife that the young Lord Balveny was misbehaving
himself, and in a typically large Douglas way. Twenty
years old, and suddenly left in command of all the Black
Douglas power, he began to wield it, setting all the
south-west in an uproar, assailing neighbours, sacking
properties in Galloway and Dumfries-shire which still
owed allegiance to other than Douglas, and then extending
his activities northwards and eastwards to Lanarkshire and
Douglasdale itself.

Bishop William Turnbull of Glasgow, a Borderer, who
was in process of copying Kennedy, his friend, in founding
a university in that city, grew uneasy as Balveny's ravages
drew near his diocese, and came to Falkland to urge
the monarch to take measures to curb this disturber of
the peace, this backed by Crichton. James acceded that
something should be done. But who to send? Angus? With
so many of the kingdom's magnates gone to the Continent,
there was a notable and unusual lack of powerful figures to
put down such lawless behaviour with any large numbers
of men. Angus was the now obvious choice; but could the
Red Douglas be relied upon to fight the Black, if necessary?
Crichton, although a shrewd operator, did not control any
large numbers of men.

James decided. He was now the ruling monarch. He
would go in person to halt and punish Balveny, taking
Angus and his manpower with him. Never had it been
more evident that the Scots sovereign's lack of any royal
standing army was a dire weakness.

Alec, although not consulted, was in some doubt as to

the wisdom of his impetuous liege-lord leading an armed assault. But he could by no means prevail on James to leave it to Angus and others. Taking leave of their worried wives, they set off across Forth for Tantallon from the little port of Kinghorn.

Angus, not a fiery or aggressive individual, was less than eager to raise his thousands and march against Balveny, although he was much upset by the depredations and follies going on. But he could not refuse the royal brother-in-law's commands, and reluctantly sent out the rallying calls. Meantime, James and Alec were entertained by the Princess Jean. A messenger was sent to inform the Chancellor of the situation.

The Red Douglas manpower was fairly concentrated on this east of Lothian and north Berwickshire area, so that the mustering of large numbers of men did not take long. Fortunately the harvest and sheep-shearing was over for the year, so the levies, mainly farm-workers, shepherds and fishermen, were not too greatly inconvenienced by the call to arms, whatever their womenfolk thought. In four days, four thousand men were assembled at Tantallon and North Berwick, a quarter of them, perhaps, horsed. The twenty-mile march to Edinburgh commenced, James at the head of his first army, royal lion rampant banner flying, and glorying in it, Angus and Alec less enthusiastic.

At the capital, they found that Crichton had gathered together a motley collection of Edinburgh citizens and his own people, to make almost a thousand to add to the total. With this reinforcement, they continued the march southwards, by the slopes of the Pentland Hills, hoping to pick up others on the way, Crichton himself not accompanying them.

It could not be a fast-moving host, with most on foot, and fifteen miles in a day were as much as they could cover, however impatient the royal leader. By Penicuik and Dolphinton, Biggar and Carnwath and Carmichael they went, Carmichael of that Ilk providing four-score additions. Nearby the Douglas Water joined upper Clyde, and up this the force turned, Douglas Castle and town ahead of them.

Although this was where the Douglases took their name, from of old, it was by no means the principal seat of the Blacks, Lochmaben and Threave, Morton and Drumlanrig, Kenmure and the Haugh of Urr being all more important, even though St Bride's Kirk, in the town, was where the earls were buried, James the Gross's dramatic interment being in most minds as they approached, when the corpse hurtled down into the crypt out-of-control. The castle, however, was nearly a mile north of the town, so they reached it first, their scouts, gone ahead, reporting that it did not seem to be held by any large force. Just where Balveny was misbehaving himself at the moment was uncertain. No doubt, however, he would be informed of the royal host's invasion of the Douglas domains.

On arrival at the castle, situated in no particularly strong position, they found the fortalice being held only by its keeper and a small garrison. At sight of the army, and at the royal command to surrender, wisely the custodian agreed to vacate it without any foolish attempt at a siege; and although James thought to hang one or two as examples, he was dissuaded by Angus and Alec on the excuse that these had caused no trouble; and they did not want Douglas town to rise in anger behind the army on its onward march. So no assault was made on the town, and it put to the flame as was the king's original idea. They did however sack, pillage and as far as possible burn the castle itself, camping the night beside it, and using its timbers, supplies and cattle to comfort the host.

Next morning they were on their way again, south by east now through the Tweedsmuir hills, rough country indeed, to the skirts of the Ettrick Forest, and on over to the Dryfe Water, and so to Annandale, ten miles in a day being as much as the terrain allowed, to James's frustration. He thought of sending his horsed company ahead, but was advised against this as giving warning. Lochmaben Castle was their next goal. This could be a very different target, Angus informed, very strongly placed amidst seven lochs, and a favourite seat of the Earl William. Alec Lyon was not alone in wondering what that man would think of all this, and how react, on his return from Rome.

It took the host six strenuous days to work their way through the great ranges of more or less empty hills to the headwaters of the River Annan, all with no sign of opposition, indeed with little sign of humanity at all, the king wondering at this unpopulated part of his kingdom which he had not known existed. Presumably Balveny was either resting from his misbehaviours or pursuing them in more distant parts, for it was surely all but impossible that he had not been informed of the royal progress by this time. James was quite enjoying this his first experience of campaigning, acting the commander, living off the land, and anticipating showing Scotland who now ruled the realm. He made good company for his lieutenants, however eager for conflict and bloodshed.

They came down to Lochmaben out of the Brunswark Hills, to find it a picturesque area of open woodlands, all those lochs amidst small hills, the largest water having a thrusting peninsula on which was perched a large castle, artificial canals and ditches cutting it off from the landward approach, making it all but impregnable save to heavy cannon, of which the royal army had none. There was quite a large castleton at the north-west end of the largest loch.

Clearly their approach to this Lochmaben revealed that it was going to be no easy stronghold to assail, much tougher than Douglas Castle. They were getting very close now to the real Black Douglas country, where they could be in danger from attack, ambush, and assault when camping at night, by a hostile folk who knew the land much better than they did. Angus pointed out that they had passed near a favoured hunting-seat of the Douglases in the skirts of the Ettrick Forest. He suggested that they should leave Lochmaben and go back to Blackhouse

Tower, a much easier target. James said that that would be a humiliation. He would make at least a gesture of requiring this hold to submit, and if necessary assail the castleton, to demonstrate that the royal authority and laws were not to be flouted. Unenthusiastically his companions went along with this, and the force proceeded down into the medley of wooded lochs.

And as it turned out, the king not only had his way but was proved right. For when summoned by the monarch in person, to the sound of trumpet and under the lion rampant banner, to surrender the castle or face siege and dire punishment, its keeper, with his lord overseas and possibly doubting Balveny's ability to save him, yielded with but little delay. Great was the royal satisfaction. Allowing the quite small garrison to betake themselves off, he there and then set about the sacking of the water-encircled stronghold, assisting in the process with his own hands, setting alight to all within which would burn, and having levelled such walling as was possible to demolish without gunpowder, and sinking all the castle's boats, all most evidently to the royal enjoyment.

The night, thereafter, was spent in celebratory fashion at the castleton, to the upset of its inhabitants, especially the women, although there were no hangings and slaughterings.

Pleased with his efforts, although disappointed that there had been no actual fighting, James allowed himself to be persuaded thereafter that he had made a sufficient demonstration of the crown's authority, and that a return whence they had come was in order and wise. His thousands of followers were well content. They had lost none of their number, and enriched themselves with the spoils of two castles. So it was back to the north, but by an easier route, from the Annan to the Moffat Water, over into Ettrick and Yarrow, and so to the Tweed at Peebles, and at length Edinburgh again, dropping off their small local contingents in the by-going. It was the end of October, and winter would soon be upon them, with a probable easing of tensions and violent activities.

The monarchial flag had been flown, three well-spent weeks for James Stewart at least, and manly exploits to retail to the womenfolk.

Bishop Kennedy was home first from Rome, the Black Douglas, now Duke of Touraine, taking time to inspect his duchy and the county of Longueville. The Primate was distinctly concerned when he heard about the royal assaults on that earl's castles, wondering, as did others, what the reaction would be. He was critical of Angus, and even Alec Lyon, for not having somehow halted James. He, of course, agreed that Balveny's misbehaviour could not be tolerated, but declared that it might have been dealt with by other means than by almost certainly grievously offending the lieutenant-general of the realm. The king considered his uncle feeble in this.

However the monarch had become otherwise preoccupied in the meantime, for Queen Mary announced that she was pregnant, and this greatly pleased her twenty-year-old husband, signalising his attainment of man's estate indeed, and allowing him to crow rather over Alec, who could not so claim. That man and Agnes were indeed disappointed that so far no offspring had come their way, and not through any failure of attempt, although it by no means lessened their joy in their union. One day they would, God willing, produce a Lyon cub.

Christmastide came and went, with a return to Stirling, Falkland being scarcely the place for the monarch in mid-winter, the Lyons having to attend there also. Not that the royal party went in for any sort of hibernation, pregnancy or none, James being almost over-actively inclined, and his wife far from molly-coddling herself. The nearby Tor Wood made excellent sheltered riding and hunting ground.

Winter conditions affected more than the king's sporting activities, this proved soon after Kennedy's return, by the weather improvement enabling two of Douglas's allies to show their resentment at the royal expedition against Lochmaben and Douglas Castles by staging a retaliatory demonstration in the Highland North. The young Earl of Ross and the Tiger Earl of Crawford joined to assail and take the royal castles of Inverness, Urquhart and Ruthven-in-Badenoch, destroying the last and occupying the other two, and the town of Inverness. Then Sir James Livingston, old Alexander's son, took the opportunity to join them, and was given Urquhart into his custody.

King James was furious, but could do little about it, other than urge the Earl of Huntly and the Earl Marischal to take action against the rebels, no easy task for the Gordon and the Keith in those Highland fastness. It was a warning, clearly, of troubles to come, and nearer home.

Then, in April, Scotland heard of the duke-earl's postponed return from France, and this even before he arrived home, for he elected to come via England, using the peace-pact situation, which he had helped to arrange, as justification to enter into his own negotiations with King Henry and the Lancaster–Gloucester faction against York. This move was sufficiently successful, to his own cause at least, to have Henry actually send out the Garter King of Arms to meet Douglas at sea, and conduct him in almost royal state to Windsor. This news was anything but welcomed at Stirling, making Douglas now look like some sovereign prince. His arrival back in Scotland was awaited with something like dread. On Kennedy's advice, James called a parliament, hoping that this, coinciding with the earl's return, would help to keep that proud character in some degree of order.

Unfortunately, because of the forty days notice, the Duke of Touraine's homecoming occurred well before the parliament, and he quickly proved that his association with the Pope and the Kings of France and England had far from lowered his estimation of his own, and Douglas, importance. Whatever his feelings about Balveny's follies during his absence, his reaction to the monarch's attacks on his castles was immediate, indeed dramatic. He not only refused to attend the parliament, and forbade all others with whom he had influence from doing so, but held what amounted to a parliament of his own, at Dumfries, summoned the king's justiciar there, Sir Herbert Herries of Terregles accused him of failing to protect Lochmaben Castle, and hanged him there and then. He also had slain Sandilands of Calder and two other knights of the king's party, and assembled his vassals to make his presence felt further north, in order to show his ire at the royal behaviour. As some further indication of his now ducal wrath and resentment, he imprisoned in Threave Castle, his main seat, MacLellan of Bombie, Sheriff of Kirkcudbright, who had refused to answer his summons to arms. It so happened that the sheriff was a cousin of Sir Patrick Gray, captain of the king's guard, and James felt bound to express royal protest at these offences against his officers of the law. So he sent Sir Patrick, a brave man indeed, to Threave, to demand the release and delivering up of MacLellan. Douglas received the monarch's emissary with grim courtesy, and while Gray was being given refreshment, sent out and had the prisoner beheaded on the spot, presently delivering the head to Gray, saying that he could have the body also, if he wished, to do with it what he would.

So much for the laws of the land.

The parliament duly met in June, again in Edinburgh's Tolbooth, in a state of considerable apprehension, and notable for its many absentees. The need for careful decision-making, with civil war most evidently looming, was emphasised by Kennedy, and even Crichton, both urging the king to be cautious and to temper wrath with discretion. The Douglas threat was the prime, all but the only, business.

James took charge from the first, the Chancellor having to give way to the throne. He began by declaring that, since he had now come of full age, certain matters fell to be changed. For one, as undoubted commander of all the forces of the realm, he no longer required a lieutenant-general. Consequently the Earl of Douglas was to be relieved of that position – this announcement received with indrawn breaths by most present. There was only some slight relief when he went on to say that in place of this appointment the new duke should be made Warden of the West and Middle Marches, which he all but controlled anyway. He added that he deplored the murders of Herries of Terregles and the others, pointing out that Sandilands of Calder was distant kin of his own, and that the beheading of Sheriff McLellan, and the insult of presenting the head to his captain of the guard, could not be overlooked, and representations must be made by parliament. Nevertheless, James thereafter concentrated more on the outrages of Douglas of Balveny, and called upon his brother to take suitable measures against him. Then he turned to the rebellion of the Earls of Ross and Crawford in the north, and gave his royal authority to the Earl of Huntly and the Earl Marischal, and all other loyal subjects in those parts, to take fullest action against the treasonable insurgents and to recover the royal castles of Inverness, Urquhart and Ruthven, and bring to justice the perpetrators.

Throughout this jerky delivery, all but a monologue, Bishop Kennedy and the Chancellor sat expressionless, the rest of the company taking their cue from them. None there could believe that all these royal directions, or almost any of them, could be carried out. The king's coming of age and assumption of fullest rule had hardly come to a promising commencement. But those who might have challenged it all were not present.

Parliament therefore went through the motions of accepting the royal decrees, passed some everyday measures and edicts, including the appointment of a new Sheriff of Kirkcudbright, and adjourned in a state of misgiving.

Alec Lyon went back to Stirling with the king, less than voluble.

22

Two weeks later, worries about the Douglas threat
were pushed into the background, at least for the royal
household, by the birth of a son, on 10th July, to Queen
Mary, with an uncomplicated delivery and a healthy and
loud-lunged infant, to be another James. Great was the
rejoicing. The king treated the event as almost unique, and
paraded the baby boy around Stirling Castle for all to see
and admire, to his wife's amusement. He had produced an
heir to the throne, and no far-out and ambitious kinsman,
such as Douglas, could now claim to be heir-presumptive.
The crown was secure.

Mary proved to be an excellent mother, and was not
long in regaining full wellbeing and activity. In fact, in a
couple more weeks they were all off to Falkland, despite the
national situation. Agnes found herself in some demand as
helper with the child.

Douglas had not been inactive in the interim. He had
put almost the entire southern parts of the country under
his control, save for the East March where Angus and the
Homes were supreme, and had moved himself and his
entourage, if not his major armed force, up to Edinburgh,
which city he and his were now all but occupying. It was
like some tide creeping in, and ever nearer to the seat of
government.

Curiously enough, it was at the capital that the proud
earl suffered a minor but irritating reverse. It so happened
that Chancellor Crichton was on his way from his town-
house therein to Leith, to take boat up Forth to Stirling,
when Douglas, who looked upon him as an enemy, sent a
group of his men to waylay and apprehend him. Crichton

managed to escape from the attack, although two of his servitors were wounded, whereupon the Chancellor hastened back to his own Crichton lands in Lothian, approached his friend the Lord Borthwick, and together, with a large party of their men, returned to the city. There they assailed the Blackfriars Monastery, where Douglas was residing. Quite a little battle ensued, but for once Douglas was outnumbered and caught unawares, and the earl had to slip away by a side door into the Cowgate, and fled the scene back to his own territories. Grimly exultant, Agnes's father was able to proceed to Stirling, the first to have made the Black Douglas look small for many a year.

King James, when he heard of this, was much gratified, and thought the time ripe to try to come to favourable terms with his *bete noire*, the new Duke of Touraine, Kennedy agreeing that something had to be done to improve the situation. He suggested that Douglas be invited to Stirling, to greet Scotland's only other duke, Rothesay – that is James's little son – and to duly acknowledge him as heir to the throne, the first officially to acknowledge the child as such. A conference could then be held to try to come to some suitable understanding over the nation's affairs. But they both recognised that the earl would be unlikely to risk entering Stirling Castle, where he could be so easily imprisoned, without some sort of safe-conduct. So James wrote a letter of invitation, signed and with the royal seal, and the seals of the Chancellor and Primate also, promising full security, and emphasising the need for amity and co-operation for the realm's welfare. This was sent by the hand of Sir William Lauder of Hatton, who had met the duke in Rome, and who himself was related, his mother having been a daughter of the fourth Earl of Douglas.

Lauder in due course arrived back from Galloway, to report that its lord would indeed pay a visit to Stirling, but in his own good time.

Scarcely heartened by that, the king and his advisers waited.

Nor were they pleased when, almost a month later, Douglas, with quite a large retinue, arrived at Stirling, and took up his residence in the town, not in the castle, without reporting his presence until the next day, when he rode up to the gatehouse, with bannermen and trumpets, to announce his presence, even with his own herald.

It was clear that he had not brought the erring Balveny with him, nor any of his brothers.

James, annoyed, forced himself to receive the man he had once admired civilly, but showed his reservations by offering only a brief audience, and inviting the earl to return the next evening to dine with him. He added that his royal hospitality did not extend to the Lord Balveny – to the other's blank stare.

The following late afternoon Douglas duly arrived, magnificently clad in continental finery sufficient to make the king, indeed all there present, appear humdrum, almost shabby. At table the host and principal guest were stiffly formal, with Bishop Kennedy having to do most of the conversing, but refraining from controversial subjects. It was noticeable that Crichton kept his distance, and indeed excused himself to the monarch before the repast was over, and left the hall. Evidently he did not desire to associate with the man who had so recently assailed him in Edinburgh, perhaps did not trust himself to keep the peace. No women were present.

Alec, watching all from well down the hall, wondered whether this meeting was going to be of any advantage to the realm.

The king, who normally had a hearty appetite, appeared to be only toying with his food, although drinking deeply.

During the subsequent entertainment, with jugglers and musicians, Kennedy withdrew also, presumably only temporarily, James on this occasion showing no urge to take part in the proceedings, as sometimes he did. Nor did Douglas display any marked appreciation.

Hardly had the Primate left the dais when James abruptly rose – and all others must rise also, to be promptly waved down to their seats again. But not Douglas, to whom the king gestured towards the dais door through which Kennedy had gone. Then he beckoned to two or three of the others at this top table, including Sir Patrick Gray, captain of the guard, his father the Lord Gray, and Sir William Lauder of Hatton, his Master of the Horse. Glancing down the hall he picked out Alec Lyon, and nodded. Then he led this little group out, with Douglas left to presume that private converse and conference was intended. Alec hurried after them, wondering. Had Kennedy gone ahead to prepare the way for some reason?

Voices led him to an anteroom behind the hall, where a fire burned, and more wines and spirits filled a table, at which the king was pouring. There was no sign of Kennedy. James thrust a tankard at Douglas, who shook his head – so James quaffed it himself, frowning. Alec got the impression that his liege-lord was already a little the worse for liquor.

The royal words, loudly spoken but somewhat slurred, seemed to substantiate that.

"You, my lord Earl – or Duke, must I now name you? – have some answering to do, have you not? Why you slew my law officers, Herries of Terregles, and Sandilands of Calder. And presented the bloody head of MacLellan of Bombie to my captain here, Sir Patrick Gray! Your reasons, my lord?"

"Good reasons, Sire," the other said briefly. "They had offended while I was abroad at Rome and France."

"Offended? Taken due action, you mean, against your brother Balveny, who was running riot over the southwest! As was their duty, as officers of the crown. Your offence was, was *un*due, and your action intolerable!" James had a little difficulty in enunciating the word intolerable.

The Douglas eyed him almost disdainfully. "I did not come here, at your request, to be insulted! Sire!" That last word was all but spat out.

"Insulted! *You* speak of insults! You who have insulted the crown and parliament. Refused to attend, and prevented others from attending. It was, is, insufferable!" Again some impediment in the flow of words.

"You name that a parliament? It was but a device to deprive me of my position of lieutenant-general! No?"

"And worthily so, I say! Had you not forged a bond with Crawford and Ross? To threaten and endanger my rule and reign? A treasonable bond. Treason, I say!"

"That bond was not treason. It was for mutual security against the rogues who you had allowed to control the kingdom – Crichton, Livingston and their kidney. Up-jumped scoundrels! Douglas does not accept such!"

The two young men stood glaring at each other, for the earl was but four years older than James's twenty-one years, the watchers all but holding their breaths.

"Accept!" James exclaimed thickly. "Accept! Who are you to accept or refuse to accept your sovereign's decisions? And parliament's. That bond with Ross and Crawford must be dis . . . dissolved. Now! Herewith! My royal command."

"Dissolved, say you? Folly! Forby, it is not in my power, nor yours, to dissolve a bond between friends. With the friends absent. And I see no cause to do so." Douglas shrugged, and half turned away.

James Stewart all but choked in his fury. Impulsively he reached down to his hip and whipped out the ceremonial dagger which hung there, bejewelled.

"False traitor!" he exclaimed. "If you will not break that bond, this shall!" And lunging forward, he raised hand to stab at the other's throat as that man turned to face him once more. And as the blood spurted out, the red flood seemed to enrage the king the more, and he stabbed and stabbed again, down to the chest now, in a frenzy of rage.

The earl staggered back, mouth wide, gulping, but no words forthcoming. He crashed against the table with all the wines, tankards and flagons falling to the floor, and there he sprawled.

All but unbelieving what they saw, the watchers stared, appalled, immobile with shock. But not all. Sir Patrick Gray, he who had been offered Sheriff MacLellan's head, strode over to the slumped, jerking figure alean over that table, snatched up one of the pewter tankards and smashed it down on the earl's head with all his force.

Douglas collapsed to the floor amongst all the spilled wine, and there lay.

For long moments there was silence in that room, save for the king's heavy, panting breathing, and gurglings from the slit throat of the victim. James was swaying on his feet now, his fiery birthmark vivid on his strangely working features. He stared down at his fallen enemy, pointing with that bloodied dagger. Then suddenly changing the direction of his gaze, he pointed it over to the window instead, jabbing the steel at it.

"Out!" he cried. "Out with him! Out, I say!" And throwing away the dagger, he stooped to grasp one of the arms of that twitching body, to start to try to drag it over the floor. Quietly Gray came to his aid, although none of the others did, and together monarch and captain of his guard hauled the Earl of Douglas and Duke of Touraine across to the window, threw open the wooden shutters below the glass, and with a sort of crazed urgency and no little difficulty, hoisted the victim up and through and over.

All could hear the thud of the fall on the cobbles of the courtyard far below. If the Douglas was not dead already, he certainly would be at that.

Lord Gray, Sir William Lauder and the Master of Glamis stood utterly aghast, witnesses to an event unique in history, with a monarch slaying a subject with his own hand, not in battle – and the victim there under the royal safe-conduct.

*   *   *

James Stewart, splashed with blood, turning, faced the others, his features suddenly crumpling. Looking from one to the other, he shook his head, wordless. None other spoke either, events over-much for speech. Then, after a few moments, the king turned and actually ran from the room, staggering a little as he went. Muttering something unintelligible, Sir Patrick Gray hurried after him.

Alec, much shaken, wondered whether he ought to go also, to be with the king. But every inch of him prevented him from doing so, even though he was Gentleman of the Bedchamber. Besides, James might well not want anyone to be with him in his present state. He stood, scarcely able to think, or to credit what had happened, almost as though it had all been but an evil dream.

Lord Gray, elderly, but a man used to military action, renowned as a fighter, took charge.

"The body!" he jerked. "Must be got away. Before it is seen by any servants. It is a back court, down there. Those leaving the hall will not see it. But it must be moved. Come!"

They hastened out, and down a back stairway to the yard, no comments made on what had occurred. There, on the cobblestones, they found the corpse of William Douglas, warm but no longer twitching.

"Where?" Gray demanded.

Alec, who knew Stirling Castle better than the others, pointed across the yard to where there was a range of vaulted cellars, used as stores. To one of these they dragged the body, themselves getting blood-splattered in the process. They pushed it inside, and closed the door on it.

"An unmarked grave. Tomorrow," Gray said. "Tell none of this."

Alec went back to his own quarters in the royal block, avoiding the king's chambers. In less than eloquent jerky words he got out the horrific story to the astounded Agnes. Practically incredulous she gazed at him, at a loss – but not so much so that she did not agree with him that he should not go to the king that night. Nor should she go to the queen. Let James tell his wife himself what he had done. They wondered what Mary of Gueldres would say to her little son's father?

It occurred to Alec that fate could work in mysterious ways indeed. The king's father had died at the hands of subjects' daggers, those fifteen years ago. Now the son had reversed the process.

23

When Alec reported at the royal quarters in the morning, he found James in a state of extreme agitation and self-abasement, not to say alarm, the queen seeking to calm and reassure him.

"I could not help it!" he declared to his attendant and friend. "God knows that I could not! It was the drink in me. I had had over-much. And he was insolent. He provoked me to it. You saw and heard him. I should not have done it. But . . ." He shook his head miserably. "God forgive me – it was the wine, I swear!"

Alec had been debating with himself what he should say, this last hour. Agnes had advised that he did not condone what the monarch had done, but not to express condemnation either. What was done was done. James was still the king, however grievously he had behaved. The rule of the land had to go on, the ship of state still to be steered, with the monarch at the helm. Last night's deed must be between James and his Maker. It was not for such as Alec Lyon to set himself up as judge. What Bishop Kennedy would say when he heard was another matter . . .

"It was all a dire night, Sire, with hot words and acts. The earl, much at fault also. His death may have been deserved. But . . ."

"Aye, deserved. But *I* slew him, man! With my own hand. The same hand which had signed his safe-conduct. God Almighty help me! What am I to do?"

"You pray," Queen Mary said. "You pray *le bon Dieu* to forgive. He will. He does love, yes. Loves you. Pray – but do not go, no. Not to go."

"I must, Mary, I must!" he cried. "I cannot stay here now. I am a murderer! I cannot rule Scotland with hands stained with blood! I am the Lord's Anointed! I have defiled the crown! Broken my coronation oath. God help me – but I am broken! I must go."

"No!" she declared strongly. "Not to go. If you go, who to rule? Our child? A babe!"

"Go, Sire? Go where?" Alec asked.

"France. The Low Countries. Mary's Gueldres. Flee the land I have failed. Anywhere . . ."

"But to what end, Your Grace? What would that serve? Would Scotland be any better without its monarch? If, if you have failed the realm in this matter, will it not be still greater failure to leave it? You, the king. There is no other to take your place. However many might shed blood, much blood, to do so."

"The meister speaks right," the queen said. "You not go."

"There would be war, the kingdom torn apart, if you left, Sire," Alec was insisting when a servant knocked and spoke from the door, to announce the presence of the Lord Bishop, seeking audience.

Kennedy strode in. "James!" he exclaimed, then turned to bow to the queen. "Your Grace, forgive me. James, I have just heard! I cannot believe my ears! You slew Douglas?"

"I did. Christ have mercy, I did. In drink."

"Say him not to go," Mary interjected. "You say him. Not to go. Must not."

"Go? What mean you – go? Go where?"

"France, he say. Netherlands. My land."

Kennedy stared. "What is this?"

"I would leave. Flee the land. For my sin. Leave," James jerked.

"Flee? Why? What good would that do?"

"I am unworthy now. To rule here. An assassin! My sin drives me out."

"Sin, yes – if you did that. Sin and folly and danger,

239

yes. But to go, to flee, to leave your kingdom for others to seek to put to rights – is that your royal duty, man? To run away from the deed you have committed will help nothing. A king cannot flee his realm, whatever he has done."

James looked from one to the other, shaking his head.

It was Alec Lyon who spoke. "How heard you of this, this deed, my lord Bishop?" he asked. "It was hoped that it might be kept secret. At least, for a time."

"My chaplain told me. All Stirling is talking of it, he says. Grievous!"

"Who informed? Last night, the Lord Gray said to bury the body in some hidden grave. That none should know. None there, at the, the deed, would speak out."

"The grave-diggers, perhaps? But that matters not. It is out, known. And we must, James, seek to limit the damage. And not by your flight. The Douglases, his brothers, will rise in rage. Nothing more sure. Join with Crawford and Ross. You must move to halt them. Prevent them joining up. Or we shall have the whole realm ablaze!"

The king wagged his head in something of despair.

"What would your father have done? I will tell you. He would have acted, and at once. As he did against Albany's son. Had him executed before he could raise rebellion. You have done enough of execution! But you can put down rebellion. Show who rules in your kingdom."

"How?" James with that one word, that question, and how it was burst out, indicated a change of reaction and attitude.

"See you," his uncle said. "Crawford is basing himself at Perth meantime. Probably waiting for Ross to join him there, before an advance on this Stirling. Huntly is harrying Ross in the north. But with all the clans he can bring to arms, the Islesman will not be easily put down. Crawford is the less strong, Tiger although he may be! Assail him at Perth, keep him and Ross from joining, and you have greatly improved the situation. You see it? Ross, with Crawford put down, or at least set back, will not come south, I think. Remain in his Highlands. And so, you can turn to face the Douglas wrath without threat at your back."

Alec wondered whether James Kennedy might not have made as good a soldier as he made a cleric.

"Men?" James demanded, showing real interest and a trace of spirit now. "Where do I get the men to assail Crawford?"

"Where you can, and must. You are the king. Call on your nearby lords. By royal command. The Erskines. The Bruces. The Drummonds. The Hays. Even Crichton himself! I shall send out messengers. In a week, less, you could have thousands, from near at hand. More later. Then march. And prove that you are the worthy son of your father!"

His nephew took a deep breath. "Yes. Yes, you are right. That is the way. I will draw the Tiger's claws!" James Stewart looked more like himself again, impetuous, positive.

His wife nodded approvingly.

Alec sought to play his part. "I will go to some of the lords," he volunteered. "And Gray will help. He is a fighter. He mislikes Crawford, I have heard. Lesser knights and lairds also, to call on . . ."

So it was decided. The King of Scots would act the monarch again, not the guilty accused.

Only four days later, a host of nearly four thousand horsed men left Stirling, with promise of others to join them from further afield. If some of the lords present eyed their sovereign somewhat warily now, oddly enough there was more of respect in their glances than criticism.

They rode north across the stripling Forth, by the bridge and causeway where Wallace had won his great victory over the English host in 1297, and on by the Allan Water to Dunblane, the lion rampant standard at their head. Alec rode behind the king and his senior lords, beside a young Trinitarian friar named Dominic, who was

Kennedy's personal chaplain, and whom the Primate had sent to represent the Church's support in this campaign – and possibly to help sustain the conscience-stricken king's resolve.

They camped overnight at Auchterarder, on the Ruthven Water, waiting for Murray of Tullibardine's very sizable contingent to join them from Strathearn; and in the morning were reinforced by another large addition under Bruce of Clackmannan. All this support greatly cheered the king, who saw it as some sort of absolution for his slaying of Douglas, his morale rising notably.

More assistance was awaiting him as they neared Perth, so that it was an impressive force which climbed over the shoulder of Moncrieff Hill, just south of the town, and they could look down into the valley of the Tay and see their goal.

Alec was probably far from the only one who wondered. Crawford, whatever else he was, was no fool, and he could not have failed to have his scouts and sentinels out, placed to warn him of any opposition; and the approach of this large army would almost certainly have been reported to him. The question was, how large a force did he have assembled at Perth? Would he select a strong position, possibly on the far side of Tay, to oppose the king? Or would he opt for discretion, and depart?

Lord Gray, who was the most experienced warrior present, no doubt warned James of such possibilities, and a scouting party was sent ahead down towards the town to try to discover the situation. The advance was halted. And before long, messengers came back with their tidings. Crawford had left Perth the previous evening, and headed off north-eastwards, possibly for his own lands of Lower Strathmore and the Mearns, Finavon, Edzell and the rest, or it might be due north to seek to rejoin Ross.

What to do, then? If he had a day's start ahead of them, and in country that he knew better than they did, was there any point in seeking to follow him? Gray advised against. Even Alec was bold enough to say the same.

If making for his own territories, Crawford would pass near Glamis, and he warned that there were innumerable places where a lesser force could hold up pursuers, at major river-crossings, of the Isla, the Prosen, the Clova and the two Esks, as well as passes where ambushes could be laid to trap them when they were necessarily strung-out in file. And northwards, into the Highland mountains, it would be even more dangerous.

Others said likewise. So it was anticlimax, all their fine array in vain, a return whence they had come, James's battle-challenge proved negative. However, it was pointed out, the effort had not been pointless. The monarch's power to rally his strength had been demonstrated. Crawford had retreated in consequence. It was a variety of victory, without battle, however disappointed was the king.

They sent out parties east and north, to discover which way Crawford had fled, and James and his leaders went into Perth to spend the night in some of the many monastic houses of the town, he avoiding the Blackfriars Monastery where his father had been murdered.

By the day following it was clear that Crawford had indeed headed off through Strathmore for his own lands. It was return to Stirling therefore, the various lords' groupings branching off for their sundry homelands, but all promising to reassemble at short notice should the need arise.

Five days after leaving Stirling, the nucleus of the army was back there, to find the town in chaos, indeed much of it a smouldering ruin. The day before, the Douglases had arrived in strength, the new earl, James, he who had intended to be a cleric, with his brothers Hugh, Earl of Ormond, Archibald, Earl of Moray and John, Lord Balveny. They had been unable to gain entry to the fortress, Crichton seeing to that, but had made their fury evident enough. They had employed the age-old Celtic usage of having twenty-four horns blown, this before the gatehouse of the castle, and announced their rejection of all allegiance to King James. They had nailed a copy of their late brother's royal safe-conduct to a board, and dragged it through the streets at the tail of the poorest horse they could find. Then they had sacked the town, looting and setting fire to large parts of it, before heading back southwards. Crichton told all this to a shaken monarch and his advisers, to their mortification.

There had been many casualties, inevitably. But at least, secure in the citadel, Queen Mary and her child, and Agnes Lyon, were safe. When, sighting the town, Alec had seen the great pall of smoke rising high and all but obscuring the castle, his heart had sunk.

Next day, after an evening of confusion and fierce debate, alleviated by thankfulness that dear ones were safe, Bishop Kennedy arrived from St Andrews by boat, where he had heard of these dire doings. He advised that a parliament be held at the earliest, to seek to enforce the royal authority. But meanwhile, there were sufficient members of the Privy Council available, with the Chancellor and himself, to issue decrees which the parliament could later endorse. Some immediate reaction was necessary.

Alec, although of course not a member, sat in at the council meeting, and heard the king, prompted by Kennedy and Crichton, announce that the Black Douglases, who had publicly renounced their allegiance to himself, were thereby forfeited, outlawed and deprived of their titles and offices as well as their estates, their persons to be apprehended by his loyal subjects and brought to trial, whenever possible. The same applied to the Earls of Crawford and Ross. Meantime, the Earl of Huntly was appointed lieutenant-general of the realm, with orders to put down all risings, in the king's name, calling upon the forces of all lords and magnates to aid him.

It was while this council was in progress that Sir Patrick Gray entered, to whisper to his father, eyebrows raised at this. Then Lord Gray announced that word had just reached Stirling that Hugh, Earl of Ormond and his brother Balveny had attacked and destroyed the Red Douglas castle of Dalkeith and burned that town, while their brother the Earl of Moray had headed north to assail Huntly's rear while he was trying to deal with the Earl of Ross.

Making decrees about forfeiture and outlawry and trials was one thing, but making these effective was clearly quite another. It looked as though the slaying of William Douglas had by no means lessened this more grievous threat to the throne, but had indeed enhanced it.

Alec was worried about his friend the Earl of Angus, the Red Douglas. Would he be the next victim, for having failed to support the Blacks? Tantallon Castle, on its cliff-top, would be a deal more difficult to take than had been Dalkeith, but the attempt might be made.

After the meeting was over, he approached the king on that subject, suggesting that Angus and his wife, James's sister Jean, should be urged to come to Stirling for safety, until the Black Douglas power was somehow put down. That was accepted. Alec could take Patrick Gray and the guard to Tantallon, as escort, to bring back Angus and the princess – if it was not too late. But he would have to be careful as to how they went . . .

24

Danger or none, Agnes insisted on being allowed to accompany her husband on this mission, concerned for her former charge. The Princess Jean should not be without a woman attendant on what could be a perilous journey to Stirling, she claimed. They would be travelling by boat from North Berwick, but if the Douglases, the Blacks, got to hear of the move, it was not beyond them to seize a squadron of vessels at Leith port and seek to intercept. Alec argued that this was all the more reason for his wife not going, but she would have none of it. She was not Crichton's daughter for nothing, and was not to be put off, especially with James agreeing that his sister might well need her.

Bishop Kennedy had come by his barge from St Andrews, and he allowed them to use his vessel, docked at Airth. Perhaps the banner of the Primate of Holy Church flying from the mast-head might help to deter any possible attack. Also it was a large vessel, capable of transporting quite a large escort.

So next day they set off for Airth, where the Forth began to widen out into its estuary, Queen Mary urging Agnes to be careful. Kennedy sent Friar Dominic with them, to give his authority. They set sail. Alec's fear was that they might be too late, that Tantallon might already be besieged, and that they might not be able to reach the castle. Would it be possible to approach directly by sea, to the cliff-foots, and somehow manage to climb up, up and then down? Angus used to fish from the cliff-top. Perhaps there was some means of scaling those heights.

Their sail down Forth, those forty-five miles, took only

some five hours, with a westerly breeze. Approaching North Berwick harbour they could see no sign of anything unusual there, although they kept well offshore as a precautionary measure. But they proceeded on eastwards, and when they rounded the headland beyond and they came in sight of Tantallon, there was only normality to be seen there, nothing of besiegery nor encampment. Thankfully they turned back for the haven.

Questions to the fishermen mending their nets there brought no word of any armed force in the neighbourhood, although their lord had issued orders to all his people to be ready to muster at short notice should there be need. So, leaving most of the escort at the ship, the party set off to walk the mile or so to the castle.

They were observed, of course, by the guards well before they reached it, and were met by armed men at the outermost of the many deep ditches dug to prevent cannon from being drawn within range of the buildings. Their identity announced, they were ushered in under the massive central gatehouse keep to the wide inner courtyard flanking the cliffs.

Angus and his wife received them gladly, Jean hugging Agnes. When they explained the object of their visit, the earl expressed some doubts, although his countess did not. She would be happy to go to see her brother at Stirling, and have a change from this cliff-top, wind- and spray-buffeted stronghold which frowned at the Norse Sea, something of a prison in the wild weather of February and March.

"I know well that the Blacks may assail me here," Angus agreed. "After what they did at Dalkeith. But I am well enough able to defend myself, I judge. This place will not be taken without heavy cannon, and even then no easy target. My people are ready to come to my aid. I cannot put so many in the field as can Hugh, Archibald and John, and now James as the new earl; but enough to make them think twice. Nor do I believe that they could take Dunbar Castle. They might burn my towns of North Berwick and Dunbar, I suppose, out of spite, as they did at Stirling and Dalkeith. But they will not take me here, I swear!"

"But is your place not with the king, in this coil in the realm's affairs?" Alec put to him. "Leaving aside this of your safety. He is much put about. He needs all leal men to rally to his side. As his good-brother, your presence would be seen as much support – the Red Douglas."

"Yes, Jamie, let us go," his wife urged. "This Tantallon is safe enough, even though you are not here. Let us go to my brother."

"Do you know, my lord, where the Douglases are, the others, at this present?" Sir Patrick Gray asked. "Are they like to be moving against you? Shortly? At Stirling we have not heard of their movements since that of Dalkeith. Save that Moray has gone north to attack Huntly and aid Ross. So at least their strength is somewhat divided."

"Aye, the word is that James and Hugh and John are gone to their own West March meantime. It is said that they are seeking a meeting with the English, with York, to ally themselves. It is even said that, having renounced allegiance to James, they are prepared to offer it to king Henry, in return for aid to unseat James! Although I can sacarcely believe that even they could go so far as that. But it seems that they are for talking with York, for whatever reason."

"Accept Henry Plantagenet as overlord of Scotland!" Alec exclaimed. "Surely not that. The Douglases!"

"It may be but idle talk . . ."

Later, after a welcome meal, they all sat round a blazing fire of birch logs in the lesser hall of the castle, with a rising wind howling and buffeting the towers and rattling the shutters, the visitors thankful that this sudden gale had not arisen while they were afloat, and enjoying the more the warmth and comfort and good company. The young Friar Dominic was proving an asset, in that he was a useful performer on the lute, and with a good tenor voice, he and Agnes partnering each other in duets, by no means all religious in content, the others, less gifted vocalists, joining in the choruses. It all made a congenial and domestic occasion, of which there had been too few, for the newcomers at least, of late.

At a lull in the music and singing, with honey wine being dispensed, Agnes it was who took opportunity to seek information.

"I am very ignorant, I fear," she said. "But all this of York and Lancaster and the English – I am unsure of what is at stake there, what it all means. I ought to know, but do not. This Duke of York, whom the Black Douglases seek to meet – just who is he? What is his connection with King Henry?"

It was the friar who answered her, a knowledgable young cleric who clearly found her to his taste. The Primate's chaplain would be well informed and read, of course. "Richard Plantagenet, Duke of York, is kin to Henry, King of England," he explained. "As is Lancaster, both descended from Edward the Third, York from his third son, Lancaster from his fourth. The king, of course, stems from the first. This Henry the Sixth is feeble in person and simple in his wits, so these cousins rival each other in seeking to control him, for their own ends. Since Gloucester, the king's uncle, died, York is slightly the nearer to the throne. But the queen, Margaret of Anjou, a strong woman, favours Lancaster. So these two are as good as at war, the white rose of York against the red rose of Lancaster. The new Earl of Douglas and his brothers appear to be leaning to York."

"The Duke of York, then, is heir to the throne of England? Senior to Lancaster?"

"No-o-o. Not quite that. For Queen Margaret has an infant son, also of doubtful health, like his father."

"York thinks to gain the supreme power, and possibly the throne, for he is more of a warrior than is Lancaster," Angus added. "He thinks to involve Scotland in his scheming. War with Scotland could see him as commander, and Lancaster as less of a soldier. And he has the strong Earls of Warwick and Salisbury on his side. So this, if true, of the Black Douglases offering him their aid, could well much please him."

"And how could it help Douglas?"

Gray answered that. "I suspect that they seek the Scots throne, no less. York to aid them unseat King James and make the new earl some sort of puppet monarch, under English sovereignty. Am I not right, my lord?" He looked over at Angus.

"I fear that is the truth," their host admitted. "They, the brothers, are descended from King Robert the Second, through the female line. Whereas I myself am from Robert the Third."

"As well that *you* have no ambitions then to unseat His Grace!" Alec put in, smiling. "For you are the closer to the throne than are they, no?"

"James has naught to fear from me, I promise you!"

"This of the Black and Red Douglases?" Agnes went on. "More ignorance, but just how did they come apart? Since both bear the same name?"

"It was back in the time of the first earl," she was told. "He, who died at the Battle of Otterburn, the dead man who won a battle, was wed three times. His third wife was the Countess of Angus in her own right, and their son inherited her earldom, now mine. His elder half-brother became second Earl of Douglas. It is quite simple. William, whom the king slew, was eighth earl, whereas I am only fourth of Angus. We seem to have lived the longer!"

"Sakes, I am dizzy with all this of families and descents and dates!" the princess cried. "Of a mercy, let us have more music and an end to it!"

"I am sorry," Agnes said. "It is my fault. I was so lacking in the knowledge . . ."

"Your father could have told you it all," Alec pointed out. "But some I was not sure of myself."

"Of your patience, one last question from this numb-skull," Agnes persisted. "This of Red and Black? Why the colours?"

"That is simple. The Douglases had been called Black ever since the time of the Good Sir James, Bruce's friend, who took his heart on crusade, who was dark-avised. But my ancestor, who inherited the Angus earldom from his mother, was red of hair. And the name has continued, whatever the hair!"

That was a suitable note for the company to return to less momentous talk and music, but what they had heard left all their minds with something of a shadow, at the possibility of not only further civil war but war with England.

The women retired before the men. But when Alec did reach his bedchamber presently it was to find it without Agnes. When she arrived, to find him bathing himself in the tub of warm water by the fire, at which process she kindly came to assist, he asked her what she had been doing all this time.

"Just women's talk," she answered.

Something about the way she said that had him glancing at her in the firelight. "A lengthy chatter, I think. Was it more of this of the Douglases and the English?"

"No, women's talk, I said." She shrugged. "The princess and I have both failed to produce a child. We were wondering why."

"M'mm. And what conclusions did you come to?"

"None. Save that we must go on trying."

"So-o-o! You do not blame your husbands?"

"Not for lack of effort, at least!"

"I am glad that you do not accuse me of . . . inactivity, at least! See you, off with your clothes and we shall show that we are not stricken with the palsy, whatever else!"

"Allow me to wash, will you?"

"I will aid you in that. To possible effect!"

"Think you that is required?"

"We shall see . . ."

They proved their strength of purpose before they slept that night, as the gale battered their window to add its own urgency.

In the morning, the tumult of wind and wave was such as to rule out any return to Stirling that day. Gray rode down to North Berwick to see that all was well with his escort of guards, while the others, wrapping themselves in plaids, climbed up to brave the elements on the parapet walk and to gaze at the drama of the Norse Sea's fearsome assault on the cowering land, in crashing breakers so high as to be scarcely believable, amidst showers of spray and spume and seaweed, even shells coming up to reach the watchers on the tower-top, not to mention the cliff-top, the shore being almost two hundred feet below them. Angus explained, having to shout, that the rage of it, in a storm, was particularly fierce, this because of great underwater cliffs, comparable to those on which his castle perched, between here and the Bass Rock, where the land ended at that lower level, and the tides, striking this, erupted in vast vehemence, spouting up in more hundreds of feet to surmount the obstacle, and hurtling on to smite the land proper in their frenzy. The Bass itself, and North Berwick Law's isolated cone, were part of the same savage rock formation, as, to be sure, were Tantallon's own precipices.

They did not watch for long, exciting as it was, in that blizzard of spray, clinging to the parapet to keep their stance. Alec looked out northwards towards the Isle of May, wondering how it fared in such conditions, and thinking that St Ethernan must have witnessed such spectacles frequently in his communions with his Maker. But the May was not to be discerned through that watery obscurity.

An inactive day was spent in talk and over-eating – perhaps the night the more active therefor.

They wakened to an extraordinary contrast, calm, no wind at all, although the sea still surged in long swells, no rattling shutters, the tide producing only a steady sighing and the screaming seafowl, not in evidence yesterday, providing the only urgency to the morning.

So, presently, it was back to the barge, this time with

Angus and Jean as companions, for the sail up Forth, leaving Tantallon in the care of a keeper, with clear instructions as to the summoning of men to its aid if need be, and sending to Stirling for the earl.

It made a jouncy voyage up to Airth, with the seas still reminding them of the previous day's sudden storm.

25

They had not been back at Stirling for more than four days when news of a great battle reached them. Huntly had caught up with the Tiger Earl on his own territory in Angus and the Mearns, and defeated him with major slaughter, this on both sides, at Brechin. Huntly's two brothers had been killed, as had Crawford's brother and Dundas of that Ilk, and over sixty knights and lairds and hundreds of men-at-arms. It was hardly a cause for rejoicing, but at least it removed the threat of the Tiger meantime, and proved Huntly's effectiveness as lieutenant-general.

James was able to go to the parliament at Edinburgh with some confidence, even though he learned that, on the morning of it, a placard had been affixed to the Tolbooth's door, signed by the new earl and his brothers, also the Lord Hamilton, renouncing all allegiance to the king, as a perjured prince and merciless monster.

That assembly's first business, however, was James Stewart's official absolution for the slaying of William Douglas. Crichton, from the Chancellor's table, declared that the earl had been in open and announced rebellion against the monarch, and was therefore due to die. Bishop Kennedy announced that papal exoneration had been obtained; and parliament, without further ado, unanimously voted the killing as rightful and deserved judgment. James was able to sit back on his throne in relief, his name cleared, whatever, on occasion, his own conscience might tell him.

There followed the necessary and inevitable adjustments, already proposed by the council. The Black

Douglases were declared forfeit, their titles stripped from them, their lands open to those strong enough to seize them, and the king's supporters rewarded; this last made a little less authoritative in that it was reported that Archibald, Earl of Moray was presently laying waste Huntly's lands in the north, and the lieutenant-general, not present, was in fact hastening thither to try to deal with it, after Brechin. However, parliament had to seem to be in control. The said Archibald Douglas's earldom of Moray was there and then bestowed upon Sir James Crichton, the Chancellor's son, Agnes's brother – with some equity, since his wife was the only child of the previous Stewart earl. The Chancellor's credit was further enhanced by his cousin, Crichton of Cairns and Barnton, being given the vacant earldom of Caithness, and created Lord High Admiral, a purely nominal honour since there was no royal fleet to command. Hay, the Constable, was created Earl of Errol; and other supporters who had rallied to the king's banner at and after Perth; Stewart of Darnley, Hepburn of Hailes, Boyd, Fleming, Lyle and Cathcart, made lords of parliament, and allotted such of the Douglas lands as they could take. All over the hall more of the members jumped up to announce their support for the king.

Angus, although not a warlike man, presumably felt that he must make the Red Douglas position entirely clear, and moved that His Grace should forthwith muster as great an army as all this support made possible, to march on the Black Douglas country and impose the royal, and parliament's, will on the south-western land, this seconded by the Lord Glamis and approved by all. Orders were given for as large a host as possible to assemble on Edinburgh's Burgh Muir in one month's time.

Up in the gallery, Alec pondered over the needs, devices and alliances required apparently for the government of realms. Were all nations so unruly and difficult to control as Scotland? Certainly England appeared to be going through somewhat similar throes. Perhaps it had always been so, mankind being controversial and unruly by nature.

The royal party returned to Stirling, to prepare for the campaign.

Alec was not the only one to be surprised and impressed by the turnout discovered at the Edinburgh assembly-point those weeks later, James himself highly elated. No fewer than thirty thousand were encamped on the Burgh Muir, and making themselves a nuisance to the capital's citizens, almost one-tenth of them Red Douglases. Never had the king seen so large an army, nor so many lords congregated in Scotland for other than a parliament, the sea of banners flying over tented pavilions a colourful legion. The monarch, to celebrate, held feastings in the abbot's house of Holyrood for two evenings, as they awaited belated but promised additions. This one would make the Lochmaben expedition look puny.

The move was made on 3rd July, the lion rampant flying at the head of literally hundreds of heraldic banners as the army headed southwards, along the eastern skirts of the Pentland Hills for Peebles-shire, their first target the Douglas properties in the vast Ettrick Forest area. These were not protected by great castles but by small Border tower-houses, strong enough for local defence but presenting little problems for a major host. Tinnis, Deuchar, Ladhope, Mountbenger, Blackhouse, Dryhope and Cramalt towers were duly taken, pillaged and destroyed, and their villages harried and sacked – their lairds and young men being mainly away with their Douglas lords.

Then over and through the lofty and empty Tweedsmuir hills for northern Dumfries-shire, not making for Lochmaben this time but keeping a line towards upper Nithsdale, the further huge province of Galloway their main objective. With so large a host progress was slow; and opposition being non- existent and looting more or less the order of the day, it was all but holiday for most there, a welcome relief from farm-work, milling, shepherding and the like.

Dumfries-shire was considered to be almost part of Galloway, although it had a different identity, its own sheriffdom and justiciary. But it was almost wholly under the control of the Douglases, despite the Maxwell, Johnstone, Herries and other West March clans' resentment. On Kennedy's advice it was James's present policy to wean these away from submission to Douglas, especially after the murder of Herries of Terregles, so no devastation was committed in upper Annandale, Nithsdale and the vales of the Waters of Ae, Kinnel, Cairns, Shinnel and Dalwhat, until the actual Galloway border was reached, near Moniaive.

Their so slow progress did have some advantage, in that it allowed the news of this mighty army to go before them, and in consequence quite large numbers of landed men came to the conclusion that it would be wise and politic to join this royal array; so that their total was almost forty thousand by the time that they reached Galloway. As it proved later, another positive benefit of the lack of haste was that it warned Douglas, well in advance of their arrival, of the size and might of the force bearing down on them – although it could have worked against the king's host.

They cut a very wide swathe through that fair land, laying waste much of what they passed, with the further delayed progress, but this all spelled out its own message. It was three weeks after leaving Edinburgh before they reached the Cluden water, where a decision had to be made as to direction of advance.

Galloway consisted of the two counties of Kirkcudbright and Wigtown. The former was the main Douglas base, with their strongest castle and seat at Threave, well to the south of their present approach. Wigtown, however, was an earldom of its own, as well as a county, also a Douglas title; and on the Earl William's forfeiture, James had presented this, with its lands, to Queen Mary, in a typical impulsive gesture. She had never attempted to visit it, but in theory, if not in practice, it was hers. So it was not to be ravaged and laid waste like the rest. A turn almost due southwards was made, therefore, into Kirkcudbrightshire, Threave their principal objective.

They always had scouts out ahead, to be sure, and Alec quite often chose to accompany these small parties, as a change from the slow riding, and seeing the burning and spoiling of the country, an activity which he did not enjoy, however necessary it was deemed to be. And on these forward sallies they learned that no large Douglas host appeared to be massing to face them; indeed one informant declared that the Lord Balveny had left his brothers at Threave, with quite a numerous company, and was heading north into Wigtownshire, the which made it look as though he was either going to collect reinforcements there, or else being sent up for that earldom's defence. Whatever it was, it made it look as though the Earl James and his other brother, Ormond, were not contemplating any large-scale encounter with the royal army, for they could not have been left in ignorance of its coming and its size.

Siege at Threave, then? Was that a practical proposition?

Down through central Kirkcudbrightshire they went, by the Glenkens to the Urr Water, which great river they followed due southwards, by Corsock and Glenlair, a score of miles, to the Haugh of Urr, where they swung off westwards for Threave. This advance brought them to the still larger River Dee, below its huge widening known as Loch Ken, and here, at last, they found what they had come so far to seek, the prime Douglas stronghold of Threave. And they saw why it was so chosen, and why defence against siege might well be contemplated.

The castle stood on an island in the quarter-mile-wide Dee, well out from the east bank, a massive fortalice, large Douglas banners flying from its tower-tops. As they came in sight of it, all in the king's party, at the head of their mile-long host, reined up and sat their horses and stared, silent. The castleton nearby, large also, was deserted. No words were necessary.

What now, then? All had guessed that Threave would be a strong place; but this, of its island-site, was a blow indeed. If the Douglases were prepared for siege, they would be well supplied with provisions, and water was all about them. Cannon, then? The king had no cannon, and even though he could find artillery somewhere in this area, which did not seem likely, mighty pieces indeed would be necessary to send effective shot to that hold, so far offshore. And its walls looked sufficiently solid to withstand battering.

James was much put out, and none there able to enlighten him as to effective action, even the Lord Gray.

The royal party took over the abandoned castleton, far from setting it alight, and the forty thousand ordered to encamp themselves nearby, as best they might. If siege it was to be, feeding this huge number was going to be a problem in itself, which had no doubt been envisaged by the Douglases, for not a cow or a sheep was to be seen on the surrounding pastures, the land cleared. Also to be seen, at the northern end of that half-mile-long island, was a major encampment of men.

The required conference took place in the largest house of the castleton.

"It is beyond all!" James exclaimed. "To have the greatest host that this land has seen for many a year, and yet to be unable to use it! Held by a reach of water. Mere water! Boats? Could we find boats? Many boats?"

"We would need scores, hundreds," Angus declared. "Where to get them? And they would be in great danger, crossing. Under fire from those walls."

"Cannon," Lord Gray announced. "Only cannon will take that hold. And they will have their own cannon. Perhaps not great. But enough to sink boats."

"Time we have, at least," Hay, now Errol, said. "We can sit here and wait until they starve . . ."

"Unless we ourselves starve first!" Keith, the marischal, objected. "Where are we to find food for our two-score thousand? We cannot hold these numbers idle and hungry, for long. They will move off, seeking meat. And many, I say, not come back."

Sir Patrick Gray spoke up. "Cannon, Father. Once, I mind you telling me that my aunt's husband, MacLellan of Bombie, he who Douglas slew and gave me the head – he had sought to build a great cannon. Did he ever do so? We are none so far from Bombie here."

Lord Gray scratched his chin. "Aye, it was his aim, yes. I had forgotten that. But whether he ever did so, I never learned."

"Was he a man for cannon?" the king demanded. "If so, there might be one or two at this Bombie, wherever it is."

"He was a man of many notions, Sire. This of a great cannon but one of them. He improved the crossbow. He devised mill-wheels with especial flaps, like fins, to double the power. More than that. My sister, who wed him, considered him crazed with all his notions."

"But this of cannon. We need cannon. Where is this Bombie?"

"It is some three miles east of Kirkcudbright town, Sire. No mighty castle. Whether there are any cannon there now, I know not. The Douglases likely would take them, after his death."

"It is worth the seeking, no? Or is there anywhere else where we might look for them in this Galloway? Not held by Douglas?"

None there could think of any castle or stronghold likely to be equipped with artillery not in Douglas hands, or not already purloined by them.

"Sir Patrick," James said. "Go you to this Bombie. Discover what you may. The Master of Glamis will go with you. We must have cannon, if it is at all possible. And quickly."

"I would not count overmuch on this of Bombie,

Sire," the Lord Gray warned. "Had anything come of my good-brother's notion, I think that I would have heard of it. And so would the Douglases!"

"What else can we do?"

None there had any hopeful solution to their predicament, other than merely calling on the Douglas brothers to surrender, offering them terms which they could find acceptable, Angus declaring that they might be prepared to yield rather than face a prolonged siege, given quarter.

Leaving that frustrated conference, Sir Patrick Gray and Alec went out to collect an escort of the royal guard, and to go in search of Bombie Castle, those three miles from Kirkcudbright.

Gray did not know the area well, but he had visited his aunt on occasion, although never from Threave. Anyone local could tell them how to get to Kirkcudbright town however.

It proved to be none so far, just over fourteen miles down Dee, due south, not much more than an hour's riding, to that walled town where the MacLellans had their town-house. It occurred to Gray that his aunt might well be there, now that her husband was dead and her son laird of Bombie. She might know about the cannon situation.

As well that they did call at the fine tenement in the main street of the ancient burgh, for they found Lady MacLellan, her son absent, but with the word that Bombie castle had been destroyed by the Douglases.

This seemed like an end to their quest for cannon. But the old lady did refer to her husband's odd project. She agreed that he had devised a great piece of artillery, consisting of heavy iron bars welded together and bound by steel hoops to form a huge gun-barrel, and had a wooden carriage on wheels to bear it. The smith, Kim Graham, at Mollance, had been making this, however little he esteemed the project – but of course work on it would have ceased on her husband's murder.

Her visitors were interested, needless to say, although

261

they were scarcely encouraged to hope that the contraption would be in a state to be of any use. But this Mollance hamlet, it seemed, was in the parish of Crossmichael, more or less on their way back to Threave; indeed they must have passed nearby it. So they could call in at the smiddy on their return journey, since there was nothing to be gained by going to Bombie.

They took their leave of the head-shaking widow, who urged vengeance upon those Douglases, and rode off up Dee again.

They had no difficulty in finding the small village of Mollance, and its smithy. The smith, this Kim Graham, proved to be a huge and hearty man, at work hammering horseshoes at his forge, and laugh heartily he did when he heard of his callers' quest. Mons Meg, was it? he cried. Apparently this Mollance was pronounced Mons locally, and Meg was his wife – why this name he did not explain. But he took them over to a stable and shed, wherein he displayed to them the source of his amusement. This was the oddity which Sir Thomas MacLellan had caused him to fashion, a waste of time and good iron he would say. He had built a couple of small cannon for Sir Thomas previously, but this monstrosity was beyond all reason, a nonsense in metal. He judged that it weighed five tons and more. It was unfinished, of course.

The visitors stared at the colossal, rusting iron tube, lying beside but not on a wooden trolley, designed to carry it. Over a dozen feet long, its mouth and breech were some twenty inches wide, an extraordinary object to be man-made in a Galloway village, lying there in a thatched shed.

"See you, Graham," Sir Patrick said, "this, this giant in iron must have been the result of much thought, as well as labour. Sir Thomas MacLellan was no fool. He would not design such as this without belief in it. You say that you forged other, smaller cannon for him, so you know how these pieces do their work, the secret of them. This mass of iron could act? Could fire ball?"

"Och aye, sir. If finished, just." The smith pointed to a corner, where a pile of iron balls, large ones, were heaped. "Sir Thomas said that it could throw one o' these near a mile! Whether it would, I dinna ken. But yon's what he said, aye – whatever he wanted it for."

"And you could finish it, man? And make it work?"

"Och, aye, sir, if need be, just. What for would it be wanted?"

"To assail a castle, man. What do you think? Threave."

"The accursed Douglases! Och then, I'll finish it right enough. Aye, wi' a will! It was them as slew Sir Thomas."

"True. How long? We need it soon, so soon as may be. Before they may have others coming to their aid. The king himself it is, besieging them."

"The king! Sakes! Then I'll be at it here and now, sirs. It is the breech just, to finish. And the trunnion."

"Trunnion? What is that?"

"A bit cradle, just. For raising and lowering the muzzle. To change the range. On yon trolley."

"Those balls? Are they for this, this bombard?"

"Aye. I made them so that Sir Thomas could judge the weight, just. To ken how much powder they would need. They're right heavy."

"Ah, yes. Gunpowder. Where will we get powder?"

"Nae bother, that. Sir Thomas ay kept powder for his pieces in the ice-house behind the stables at Bombie. The Douglases would never think to search yon when they burned the place. Plenties there."

"Good. You will be well paid for this, I promise you. How long?"

"Gie me three days, just."

"You will be able to bring it to Threave? Oxen?"

"Na na – horses, sir. Twa plough-horses. Quicker. And nae oxen here."

"His Grace the King will thank you, Graham."

"Friend," Alec put in, as they were returning to the

waiting escort, "why do you name this Mons Meg? After your wife, did you say?"

"Aye." The man grinned. "My wife Meg hasna gien me a bairn. And this cannon hasna fired a ball! No' yet." He hooted. "Maybe, if it fires right, she'll fire too! She's no' that auld."

Alec perceived that he and the Red Douglas were not the only would-be fathers.

This Mollance was only some four miles from Threave, so they were back before nightfall. And great was the elation of James Stewart when he heard their report, so much so as to have his messengers praying that the smith, Graham, might be as good as his word, and the bombard came up to its designer's intention. They were informed that while they were gone, some of the army's scouts, looking for cattle and sheep for food, had found a small boat a mile or so up towards Loch Ken, and bringing this back, the king had used it to row out halfway to the castle island, under the lion rampant standard, there to shout a summons to the Douglases to surrender. He had been answered by abusive threats, and to emphasise the defiance, just as the boat returned to the shore, a single cannon-blast had resounded, blank-shot probably but enough to make the message clear.

So it was settling-in there by the Dee-side, to await Mons Meg.

Kim Graham proved to be even better than his word, in that he arrived at the encampment in the late afternoon of only two days later, with his great bombard being dragged by a pair of heavy horses on its cradle trolley, and two other men leading pack-horses laden with sacks of cannon-balls and of gunpowder.

The king actually ran to greet them, and to stare at the monstrous piece of artillery, fully twice the size of the largest cannon even at Stirling Castle. James being James, of course, nothing would do but that the thing should be tested there and then, Graham nothing loth. So, before an interested audience, the smith and his helpers set to work to position the heavy piece on its trunnion, raise the muzzle to the required elevation, this aimed at the Castle's main keep, put a ball down the barrel, ramming it home with a rod, and filling the covered breech cavity with powder, much powder, lead a fuse-length thereto – and all ready, warn king and onlookers to stand well back. He then struck steel and flint on to tinder, blew this into a little blaze to light the fuse, and then hastily withdrew to a safe distance.

Fascinated, all watched the slow-burning fuse work its way to the breech cavity, in anticipation. But despite their hopeful expectations, none there was prepared for quite the violence and ear-piercing blast of the explosion, the rush of hot air which all but knocked those nearest over, and the major backwards recoil of that massive weight of iron, all alarming in the extreme, even to the nearby horses, which shied and sidled.

Amidst the cries, the staggering, the ear-clapping and coughing from the billowing smoke, it was the Lord Gray who shouted loud, and pointed. There, on Threave's massive tower, a cloud of dust was rising from just below the parapet walk. When this cleared a little, a gaping hole could be seen in the masonry, discernible even at that range.

At the sight, cheers arose from the watchers, and the king strode over to fling his arms around Kim Graham, in an embrace, a royal reaction hitherto reserved only for female persons. It was all acclaim, then, and congratulations, Alec as well as others going over to shake the smith's hand, that grinning giant the hero of the hour.

James duly demanded a second shot, this to be aimed lower, at the enclosing walls of the courtyard, which would demolish more easily, it was hoped. So the trunnion was adjusted, the loading and priming process repeated, but this time the onlookers all moved heedfully further back, and a man sent to lead the horses off.

The second blast was no less deafening and breathtaking, however much they were all prepared for it; but the aim was less accurate, the ball striking first the summit of the courtyard wall and then smashing on to demolish some of the outbuildings beyond – not the target, but an effective demonstration nevertheless.

What would be the reaction thereto within Threave Castle? all wondered.

They had not long to wait to find out. Two cannon-shots boomed from over the water. One ball came almost to them, to throw up a shower of earth near the shore, near enough to have all the king's party backing hurriedly; the other created a spout in the river. But the one which had landed dug no great hole. Almost certainly the size of these Douglas pieces was insufficient for any long-range bombardment, their purpose no doubt to defend the castle from attack over the water.

James laughed aloud and shook his fist at the enemy, ordering Graham to fire more ball, and to see if he could put a shot as far over as the encampment of the men further over on the island. That man declared that he would move his Mons Meg back some way, just in case some other shots from the foe reached further; his own monster would be none the less effective, and could almost certainly reach the Douglas men yonder. Sir Thomas had hoped that its range would be all but a mile.

So the horses had to be brought forward again to move the cannon and reposition it on a slight grassy hummock.

Then there commenced the battering of Threave, a steady pounding at fairly regular intervals, loading, ramming, priming, fusing, firing. Not all of the shots were seen to register, but enough did to have major effect, smashing gaps in the curtain walls mainly, but some making more holes in the keep and the secondary towers, one of the flagstaffs with the Douglas banner brought down, to cheers. Two were seen to cause a great scattering in the crowd of men at the far end of the island. One or two return shots were offered, but with these clearly ineffective, out of range, they ceased. The onlookers were greatly pleased, whatever the assault on their ears.

It was the Lord Gray pointing out to James the rapid diminution of the pile of cannon-balls, and the emptying of the powder-sacks, which caused a halt to be called in the bombardment. The sun had set and the dusk beginning to settle. Better to reserve some shots for the morning, it was suggested. Let the Douglases have the night to ponder their situation. A start of the battering with sun-up would be more effective than using up all their fire-power this night.

Reluctantly the king had to agree. He asked Graham whether he had any more balls back at his smithy, and when he learned that all had been brought, wondered how long it would take to fashion more. That had the smith shaking his head. These great missiles took much forging. It would be days before he could replace any number of them. There was more powder at Bombie, but . . .

The bombardment ceased then, and the besiegers readied themselves for the night, food scarce. Almost certainly they fed better over in that castle. James Stewart was so encouraged by the situation that he insisted that Kim Graham and his two helpers spend the evening in the royal company – to the embarrassment of those worthies.

The sentries watched heedfully, as on the previous nights, for any move from the castle island. None developed.

The sun had barely risen when Graham sent another two shots smashing into the two targets, the walls and the encampment. And not long thereafter, a large white sheet appeared, to hang from the battered parapet of the keep.

There could be little doubt as to the meaning of that. The Douglases desired, required, to parley, to come to terms. They recognised that their present situation was untenable. James punched fist into palm in satisfaction. He had them, he had them!

Lord Gray warned not to be over-sure. These Douglases were not so easily put down.

When a second white sheet was displayed from a keep window, it was clear that a parley was desired.

James ordered their single boat to be brought downriver to him, entered it, with five others, Lord Gray and his son, Angus, Kennedy's chaplain Dominic, and Alec Lyon, the last bearing aloft the royal standard. They were rowed out across the river to within hailing distance of the castle.

On an undamaged section of the curtain wall's parapet walk they could see figures standing. These waved.

Sir Patrick blew a blast on a horn, and the king called, "I, James, your sovereign-lord, speak. Do you yield?"

Promptly the answer came back to them. "On conditions, Sire, we will so consider, yes."

"Consider! You have had sufficient time to consider, sirrah! Yield, I say. Or be pounded to dust! As you deserve!"

There was silence from the castle.

Gray spoke urgently. "Hear them, Sire. We have little ball left. Four or five more shots and we fall silent. For days it may be. And our thousands are hungry, restive. And Balveny could come back, in force, at our rear. Hear them, I say."

"Highness," Friar Dominic said, "my lord bishop told me that I might advise Your Grace, in his name, to come to terms, if at all possible. For the realm's sake. Make it not over-difficult for them to yield. They have great powers still, in the land, other than this Threave. They still could do much hurt to your kingdom."

"I agree," Angus put in. "Douglas and his brother could make their escape by night. They will have their own boats on that island. Once free of it, they could raise more thousands. Rejoin Balveny. Wise, Sire, to come to some agreement. Since they seem to ask for it."

268

James frowned, then shrugged. He shouted again. "Yon white banner? What does that mean, Douglas?"

The answer came at once. "We would come to agreement. If we can, Sire. We, my lord of Ormond and myself, Douglas, will make submission. If you will heed us."

"Heed what, man?"

"This, Your Grace. We will pay you, as our sovereign-lord, all honour and worship. We will forgive" – a slight pause – "forgive all who had hand in the slaying of our brother, the Earl William."

James Stewart drew a quick breath.

"We will restore all lands and goods taken from others in this realm. Revoke all leagues and bands made with other lords, and agree to make none in future. And, and this of the earldom of Wigtown, ours by inheritance, we will not seek to reclaim it from Your Grace's royal wife. Nor the lordship of Stewarton, which also you have made over to her."

"Think you that is all that I require of you!" the king cried back hotly.

"As well as that, Sire, we will well defend your borders, act wardens to our best ability, and keep the peace with the Marchmen. Also keep the truce, as much as we may, between the kingdoms of Scotland and England."

James looked at his companions. "Hear you that?" he demanded. "What in insolence he offers!"

"It is most of what you require," Angus said.

"It is better than I feared," Gray agreed. "Accept it, and you are spared further battle, bloodshed, the realm in turmoil. There are times, Sire, when a commander in the field has to take the longer view."

"I believe that my lord Bishop of St. Andrews would say the same, Your Grace. He would have peace and unity in your realm, not strife. And this would seem much helpful towards that," Friar Dominic said.

"Forty thousand men! And thus to yield!"

"It is they who yield, James, not you," his brother-in-law reminded. "And I would say that it is not the forty thousand that has brought them to it, but MacLellan of Bombie's mighty bombard!"

James shook his head at this all but unanimous advice. "How can I ensure that they mean it? That Douglas but says the words, and they mean nothing?" It looked as though he was weakening.

"Ask him that, Sire," Alec put in.

"I will, yes." The royal voice was raised again. "Words, Douglas – words! How know we that they are not only that? That deeds, sure deeds, will follow?"

"I swear it on the Holy Gospels," came back.

"M'mm." James looked a little uncertain at that.

Swiftly the voice came to them again. "In token whereof, Sire, I seek your good offices. I beg you to speak with the Primate, the head of Holy Church in this land, to obtain from the Pope in Rome dispensation for myself, Douglas, to wed my brother's widow and my cousin, Margaret of Galloway."

All in that boat stared at each other at this extraordinary request, the Douglas actually seeking the royal aid in a private matter, in such circumstances. James all but choked.

It was the Church's representative who made sense of it. "Sire, I have heard that this earl doted on that young woman – all the brothers did, although the eldest won her. But here is good. Aid to Your Highness's cause, I judge. To wed his brother's widow is proscribed, not possible without especial papal permission. On Bishop Kennedy's especial recommendation, and that of the nuncio, that probably would be forthcoming. Without it, no. So here is Your Highness's earnest, assurance, that the earl will keep his word. At least until he is wed! If you refuse, the Fair Maid of Galloway is not for him, or any of his brothers. You have him, Sire!"

"Lord!" Sir Patrick jerked. "Here is a gift indeed! Better than any swearing on holy writ! If the bishop will agree to this, then you have won over Douglas, Sire."

Lord Gray nodded grimly. "A man's weakness for a woman! It can cost dear indeed!"

James was grinning now. "Aye," he said. "I see it. I will tell him so." He raised voice once more. "Douglas, I hear you. Yes, I will speak with the lord bishop on this. Perchance he will heed. And if you fail me in your word, you will know what to expect!"

"I thank you, Sire. You have my word."

After that, there seemed to be nothing more to say. The compact, such as it was, appeared to be made. The royal party were not going to put themselves into Douglas hands by proceeding on to the castle, white flag or none. And the opposition gave no indication that further negotiations were envisaged. Indeed the figures disappeared from that parapet.

The boat was turned, to head back for the shore.

A hasty council thereafter decided that there was nothing to be gained by remaining where they were. Balveny might appear and attack their rear, not knowing of the curious accord – and although their thousands could almost certainly defeat him, it might well be at a price in blood. And to what end? The day was young yet, their host was hungry, and the sooner they could win to a source of food, the better, a town preferably. They would move.

Before leaving the Threave castleton the king had a word with Kim Graham. As well as rewarding him and his helpers generously, he told him that he wanted that cannon, Mons Meg, for himself. He would pay well for it, and for a supply of the necessary balls. Let them be delivered in due course to his castle of Edinburgh. The royal thanks were typically impulsive.

So the host turned its face eastwards in search of sustenance, leaving three men, two horses, five cannon-balls and a massive iron monster on the site of the siege of Threave.

It had all made a very odd campaign.

26

A parliament was called for late August, in Edinburgh, to confirm and substantiate all that had been gained with regard to the Douglases. Meantime, with those forty days to wait, on Kennedy's and Crichton's advice, James made an expedition to the north. This was more of a royal progress than any armed campaign, to impress on those parts, unruly as they could be, the significance of the humbling of the Black Douglases and the great increase of the king's power and dominance over his realm. Indeed both advisers, Crichton beginning to show his age, accompanied the monarch, Kennedy having despatched his plea to the Pope regarding the Fair Maid of Galloway, no longer maiden as she was.

They picked up Huntly, the lieutenant-general, at Perth, and he informed them that Ross, John of the Isles, duly warned by the defeat of Crawford at Brechin and the latest collapse of his allies at Threave, would come here to Perth in a few days' time, to pay his own humble duty to his sovereign-lord. Clearly nothing succeeded like success.

So the distinguished company moved on north by east, by the northern slopes of the Sidlaw Hills, past MacBeth's Dunsinane to Coupar Angus and into Strathmore, where Alec's father joined them at Glamis, indeed entertained them all overnight, quite a major undertaking, Lady Glamis in a great old state. And in the morning, as they were preparing to move on, there was an unexpected development. Servitors came to announce that a ragged barefoot train had arrived, allegedly seeking the King's Grace, some sort of gangrel band. They had tried to send them away but they had persisted. They were round at the back quarters of the castle.

James, intrigued, went to see what this was, Alec and his father, with others, also. And there, at the head of a beggarly gang, clad in torn old clothing, unshod and bareheaded, was the Tiger Earl of Crawford himself, his lairds and knights behind him, all similarly dishevelled.

At sight of the monarch, Crawford came forward, to fall on his knees, arms outstretched, to announce his regret and remorse for the sins of himself and his people, and to plead forgiveness, tears in his eyes.

Astonished, uncertain, the king shook his head, scarcely believing that this could be the fierce Tiger. Huntly had come up behind them, and he, who had so recently defeated Crawford in battle, unsure of James's attitude, urged royal forbearance and clemency, Glamis adding his voice, for he, as justiciar, knew all too well the strength that Crawford could still wield in Strathmore and the Mearns.

The king, distinctly doubtful, at length held out his hand to the kneeling earl to take between both his own in the fealty gesture, he declaring gratitude, thankfulness and praise.

Abruptly James turned and hurried back into the castle, leaving the ragged crew to retire whence they had come, not entirely sure of the impact they had made and what the consequences would be.

Kennedy and Crichton, when they heard, were both well enough pleased by this odd episode. If such as Crawford could so act, and before his people, and with John of the Isles coming to make his peace, there would be few indeed who would now think to contest the royal authority. There was scarcely need to go on with this progress.

But Glamis urged some further advance, on into the Mearns, his justiciarship, where indiscipline and unlawful behaviour amongst the Ogilvys, the Carnegies, the Lindsays and others were his constant headache, lesser folk these perhaps, but still the better for some evidence of the royal concern. So, the weather being fine, and the all-important harvesting not yet a preoccupation with magnates and their tenants alike, the quite pleasant journeying was continued down Strathmore and over the Esks, northwards into the Howe of the Mearns and along the skirts of the Highland hills into the Fettercairn and Drumtochty area, none so far from the Aberdeenshire border, James seeing this as an opportunity to inspect the ancient royal castle of Kincardine, more or less abandoned now but with its own colourful history. For there King Malcolm Canmore had sent his Queen Ingeborg and their three sons when he fell for the beauty and talents of Margaret Atheling, and where the queen died shortly thereafter, not without suspicion of poison, and he was able to wed the said Margaret, queen and saint; there too, another determined woman, Fenella, engineered the strange death of King Kenneth the Second.

Kincardine Castle, however, when they reached it, scarcely gave the impression of being the scene of dark and dramatic deeds, set peacefully in pleasant wooded country near the hillfoots, comparatively small, empty and part ruinous, something of a disappointment to the romantically minded monarch. Why had it been let get into this state? Had not William the Lyon and Alexander the Third made it their hunting seat?

Here they turned back, without having made any very obvious impact on the area, apart from the company landing themselves on sundry local lords and lairds for meals and overnight accommodation – which perhaps had its own effects.

On their return journey, taking a slightly different route by Stracathro and Brechin, to see the site of Huntly's great victory, entering Strathmore again, they were met by a small party of Crawford's people, by no means raggedly dressed this time, who brought their lord's pressing invitation for His Grace and company to visit him at Finavon Castle. A little doubtful about this, James consulted Kennedy, for once he had vowed to take

Finavon and "make its highest stone its lowest". But he was prevailed upon to accept this offer of hospitality, for the sake of gaining the hearts as well as the swords and lands of his people, as the bishop put it.

At the tall and commanding castle they met with great magnificence, in such marked contrast to the beggarly trappings of the former encounter, Crawford himself resplendent, his chamberlain almost as fine, his servants faultless, the great hall prepared for a banquet and entertainment. But before he allowed anything other than an initial greeting, James Stewart ordered his host to take him up to the topmost parapet walk of the main keep. And up there, the king drew his dagger, to the earl's wide-eyed alarm, but with it proceeded to chip away at the mortar holding one of the coping stones in place – to the disadvantage of that blade, possibly the same with which he had slain another earl. But at least it loosened the mortar, and the king was able to push the stone over, for it to fall with a crash to the courtyard below, and thus to fulfil his vow about making the highest stone of Finavon the lowest. When the Tiger had this explained to him, he roared his relief, slapping his knee, and all could descend to the festivities prepared below in more relaxed and amicable fashion.

They made a convivial night of it.

On back to Perth the next day, they found the Earl of Ross awaiting them. No coming to meet them for this one, a very different character from his late fellow rebel. A proud and handsome Highlandman was John of the Isles, descended from the mighty Somerled, and come to establish peace, as it were, between two princes rather than making any submission to the King of Scots. The meeting, held in the Greyfriars monastery, was brief and to the point, and very formal, James in fact seeming all but in awe of this lofty and dignified character, however lispingly soft was his Highland tongue. Ross made no gestures of fealty, offered no apologies for having been in arms against the forces of the south, but declared that in the present situation he and his would sever all links with sources below the Highland Line, including the Douglas and Crawford earldoms. And he would expect the man, Huntly, to pay due respect to his own and his friends' territories. That was all, and James Stewart had to be content with it, at Kennedy's instigation, even Huntly's own, for if there was one certainty in the affairs of the realm, it was that by no means could the Lowland forces, however powerful and well led, master the Highlands and the Isles.

No celebratory festivities here, merely a coolly mannered parting, John MacDonald leaving Perth with his train of chiefs forthwith, giving the impression that the king had been fortunate that he had been prepared to wait for him there. But James's advisers, even Crichton, said thereafter that this was nowise unsatisfactory, peace with the intractable Highlanders, without a drop of blood shed.

So it was back to Stirling, to prepare for the parliament which was, as it were, to put the official seal upon the king's establishment of authority over his difficult realm.

With the monarch preoccupied with plans for the assembly, honours to bestow on his supporters, new offices and officials to appoint for the various areas now at last under royal control, at least in name, and other parliamentary business, Alec and Agnes took the opportunity to pay a visit to Pitteadie, and not only that, but to take the queen with them, her little daughter now old enough to be left with her nurses, and Mary, an active creature, having had more than enough of being cooped up in Stirling's rock-top fortress. With a very small escort, then, the three of them rode off for Fife, rejoicing to be free, for a week, from duties and commitments.

Mary of Gueldres made excellent company, cheerful, unassuming, interested in all that she saw and what went on, her command of her new language much improved. She announced that she believed that she was pregnant again, declaring that it was going to be another boy.

They spent a happy time at Pitteadie, exploring much of Fife, most of it as new to Agnes as to the queen, indeed some to her husband also, Mary being particularly enchanted with the fishing villages of the East Neuk, with their red-tiled and whitewashed houses and pier-guarded harbours; Largo, Earlsferry, Elie, St Monans, Pittenweem, Anstruther, Kilrenny and Crail, from these last being able to look out to the Isle of May, seen from a different angle, her first footfall on Scottish soil. So much taken was she over that isolated outpost of her husband's kingdom, that she prevailed on Alec to have some Pittenweem fishermen agree to take them out to the island, two days hence, conditions permitting. After all, it was from here that St Ethernan had had his timber fuel ferried out regularly to keep his lighthouse beacon burning on the May to warn shipping of danger, and possibly by the ancestors of these very fishermen.

Their boat-trip, with the weather kind, was a great success, the boatmen soon overcoming their awe at having their queen as passenger. The seas were not rough. They had to sail round to the southern end of the island to make a landing, the young women exclaiming at the seals they saw basking on cliff-foot rocks, the towering precipices, and the screaming, circling seafowl.

Ashore, they tramped and clambered over every yard of the isle which gave them foothold, female skirts hitched high. Although it had not seemed windy on the water, it was blowy here, and with that, and the noise of the multitudes of birds, some of which swooped down on them without ever actually touching them, even though occasionally their droppings did, they had to shout – and there was much to shout about, it proved. They saw eider ducks' nests, lined with down, some of which Mary pocketed, guillemots perching on precarious ledges and glaring at them, cormorants and shags hissing at them from notably untidy nests of grasses and seaweed, puffins peering at them, comically tame, and lots of low-growing flowers, which Alec named as sea campion and milkwort and even primroses, hardly to be looked for in such an exposed position.

It was all a remarkable and welcome change from the formalities and restrictions of court life, and as such acceptable indeed. They left the May almost reluctantly.

Not that their other activities from Pitteadie failed to give enjoyment also. As well as exploring, they visited neighbouring estates and their lairds; examined the coastline caves at Wemyss, which gave that area its name, in the Gaelic; the women tried their hands at milking the Duries' cows; and they practised archery. Their escorts were left very much to entertain themselves, mainly down at the village of Kinghorn, making no complaints.

Their week over, they returned to Stirling and the constraints thereof.

This parliament, being in the nature of a celebration, the queen was to be present, and therefore Agnes. Being larger as to attendance, it was to be held not in the Tolbooth but at Holyrood Abbey, suitable as giving thanks to their Creator, the King of kings. But James's first call on arrival at Edinburgh nevertheless was up at the castle, to see whether his Mons Meg had arrived. Sure enough, there it was, up on a commanding site, a heap of great cannon-balls beside it. Those accompanying him found it difficult to win him away from the thing, to go down to Holyrood to greet the envoys and visitors invited to join the queen in appreciating this especial parliament.

The Abbot of the Holy Rood laid on a magnificent banquet that night for the monarch and his guests.

Next day the parliament, so carefully prepared, was no disappointment. Watching from up in the clerestorey gallery of the great church, especially granted by Holy Church for the occasion as a celebration of the God-given peace in the land, Alec, who had observed many assemblies, had never known one like it. The preliminaries were more like a major religious occasion than any state council or convocation, Bishop Kennedy leading, with the abbot and other prelates assisting, prayer and thanksgiving and addresses, even a choir contributing. When Crichton, as Chancellor, took over, even that stern authoritarian seemed a little uncertain as to procedure, and after announcing that this parliament was now in session, and saying that it was a notable event with much to the advantage of the nation to declare and establish and endorse, turned to the throne and more or less handed it over to the king.

Nothing loth, James jumped up, remembered that if he stood all others must do so likewise, sat down again, and jerked out a series of statements, words rather more forceful and vehement, even disconnected, than coherent, but with their own eloquence in emphasising the monarch's enhanced authority and prerogative. He asserted that, for the first time since he had succeeded to his royal father's throne, he could declare peace in his kingdom; that he intended that peace to continue, for the benefit of all his people; that the laws of the realm would be applied and enforced hereafter, and if necessary parliament should pass new laws to maintain the peace and cherish his subjects, from the lowest to the highest. As witness to which, by his royal will and command, he called on the Chancellor to detail his proposals for parliament to enact.

Crichton, more assured now, with his papers before him, commenced by reading that, in the interests of the king's peace and good relations, all forfeited lands of whomsoever, including former rebels, would be held in the royal care for one year only, whereafter, assuming that the former owners remained true to their allegiance and given word, they would be returned to them. Second, that a force of armed men from each county and jurisdiction and town of the land should be enrolled, to form a ready army for the lieutenant-general, to enforce where necessary the royal prerogative and sway, this to be paid for by a levy on

279

lands according to their wealth. Third, the appointment of all law officers, justiciars, sheriffs and the like should be supervised by a committee of parliament, this to ensure equity and fair judgment for the common folk of the land. Fourth, trade and commerce were to be encouraged by the formation of guilds and associations, of merchants, smiths, woodworkers, millers, spinners and all makers of goods, for the increase of the wealth of the nation; and foreign dealings and exchange to be improved and enlarged by the welcome of traders and visitors from other lands, as demonstrated by their friends from the Low Countries – and he turned and bowed to the queen, where she sat at the side of the chancel.

In the circumstances, none present could very well question nor debate all this. Alec smiled, as did others, when it was the Earl of Crawford who rose promptly to move heartily that these excellent provisions be endorsed by parliament. And when his former foe, Huntly, seconded that, the smiles were the broader. No contrary motion was forthcoming, and the list of resolutions was passed unanimously – an unusual departure for any Scots parliament. Factions undoubtedly remained, but they did not assert themselves on this occasion.

Thereafter the proposed changes in and nominations for various offices and roles were accepted, although the appointment of Sir James Livingston, the old lord's eldest son, as High Chamberlain raised some eyebrows, this having been advised by Kennedy in order to keep that difficult house in order, the chamberlainship being a prestigious post but not significant in the rule.

Strangely, perhaps, the one slightly critical note in the entire proceedings was sounded by none other than the Primate himself, probably as a gentle warning to his nephew. It was that Holy Church requested some restriction on the royal use of its funds and revenues in the realm's secular affairs. After a brief silence, and then James's nod, this was accepted likewise, without discussion.

The assembly was prorogued, after a final prayer and general benediction.

The king took his wife and friends back up to the castle to show off his wonderful new acquisition, which, he asserted, could be almost credited with making his present triumph possible by bringing down the Douglases. He would have wished to make demonstration of its power and excellence, but he could hardly fire a ball from here without causing damage, even out over the Nor' Loch. He had to content himself with having the breech cavity filled with powder, a fuse applied and lit, and firing a thunderous blank shot, which sufficiently impressed the watchers, had them staggering back coughing amidst clouds of smoke, and was echoed from the heights of Arthur's Seat. Not content, after all, with that, he had to have a second discharge which, warned, had them all covering ears with hands. What the citizens of Edinburgh thought of this alarming din was not to be known, but at least they were spared a third aural assault by the queen's pleas. It is to be feared that her husband's enthusiastic explanations of the construction and special features of this huge cannon fell rather on deafened ears as they returned to the abbey.

On the morrow it would be back to Stirling.

27

The period of peace and comparative harmony which
ensued was welcomed by most, especially those about the
court. James was able to spend much time at Falkland,
and the Lyons some at Pitteadie. News arrived from the
Vatican that the Pope was prepared to give dispensation
for the marriage of James, Earl of Douglas to his brother's
widow and cousin, the which promptly followed, although
it was rumoured that the bride herself was anything but
joyful over it all.

But after Yuletide, with its celebrations, happier than
usual, a strange and unlooked-for series of happenings
cast some shadows over those concerned with the rule of
the land; deaths, and from natural causes, not hostilities.
The first, early in the year, was that of none other than the
Tiger Earl, reported to have passed away in his own house
of Finavon from a fever. How many actively mourned him
it would be hard to say, but he did leave a gap on the
national scene. He left as heir only a child son.

The next death, only a few weeks later, had a considerably greater impact on the nation, for it was that of
William Crichton, the Chancellor, a blow indeed, for he
had become, in these last years, a major support for the
monarch whom he had so sorely offended earlier. Agnes
had never been close to her stern father, but she could
not be other than saddened by his passing. Much more
distressing to her, however, was the sudden death of her
brother James, the new Lord Crichton, only weeks after
he had succeeded to that title, this the result of being
thrown from his horse. So two funerals for the Lyons to
attend, so woefully close together. And if that was not

enough, her kinsman George Crichton, the new Earl of Caithness, also died shortly thereafter, he who was titular Admiral of Scotland; a year of disaster for that family.

There was still another loss to the nation; William Turnbull, Bishop of Glasgow, who had founded the university there, and whom Kennedy, who saw him as a possible successor as Primate, had had James appoint Lord Privy Seal. The most promising of all the younger prelates, he passed on at a comparatively early age. Many mourned him.

It all made a sorry spoiling of the king's acclaimed peace and establishing of his authority. He, and those around him, found themselves wondering who would be the next in this grievous catalogue.

In the event it was not further deaths which brought an end to Scotland's interval of concord, but the threat of war, major war, national as well as civil. It was the Lord Hamilton who was involved, married to the former Countess of Douglas, widow of the fourth earl. One of the West March Maxwells arrived at Falkland to inform the king that the word was that Hamilton, who had always supported the Douglases, if not necessarily in arms, had been sent by the earl to England, to the Duke of York, to renew the treasonable alliance, and seek funds and an English army to help unseat King James, for him, Douglas, to take over the throne as a puppet-king, again promising allegiance to King Henry, whom he would acknowledge as Lord Paramount of Scotland, thus fulfilling that centuries-old English aspiration. Presumably, now that his marriage to the Fair Maid was secure, Earl James no longer felt the need for his sovereign's clemency. Hamilton was thought to have brought back promises of armed support and a large sum of money.

James Stewart's hurt and fury was such as Alec Lyon had never before seen. He stormed and raged, so that his Mary feared for apoplexy, seeking help in her efforts to calm him down. Nothing would do but that the Douglas must be put down, once and for all, not only the earl but all his treacherous kin, Hamilton included. The nation must be called to arms to achieve this, forthwith, and to demonstrate to the English that Scotland was not ripe for picking. Whether his Mons Meg would be able to assist in this final task remained to be seen. Douglas should never have been spared at Threave. Kennedy was to be blamed for so advising.

It was back to Stirling at once, to issue the summons to the royal standard, no reluctance nor excuses on the part of his nobility and supporters to be countenanced. He would lead his greatest army in person, not Huntly, no mercy to be shown to the blackguardly traitors. Then on to Edinburgh, for the assembly on the Burgh Muir. This was to be the end of the Black Douglases.

For all James's impatience to be up and at them, it took time to assemble the size of force he demanded, from all over the land, even parts of the Highlands. But he was in no mood to kick his heels waiting; so taking a thousand or so of those already mustered, he set off westwards, leaving Huntly to see to the rest, and ordering Mons Meg to be brought on behind, as quickly as its ponderous weight would allow, heading for the nearest Douglas castle, that of Abercorn. This was a stronghold of Balveny, the youngest of the brothers, and lay about a dozen miles westwards near Queen Margaret's Ferry.

Needless to say, they quickly outpaced the heavy cannon and its great lumbering horses, and those with the cannon-balls and powder. They found Abercorn Castle, although not large as such strengths went, likely to be a hard nut to crack, this because of its strong position within an area of marshland near the ancient parish kirk, an extensive bog, with only a zigzag causeway through the mire to give access. Whether Balveny was therein or not they did not know; but others were, and sufficiently aggressive, for when a group under Lord Gray were sent forward from the host to investigate that causeway, they were promptly fired on, albeit by only modest-sized artillery, probably sakers, the shots not reaching them but sufficiently effective a warning to make any approach over that narrow, twisting firm track highly dangerous. And soundings of the marsh itself proved it to be soft, a quagmire indeed, and wide enough all around to keep attackers well distant. Abercorn was not islanded in a river, like Threave, but it might as well have been so.

James was very frustrated, waiting for Mons Meg, although he, and the others, feared that even that piece would be out of effective range, save by using the causeway. The royal summons to surrender was answered by further cannon-fire, although the balls did not anything like reach their firm ground. There was nothing for it but to seem to besiege. James was never good at waiting, patience not one of his virtues.

It took hours for Meg and its ammunition to arrive, and when it did, the king was incensed to discover that only eight balls had been brought with it, even these making a heavy load for horses. It was early evening, but James insisted on a trial shot being fired from the marsh edge, almost at once. Whether the ball hit the walling or not was not evident, no cloud of dust nor gap showing; most, watching, said that it had not, the range over-far even for Meg. Hotly, the king declared that the gunner – who of course was not the expert Kim Graham but one of the Edinburgh Castle garrison – had not used sufficient powder. So another discharge was tried, with the breech all but overloaded with powder. And despite the enormous crash and the heavy pall of smoke resultant, they did see the fall of the ball. It threw up a spout of wet mud some way short of the castle walling. So clearly they were not within range.

Nothing for it, then, James declared, but for Mons Meg to be taken out along that causeway, nearer to its target. But Gray pointed out that the zigzags of that narrow stone-paved approach were subtly designed to trap unwelcome and unwary visitors, with the twists and turnings uneven and erratic, with false offshoots ending in mire. This dusk was no time to try to venture the heavy and clumsy monster, dragged by its horses, out on to such a corridor.

But the monarch was insistent. The King of Scots and his army were not to be held up and kept at bay by this small fortalice in the midst of a bog. Get the cannon out along that track, however carefully, and they would pound the wretched place into submission in a short time, even with their six remaining balls. It would not be fully dark for an hour or so yet.

So the horses were yoked up again and the move made. Alec pointed out to Sir Patrick Gray that unless the cannoneer was very efficient in his elevations and aiming, those six balls were unlikely to achieve their objective. They certainly could not afford to waste any. How long before others could be brought? Or even made? Were there more at Edinburgh? The other shrugged eloquently.

The first thirty yards or so of that causeway were covered slowly, but successfully, the horses being led cautiously indeed, men out in front testing every foot of the way. A steep bend to the left was negotiated, with some difficulty, for the solid paving was no more than ten feet in width, and the horses and the cannon required space to swerve and deviate. And almost immediately thereafter there was a tight thrust to the right, not so difficult for a single horseman but awkward for such a dragged and lengthy weight as this. Heedfully, with much backing and testing, they got beasts and burden round, and with sighs of relief started along the next section. But, only a few yards, and disaster – the right-hand horse plunged over the edge as the men in front yelled that this was only a false spur. And as they cried out, the wheels of the trolley and trunnion on that right side tipped over after the floundering animal, and the weighty mass of iron lurched over into the bog.

Great was the consternation, especially that of James Stewart. His precious Meg! Save it! Save it! Get it back up on to the causeway. Up with it. Suddenly Abercorn Castle was all but forgotten. Mons Meg became all-important. Rescue Meg!

That proved to be none so easy. Fortunately not all of the trolley was over the edge, the left wheels still precariously on the paving-stones, the cannon itself at a critical angle. The fear was that it would sink further, even be pulled over by that unfortunate horse which was still roped to it. How deep was the mire? Could it engulf Meg altogether? The wretched horse, plunging, was almost up to its belly.

Somehow that sorry beast had to be got out first, not so much for its own sake as that it could pull over the trolley completely; and anyway it was required to aid the dragging process to safety. The scanty width of the causeway prevented any large number of men from assisting in this, especially with the king fussing and fuming and himself trying to pull at the rope between horse and trolley. It was chaos, muddy chaos.

Eventually they managed to get the animal out on to the stone slabbing, and an unhappy and difficult creature it had become, the manoeuvring it to the correct position to aid the now agitated other horse a task in itself, and then trying to have the two to pull together in that limited space still more of a problem.

James, angry and humiliated, was persuaded to retreat therefrom, but not before he had been informed that his Meg's wide mouth, or muzzle, had filled up with mud and slime. That was the finishing touch.

Making for his own horse, he sent for Lord Gray, still out on the causeway. He was to remain here, with a sufficiency of men, to see to the recovery of the cannon. He was going on, with most of the force, to Inveravon, another ten miles or so, westwards still. It was one more Douglas house, reputedly not strongly fortified. The folk there would not be expecting an assault by night. He would take that, and then come back here to deal with Abercorn.

However authoritatively that was declared, Gray looked at him doubtfully, as did others. But clearly the much upset monarch was anxious to redeem his credibility as a commander, and to remove himself from this mortifying situation of having to sit and watch while his artillery was being salvaged from the morass into which it had gone at his orders.

Alec and Patrick Gray went with the king, of course, however questioning of this move by night. Admittedly they knew the country hereabouts fairly well, for it was on the direct route from Stirling to Edinburgh which they had to use so often. Inveravon itself was a mile or so off the road, on the other, northern side of the very winding River Avon some four miles west of Linlithgow, not far from where it entered the upper firth almost directly opposite Culross, the famed birthplace of St Mungo, and near the end of the likewise famous Roman Wall of Antonine. The Romans had at least done these parts a good turn in constructing a substantial ford across the river, for they had camps on both sides for their wall-builders, and this survived. Indeed Inveravon Castle was said to be erected on the site of one of their fortlets. So the ten-mile ride in darkness would not be too difficult. But what would be achieved at the end of it remained to be seen.

The king was very silent as they went, his companions reining back somewhat to leave him to his thoughts.

They in due course passed through a silent and benighted Linlithgow, although the passage of several hundred horsemen must have awakened much of the citizenry.

The finding of the ford in the darkness was the problem, for the road did not follow the riverbank, liable to flooding. They knew that it was before they came to Polmont. Fortunately the Romans came to their aid again, for near Gilston they came across traces of an ancient road running north and south, evident even in the dark, which could only be Roman; and since the river lay to the north this probably led to the ford. It did, and they were able to splash across just as dawn was beginning to lighten the eastern sky.

Despite the weariness of his men, James was determined on immediate attack. There were forts on two mounds only half a mile apart, and the half-light revealed building on the western one. They rode for this.

There was little subtlety or artifice about this assault. They found that there had been a deep ditch around the base of the mound, but this was dry, and the horsemen, dismounting, were able to cross it at various points and climb up the grassy slopes to the very walls of the castle. It proved to be a larger place than Abercorn, but much less defendable. If guards there were on duty they presumably were asleep, for no alarm was sounded. At the gatehouse in the curtain walling, right and left, the king's people hid themselves close against the masonry where they could not be seen from the parapet. Sir Patrick went forward alone, to hammer on the great gates with his sword hilt. It took a while for him to gain any attention, but at length a man peered down from the parapet, alone, to demand what was to do? Gray shouted up that he was from the castle of Abercorn, with urgent tidings. That seemed to be accepted, and the guard disappeared.

Presently they all heard the noise of a drawbar being removed, and men on either side of the gateway moved closer, James and Alec amongst them. Then the postern, or minor door in the main massive gates, was opened, and a single man stood therein. Gray threw himself upon him instantly, sword smashing down, and as the unfortunate fell, the attackers ran up and over and in, weapons in hand.

Another guard came down the winding stairway from the gatehouse chamber and was promptly felled. The rest of the king's force came pouring in. The courtyard was empty.

James, all warrior now, led the way over to the square, high block of the main keep. The door to it was shut but not barred nor locked. He flung it open, and in the invaders surged. Clearly all the occupants were asleep.

Splitting up, with a minimum of noise, groups went to deal with the slumberers on the various floors, Alec and Gray preceding the king upstairs.

Noise there was very quickly thereafter, yells and screams and groans, but quite soon the shouting was triumphant, the opposition either struck down or cowering in surrender.

Surely seldom had even a moderately sized castle been taken with so little trouble as Inveravon.

There were no large numbers, as garrison, if that it could be called, and these, such as had not died in the assault, were sent off to the nearby village of Nether Kinneil, with their wounded, their few womenfolk not neglected by some of the attackers. James gave orders for the castle to be sacked and burned, but said that they would rest awhile therein first, as was indeed called for. They found no great store of provisions for his hundreds, so it was a hungry as well as a weary company which eventually left Avonside to return whence they had come.

Back at Abercorn they found all more or less as they had left it, save that the supply of cannon-balls was exhausted, and this without the fortalice showing any sign of yielding. Lord Gray said that they had managed to clear Mons Meg's muzzle and barrel of the mud and slime, no easy task with its lengthy funnel. They had got it firing again, but with obviously scant effect at that range. However, he for one was not going to try to get it out on that causeway again, and strongly recommended his liege-lord not to do so either. He had sent for more balls from Edinburgh, but whether such were available he did not know. And forging a new supply would take time undoubtedly.

James, able to announce his success at Inveravon, was more amenable now to good advice. He declared that, since word had come to Gray in the royal absence, a large force of Highlanders had reached Glasgow, under Colin, Lord Campbell, in response to his appeal to some of the chiefs, he would go there now and use them to assail some of the Douglas strengths in the west, Gray to come with him. They would leave a company of men to besiege this Abercorn; the Constable, the new Earl of Errol, to be sent for from the muster at Edinburgh to take charge. The king was very much in command again. They would starve out those rascals in the castle, even if they were not able to bombard them out.

The force started on the quite long ride to Glasgow.

They found large numbers of men awaiting orders in Glasgow, indeed two armies, Highlanders and Lowlanders – but not together, advisedly, for there already had been scuffles between them, so their commanders were concerned to keep them apart, Campbell's Argyll men, Macfarlanes, Colquhouns, Lamonts and the like basing themselves on the northern bank of Clyde, the Cunninghams, Montgomeries, Lyalls, Lockharts and Dalziels, under their lords, well to the south. It was hoped that the presence of the monarch would keep these quarrelsome subjects from each other's throats, always a problem in Scotland. Their leaders agreed that action, military action, would be the most effective means to this desired end; so no time was lost in heading off southwards, up Clyde, for Lanark and the Hamilton country, allies of Douglas.

Strangely enough, their first assault was on a new castle built by Balveny, called Avendale, beside a second river of that name – not so strange in that the name was taken from the Gaelic word for a stream, *abhainn*, and there were many variations of it throughout Scotland, Avon, Aven, A'an, Almond, Allan, Ale, even Devon and Deveron. This one was a tributary of the Clyde, a dozen miles west of Lanark. The castle, not long completed, fell to the king without overmuch delay, its keeper, unsure of its defensive state, putting up only a token resistance. There was no real slaughter here, but quite a lot of booty. And James had his first experience of losing part of his army, not through casualties but by Highlanders departing overnight with cattle they had looted from the property, heading back home with these.

The next target was Draffane Castle, high above the south bank of Clyde itself, near Crossford, Draffane of that Ilk being a vassal of the Hamiltons; perhaps not a very enthusiastic vassal, for when he saw the size of the force come against him under the royal standard, he yielded almost at once, protesting his loyalty to the crown. So Draffane was largely spared sacking. So far, the required military action for uniting the force was scarcely forthcoming, however profitable the booty.

The small Douglas strengths of Hallbar and Waygateshaw were then assailed and easily taken. In this Clyde valley, however, a very fertile area, being populous and rich in cattle, the size of the army did diminish, some of the Lowland levvies taking their cue from the Highlanders, departing in darkness with loot; also, it is to be feared, womenfolk.

It did not take very long to reach Lanark. James had thought to make something of an example of this county town, long dominated by the Douglases and the Hamiltons. But the Lockharts and Dalziels had properties and influence here also, and were concerned that the area should not suffer the royal wrath, Carnwath, Carstairs, Cleghorn and Covington being all Lockhart houses, and Walter Dalziel holding the office of Sergeant of Lanark, and owning land there of the former hospice of St Leonards, or Lazarus, a leper colony. Also, it was pointed out to the king that Lanark had been the favoured town of that great patriot William Wallace, who had helped the Bruce, the monarch's distant ancestor, to gain the throne. So Lanark was spared, with only the town-houses of various Douglases destroyed. The now reduced host moved on eastwards, up Clyde still, to make for the original Douglas country, which gave the family their name, Douglasdale, and such as Sandilands, Watchknowe, Uddington and Douglas itself therein.

And here again the king was faced with something of a problem. For this area Angus and the *Red* Douglases looked on as their calf-country, and they must not be offended. So the force contented itself with a progress through the dale, making only token gestures at burning one or two places undeniably Black, spending a night in and around Douglas town itself, and returning northwards, heading back for Abercorn, the army losing detachments all the way. James was the more determined that he must somehow set up a standing army under his own command, and not be dependent on the levvies of his lords and lairds over which he had so little real control for any length of time.

At Edinburgh they found the main assembly, under Huntly and Angus, still awaiting orders, all but settled by now into their encampment on the Burgh Muir. Clearly, as commander-in-chief, the king ought to have sent instructions to his lieutenant-general as to the movement of this large force. On the word that Abercorn was still holding out against Errol, James decided that he must use this waiting host, give it some task forthwith. The Douglas brothers were said to be still basing themselves on their own redoubt-country of Dumfries-shire and Galloway, and must not be allowed to remain there unassailed. So they would head thither, going by Selkirk and Ettrick and over to Lochmaben as before, but sending Huntly, the most experienced soldier, somehow to bring down Balveny's stronghold of Abercorn.

Alec Lyon, like many another there, wearied with all this campaigning, sighed as he turned southwards again with this enlarged army.

They were burning and sacking their way down Ettrick and Yarrow when there was a very significant development, and nothing to do with their warfare. A courier arrived from Stirling, exhausted after seeking for them, sent hot-foot to the king by his wife. Mary of Gueldres had been brought to bed earlier than expected, and had given birth to a son.

James Stewart was a man transformed. A son! He had fathered another son! Abruptly, bringing down the Black Douglas could be left to others. He was for Stirling, to see this latest in the long princely line of the oldest monarchy in Christendom – and to congratulate the mother, to be sure. Angus, his brother-in-law and the senior earl present, with the Lord Gray as adviser, could carry on to the south-west to deal with the Douglases; *he* was for Stirling, and forthwith.

Taking Alec and Sir Patrick, captain of his guard, and a small detachment as escort, the King of Scots turned and rode back whence they had come, at all speed.

Avoiding Edinburgh, they had to pass near to Abercorn, and James almost reluctantly did rein aside to go and see how the siege there progressed. They found the castle still holding out, but Huntly making good use of the idle besiegers by quarrying stone from a nearby escarpment, and bringing it to use to widen, reinforce and realign that causeway, so that it would carry Mons Meg out to within effective range of the fortalice. He had also had a supply of large cannon-balls made at Linlithgow by smiths. A few more days, he asserted, and Abercorn would fall.

Thankful for that assurance, James pressed on his urgent way.

At Stirling it was all excitement, joy, pride and triumph. The precious infant was healthy, well formed despite being somewhat premature, and certainly strong of lungs. The queen was well and cheerful, a born mother. Their little son James was highly intrigued with his new brother – altogether a happy family with much to celebrate.

Alec, reunited with Agnes, made no complaint when James announced that, so soon as the queen was fit to travel, they would be off to falkland, his favourite domicile, much to be preferred to the rock-top fortress, and splendid for hunting and hawking. No enthusiast for burning and sacking, his Gentleman of the Bedchamber did not criticise. Let the warriors elsewhere get on with it without the monarch.

Two weeks at Falkland and the Earl of Errol arrived in person with the news, excellent news. Abercorn had fallen at long last, battered into submission by the great cannon from its advanced position made possible by the vast amount of quarried stone laid down by Huntly. And not only that, Angus had won a decisive victory at a place called Arkinholm, on the West March, where the Ewes Water joined that Esk near to Langholm. Why the Douglas brothers had been so far south-east of their own territory was not explained, possibly heading for over the border into England to link up with the English Warden, the Earl of Northumberland, in their treasonable alliance. But, at any rate, the royal army had triumphed, and totally. The Earl of Moray fell in action, Ormond was captured, and Douglas himself and Balveny had fled for the north, probably to take refuge with their friend, John of the Isles. Angus, an unlikely victor in battle, but no doubt guided by Gray, was proceeding on to Galloway to make clear to all in those parts that their lords' power was shattered at last. The Red Douglas had put down the Black.

James Stewart, exultant, gave orders that the Earl of Ormond was to be hanged and his head brought for exhibition at the Market Cross of Edinburgh, as sign to the nation that an era was ended.

The King of Scots reigned supreme in his kingdom, for the first time since his father, James the First, had died – and with a James the Third, God willing, there to follow on in due course.

PART THREE

28

A hopefully prolonged era of peace in the land was something new for the Scots, none alive having experienced such previously. A parliament met to celebrate it all, the best attended assembly in living memory, and great were the congratulations, the honouring of loyal supporters, the appointments to new offices, and at least the accepted proposal to start creating a standing royal army. They necessarily had a new Chancellor to succeed the late Crichton, and William St Clair, Earl of Orkney, was appointed, a rather remarkable choice in that he was the brother of Beatrix, Countess of Douglas, mother of the rebel earls; but he had always held to the crown against all pressures from his nephews, and now was rewarded, and not only with this prestigious office but with the earldom of Caithness as well. His first act, as Chancellor, on the advice of Bishop Kennedy, was to present a deposition to parliament, a huge document congratulating the king on his triumph over the forces of anarchy and evil, and the production of a second male heir, and swearing lifelong allegiance to the throne, this to be signed by all present, their various seals to be appended later. Quite a lengthy ceremony was made of this signing, the prelates first, the Bishops of St Andrews, Dunblane, Dunkeld, Ross and Argyll, followed by the Earls of Athol, Angus, Menteith, Errol, Huntly, the Marischal and Orkney himself; then the Lords of Lorne, Erskine, Campbell, Graham, Somerville, Montgomery, Maxwell, Leslie, Glamis, Gray, Boyd and Borthwick, with a last highly dramatic addition, that of Hamilton, brother-in-law of the Douglases who, on the fall of Abercorn, had seen the error of his ways and come to present himself to Huntly in surrender, and, again on Kennedy's suggestion, had been diplomatically pardoned, this removing powerful support from the rebels, and demonstrating to others to do likewise, probably part of the reason for the defeat of the Black Douglases at Arkinholm. Now he was accepted before parliament, however doubtfully he was eyed by many there.

There was no room on the scroll for all the lairds and knights and commissioners of the shires, not to mention the royal burghs' representatives, to sign, but a few chosen ones added their names in lieu of the rest. The royal burgh of Haddington's provost appended his mark in the same way. When all the seals were duly attached, this historic document was to be presented to the king as token of the royal achievement.

It then fell to the new Chancellor to move the forfeiture of the lives, titles, estates and chattels of the two surviving Douglas brothers, and of their mother, his own sister likewise, an unprecedented happening, for she had aided them, but omitting the Fair Maid of Galloway, unwilling wife of the Earl James, whose dispensation from the Pope had been so significant in the fall of Threave; she was spared, and another dispensation was to be sought from the Vatican for her to have her marriage annulled.

The next business was to have the wardenships of the Marches made non-hereditary, so that never again would the so important borderline be at the mercy of rebels and traitors who were secure in their authority.

All this was passed unanimously, although the lengthy list of new appointments, which took up the rest of the session, did arouse some debate, controversy and exchange.

It was not long after parliament stood down that word of a highly remarkable, not to say alarming, occurrence reached the royal court. John of the Isles and Ross, with whom Douglas and Balveny were sheltering, had assembled an enormous fleet of galleys, such as only he could do, and embarked thereon allegedly five thousand clansmen, to sail down the West Highland coast as far as Bute and Arran, in a leisurely progress, calling at many places, to show who ruled these parts. The king and his advisers were at first much concerned over this – for there was no royal fleet to challenge it – and they feared that the Lord of the Isles had gone back on his oath of allegiance made at Perth those years before. However, it was Kennedy who learned the truth of it, as Primate of Holy Church, that it all was in fact a demonstration, not against the king but against the appointment, by the College of Bishops, of George Lauder, a Lowlander from Fife, to be Bishop of Argyll. Apparently the Islesman had his own nominee for the vacancy; and the unusual protest was that this interloper could not even speak the Gaelic language and so was unintelligible to most of the clergy and people. Thankfully James passed this matter over to the prelates to deal with. But one item connected with this demonstration did concern the civil power. It was reported that one of the galley fleet had progressed on southwards well beyond Arran, carrying Douglas and Balveny to refuge in England. This might or might not lead to trouble, it was recognised.

It was not long before they heard the results of this Douglas escape from Scotland. The brothers had been well received, indeed with notable distinction, by the Duke of York who was at present in supreme power at London, controlling King Henry, so much so as to present the earl with a pension of five hundred pounds, and promises of military aid. James, of course, was angry. On Huntly's and Gray's advice, he commanded permanent precautions to be taken all along the borderline, the strengthening of castles and garrisons, making Roxburgh's royal fortress their headquarters, and going himself to supervise. All the fords across Tweed which could be used by invaders were guarded, and plans devised to make them impassable at short notice, all the way from Berwick to Roxburgh. An elaborate chain of beacons was established, to be manned day and night, placed on high points all the way across the

Borderland, from Berwick and on right up to Edinburgh, with certain key points at Home Castle in the Merse, Smailholm Tower near Melrose, the Eildon Hills, up Lauderdale to Soutra, and so over Lothian to North Berwick Law, the Garleton Hills above Haddington, Dalkeith and so to the capital. A recognised code was imposed on the beacon-watchers. One fire was to represent an enemy's possible approach. Two fires that they were coming on certainly for the border. Four, that there be no doubt, that they were actually invading in strength. From Edinburgh's heights, Arthur's Seat in especial, signals could be seen over in Fife, smokes by day, fires by night, and from Fife transmitted westwards to Stirling and north to the Sidlaws and Perth. It was reckoned, perhaps optimistically, that one hour after beacons were lit at Tweed, all of Lowland Scotland would know of possible invasion. This was James's own formulation, and he was very proud of it.

But, as ever, his wise uncle urged other and less militant moves should also be tried to deal with the English threat. He should write to King Henry, as one monarch to another, declaring his peaceful intentions but pointing out that the harbouring and encouraging of traitors could be harmful to good relations between the kingdoms, and requesting that assurances would be forthcoming that no military aid should be given to rebels, a sentiment in which their fellow monarch, the King of France, would strongly agree – this the sting in the tail.

James did as suggested, and in due course got a letter back from Henry, although, since he was liable to bouts of insanity, it might have been dictated by York, even though signed by the monarch. This was not such as to promote confidence, however superficially amicable its wording, for it began thus: "The king, to an illustrious prince calling himself King of Scots, sends greeting." And after assertions of goodwill, ending: "The homage of the said prince to the King of England is required as monarch; and might the Lord Jesus Christ reclaim him,

James, from error and set him in the paths of justice and truth. The king bids the said prince a cordial farewell."

The effect of this communication on the King of Scots could be imagined. It resulted in still sterner provisions being enforced along the borderline, and arrangements made for the speedy mustering of forces in all parts of the country. Also the nucleus of the new national standing army to be established at Stirling, which could head any assembly of the lords' levvies.

Kennedy was grievously disappointed, James all but mocking him.

Then there was a relaxation of tension when the news came that the extraordinary Wars of the Roses were not over, and York had suffered an eclipse again, this through the machinations of Queen Margaret of Anjou who was proving a strong-minded woman, however feeble her husband, and who engineered the release of the Duke of Somerset and his overthrowing of York. Somerset was known to be much less aggressive towards Scotland. How long this improved situation would last, of course, was anybody's guess; but it did relieve the pressure meantime. Nevertheless the border controls remained in force.

Another parliament was called that late autumn, at Stirling this time, James quite the most parliament-concerned of his line, largely to establish and regularise the army situation and the border preparedness, where vigilance had tended to slacken with York's downfall, and harvest-time, as always, preoccupying manpower. Alec missed this assembly, for he was summoned to Glamis where his father had fallen seriously ill, and the physicians were despairing for his life. It was some sort of liver complaint, it seemed, and the family was greatly worried. Alec was shocked when he saw his parent, so shrunken and drawn was he who had always been a big and robust individual. Nevertheless the thane declared, however weakly, that he was not done yet, and his eldest son had not to count on becoming Lord Glamis over-soon – a worthy spirit.

Alec and Agnes stayed at Glamis for a couple of weeks. While there they made their first acquaintance with his brother John's fairly new wife, Elizabeth, daughter of Sir John Scrymgeour of Dudhope, a Dundee magnate descended from Wallace's standard-bearer; and they did not fail to notice that she was already pregnant. This, to be sure, distinctly emphasised their own sad inability to produce offspring, but Alec made the best of it by declaring that he hoped that it was a boy and so the onward march of their ancient line of Lyon would be maintained, even though diluted by such as Scrymgeour, this with a smile.

With Lord Glamis looking neither better nor worse but claiming to feel some improvement, they eventually returned to their duties with the king and queen at Stirling, promising to be back promptly, if summoned.

It was a little galling, that Yuletide, to learn that Queen Mary was once again with child, James positively crowing about it, seeing it as evidence of his own masculine prowess. However, at least their friend Angus and his princess wife remained infertile. They consoled each other by agreeing that childlessness was no reliable sign of lack of love and affection.

Soon thereafter there descended upon Stirling Castle, all in the course of a few days, three ladies, these unconnected with each other but all in approximately the same position and all desirous of royal help. The first was the Countess of Douglas, the Fair Maid of Galloway, a beauty indeed but an unhappy one. She was relieved that her unwilling marriage to the exiled Earl James had been annulled, but with all his lands, and formerly her own, forfeited, confiscated and ravaged, she was all but destitute and homeless. She sought the king's mercy. Queen Mary took to her at once, and James was not unimpressed by her good looks. He promised full restitution of her former lands and gave her the barony of Balveny; and noting the admiring glances of his stepfather, the Black Knight of Lorne whom he had created Earl of Atholl, and who was apt to be about the court, suggested that he might make a worthy husband for her. Margaret Douglas, only too well aware that she required some sort of protector, and also of the Black Knight's reputation as a reliable character, agreed to consider the proposal.

The second arrival was none other than the Countess of Ross, wife of the Lord of the Isles. She was a daughter of the chamberlain, James, second Lord Livingston, but had been little more than a child when she was wed to John MacDonald, who had never shown any affection for her and had a positive court of Highland women to wait on him, and a number of illegitimate sons, all but abandoning her. Mary of Gueldres took pity on her also, and made her an extra lady-in-waiting.

And if that was not enough, his own sister Annabella arrived back from Savoy, divorced, apparently at the behest of the King of France who, it seemed, had other plans for the heir to the Duke of Savoy. Of such were the arranged marriages of high-born women. The king would have to find one more husband for her. Would the Earl of Huntly do? He had been a widower for years.

The queen, pregnant, declared that she was thankful to be so, in case her royal spouse decided that he could do with another wife! And Agnes Lyon asked whether Alec was going to dispose of her, because she had not produced an heir, although the failing might well be in himself!

At least all this made for a change from matters military.

29

The need for heedful defence of the realm, however, was reasserted in the early summer of 1456 when, at Falkland, they were celebrating the king's twenty-sixth birthday and the queen expecting any day to be delivered of the latest progeny. Word was brought that, despite all precautions, the Earls of Douglas and Northumberland had managed to cross the borderline and were laying waste the Merse. Whether this indicated that Somerset and Margaret of Anjou agreed, or possibly a return of York in the English seesaw of power, they did not know; but it was none the less grievous. In the circumstances, James was reluctant to leave Falkland and his family, so he sent his brother-in-law Angus instead, with Lord Gray, to use the new small standing army at Stirling, while he ordered a readiness to muster for a large host, under Huntly, should this prove to be the start of a major English invasion rather than just some sort of raid. Alec was sent, with Sir Patrick, to patrol the entire borderline, to discover whether any other and subsidiary raids were being made, although the beacon system was not warning of any such.

So from birthday celebrations to hard riding and possible conflict, with a modest company of fifty men they headed for the Borderland, to reach the Tweed where Teviot joined it, at Roxburgh, the headquarters of borderline defence. No word of other raids than the Merse one to the east was forthcoming there, and it surely would have been known had there been any, at least in that easterly direction. So they turned off to follow Teviot westwards, by Hawick. They went as far as the edge of the West March at Carlanrig, and here they were assured in the Johnstone, Maxwell and Armstrong country, that no invasions had taken place between there and the Solway Firth. So it was back to Roxburgh, there to meet sundry Turnbulls, Elliots and Pringles who had been supporting Angus in the Merse, and to learn of another notable victory. The invaders had been soundly beaten, losing almost one thousand dead and over seven hundred prisoners taken, to be exchanged for handsome ransom, although unfortunately Douglas and Northumberland managed to escape. It was strange that the Red Douglas was earning a reputation as a commander in the field, he who had never had any ambitions to be a soldier, although it was quite possibly Sir Patrick's father who deserved most of the credit, as adviser.

Presumably this raid had been in the nature of a testing of the waters by the English? If so, it was to be hoped that the lesson learned was sufficiently clear.

Back to Falkland, then, much relieved.

The king took this incident, however successful as far as the Scots were concerned, as warning that the English threat, whether Douglas-inspired or otherwise, was not to be dismissed or belittled. There were ten times as many English as Scots, and although they seemed always preoccupied in fighting each other in these Roses wars, they could still mount a dire offensive against the northern kingdom to seek to impose the false claim to overlordship. So James, now with a second son, to be named Alexander, Duke of Albany, adjourned celebration and devoted himself to ensuring the defence of the realm.

The marshalling and training of armed forces was of course the priority. But Huntly, Angus, Gray and others could oversee the details of that. He himself had this other especial interest, which had almost become an obsession with James Stewart; the manufacture and provision of powerful cannon. Mons Meg had cast its spell over him.

So he assembled at Stirling a group of blacksmiths, and

sent for Kim Graham from Galloway to come and instruct them, meanwhile seeking to learn all that he could as to the theory of artillery and ordnance. He learned that in France and the Low Countries there was quite a variety of cannon in use, variously called cannon-royal, whole-cannon and demi-cannon, ranging in size and the weight of ball they could fire from twenty pounds up to sixty; Mons Meg, however, using balls of nearly a hundredweight. There were different kinds as well as sizes, bombards which fired the heaviest shot but with very short range, to culverins, which had very long barrels, with range to match, but which threw only small shot. These last, James reckoned, would be an excellent provision for use in the field, with his armies, fired against enemy troops, but little use in siegery. They would have to be made more readily movable, however, on better carriages and larger wheels, to keep up with the army. Even Meg and the new guns that he planned to have made should be given improved trolleys, so that they could be drawn over rough country by teams of horses, not just couples, and at greater speed.

While considering and working on all this, even designing his own gun-carriages, James was told of one of his own lords who was also interested in cannon, and learned this from none other than Agnes Lyon, for the said lord was her late father's friend, Borthwick; she had heard them discussing artillery as a girl, and declared that the fine castle at Lochquariat, now called Borthwick, had been constructed with a view to making it all but impervious to cannon-fire. This information, which the king declared ought to have been given to him long since, had him eager to see Borthwick and his castle forthwith, to discover whether there was anything new to be learned there.

So a royal visit was paid to south Lothian, something over a dozen miles south-east of the capital, amongst the western foothills of the Lammermuirs, Alec and Sir Patrick in attendance. They were all greatly impressed with the castle, tall, rising to over one hundred feet at its parapet with walls as thick as fourteen feet, and these not narrowing as they rose, as was usual, and so offering no weakening to cannon-fire. And the site chosen was on a mound amongst hollows and the twists and turns of the Gore Water, which would prevent any artillery being placed advantageously, making elevation of muzzles difficult. Lord Borthwick himself, elderly as he now was, but much intrigued by his sovereign's interest and knowledge, very willingly shared his information with James, to the latter's profit and satisfaction; so much so that there and then he nominated Borthwick as his Master Gunner. He urged him to advance his knowledge further, suggesting that he sent for information to the Continent, not necessarily going himself but perhaps sending one of his sons. The youngest of these, James, of Glengelt and Ballencrieff, listening interestedly to the conversation, promptly volunteered to be the enquirer overseas, and was as promptly appointed Gunner-Depute of the realm.

Improvements in gun carriages were also discussed, all well into the night. James, the enthusiast, returned to Stirling next day, more ardent a cannoneer than ever.

Bishop Kennedy did not allow his nephew's interest in artillery to exclude due concern for the improved welfare of the people of his kingdom, making many suggestions as to betterment, reforms and new developments. That year of 1458 there were two parliaments, the first hurriedly called, the forty days' notice overruled, this to try to deal with a sudden but widespread visitation of plague which hit the cities of Edinburgh, Glasgow and Dundee, also some smaller townships. The cause of this was not known, some clerics declaring that it was God's judgment on the nation for various sins, particularly failure to render sufficient tithes to Holy Church. The Primate would have none of that, and advocated all possible steps to alleviate the distress and to seek to prevent any further spread of the pestilence, this on a national scale, requiring a parliament, according to Kennedy. So a number of decisions were made, such as confining the families of sufferers in their houses for a time to prevent the spread of infection; any who disobeyed were to leave their town or village for the time being, none to return while any of the household were sick; no burning of contaminated houses, as was being done, causing danger to adjoining properties; local clergy to proceed through streets and occupied areas twice every week to inspect and help, such clergy to be granted indulgences therefor.

The second parliament was held just before harvest-time, thankfully with the plague banished; and at this many and far-reaching improvements were passed, again mainly on the instigation of Kennedy and his bishops. The imposition of undue and punishing levies and dues, what were known as distresses, on goods bought and sold at markets and fairs within baronies, by the barons, was prohibited, sheriffs and justiciars to ensure compliance. Trade was to be aided by every possible means, and the lords to see to this, however much below their dignity most of them conceived it to be. An increase in the number of mills was to be stimulated, to deal with a hoped for extra cultivation of grain and the reclaiming of barren land; and individual farmers were to be encouraged to set up their own little horse-mills, circular buildings in which a single horse pacing round and round could grind corn into meal, something Queen Mary declared was done in Gelderland.

A most notable and ambitious plan was put to the assembly, and passed; a reform of the currency, indeed a new coinage, this to stabilise prices, again improve trading, limit the importation of foreign moneys, and end a sort of smuggling exchange, which had become common at ports. The new coinage was to be all of silver, conforming in weight to the English money, none in base metal, and to consist of groats, that is eight-pence, half-groats, pennies, half-pennies and farthings, all bearing the king's head, and this making it a punishable offence against the crown to chip or chisel off any of the metal, as was frequently done, which would be considered an assault on the royal person. The Church, ever the principal producer of wealth in the land, from its abbeys, friaries, monasteries and hospices, with their granges and mills, to oversee this development, and largely to advance the necessary silver to make it all possible.

The churchmen were indeed in good fettle and spirits this year, and optimistic for the future. For Kennedy's old friend, the nuncio, had ascended to the papal throne as Pius the Second, and his fondness for Scotland, even though he reputedly cursed its rain for giving him rheumatism, was such that the northern kingdom could look for considerable advantages, not the least that the King of England would be urged to renounce all claims to overlordship. Commissioners, led by the Primate, were to go to Rome, to perform due homage, and seek the Pontiff's good offices, parliament adding its respects and sending gifts.

The final business of this unusual meeting was concerned with the world of nature and its usefulness for mankind – none thereat could ever recollect any similar subject for national debate. Again it was the churchmen who initiated this, and assured the doubting magnates and delegates that it was wise, needful. The wholesale cutting down of trees must stop. The planting of replacements, shrubs and hedges was to be encouraged, in the interests of shelter for crops and beasts and the provision of timber for future use. Birds, particularly wildfowl, partridges, plover, wild duck and geese, were to be enabled to breed and increase in numbers, their nests and eggs not harried, for they were of benefit to man's sustentation. The breeding of pigeons was to be encouraged also. Creatures which preyed on these were to be put down – crows, rooks, buzzards, gleds or hawks. Salmon and trout were forbidden to be taken during the close season. And wolves, where these still existed, were to be hunted down, the sheriffs and bailies of the area to be held responsible for this. Any man who slew a wolf was entitled to receive a silver penny from every household in the parish, on presentation of the head to the sheriff, and for a fox a lesser reward.

Alec Lyon was not alone, when that session was finally adjourned, in remarking that he had never known a parliament quite like it.

The Primate and the other commissioners would depart for Rome in the course of a few days.

30

It was early spring of 1459 before Kennedy and the others got back from the celebrations at the Vatican, having visited London on the return journey, bearing the new Pope's strong advocacy of peace between England and Scotland, and an end to assertions of paramountcy. King Henry was undergoing one of his frequent spells of wandering wits, but his Queen Margaret and the Duke of Somerset were reasonably friendly, and while not actually agreeing to drop the offensive overlordship claim, did get the feeble monarch to sign a four-year truce.

Another very useful result of the Rome embassage was a letter brought back from Pope Pius to John of the Isles, Earl of Ross, urging him to render due service and deference to his Lord's anointed monarch, King James. Piccolomini, when nuncio, had been very much aware of the Highland–Lowland dichotomy, and the problems that produced for the Kings of Scots. And, however much the MacDonald saw himself as an all but independent princeling, he was apparently sufficiently religiously inclined to be in some awe of the pontifical authority, for it took only some five weeks for him to arrive in person at Stirling, admittedly with quite a magnificent train of clan leaders and chieftains, to announce his allegiance and support for James Stewart, and to offer his aid, if required, in the national cause, so long as it was not contrary to the interests of any of the clans who owed him obedience. James saw great advantage in this, needless to say, and treated the other almost warmly, particularly concerned for the possible use of the Lord of the Isles' great galley fleet, he having no naval force of his own. He introduced and commended him to the Earl of Orkney and Caithness, who was now Lord High Admiral, in name at least, in the hope that some suitable arrangement would be forthcoming. This aspect of affairs had its present relevance, for it was reported that the Duke of York, ousted meantime from power, had gone to Ireland and was basing himself there, no doubt with a view to bringing over an Irish army to aid him recover his sway in England – and Scotland might well become involved in such an effort. In that case, a fleet of war-galleys would be invaluable.

James confided to his secular friends that Holy Church could be useful indeed at times.

Less favourable news from England was that the Earl of Douglas had transferred his allegiance to the Lancastrian party, and they had renewed his five hundred pounds pension.

Mary of Gueldres produced another son, to be named John and created Earl of Mar, making the throne still more secure as to heirs. As a mother she was as fond as she was prolific and good-natured, and her one daughter growing up as attractive as she was effective in keeping her brothers in order.

James Stewart was a proud man. He had his kingdom in order, even the Highland parts. He had created five new earldoms including the Red Douglas of Dalkeith to be Earl of Morton. He had appointed eleven new burghs of barony, including his own castleton of Falkland, all sources of revenue and trade. He had fathered three sons. And he had produced a number of cannon, of different weights and calibre, and was particularly proud to have made three long-barrelled pieces, demi-culverins, set on large-wheeled carriages, which ought to be of great assistance to his army, although he was disappointed not to have been able to improve on, or even rival, Mons Meg with his heavier bombards, despite Kim Graham's know-how.

The Scots crown, he claimed, and rightly, was stronger

than it had ever been since the death of Robert the Bruce, even though much of that strength could be credited to James Kennedy.

But satisfaction and congratulation were somewhat damped that early summer of 1459. York was back in England. He had landed from Ireland, not in the north at all but in Kent, oddly, so there had been no calling on the Lord of the Isles' fleet. And the duke had managed to bring over from exile in France the Earl of Warwick, probably the most talented English soldier alive, and with the Earl of Salisbury and others was presenting a major challenge to the ruling Lancastrian faction. In the circumstances, Somerset and Margaret of Anjou could be anxious indeed, however peculiar King Henry's state.

That English anxiety took the form of a message to the King of Scots, in July. Would he make a demonstration of Scots support for their truce by leading an army over the border, to give York and Warwick pause, and hopefully ease the threat on London?

In the mood that he was in, James was almost glad to agree to this. The Earl of Northumberland, Douglas's ally, had been requiring to be taught a lesson for long. Here was opportunity, and at English request. Opportunity also to test his standing army, in leading a great force of the lords' levies, and also his new culverin artillery.

Bishop Kennedy was less enthusiastic. If York did indeed regain control in England, then this gesture could result in stern reaction. The fact that he was concentrating this new attempt in Kent and the south did not mean that he could not also come north, especially if provoked. The Primate was unhappy about the known prowess of Warwick.

James was not to be put off. He respected his uncle's judgment in affairs of state, and had reason to do so; but matters military were not the province of the clergy. Orders went out for a major muster of forces at the Burgh Muir of Edinburgh in two weeks' time.

*   *   *

Great was the ardour and confidence at the capital as the host assembled. Never in living memory had so large an army been seen, sixty thousand it was reckoned, two thousand of them Islesmen, come by sea to the Clyde estuary under John MacDonald himself. The lords had vied with each other to produce numbers, although not a few of them looked at the Highlanders askance, especially as these were not mounted, horses being little used in clan warfare, where mountains and lochs made them of little value. Doubtful glances were also cast upon the king's three culverins, such as had never before accompanied an army on the march in Scotland. However, it was reckoned by most that these two novelties, Highlanders on foot and wheeled cannon, would soon be left behind by a mounted force, so they could be all but ignored. For the rest it was all flourish, prideful competition, flying banners and cheer. This was all going to be something of a diversion, with no major army to face, the northern English to be put in their place, and much spoil and booty likely to come their way.

Alec and Patrick Gray were allotted the duty of leading scouting parties, they being well acquainted with the lower Tweed area, for it had been decided to invade over the East March into Northumberland, where the Percy earl deserved a drubbing. They might return by Cumberland and the Middle or West Marches, depending on how the campaign went, and how far they proceeded south into England. James was talking about possibly probing as far as Durham.

So it was down to the Borderland, by Soutra, Lauderdale and over into the Merse, the Lowlanders distinctly surprised to see how well the Islesmen kept up with the mounted thousands, the running gillies, as they were termed, living up to their name, seemingly tireless. Even the cannon, each towed by its team of six horses, were not far behind, to the king's evident satisfaction.

Alec quite enjoyed the scouting, well ahead of the army, riding free, for no large force can travel very fast and far in a day. The scouts, assured that the way was clear, returned to the main body of a night, for good feeding and easy sleeping, making the best of both worlds.

The first night was passed at Lauder Common, that small burgh being saddled with the loyal duty of providing food and comfort for the royal host, to its sorrow.

Across the Berwickshire Merse, by Home Castle, pivot of the beacon system, they reached the Tweed near Ednam, or Edenham, the first parish in all Scotland, founded by David the First, and turned downriver past Coldstream to the Lennel Hill area for the second night. Here they were about a dozen miles west of Berwick town, its castle, sadly, permanently in English hands these days. It could be besieged, but it was very strongly sited and even the culverins would be unable to breach its walls – and this would only hold up the advance. So no attempt to cross there was advisable, James declaring that one day he must bring Mons Meg down here, and some of his bombards, and win Berwick back into Berwickshire where it so obviously belonged. They could cross Tweed near this Lennel on the morrow, and commence their demonstration.

Alec and Patrick went ahead as usual at first light, the wide causeway-based ford cleared for them, to make for the entry of the English tributary, the Till, and follow up its valley on their way to the Northumberland moors. They were careful to keep well back from the river, however, and not to pass over-close to the quite numerous tower-houses and lesser castles of this area, Twizel, Castle Heaton, Tindel, Etal, Ford and others, not to give warning of the army's approach, for almost certainly these would be targets of James's strategy. They saw no indication that word of the approach of a host had reached these parts.

By the time that they had got as far as Ford Castle, a dozen miles or so and on higher ground now, it was backwards as well as forwards and to the flanks that they were apt to look, the distant boom of gunfire reaching them, and seeing the columns of black smoke beginning

317

to rise, sufficient warning indeed to all the area that major trouble was on the way. So now the scouting party had to go more warily, anxious not to be spotted by other than shepherds, cattle-herders and the like, for quickly the land would be roused, used as these parts were to cross-border raiding.

Hereabouts they decided to wait for the main army, for if they followed the Till further it would lead them ever south-westwards into the hills, whereas they understood that the king and Huntly desired to menace the Earl of Northumberland in especial, and his great castle was at Alnwick near the coast. Not that they could hope to take that huge stronghold itself, but they could harass the areas nearby and thereby threaten the Percy. So probably a turn eastwards here was indicated.

It took a considerable time for the force to arrive, and then in sections, for it had spread out to deal with the scatter of towers and great houses of Northumberland's vassals and squires, the victims of those smoke columns. When James and his principal grouping did arrive, it was to announce that they had sacked the castles and towers of Twizel, Tillmouth, Heaton, Duddo, Pallinsburn and Etal; and the others were dealing with further-off Branxton and Learmouth. They would assail this Ford Castle, and settle here for the night – a very satisfactory first day. The culverins were only an hour or so later in appearing, their traction remarkably successful.

In the face of such a mighty array, the Heron fortalice of Ford capitulated fairly promptly, on condition that its owner and occupants were permitted to leave unharmed. Since slaughter was not the object of this exercise of power, this was agreed; and the monarch and his leaders were able to spend the night in comfort in the undamaged and well-provisioned house, well pleased with themselves. It could be burned in the morning. Admittedly hereafter the countryside would be warned, and their progress the less easy; but with sixty thousand descending upon them, the Northumbrians were unlikely to put up much in the way of armed resistance, most electing to flee probably down to Alnwick, or even beyond to the city of Newcastle. So, yes, they would hereafter head eastwards, for the coastal areas.

In the morning, the scouts rode off in the direction of Lowick town therefore, passing near the castles of Watchlaw and Barmoor. They saw no massing of defenders, but did come across a number of small groups hurriedly herding cattle off into the nearby low hills to the west. They avoided Lowick itself, making for the Kyloe area and Fenwick, from the higher ground of which they could see the blue of the sea, and with what must be Holy Island and the Farnes none so far offshore. The powerful castles of Haggerston and Bamburgh were near here, they understood, but probably these would be left unassailed meantime, even any brief siege meaning unwanted delay. Telltale smokes were arising again behind them all the time.

They halted at Belford in the late afternoon, Bamburgh only about five miles away. They would have to see whether the king would bypass this also.

That night James held a council of his lords. They decided that over-much warning was being given, allowing Northumberland possibly to muster his strength and rouse much of the land against them. No major battle was their objective; this was to be a presentation of Scots power, not the start of a war. So, head straight for the earl's seat of Alnwick, most of the army to remain there threatening town and castle, under Huntly and Gray, while James himself, and Angus with perhaps some two thousand, made a dash southwards, passing but not attacking Newcastle, and on to Durham before turning back, this in the nature of a gesture, a lesson to the entire north of England, a hard-riding sally by the King of Scots.

Since scouts would not be required on this southwards drive, Alec and Patrick Gray were to be given the task of patrolling a wide area in an arc west of Alnwick to ensure that no forces from Cumberland and the English

West March descended on the stationary Scots army unannounced.

Next day, then, it was on to the River Aln – another indication that the Celtic people had dwelt here long ago, and given their *abhainn* name to this stream also – and at Alnmouth turning inland for Alnwick itself, some five miles. Nearing the walled town, they got their first glimpse of armed men, a party of some hundreds watching their approach from a height above the river. But at sight of this mighty host bearing down on them, these hurriedly made off, no doubt to inform their earl of the danger. Alnwick Castle would be well prepared for siege.

Well aware of what havoc this army could wreak on a town, even one defended by walls, and desiring no unnecessary carnage or massacre – for the English queen had required only a demonstration – James ordered his force to encircle the place but not to attempt to enter it. The castle stood on a mound within its own parkland some way east of the town, at a bend of the river.

With a party of lords and knights, banners much in evidence, and taking the culverins, the king rode forward towards this extensive, almost palatial fortalice, larger than any private hold Alec had ever seen in Scotland, the five golden fusils in fesse, for Percy, flapping from four towers.

They had not got within three hundred yards of the castle when the bang of a cannon and a puff of smoke halted them, almost certainly a blank shot, for no whistle nor fall of ball was evident, but the message clear. James ordered his three culverins each to fire a shot in return, not that that would do any real damage at that range to stone walling, but would be equally eloquent. Then he sent further forward a herald, with horn-blowers, under the lion rampant standard, to announce that James, King of Scots required the Earl of Northumberland to yield himself and his castle, as required by his King Henry, Queen Margaret and the Duke of Somerset. This brought forth no response other than two more cannon-blasts. So the position was clear, and as expected. The Percy was defiant but boxed up in his hold, and the Scots army could settle down around castle and town, and James could set off on his desired expedition southwards. It was reckoned that Durham was not more than fifty miles away, going by Morpeth and Chester-le-Street, avoiding Newcastle, so the king's party ought to be there and back in no more than four days. If any serious trouble was encountered, they would either turn back or send messengers for aid. The Lord of the Isles elected to accompany the monarch, leaving his Islesmen under the command of his kinsman, Donald Balloch of Islay.

In the morning this programme was put into operation, James and his two thousand setting off for Morpeth, and the scouting group to start their patrolling westwards, leaving Huntly and the bulk of the army encamped. No doubt the folk of Alnwick quaked.

Alec Lyon and Patrick Gray, who had become friends over these past months, quite enjoyed those next four days of ranging the Northumbrian uplands, doing nothing very demanding, just exploring the hillfoots area of the southern Cheviots and the valleys of Breamish and Rede and Coquet, going north almost as far as Wooler and south to Rothbury and west to Alwinton, and keeping a keen lookout all the while. They encountered nothing to give cause for alarm, although they themselves may have alarmed not a few of that fairly scanty population – not that they did any attacking, however many sheep and cattle they found it necessary to slaughter for nightly roasting over their camp-fires. Their duty was to keep watch, not terrorise. From Rothbury vicinity they did make a diversion to visit the site of the famous Battle of Otterburn, which the English called Chevy Chase, the conflict won by a dead man, he the second Earl of Douglas, stabbed in the back by his own armour-bearer for some grudge at the very start of the night-time engagement, but carried forward dead by his aides, these shouting "A Douglas! A Douglas!" The enemy then had been another

Percy, from Alnwick, Hotspur, defeated and captured those seventy years ago.

In due course they returned to the army, to find the king already back, having made a successful and satisfying flourish, meeting with no major opposition, reaching Durham, not assailing its castle or cathedral but announcing his presence and royal identity, and burning a few lesser places on the way back.

All the Scots leadership was pleased with the entire expedition thus far, even though they had steadily lost quite substantial numbers of men, who kept disappearing overnight to collect and drive homewards herds of cattle, which they looked upon as their legitimate spoil, reward for armed service. But Huntly, for one, had become somewhat anxious. All the north of England by now must be in a state of alarm and alert, and these no feeble folk but doughty fighters, the Forsters, Robsons, Dunns, Nixons, Ridleys, Charltons and the rest, under their lords. They would not lie low in this invasion, but would raise the land in retaliation. Admittedly, if it came to outright battle on a major scale, the Scots probably would win, but at a cost. And was that the objective? Had they not done what they set out to do? Made their demonstration, and most effectively. He advocated a prompt return over the border, Lord Gray backing him.

James Stewart had to agree. He had made his mark. To risk serious bloodshed for his force now would be to no gain. So the order was given to pack up and head northwards by the most direct route, by the Till to the Tweed at Coldstream. They would, needless to say, pick up an adequate supply of cattle on the way, to satisfy everybody.

31

Agnes had sad news for her husband when he arrived back at Stirling. His father, who had never regained his strength after his illness of three years before, had suddenly died. The word had been brought two days earlier.

So it was Strathmore for the Lyons, and at once, for the funeral. In his sorrow, they were well on their way before the consequences made their full impact on Alec's mind; he was now Lord Glamis, and thane, and this was inevitably going to make big differences in his life. He and Agnes would have to review their future with some care.

At Glamis Castle, his father's death had come as no great shock, however sudden the end, for he had been a failing man for those years. But the grief was there, the widow bereft. The funeral had been delayed until the new Lord Glamis could be present. A notable occasion it had to be, then, nearly all of Strathmore and the Mearns appearing to be there, including the new Earl of Crawford from Finavon, even the Lord Gray and his son, near home at Broughty Castle near Dundee as they were, for the late thane had been popular, and represented one of the most ancient and illustrious lines in the land. Indeed the only other thane in Scotland still using the traditional style, that of Arbuthnott, from the Mearns, was present. So there was much mourning, and much entertaining to be done at Glamis Castle that night, perhaps no bad thing, gloom and grief temporarily suspended.

Thereafter, however, decisions fell to be made. As lord of Glamis now and head of the family, Alec abruptly had new and pressing duties imposed upon him, with large estates to manage, not just small Pitteadie, and a prominent role to play in Strathmore, consonant with his traditional title, for Glamis was the foremost family of the area in terms of line and ancestry. Admittedly his brother John had been largely deputising for their ailing father for some time, and might still do so in some measure for Alec. But inevitably his new situation would conflict with the duties of Gentleman of the Bedchamber and close attendant on the king. And there was Agnes's position as lady-in-waiting to the queen to consider also. Could they both just resign from these royal commitments? And did they want to? James and Mary might well demand their continued attendance. Alec had become accustomed to taking some part in national affairs, and would miss such activities. Would the management of the Glamis properties and lordly responsibilities in Strathmore provide adequate alternative compensation and interests? And Agnes had grown very fond of Mary of Gueldres; they were in fact now close friends. So – what?

It was decided, after much debate, that no firm conclusion could be reached at this stage, especially with the royal will to be ascertained. Brother John should continue with his role of deputy lord meantime, the other brother, William, aiding him, although Alec would endeavour frequently to visit Strathmore and act the thane on occasion. Their sister Elizabeth was now betrothed to Robertson of Struan, chieftain of a Perthshire clan, so no responsibility saddled them in that direction. Their mother, much younger than had been her husband, would be glad enough to remain mistress of Glamis Castle instead of being displaced by Agnes. And John could use the style of Master of Glamis, as the heir, until Alec produced a son, which seemed less and less likely. The property of Ogilvie, a detached estate south-west of Perth, was bestowed on William, to give him some authority. Pitteadie would remain Alec's own, and the couple's favoured residence.

All this resolved, to general acceptance and satisfaction, Lord and Lady Glamis returned to court at Stirling.

* * *

The royal couple, and indeed the young Princess Mary, were obviously glad to see the Lyons back, saying so, and James making it clear that he expected Alec to continue to remain at court. He did change his style, however, from Gentleman of the Bedchamber to Lord in Waiting, as had become suitable. And he acceded that visits to Glamis would have to be fairly frequent.

So all was well meantime.

But it was less so on the national scene, for the news presently reached them that York and Warwick had defeated the Lancastrians, not in Kent but in a major battle at Northampton, with great slaughter. Somerset was dead, and King Henry now firmly in York's hands, indeed a prisoner in his own palace, York being called Constable of England. Queen Margaret and her son, the child Edward, Prince of Wales, had fled, whither was not known.

This development was greeted with considerable alarm in Scotland, for York's animosity to the northern kingdom was known by all, and Northumberland having always been Yorkist in sympathies, the recent Scots sally therein might well provoke strong retaliation. Border controls, therefore, were reactivated and strengthened, and readiness to muster another large army ordered.

The whereabouts of Margaret of Anjou and her son was not long in being ascertained, for they in fact arrived in Scotland, by ship to the Clyde, with a small entourage, and promptly made their way to Stirling. This, needless to say, was something of an embarrassment, however sympathetic James Stewart might be to the visitors' cause, for of course it made the possibility of a Yorkist attack over the border the more likely.

Margaret was a strong-featured woman of nearly thirty years, and clearly as strong-willed, her son Edward a bewildered six-year-old. She was the daughter of René of Anjou, titular King of Naples. Most evidently she was not considering this flight to Scotland in any way as a giving in to Richard of York, but merely a breathing-space in her efforts to have him ousted once and for all. Indeed she was not long in making it clear that her coming to James was no mere seeking of refuge, but to request his military aid in the Lancastrian cause, he who had shown his mettle in the demonstration she had sought into Northumberland.

Even James Stewart, enthusiast as he was, had to be cautious in his reaction to this suggestion, for it was evident that it was not just another raid or gesture that she wanted but a full-scale invasion of England, to give a lead to her side in this War of the Roses. The king's advisers, needless to say, were strong in their objections to any such venture, few seeing it as wise or to the realm's advantage. If York himself attacked Scotland, that was different; then all their strength to be used against him. But major onslaught on England, no. Queen Margaret was disappointed, but she did not take her departure.

It was not long before there were repercussions from the south to Margaret's Scottish visit, York presumably guessing that she was there of a purpose, not merely seeking asylum. The beacons began to blaze along the border, and not in any single warning. Raiders came over Tweed, at various points, not large-scale attacks but sufficiently widespread as to indicate a planned strategy. At first it was assumed that this was some sort of retaliation by the Northumbrians for their recent sufferings. James sent sections of his standing army to deal with these forays. But when these developed along the West March as well, it became evident that this was more than just Percy exacting revenge. Some larger project was probably involved. A general muster was ordered to cope with it, amidst national concern.

But such assembling of the lords' manpower, from all over the land, took time, especially as this was early August, the time of the grain harvest, with so many of the warriors-to-be involved in that essential labour. It was a strange time for the English to be attacking, all agreed, since they also could not be finished with their

326

harvesting, which made it all the more serious, not to say alarming. James fretted.

He did more than fret. For word reached him from the Middle March that there had been a quite large-scale attack over Carter Bar down into Jedforest, and crossing Teviot before that river reached Tweed, the invaders were laying waste to Jedburgh and Kelso, and even besieging Roxburgh Castle itself, the hub of the borderline defensive system. Much concerned, the king rode for Edinburgh to collect such of his forces as had already gathered there, to lead them southwards, with orders for others to follow just as soon as available.

Alec, who had gone to Strathmore to raise men there, from his own estates and others, learned of this from a messenger sent by Queen Mary, urging haste.

When he arrived back at Stirling, with almost six hundred men, Agnes at his side, it was to find Mary awaiting them with her husband's cannon ready, or some of them, these the heavier pieces, for he had taken only his culverins with them. But on reaching Roxburgh he had found his royal castle taken by the enemy, just how was not reported, and now he was besieging it in turn, a sorry state of affairs. He needed more than culverins.

Alec, ready to take these bombards south as required, was astonished to learn that Mary of Gueldres intended to accompany them. Whether this was at the instigation of Margaret of Anjou, or of her own desire, was not to be known; but that warlike lady was going also. Just why this feminine involvement was unexplained; it could scarcely be at the king's urging. So Alec set off from Stirling with two queens, almost a thousand men, six bombards of varying sizes – Mons Meg not amongst them, for it was being fitted with a new trunnion trolley to improve its mobility, weighty as it was – cartloads of cannon-balls and sacks of gunpowder; also his wife, for Agnes was not going to let her friend journey lacking her lady-in-waiting.

Never had the new Lord Glamis gone to what was probably war in such unusual style.

In the circumstances, and with the cannon, they did not travel very fast, however good on horseback were the women. It took them all day to get to Edinburgh, and on the Burgh Muir there they found the Lord Gray assembling more troops. That man eyed the ladies askance, but could not contest their decision. He found them overnight quarters at Holyrood – but where they would rest the following night he knew not, for they would not reach Roxburgh in one day's riding, he feared, with those cannon. He was hoping that Huntly, with major reinforcements from his northern parts, would come within the next two days. And the Lord of the Isles was reputedly on his way.

So at least they were able to spend one comfortable night.

Next day it was onwards through Lothian, for the Lammermuir Hills at Soutra, and over that steep pass, hard work for the cannon-horses, into Lauderdale, the two queens interested in all that they saw, and far from holding up progress. Indeed, at Lauder, Alec suggested that there was no need for them to remain with the slow-moving artillery. If they rode on ahead they could probably reach Roxburgh by the evening, another twenty-five miles or so, join the king, and leave his cannon to come on next day. This was agreed, and pace much improved, down Leader to the Tweed near Melrose, then on by St Boswells and south-east by Maxton to the river's junction with Teviot, the women being no handicap as to speed, and quite unabashed over responding to the calls of nature, these tending to be less frequent than the men's.

Well before sundown they arrived at Roxburgh town, a little way west of the castle which stood in a very strong position at the apex of the narrow peninsula formed by the junction of the two great rivers.

They found James there with some of his lords, although his small army was encamped where it could settle itself in its siege of the castle, no simple matter apparently on account of the difficult site, more water than land.

James was, of course, surprised to see his wife and Queen Margaret, but he was not critical, his concern being for the arrival of his cannon, his impatience manifest.

So the newcomers, at least the lofty ones, were able to pass another night in fair comfort, in the house of the town's provost.

In the morning they were taken to see the siegery, and did not have to be schooled in such matters to perceive why the taking of this hold was not easy, although it did make them wonder how the castle had fallen to the English in the first place. James declared that it was folly, if not worse. The keeper had failed in his duty, shamefully. He had apparently allowed large numbers of the enemy to come down Teviot on rafts of logs, by night, and these had managed to land on the narrow banking under the walls, all along the southern side of the elongated site where the fortalice occupied the very narrow V-shaped position, with a river on either side. Because of the length of these lateral walls, the English had been able to scale the high masonry with grappling-irons and ropes, in many places. There should have been fires lit all along, of course, to give the guards due warning, but evidently there were not. In the darkness sufficient of the attackers won entry to overpower such sentries as were on duty and awake, and the sleeping fortress fell, a dire example of failure and incompetence. The keeper was now no doubt a prisoner therein – if the enemy had not hanged him, and saved his liege-lord the trouble of later doing the like!

The king was now concerned over where to try to site his cannon when they arrived. He had tried shots with his culverins, but they were useless against thick walling at that range, at any range. And that peculiar situation made the effective placing of artillery, however powerful, extremely difficult – as, to be sure, had been the reason for building it there, as it had been at Threave and Abercorn and others. Both rivers were so close to the steep slopes up to the castle that cannon could not be used thereon, even on the north side, because of the required elevation, the barrels at an impossible angle. So it had to be the far side of the waters; and strangely enough, although the Tweed was the greater stream, the Teviot was considerably wider at this stretch, shallower but wider. So there was no option but the north bank of Tweed, and that was a long way from the castle walls. Further to the west, there was just no way up for cannon on that rocky ridge. James was, in fact, doubtful whether any of his bombards would be within effective range, although there was one piece, purchased from Flanders, reputed to be of long range, but not yet tested out. The Flemings had named it the Lion, and were very proud of it, whether justly so remained to be seen. It would have to be good to be better than the absent Mons Meg.

Gazing at that lengthy fortalice, with its row of towers in line, James clenched his fists and shook one of them at it. That was *his* property, built by his ancestor, one of the keys of his kingdom; and here he was having to seek to destroy it!

They returned to the town, Mary seeking to soothe her husband's ire. The castle would not be equipped for a long siege, she pointed out. James had a large enough force here to prevent any help or food supplies reaching it, even by river. So it would have to yield, in time, the Frenchwoman agreeing with her.

They had another evening and night in the provost's house.

With no sign of the cannon the next morning, the two queens, with Agnes, and escorted by Alec and Angus, went to visit the nearby abbey of Kelsaugh, or Kelso as it was commonly called, down Tweed. David the First, the youngest and best of the Margaretsons, had built it, oddly enough to replace one he had erected at Selkirk, in the Ettrick Forest, fifteen years previously, but which had proved to be too remote for much usage. He had later, of course, founded many another, from Jedburgh, Melrose, Holyrood and up to Cambuskenneth; but this was the model. The visitors greatly admired the handsome building, although it had been damaged many times by English raiders. In consequence, the abbot there, although he made a proud host, did eye the English queen doubtfully.

Back at Roxburgh in the afternoon, they found an increase of strength, with the arrival of Huntly, Gray and the Lord of the Isles. Actually this large reinforcement was of no great advantage in the circumstances, with little that it could usefully do to contribute to the siege, and the numbers adding to the ever-present problem of food supply for an armed force. The cannon had still not arrived, but were expected to be there by nightfall.

The newcomers also were taken to see the castle situation, and could not propose any more effective course than prolonged siege. James, at Huntly's suggestion, sent most of them off east and west to patrol the borderline, in case of other Yorkist attempts.

The artillery train did eventually reach them, weary in men and beasts. Tomorrow, then, they would be put to the test, the king professing himself hopeful; for even though the range might be extreme, the very fact that major cannon were now to be employed against them might possibly bring the besieged to surrender.

The royal party and the six bombards were off, by sun-up, for the castle, James all impatience now. They went along the north side of Tweed, the queens and Agnes insisting on accompanying them, however unsuitable some of the lords considered it. James explained the different strengths and weaknesses of the various pieces, five of which had been made under his own orders and supervision. The sixth, the Flemish Lion, was the one on which he pinned his highest hopes. It had never yet been fired, at least since coming to Scotland, for no ball had come with it, and its calibre was different from any of the others, Mons Meg included, so that special missiles had to be forged for it. No great number of these had yet been made, so it would be a matter of making every shot tell – that is, if indeed its range was sufficient. It was not so long in the barrel as was Meg, and slightly less as to bore; but great things were claimed for it. The construction was somewhat different, with an enlarged breech to take more powder, and a swelling at the muzzle, said to give extra strength where the vibrations of the ball leaving the barrel could affect the range. Also, because of the force of the explosion, the steel rods forming the barrel could expand, and the iron rings along it were made somewhat slack to allow for this, held tightly in place by wooden wedges until the blast. These explanations, it is to be feared, fell on rather deaf ears.

Opposite the castle, the procession of pieces and cart-loads of shot and powder positioned itself as close to the edge of the river as possible. It was to be hoped that the enemies' hearts would sink at the sight. The king's cannoneers, under young Borthwick, used to their own bombards, were not long in positioning, loading, priming and fusing. The Lion, needing more heedful handling, would be tested thereafter.

James, very much in charge, had the five lined up in a row, his intention to have all fired simultaneously, the mighty crash of it hoped to strike terror into the English. In fact, synchronisation was not quite achieved, some fuses burning more quickly than others; but the all but continuous roar and blasting was possibly even more ear-splitting and alarming, so much so that the onlookers staggered back everywhere, the women's mouths open in unheard screams. So much smoke was generated by all this that it took a while to clear sufficiently for the attackers to be able to see results. There was no obvious gap in the castle walling, but two black holes were to be seen in the grassy bank just below, so the balls were at least reaching that far.

A reloading was ordered, and, leaving Borthwick to see to it, James turned to the Flemish piece, with his principal cannoneer.

All were interested in this untried weapon, needless to say, but after the deafening and almost terrifying blast which they had just experienced, most stood well back, for this was a larger gun and would no doubt use more powder and make the still louder discharge. Not so Angus, who had become interested in this of artillery, seeing such as a means of making his Tantallon Castle impregnable. The king pointed out to him that the breech cavity for containing the powder was almost twice the size of that on the other bombards, which ought greatly to improve the range and hitting power of the shot. The balls for this were seventeen inches in calibre, as against nearly twenty for Mons Meg, but the powder basin was larger. So they would be wise to hold their hands over their ears as this piece was fired.

Ball already in the barrel, the chief cannoneer filled the breech as full of gunpowder as it would hold, and clamped down and locked its lid. Then James himself struck flint to tow, blew the glow into a blaze, and lit the fuse. All around, hands were already covering ears.

The sizzling fuse was like a wriggling red-tailed snake.

The violence of the explosion was beyond all experience, an eruption scarcely to be comprehended in the shocked minds of all present, with even those standing well back having difficulty in keeping their feet in the blast, fragments of metal flying in all directions, the smoke-cloud enveloping all. Pandemonium.

When the dust-storm and fumes cleared somewhat, it was to show that cannon pitched sideways, part off its carriage, barrel part burst open and at an odd angle, and three bodies lying beside it, the cannoneer, the Earl of Angus and the King of Scots.

When the onlookers could take it all in, and rushed forward, it was to find Angus writhing and groaning, but the other two still. James Stewart had one leg bent and obviously broken, but he was as obviously dead. Cannon he had claimed, and cannon had claimed him.

Shocked beyond all belief, those who crowded round made way for the queen. Sinking to her knees she gazed down at her husband's body, his bloody features and shattered lower half, the groin in especial. On his face, the reddish mark which had nicknamed him Fiery Face now was overlaid with scarlet. Stroking back his hair, Mary raised his battered head and shoulders in her arms and rocked him to and fro, crooning as though to a child.

32

In the utter consternation, all but disbelief, which followed, despite the presence of seasoned warriors such as
Huntly and Gray and the Lord of the Isles, it was Mary
of Gueldres who took charge, a woman suddenly schooled
to calm authority, set-featured but assured. She ordered
the king's body to be wrapped in her own travelling cloak
and to be taken to one of the carts, she walking beside
it, holding one limp hand, Agnes Lyon with her, but as
she went, she commanded Huntly to proceed with the
cannonade of the other five bombards. James would wish
it, she said level-voiced. He was not to have died in vain,
in his bringing down of Roxburgh Castle.

Alec, appalled, went to kneel beside his friend, Angus.
He had a gash down the side of his face, but did not appear
to be otherwise injured, only part stunned by the blast.
They carried him to the carts also. The cannoneer was
just a crumpled heap, he the closest of all to the burst
weapon.

Although few there were in a state of mind for continuing siegery, the queen's orders were obeyed, she telling
the lords that she, and they, owed it to her husband to bring
down this stronghold, his final objective. She and Queen
Margaret, with Agnes, went off with the two bodies and
the semi-conscious Angus for Roxburgh-town.

The bombardment continued, all the cannoneers now
standing heedfully back from their weapons once fuses
were lit, the watchers likewise. The battering, unfortunately, did not seem to be having much of an effect on
the castle, the range too great.

When Alec and most of the other lords got back to the

town that evening, it was to further astonishment. None of the women were there. Queen Mary had already departed for Stirling, ordering the king's body to be taken by cart to Edinburgh, where she evidently intended to have him interred at Holyrood Abbey. She was going for her son, who was now James the Third, King of Scots, and her other children, to bring them all back to Roxburgh. Since his army and nobles were here, the boy king should be enthroned forthwith and in their presence. This could be done in Kelshaugh Abbey. Scotland must have its crowned monarch; she owed this to the two Jameses, father and son, and to her adopted country.

All there were much impressed by this assertion of devotion and authority by the suddenly widowed queen. She had always been recognised as a fairly strong character, but her kindly and friendly nature had to some extent overlaid its evidence. Now they knew it.

The siege continued. The Abbot of Kelshaugh was warned that he was going to be involved in important affairs. King James's corpse was duly escorted off to Edinburgh by Sir Patrick Gray and a troop of the royal guard.

From Roxburgh to Stirling was some eighty miles by the shortest route, and it said much for Queen Mary's resolution and ability that she was back on the fifth day, with her three sons and two daughters, and Queen Margaret with the Prince of Wales, hard riding for children. Bishop Kennedy, she reported, with other prelates and some of the older lords, were on their way and should arrive at Kelshaugh next day.

It was satisfactory, at least, to be able to tell that able widow that Roxburgh Castle had indeed fallen the day before. Almost certainly it was not the bombardment which had forced the yielding, although it may have helped to sap morale, but hunger, food supplies run out. The English commander had sent men under a white flag to the opposite river bank, to shout that they would surrender the hold provided that they were permitted to return to England unharmed. In the circumstances Huntly, in charge, had agreed to this.

Mary of Gueldres, in the son's name, gave orders that the castle was to be demolished, never again to be taken by enemies from over the too-nearby border and used against Scotland.

The move was made, at least by the important folk, eastwards to Kelshaugh, to await the arrival of the Primate and his party, Agnes in charge of the royal children, the nine-year-old Princess Mary helping.

Kelshaugh Abbey in 1460 at least made a fine setting for the coronation of David the First's successor at eleven removes, however undistinguished a little boy the eight-year-old James Stewart might be, the least lively and positive of the family. He was two years older than his father had been when he succeeded to the throne twenty-two years before.

The ceremony was perhaps less splendid and colourful than usual, in the circumstances, few there being dressed for the occasion, travelling clothes and armour being more in evidence than velvet and silks and satins. But Kennedy had brought the crown, the sceptre and the sword of state, with the elderly Lord Lyon King of Arms in charge of them. The abbot's seat could be used as throne. And there was a sufficiency of earls, lords, officers of state, knights and prelates present to witness the great event, even Angus himself, head bandaged and unsteady on his legs.

With Queen Mary and her other children sitting in the choir stalls of the chancel, and Queen Margaret and her son at the other side, young James was conducted to the throne by the Lord Lyon, to the chanting of choristers, looking exceedingly uncertain, not to say alarmed, and glancing over to his mother and sister throughout. The Primate conducted the service and ceremony, assisted by Bishop Durisdeer of Glasgow and the abbot. He in due course anointed with sacred oil, and when it came to the actual crowning, Angus, as probably the senior earl present, and uncle by marriage of the little monarch, came forward so shakily to perform this that Alec Lyon hurried out to take his arm and aid him. Angus took the ancient crown from the Lord Lyon, to hold it over the boy, and with the Primate's blessing, touched the brow with it – too large, of course, for James's small head – murmuring the required formula, this to the cheers of the great company.

All stood, to the shouts of God save the King! God save the King! the boy standing also, and being gently pushed down by his uncle.

So it was done. Scotland had its crowned monarch again, of the most ancient line in Christendom, some said the seventieth, others the sixty-eighth, certainly the thirty-fourth since Kenneth mac Alpin united Alba and Dalriada to form Scotland. On this occasion they dispensed with the King of Arms, representing the High Sennachie, reading out the lengthy list of names.

Then it was the impressive but also lengthy process of the traditional fealty-giving, as the lords and magnates came up in order of precedence to kneel before the monarch and take his small hand between their own two palms, vowing their loyal duty and deference, Angus leading in this, although there was some hesitation, with the Lord of the Isles seeking to be first, as of right, not as the Earl of Ross but representing the ancient and semi-independent kingdom of the Isles founded by Somerled. Huntly, who should have been next, as lieutenant-general, not to spoil the occasion, yielded place.

This prolonged performance over, undoubtedly the first time that a Queen of England and a Prince of Wales had ever attended a Scots coronation, it was for outside into the August sunshine for another traditional ritual, the knighting. It was the custom, at such an occasion, for the new monarch to confer knighthoods on a large number of his supporters who were not as yet so honoured. But in this case, since only a knight can make a knight, and young James himself had not been knighted, this had to be done first. Angus performed this duty also, however weary, the boy looking terrified at the sword which his uncle had to bring down, however carefully, on each small shoulder, dubbing him knight and instructing him to arise Sir James, and remain a good knight until his life's end. The sword of state being far too heavy for the child to wield, a lighter weapon was brought, and even this being too much for James, Huntly stepped forward to replace the wounded Angus, and manipulated the blade, holding the boy's hand upon its hilt, for the shoulder-tapping process, uttering the required words at each dubbing.

Alec Lyon was the first to be accorded the accolade, he oddly enough, despite his fairly lofty rank, never having been knighted. So he knelt before the new monarch for the second time, and was told by Huntly to arise Sir Alexander, Thane and Lord of Glamis.

Scores of recipients followed him, for, with the army assembled nearby there was no lack of candidates, James quickly tiring of the business but being kept at it by his mother who came to stand alongside.

This concluded the ceremonial, and the royal party could retire for rest and privacy before the customary banquet which the abbot was providing in the town hall, since there was no apartment large enough in the abbey precincts.

It was a strange feasting thereafter, with everyone very much aware that it was mourning rather than celebrating which ought to have been their preoccupation. But the queen, by her example, led them all in at least a superficial cheerfulness and cordiality, with the ongoing entertainment limited to choir-singing. And because of the children, an early retirement was acceptable, leaving those so inclined to linger over their wine.

It had been an important day, however taxing for the royal family – as indeed would be the two days to follow.

In the morning, it was the road for most, northwards for the royal party, westwards for Margaret of Anjou and her son, for they were not going back to Stirling but to the Solway shore, where they would await developments, either Lancastrian victory and return to England, or going to Ireland to seek to promote the cause there. Lincluden Abbey, it was advised, would be a convenient refuge meatime.

So it was parting, much of the army remaining in the Borderland, under Gray, in case of further Yorkist attacks, the queen and the Primate leading the new monarch and court attenders for Edinburgh.

The capital was in a stir, next day, over the death of the king, fears for the realm rife, a child monarch ever the recipe for trouble. Kennedy, Huntly and others sought to calm apprehensions, declaring that a parliament would be called forthwith to stabilise the situation, and that the nation's government would remain firm under the young sovereign-lord, indeed unchanged save for the occupant of the throne.

At Holyrood Abbey, the late king's body, coffined now in lead, lay in state before the high altar under the lion rampant banner.

The funeral service, this again conducted by the Primate, was a taxing occasion for all who had been close to James, and here Mary of Gueldres did break down in tears, to the upset of her children who had never seen her thus, the elder daughter doing much to try to comfort her, aided by Agnes Lyon. The actual interment in the abbey's crypt could be attended only by a few, for there was little room therein amongst all the other coffins, and Kennedy shepherded those few out again fairly quickly, leaving the widow to remain alone for a while, kneeling beside the remains. Alec and Agnes wagged heads to each other, outside. To attend a coronation of one's son and the funeral of one's husband within two days was a daunting experience, and for more than the family, although they agreed that it must have happened before in the land's troubled history.

The Abbot of Holyrood did not have to produce any banquet that night.

It was for Stirling in the morning, the queen having recovered her composure. On the way the Lyons wondered what would be their own future now. Young James, in the midst of his family, would not require any lord-in-waiting as close attendant, although his mother might still wish Agnes to remain with her, which could be awkward. There was a sufficiency for Alec to do awaiting him at Glamis, but he wanted to have his wife with him, not sixty miles distant.

In this situation, the forty days' notice for a parliament had to be dispensed with, and one was called for a week hence, messengers sent south again for many of the army commanders to return for it. The queen, practical as she was, in command of herself and concerned for her son, was for having parliament set up a council of regency, herself sitting thereon, with Kennedy, the Chancellor, Huntly, Angus and others. Huntly could remain lieutenant-general, Gray his deputy and Sir Patrick still captain of the royal guard. This was agreed.

So much for affairs of state. The Lyons were reluctant to press the queen on their own situation, but in only a couple of days Mary herself raised the question, that evening, after saying goodnight to her children and coming downstairs with Agnes to the withdrawing-room off the private hall, where Alec and Patrick Gray sat at cards, a game which Mary herself had brought from the Low Countries.

"You and your husband, my dear?" she said. "Will you be to leaving me, now? To my loss! You are the Lord and Lady Glamis, with much lands to look at and peoples to keep in goodness." She still had these oddities of speech even after eleven years in her adopted land. "He has no more my husband to attend on. Will you be gone to your Glamis?"

"We, we await your royal will, Highness." Agnes sounded hesitant, and looked over at Alec.

He, risen at the royal entry, inclined his head. "I have neglected my duties in Strathmore, Your Grace, these months," he admitted. "My duties with my royal master coming first, I judged. My brother acting for me at Glamis. But, now? Your royal son scarcely needs such as myself. And I would wish to play my part as Thane of Glamis."

"So I did think it, my lord. And you will wish your wife to be with you, as she should be, yes? So I must bear my loss. But you will not be so distant, no? How many leagues, miles? A day of riding? And from Falkland, the less – where we shall be much dwelling. Your Pitteadie near to that. St Andrews also, for Jamie will have to see much his uncle the bishop, who becomes old."

"I shall come to you often, Highness, if you so wish it, and blithe to do so!" Agnes declared. "It will be my joy, that I swear!"

"That is good. There is a word I have heard my husband to use – extra. You will be my extra lady-in-waiting still, my dear Agnes. And you, my lord, extra lord-in-waiting to my son. How say you? I am not to lose my friends?"

"I say praise be!" Alec exclaimed, and stepped forward, to take the queen's hand and kiss it.

Agnes did better. She kissed Mary's cheek, and had her salutation returned, with warmth, even an embrace. Queens, especially widowed ones, can know loneliness.

Sir Patrick Gray quietly slipped out of the room.

HISTORICAL NOTE

James the Third proved to be no potent monarch, lacking his father's drive and his grandfather's strong character, more like his weak great-grandfather Robert the Third. He required all his able mother's direction and support; and when she died, he was fortunate to have his sister Mary's guidance and care, for she was an effective and talented young woman, as well as beautiful, and in fact would have made a good queen-regnant. James got less aid from his brothers, Alexander, Duke of Albany, and John, Earl of Mar, the former indeed eventually challenging him for the throne.

So this James Stewart, although he had abilities, if scarcely kingly ones, did not rule his nation well; in fact he left the ruling mainly to others, and ill-chosen others. But at least by his marriage to Margaret of Denmark, this largely contrived by his sister Mary, he gained the isles of Orkney and Shetland for Scotland, and produced a son, another James, who was to become the fourth of his name and one of the best kings that Scotland ever had.